The War of Vengeance: Vampire Formula #1

P.A. Ross

SCARLETT THORN

http://www.thornsneedles.com/

Scarlett-Thorn Publishing

2nd Edition

ISBN-13: 979-8413776797

TABLE OF CONTENTS

Chapter One

The engines vibrated and the wind rattled the fuselage. My twitching muscles kept in tune while I held myself steady and tightened up the seatbelt.

We had boarded the plane a few hours earlier and stored our gear in the green webbing along the inside of the plane. We took our seats against the sides and under the storage. The shutters on all the windows were firmly shut to stop the dim light from escaping.

Fingers squeezed my knee, and I twisted around to meet Ruby′s light green eyes. She smiled and tucked her red hair back under her helmet.

"Don't worry, Jon. You have practised this many times," she said, shouting above the din of the engines.

"I am not worried."

"I may not have your psychic skills, but I have seen that look on people's faces before."

"Maybe, just a little," I admitted.

"Stand up and let me check through your gear. It will help reassure you," she said, her face tinted red from the glow of the jump lights. I unbuckled my seat belt and stood up. She did the same with the top of her helmet level to my chin.

She knelt and checked my boots were fastened up and wingsuit trousers in the correct position. Next, she tugged on the gun holster strapped to my thigh and checked the clip in place over the pistol. She grabbed the parachute straps around my groin and across my chest and yanked them tight.

'Oh please, she is doing that on purpose. I checked your gear before we left,' Thorn's psychic thoughts jumped into my head.

I looked across the dark plane, illuminated only by the red of the jump traffic-lights, to where Thorn sat on the side bench with her human training buddy, Dunk.

'Thorn, she is just checking my equipment, as I am a bit nervous. It is her job. She is supposed to train me and learn from me.'

'Ha, I am your mentor. Don't you ever forget that.'

'Different type of mentor. You know this. You have Dunk to teach you

squad tactics and Special Forces techniques and for you to teach him how to fight vampires.'

'But Ruby is obviously there to annoy me. The red hair and the code name is supposed to remind you of Scarlett. To remind you of being partly human.'

Ruby patted my chest. "Turn around and let me check your parachute and rifle are on properly."
I turned around and continued to talk to Thorn psychically.

'This again. You are jealous of her working so close with me.'

'Not of her, but of what she represents. MI5 are continually trying to get you to join them.'

'They haven't asked me to join them.'

'The actions they have taken infer it, refusing to let you use the formula while on their base, offering you the reversing formula that could make you human again. Naming your training buddy Ruby and dying her hair red. All of it is to keep you human and remind you of your past.'

'Maybe. Do you think I would fall for it and try to seduce her?'

'No. I don't. You're not Ruby's type. I am.'

'I know. I don't think Mary's MI5 team knows that.'

Ruby patted my back and I spun back around. She checked the helmet strap and stood on tiptoes to pull the goggles off my helmet onto my eyes. She held a thumbs up and I responded with the okay sign. I sat back down and buckled in, and Ruby sat next to me. Directly across the plane, Rip sat with his training buddy, Bradders.
Rip nodded. *'Is Thorn still in a state about Ruby?'*

'Every day.'

'Don't worry. The training is nearly over. This is our first proper mission

altogether. Hopefully, this will get us the information we need to take the war to the Turned and Hunters.'

'I hope so. It has been a long six months of training with these guys.'

'They will need to pass on what they have learnt from us if they are to set up a new Hunter's organisation. And we need to focus on practising the control of magic and putting this military training into action,' Rip said.

'I agree.'

Six months ago, following our fight with the Turned and the revealing of Cyrus to be South, the Dragan leader of the Turned army, we spent a few days recovering and enjoying the relative peace and quiet. Then a couple of nights later, a private jet flew us to England from the Spanish Air Force base.

We landed at a military airfield and then were escorted straight into an army transport helicopter. We flew over the speckled lights of towns and cities, linked by a network of half-lit roads and surrounding areas shrouded in the dark of night.

After a while, a patchwork of dark green fields, forests and mountains replaced the urban sprawl underneath. The helicopter descended into a valley towards half a dozen brick buildings, and through the trees, four houses lined down either side of a fake street.

The pilot radioed through. Floodlights focused into the centre of the camp, and out of the buildings, a flurry of figures appeared, steam rising off their bodies as they hit the frosty night air. The group of soldiers formed a circle, with guns held at their waists, ready to fire. We landed in the middle of the welcoming committee.

The blades kicked up dust and dirt, buffeting the surrounding soldiers, who stood their ground and covered their eyes. To the side of the helicopter, Mary stood next to a line of four soldiers clothed in green combat gear, who stood to attention. Mary had also dressed in military green combat clothes, but her top button was undone and sleeves rolled up, and she wore earrings and rings.

The engine turned off, and the blades slowed down. The pilot gave us the thumbs up, and we unstrapped and stepped out. We had dressed ready for training in urban grey combat gear borrowed from the Spanish military.

Thorn pulled me to one side. "Be on your guard. Sooner or later, these people will betray us," Thorn said, smiled over to Mary, and held out her hand. Mary walked over and shook it.

"Flight okay?" Mary asked.

"Fine, not so sure about our welcoming committee," Thorn said, looking around at the armed soldiers encircling us with fingers on triggers.

Mary shook her head. "They insisted. It is standard practice when soldiers from another country arrive. It's a reminder of who is in charge."

"Well, that is pleasant."

"Please, don't take it personally. They are scared of your group. This show of strength is to make themselves feel more comfortable."

"I will try my best. But don't get any silly ideas about who is in charge. This is an alliance. We agreed on a set of rules. We train you and you train us, and we work together to defeat the Turned and build a new Hunter's organisation. The command is fifty-fifty between you and me. We both need to agree on any joint actions."

"No worries. I understand the agreement," Mary said and escorted us over to the four soldiers lined up. "Let me introduce you to your training buddies. During your stay, your training buddy will personally look after you. They will train you in special forces tactics and weapons. In return, you will teach them close combat against vampires, their history and behaviours."

"Agreed."

"First in our line-up is Captain Ruby. Ruby is not her real name. She was one of the first female entrants in the SAS and has distinguished herself in combat. She is a specialist in combat tactics and strategies. And she is the leader of your training buddies and reports directly to me."

Thorn smiled and stepped forward and held out her hand. But Ruby saluted her instead. "Ma'am."

"Ruby will be Jon's buddy," Mary said.

Thorn glared at Mary. "Are you joking? Ruby with the red hair is Jon's buddy."

"No joke. I have matched the buddies to each of you based on psychological profiling. Jon responds well to older and more experienced women, as he has issues with authority father figures."

"What do you mean, father figure issues?" I said.

They both just raised their eyebrows, and Mary pushed onto the next soldier in the line-up.

The next person was a dark haired man, about Thorn's height, with broad shoulders to a tapered waist.

"This is Dunk. He is an unarmed combat specialist. He is your training buddy, Thorn."

Thorn nodded and Dunk saluted. "Pleasure to work with you, ma'am."

"Good. I will look forward to getting close and uncomfortable with you," Thorn replied and moved on to the next person, another man, shorter with a lean frame and shaven head.

"The next buddy is for Rip. His name is Bradders. He is a specialist sniper," Mary said.

Rip stepped up to the man and sniffed him. "Garlic doesn't work."

He grabbed the man's crucifix necklace. "Nor do crosses or holy water. Not on us. But on vampires like the Turned, they might."

Bradders smirked, his blue eyes glinting. "Sorry, sir, but aren't you a vampire?"

"That is enough, Bradders," Ruby shouted. "Sorry for Bradders. We briefed him before your visit. He thinks he is funny."

"Ah. The class clown. This is why I have him as my buddy. You think we are the same?"

"No. We were hoping you could wipe the smirk off his face," Ruby answered, and Bradders straightened up and frowned.

"Lastly, we have Smash. He is a specialist in comms, first aid and explosives."

Cassius stepped forward, eye to eye with the other man, both at the same height and size. Cassius had to be paired with someone he could respect, as per his profile.

"This little man is for me?" Cassius said.

"Little!" the man replied; his big beard bristled.

"You are at least one centimetre shorter than me," Cassius said and roared with laughter.

"Or maybe you are wearing your mommy's high heels," Smash replied, head leaning forward.

Cassius stopped laughing and his eyes turned red. Smash eyeballed him without flinching. Cassius pushed through his fangs and contorted his facial muscles. Smashed stared ahead, unblinking, hands at his side and relaxed.

Bradders held up his hand. "Miss, can I un-volunteer, please?"

"You didn't volunteer, remember? You signed a contract," Mary responded.

Cassius stopped and stared at Smash, then laughed again and patted his hand on Smash's shoulder. "I like you. We are going to get along just fine."

"Good. Introductions are over. Let me tell you the ground rules. Number one, we don't want Jon to be using the vampire formula while on the base."

"What! He needs to complete his transformation," Thorn yelled.

"We disagree. He is a human, and we would like him to re-think his current path. We are working on a formula that would reverse the transformation. When it is completed, it is on offer for him to try," Mary said.

"No way. You can't force him not to take it or use this reversing formula. How are you going to stop us?"

"Thorn, it is okay. I have more than enough power when using Rip's training. When we leave, I can finish taking it. There are only two injections left. Let's not turn this into a big issue," I said.

Thorn growled under her breath. "Fine. We will let you have that one."

Mary smiled. "Thank you, Jon, for humouring an old friend. Rule number two, everyone is to stop in the one barrack room."

"No way. We have private rooms," Thorn said.

"Private rooms," I repeated, along with Cassius and Rip.

"It would be better for team bonding," Mary said.

"It is a definite no," I said, "I let you have the no formula taking."

"Okay," Mary replied, and Ruby's breath streamed out in a sigh of relief.

"Number three, no feeding on any of the humans at the base. We will bring you blood."

"Oh please, have some respect for us. I would not treat my hosts with such disrespect. Of course, we will not feed on anyone here unless they ask us to," Thorn said, and crossed her arms and grinned.

"I don't care if anyone asks. No feeding on us."

Rip put up his hand. "Not even if it is part of the training?"

"How is that training for us?"

"Who said it was for you?" Rip said. Cassius laughed again, and I clamped my hand over my mouth to stop myself.

"Yes, Rip. We definitely paired you with the right person. Just to be clear, no feeding. If you want to train us in detecting a vampire hunting for a meal, then please do so, but without the actual biting and blood-sucking part."

"Are we done with your rules now?" Thorn asked.

"Yes."

"Okay. My turn. Rule four, we train at night, so kiss the daylight goodbye. Rule five, none of these lights better have UV bulbs hidden in the background. Rule six, anyone attacks us, and it will be a full on massacre. Rule seven, don't call us vampires," Thorn said and glared at Bradders, who stared straight ahead to avoid her gaze. "Rule eight, we want the wi-fi password with unlimited data."

Mary nodded along. "I agree with all the above. But the internet access is monitored but feel free to use it. The password is vampires_suck. Oh, I forgot one, rule nine, no seduction or psychic control over the personnel at the base. Remember, we are your allies, not your playthings. We are working on countermeasures to block out psychic interference."

"Understood," Thorn said.

"Good. Let me show you to your rooms and get you settled in before we train."

Rip coughed. "Excuse me, have you brought the training supplies I requested?"

Mary looked at the helicopter where two soldiers were unloading crates. "They are getting it now."

"You got the good stuff?"

"Yes, we got the vintages and years you were asking for. I hope this isn't a joke. Thorn has assured me that red wine is essential for your training."

"Of course, I would not lie to you. But this is Dragan training only. Unless your team would like to learn how to taste test red wine, then I can spare some time."

Mary headed off to a long, one level brick building. "This way."

We followed her in and she showed us to a set of private rooms. Thorn's and my room had a double bed, table, wardrobe, fridge and TV mounted on the wall. A basic army bunk room. Nothing fancy and all painted a dull military grey. The rooms were already prepared for us, as if they knew we would refuse to stop altogether in a barrack room. It was just a negotiation tactic. The others all had similar rooms down the same grey soulless corridor.

We had a little night left, so Rip broke open the crate of red wine in the common room and started training Thorn and Cassius on controlling their magic. I assisted Rip by demonstrating how to withhold the natural course of magic to heal my body. Firstly, I cut my arm and prevented the healing and then burnt off the alcohol. It took a few attempts and glasses of red wine before Thorn and Cassius prevented the healing. They didn't adapt to it as quickly as I did.

Rip explained he was the same. Hundreds of years of letting magic find its own way made it difficult to break their natural instincts. In contrast, I only had a few months of bad habits to break. I enjoyed training Thorn for a change and being better than her at something.

The following night, an alarm woke us and our training buddies appeared at our doors.

"Get dressed and meet in the courtyard in ten minutes!" Ruby shouted.

We pulled on our combat clothing and hurried outside. Rip sauntered out five minutes later while lighting a cigarette. Our training buddies were already lined up, and they waved us to stand next to them. At the front, a man stood on a box, flanked by another two men dressed in black clothes. Once we were all lined up, the man on the box scanned up and down the line.

"Rip, take that cigarette out of your mouth. This is a training camp, not a holiday park."

Rip took a long drag and slowly blew it out, and then flicked the cigarette onto the wet, muddy ground.

The man continued. "I am your instructor. I will run your first night's training program. Tonight, you will pair up with your buddy and compete against the other pairs through a set of physical challenges. Firstly, let's get your blood pumping."

The instructor yelled out exercises and tried to beast us. He soon realised he wasn't tiring us out. Next, we buddied up and went off in intervals for a run in the forest. Along the route, we tackled an assault course, climbed over walls, crawled under wire fences, swam under obstacles, carried each other, and then carried a massive log between us. At the end of the course, they handed us a rifle and we had ten shots at a range of targets. They added the scores up and converted it into time off our run. Rip and Bradders won, mostly down to the shooting at the end.

The next night, Ruby led us in squad formations to perform house clearances down the fake street next to the base. The other Dragans and I watched our human buddies perform it on CCTV, breaking into the houses, covering the entrances and exits, clearing out each room. We then completed a walk through with them.

Thorn asked them to run through it again and if during it, they would allow us to link to them psychically. We could be in the moment and learn a lot faster. After some discussion, they agreed, and we sat down and closed our eyes while our buddies ran through the exercise a few more times. We lived each thought and movement as the squad worked together. After a few runs, we had developed a level of psychic muscle and memory. Next, we ran physically through the exercise close to perfection.

The psychic linkage set the tone for the rest of the training. Whatever they showed us, we could live the moment and then repeat. We did the same for them. We showed them how to fight a Turned, linking them into our thoughts and movements, so they could feel and react the same way.

We accelerated through the training programs and covered everything from weapons training, explosives, comms, high altitude parachute jumps, wingsuits, scuba diving, and hand to hand.

In return, we taught them how to fight vampires, how to detect vampires, the behaviours of a vampire and how to resist a vampire's powers. Towards the end of the training, we worked out joint battle strategies; how could Dragans and Humans fight together.

We also fitted in some Dragan only magic training. Rip continued with his basic drinking training until Thorn pushed him into something more practical. We used it to re-run the assault course, accelerate our healing, block our recovery, and power up our combat skills.

It had been six months of intense training with our buddies, when a call had come in that MI5 had located a target, The Original. He was the first-ever Turned created by Cyrus, the General of his army, and the leader of the Turned Revolution until overthrown by Bramel.

We geared up straight away and soon found ourselves flying over Argentina, wearing wingsuits, parachutes and weapons.

#

In the plane, the human buddies checked over their Dragan counterparts, who then returned the favour. I stood up to do the same with Ruby.

"No need. I am fine," she said.

"Come on. You are making me look bad."

She stood up, and I performed the same checks on her wingsuit, parachute and weapon straps, and then her helmet and goggles.

I sat back down when the jump lights turned from red to amber. Bradders leapt out of his seat and hit a button at the back of the plane. The end of the aircraft unfolded down to a ramp, with the wind whistling through the plane, tugging us towards the exit. We all unbuckled and lined up, tensing our muscles to stop the pull to the rear of the aircraft. I put my goggles on and checked the GPS on my wrist.

"Comms links on," Ruby shouted. I flicked the button on the wire leading to my earpiece.

"Thumbs up if you can hear me," Ruby said. We all responded.

The jump light turned green, and Bradders turned to us and pumped the air with his fists. "This is when the fun begins." He spun back and ran out the back, shouting as he leapt off the ramp into the night.

"Idiot," Rip said and walked down the ramp and dropped off the edge.

Smash and Cassius nodded at each other and ran down the ramp and jumped off.

Thorn slapped Dunk on the shoulder. "You first."

Dunk jogged down and jumped off. Thorn walked backwards to the end of the ramp, smiling the entire time.

'See you down there.'

On her last step, she crouched down, back flipped into the air and flew away, looking back as the darkness engulfed her.

"You're next," Ruby said. "As the captain, I always go last to make sure the plane is clear."

I walked down to the end and leaned forward into a handstand on the edge of the ramp. I held it for a second, lowered down, and then thrust up and out, letting the wind snatch me away from the plane and into the dark expanse.

Chapter Two

I spun head over heels for a few seconds and stretched out my arms and legs to level off. A figure flew past, Ruby, and I angled my body towards her and followed in her slipstream. My GPS highlighted the landing area and showed my position on the map. We were a few miles off and had to glide in on the wingsuits.

The Argentinian government had links into the Turned organisation, so we hadn't sought permission to fly over. However, the vineyard that The Original lived in was near the border, so we had gained permission from the neighbouring country to fly over.

All we had to do was gracefully fall and glide into Argentina, locate the vineyard, and kill The Original while trying not to get spotted by the local security forces and cause a diplomatic incident due to invading British Special Forces.

We had to overpower any Turned guards if necessary. We hoped to assassinate The Original without engaging the rest of the Turned, but it was unlikely, as he would be guarded by a hand full of third-gen Turned. It was likely we would have to kill all the guarding vampires and not let The Original escape. Not the easiest of first missions together. I had hoped for something a little simpler.

The cold air blasted my face and my wingsuit rippled under the force. I checked the GPS. We were dropping at 53 mph and flying over the ground at 72 mph. This wouldn't take long. Below, I could make out the white edges of the mountain range we had flown over that created the natural border to Argentina.

"This is Bradders. I have reached the deployment altitude. Deploying parachute. See you on the ground," he said over the radio comm link.

I checked my GPS and only had a few more seconds before I deployed as well. In front, I saw another chute open, and I angled away and pulled the handle on my chute. I always hated this part, waiting to see if it would open.

I counted down and the chute yanked me out of my dive. I grabbed the steering toggles and swung the parachute around, following the directions on my GPS and the faint black figures of my unit.

To my side, a large white building, with faint lights emitting out of four square windows. At the front, a few cars and buses were parked in a square patch of dirt. Fields of grape vines encircled the building, with a single road cut through the middle to the front of the ranch and the parked vehicles.

We flew in parallel and over the treetops lining the edge of the vineyard. I passed over the trees and around to the side, looking for a space to land, close to the other team, but not too close as to avoid getting tangled up in their chutes.

"Jon, turn left. Good, now straight ahead. Excellent. You can drop there," Bradders said over the commlink.

The ground rushed up, and I pulled the steering toggles down, stalled my flight, and soften my knees for impact. I hit the ground and ran along, letting the chute take the momentum out of the landing.

I unstrapped and gathered up the chute in a bundle. I removed the rest of my gear, unzipped the wingsuit, stuffed it inside the chute and wrapped it up. Underneath the wingsuit, I wore green and brown combat camouflage clothes. I buckled up my pistol holster and swung the rifle around my neck. I grabbed the chute bundle and walked back to the glowing images of my unit.

Ever since the last injection of the formula, the Dragan sight had remained, although fainter than fully transformed. I could see in the dark and pick out the different heat and scents of Humans and Dragans. They were all dressed in the same green and brown combat gear, standard issue clothing, but I could tell them apart from a distance.

The unit had gathered and piled all the chutes and wingsuits together. Smash placed some incendiary devices around them to burn the evidence of our visit.

Ruby gathered us together in a huddle. "You should have all seen the vineyard and the white ranch building in the middle. We follow the plan. Back through the trees, each in our pairs, and take up four positions at each corner of the building. We rely on the psychic abilities to relay comms at this point. They have no chance of picking up the signal. The Dragans use their abilities to work out the numbers of Turned and Hunters inside. We humans have night vision goggles to help. Before we head off, we all need to spray down and cover our scent."

We all pulled out a canister, sprayed ourselves, and threw the empty cans onto the pile with the chutes.

"What is this stuff again?" Rip asked, wafting it away with his hands.

"It is a mixture of local wildlife scents. We don't want the Turned detecting us before the party starts," Ruby said. "Everyone clear."

"Clear," I said, and everyone responded apart from Thorn. We all stared at her.

"Yes, boss. I am clear. I go with Dunk to the far right corner and relay back the info. Then we decide what to do next."

"Thank you, Thorn. Good, let's move."

The other pairs peeled away into the dark, and Ruby waited as the last figure disappeared out of sight.

"Jon, we go straight ahead. Let me know as soon as you can see them. From our experiments, it should mean we are out of their sight. The Turned don't have such a long-range of sight or smell. If we stay on your limits, it should be good enough to gain the advantage, especially with our scents covered."

"Okay. I am ready to go."

"Follow my lead," Ruby said and pulled down her night vision goggles.

We headed off through the trees and into the field of vines. I walked down the dry dirt path behind her, looking ahead at the white wooden building. It reminded me of an American cowboy ranch. At the front, a big pillar porch with a large light casting shadows. A veranda along one side with a couple of tables and chairs. The main structure had a square front to a second level and other buildings angled out of one another, which looked to have been added over the years.

Although at night, the ground kept the day's heat, and humid air hung in between the vines. Flies buzzed at the sweat and the fake animal ordure spray covering our scent. I mopped the sweat prickling on my forehead away with my sleeve.

As we got closer, Ruby crouched down in her walk and I copied, keeping us below the tops of the vines, but the white porch in sight. Luckily, it was nearing harvest and the vines were thick with grapes and leaves, providing us with plenty of cover.

We walked on, and I caught sight of a glowing figure patrolling the grounds. I tapped Ruby on the shoulder. "Patrols up ahead."

She bent down onto one knee and stared ahead through the night vision goggles.

"Two guards patrolling the perimeter of the house. I can see a few more inside as they pass the windows. Check-in with the other Dragans to get the full picture."

I psychically reached out. *'What is your situation? We have patrols. Several armed Turned inside. I can't sense any humans at all.'*

'Same here. Two guards are patrolling and several hostiles inside. I detect some second-gen Turned inside and third-gen patrolling,' Thorn said.

'And this side,' Rip said.

'Here as well,' Cassius said.

"Ruby, they are all seeing the same. It is more heavily guarded than we expected. Something is happening here. The buses look like they have brought in groups of vampires."

"This is more than we expected. We expected The Original to have some guards, but this is an entire unit, not a handful of vamps. We didn't think there would be any second-gen Turned."

"So, what is the plan? Do we abort?"

"We switch plans. We use attack pattern beta. What does Thorn think?"

'I haven't come all this way just to fall out of a plane.'

"Thorn agrees. Let's finish the job."

Ruby grabbed some loose earth and let the breeze blow it away. "The wind is coming off the mountains and blowing towards us. This is where you, Thorn and Rip will attack from. I will circle round and meet up with my unit and Cassius, and let the wind carry in our scent."

'We are on our way. I will tell the others to stay here,' Thorn replied, as she had been psychically listening in to our conversation.

Ruby went around to the right, circling the white building, keeping her distance. After a few minutes, Thorn and Rip appeared and crouched down at my side.

"Remember, wait for the signal from Cassius," Rip said. "In the meantime, draw in your magic and connect to your emotions. Build it up into a big ball, ready to explode."

I sat cross-legged on the floor and closed my eyes. My emotions were easy to find: exhilaration, excitement and fear.

"V, wait. I have something for you," Thorn said, and I opened my eyes to see her holding a vampire formula needle.

"But they said I couldn't take it?"

"They said you couldn't inject it while on their base. We aren't on their base. This is a perfect opportunity to take the next step."

I took the needle straight away, keen to finish and fully transform into a Dragan. I lay down in the dirt, plunged the needle into my neck and forced in the formula. My eyes closed, as I awaited the usual pain, terror, and blankness of a temporary death to be re-born a full Dragan.

My muscles twitched, and my hands closed and opened as the fire of the Dragan DNA coursed through my blood. My heart raced fast and head thumped. My stomach tightened and headache increased to a blinding pain. Then it stopped, my heart slowed, the muscles relaxed and the headache eased. I opened my eyes and my senses had heightened. I stared at Thorn.

"Are you okay?" she asked.

"I didn't die?"

"No, of course not. You are a full Dragan."

"No. I mean, I didn't have to die to become a full Dragan. Normally, I get a heart attack and drift out of my body to a warm glowing light with my parents waiting for me. But not this time. I approached the edge of death and it was completed before I started to crossover."

She smiled and patted my shoulder. "This is good news. This means you are nearly finished, and you no longer have to go through that pain."

I nodded. I could live without the pain and terror of dying every time. But I didn't get to see my parents. I looked forward to seeing them on each injection despite it coming with incredible pain. I thought I would have more time, a chance at least to say a quick goodbye. However, the fact I saw them at all held out hope I would see them again one day. But that could be an extremely long time as I was becoming a Dragan with a near-immortal lifespan. "You are right. I am nearly complete."

Thorn smiled and kissed my cheek. "This should be a good thing. So cheer up and we can celebrate later. But for now, we have a mission to complete, so get up and draw in your magic."

I sat cross-legged and used the joy of the easier transformation, nearing the end of my journey and the sadness that I didn't see my parents again, to build up my magic ready for the assault. Inside, my sphere of purple magic pulsated, preparing to fuel my Dragan powers.

Cassius' thoughts spoke to us. *'We are starting. Good luck.'*

He opened a connection into his mind, so we could hear and see what was happening. He poured water over his head and washed off the scent mask. Smash stood at his side, holding a bag of grenades. Bradders had nestled in between the vines for cover and lay on the ground, looking down the sights of his sniper rifle. Both Dunk and Ruby flanked Smash and Cassius in covering positions. Cassius walked forward and Smash, Ruby and Dunk followed. The wind blew off the mountains and pulled the scent off them towards the ranch and the Turned.

The yellow glowing figures of the patrolling guards stopped and sniffed the air. Their focus turned towards his approaching figure.

"Dragans and Humans," a guard screamed. They both fired off a volley of bullets. A guard's head exploded from Bradder's shot and Cassius took cover. Smash pulled the pin on a grenade, threw it over the guards, and it exploded on the back porch. Wood splintered out in a shock wave, the flames devouring the white wood. A couple of figures stumbled from the burning hole, and Ruby and Dunk fired. The Turned crashed to the floor, screaming and clutching at their bullet wounds.

Thorn tapped my shoulder. “It’s our turn.”

I disconnected from Cassius’s mind and stood up next to Rip and Thorn.

“Rip, take the top floor. V and I will clear out the bottom. V go left. I will go right.”

Thorn and Rip coiled their legs and leant forward. I bent my legs and tilted forward, ready for the signal. I focused on the door of the ranch. The two patrolling guards and other Turned inside had gone to fight against Cassius and company out the back on the other side. No one blocked our path.

“3..2..1.. go,” Thorn said.

Thorn and Rip dashed off, and I released my crackling sphere of magic into my limbs and sprinted through the vines. Rip launched up and smashed through an upstairs window. Thorn ripped off the front door and went inside. I bolted through the broken doorway and went left.

I gripped a silver knife and went from room to room down the corridor, making sure we weren’t cut off when we attacked the rear of the Turned defence. I checked a study with bookshelves against every wall and a large oak desk. A games room with pool table and table tennis. An entertainment room with a massive TV, games consoles, and fridge and cupboards. The rooms were empty of people, as all the action was out the back of the ranch. I headed towards the noise of gunfire to join the battle.

I swept around the corner of the corridor and crouched against the wall. Up ahead, a Turned was using the doorway as cover. He popped his head around, fired off a few shots at Cassius and co, and then hid again. I aimed the automatic rifle and padded up to his back. Once close enough, I switched to the knife.

He swung back from a burst of gunfire, and I grappled my hand across his mouth, slammed the knife into his back, and yanked him out of sight. I pushed him down the hallway as his body burned and forced him into an empty room and shut the door. The dull thud of his explosion rattled the door, and I hoped it hadn’t alerted the other Turned. I went back to the doorway, knelt to the floor, and peeked my head around.

Four vampires took cover at the sides of a smouldering hole in the wall and returned fire into the vines. The explosion had flung the tables and chairs to the sides, and ash had scattered across the floor. Flames flickered on the furniture and smoke enveloped the room. In another room down the hallway, a battle cry and an explosion rang out.

Outside, two vampires fell from above and hit the ground, kicking up a wave of dirt. They writhed on the floor as flames erupted until they exploded into a fountain of ash.

Rip jumped down through the ash and onto the porch. The vamps, who were barricaded behind the railings and upturned tables and chairs, scrambled backwards to aim. Rip kicked the barricades out of the way and spun a knife into a vamp's chest. The other vamp jumped up to shoot when a sniper's bullet shattered its skull.

The vampires in the room took aim at Rip. I stepped in and threw a silver knife into the back of a vampire's head. The others spun around and I fired off two bursts into the next two vamps. The last one charged in with a sword, and I blocked with my rifle. They swung back, and I spun the rifle around to parry each blow as they launched a series of hacks at my body. I forced the vampire back and front kicked it into the wall. Then I squeezed the trigger, nailing it between the eyes. The bodies flamed and exploded. I ducked into a ball to take cover.

Thorn appeared at Rip's side, and I uncurled and stepped through the flaming hole in the wall.

"Are there any others?" I asked.

"I can't sense anyone else nearby. Secure the back of the house and get the others inside," Thorn said.

I climbed back through the hole and guarded the doorway, checking down the hallways and opening up my senses to the smells or sounds of other Turned still lurking about. I couldn't sense anyone else apart from our unit. But this was a concern, as I couldn't detect The Original. A first-gen Turned would give off a distinctive scent and aura that I would recognise from meeting Bramel.

The others climbed through the smouldering hole and huddled up.

"We split into our pairs and go room to room looking for The Original. Keep radio silence," Ruby said.

Thorn and Dunk went right. Cassius circled around outside with Smash. Rip went outside and jumped back onto the first floor. Rip reluctantly climbed after him.

Ruby and I headed left, down the opposite hallway I had checked earlier. Bullet holes and blood marks riddled the first room backing on to the porch.

The room that Thorn had cleared earlier.

We checked the rest of the rooms, a TV room, a dining area, a bedroom, and a toilet, which were all empty. We reached the end of the hallway through double white doors and entered a large conference room. They had set long rectangle tables around the edges of the room, with red bottles labelled, empty glasses, clipboards and pens. In the corner, chairs were all stacked up and tucked away.

I went to inspect the bottles. Each bottle had a different label: rabbit's blood, rat, cat, dog, cow, horse, adult human male, adult human female, teenager, and virgin. The clipboard had a form on it with a space to write the name of the blood and tick boxes to rank its taste, smell and power. It looked like we had interrupted the party, as none of the forms had been filled out and none of the bottles opened.

We moved through another set of double white doors into a kitchen area. The walls had large fridges down one side containing more red bottles. On the other side of the kitchen were hobs and ovens, and down the middle a black marbled worktop. We walked through another set of double doors into a room with four sofas and a large TV.

'We found him. Come around to the other side. There is a secret passage leading down into a basement and a study. We detected a draft coming through the bookshelves,' Thorn spoke into my mind.

We headed back to the main hallway, and I followed the signals from Thorn, to go back down the hallways and rooms I had swept earlier on.

Within the study room I had looked in earlier, a bookcase was swung back, leading to a wooden stairway inside the walls. We walked down into another study almost identical to the one upstairs.

Dusty bookshelves lined every wall, a desk in the middle, and a table with red bottles and empty glasses to the side. The others all stood in front of the large oak desk strewn with maps and documents, with a man sitting behind it, The Original.

"At last, here is the cause of all my pain. The infamous hybrid, V," The Original said, holding a glass of blood which he sipped and then grinned.

The man was of average height, bald, and sturdy. I got the same signals from when I met Bramel. The aura and glow were higher than the other Turned but not the same as a Dragan. This had to be him. He wore a green paisley smoking jacket and wore a red cravat around his neck.

"And you must be The Original, the first of your kind, the first Turned."

"Please, call me Ovidiu. The Original is such a long title and not technically true. Let me tell you a story. I might as well come clean," he said and put the glass down on the table.

Thorn pulled out a chair from the other side of the desk. "Please continue. But don't think you can stall us for too long. I know you too well."

"Thorn, it is such a pleasure to see you again. I should have known it would be you to kill me. I deserve the true death at the hands of royalty.

"So to the story. After Cyrus left the Union with Thorn, he travelled across Europe to reunite with his family and eventually reached the edge of a small town in Transylvania, which is now part of Romania. He needed to feed and spotted a lonely shepherd boy. He fed upon him until the boy was nearly dead. Cyrus taunted the boy at the edge of death and offered him something to drink. He cut his arm, poured blood into a cup, and offered it to the dying boy. He drank it down and then died.

"Cyrus laughed at the dead boy and rested in the hills after his meal. Five minutes later, the boy came back to life, with eyes and claws similar to a Dragan. Cyrus was freaked out and killed the boy immediately, despite the boy's submission and pleading. The next night, he journeyed into the town, contemplating what had happened. The realisation that the blood brought the boy back to life and created a new type of Dragan. He understood the power he had discovered and tried it again, but this time on someone that could assist him. That night, he broke into the Mayor's house and turned him. It was clear the Mayor would follow the orders of his creator and had some ability to control his appearance the same as a Dragan. They experimented by turning the Mayor's servants and tested their strengths and weaknesses.

"The next day, the Mayor called a meeting of the town's most influential people. Cyrus, the Mayor and servants, turned these people. The next night, the new vampires brought together their own servants, workers and families and turned them. Within a few days, the whole town was killed and brought back to life. This was Cyrus's first army, and I was the Mayor. He placed me in charge of his army. We were going to kill the other Dragans, so Cyrus could become King. Then I believed Cyrus wanted to extend his rule to cover humans as well."

"He intended to rule over everyone?" I asked.

"Yes, of course. You have met Cyrus? He loves power. Just being in charge of a handful of Dragans would never have been enough. Regardless, the Dragan civil war attracted the attention of humans. They were happy to let it play out, as long as vampires were killing vampires. They even evacuated areas for us to fight in. But they were concerned about what would happen when the war ended. War with humans seemed inevitable once we had settled the Dragan war."

"This is true. We had done some deals to stay out of certain areas. In return, they gave us land to fight on. But they were building their armies to defend against us in the meantime," Thorn said.

"So after Thorn beat Cyrus. You rebelled against your master," I asked, the perfect opportunity to get the truth straight from the source.

"Yes. We were beaten, but Cyrus couldn't see it. He kept sending us on suicide missions. In the end, we had enough and left. The other vampires pronounced me, King of the Turned. The humans attacked us when they heard the war was over. We fought back and took over a town. But they kept coming for us. We built up our defences. Then Bramel arrived one day with Thorn's Turned army. We joined forces, but we couldn't agree on who was in charge. We fought for the position of King and Bramel won. He let me live and put me in charge of the army," Ovidiu said, and took a mouthful of blood.

"And the war with the humans?" I asked.

"Somehow, Bramel negotiated a peace treaty with them. We could leave unharmed as long as we agreed to keep the vampire numbers in check and not gather in large numbers. There would be no war. To ensure we stuck to the deal, the humans started up their own forces to monitor us and cull the numbers when necessary. These were the original Hunters, and it is why you find them in every country. They spread the word and followed us."

"So Bramel saved you all," I said.

"You could say that. I think we should have attacked at the very beginning while they were still weak. We have only given them time to prepare and organise themselves. We could have invaded at night and recruited their leaders and armies onto our side. Just as Cyrus did in my village. But Bramel was King and had other ideas. He believed in co-existence and not out right rule."

It was strange to hear the history from the Turned point of view. I even had some admiration for Bramel. He had probably stopped an all-out war and saved thousands of human lives. Maybe millions in the long term of all the people that wouldn't have been born. Without him, we could be living in a vampire controlled world and existing as slaves or as blood bags.

"So I should thank Bramel and work with him," I said.

"You may not be alive today without his actions," Ovidiu said.

"So what has changed?" I asked.

"You know this answer. Everything was in the balance until the world became a smaller place through advances in technology. There are fewer places for vampires to hide. Cameras are everywhere. Sooner or later, the existence of vampires will become known. I believe war with humans has only been stalled. Bramel has come around to our way of thinking. He believes there must be a change in the balance of power. Recently, magic has returned to the world and this has implications. Everything will change. There is no stopping it. There will be a supernatural arms race, and genetic engineering is the key to allow us Turned to realise our full potential. And you, my friend, are the key."

I sighed. It always came back to me.

"What about South?" I asked.

"South?"

"Cyrus is South and has been controlling Bramel all along. You aren't in control of your own destiny."

"South. We heard the rumours as well. Bramel used to speak secretly with a lot of powerful people. We could never prove it to be some overlord. Those that looked into it too long and hard inevitably disappeared," Ovidiu said.

"Even I didn't know you weren't the first Turned," Thorn said, interrupting the flow of the conversation.

"Well, not the actual first, but the first true Turned. The boy was just an accidental experiment."

"Well, that was an interesting history lesson, but we have a job to do," Thorn said.

"Have a drink first. I have a whole host of fantastic bloods to try. It would be a shame if none of them got drunk after you gate crashed my party."

"What is going on here? There are loads more Turned than we expected, and upstairs there is a room full of different types of blood," I asked.

"Every four years, I host a blood tasting festival. The cream of the Turned society comes to my little house and tries a range of bloods collected from across the world. Unfortunately, due to recent hostilities, the normal collection of first and second-gen Turned could not attend. I had to put up with a heavy guard of third-gen Turned and a few second-gen Turned being spared from the war effort. I refused to waste good blood on these lower vampires, so I collected other types of blood for them to try, animal blood."

"So we have ruined your party?"

"It was already ruined by having these others here. They wouldn't appreciate a good full-bodied blood. I told them the animal blood was like having a child's soft drink and to savour the sweetness of the rabbit's blood. It would ensure they wouldn't get over-excited while on guard duty. But the truth is good blood would have been wasted on them."

"Well, the party is about to get worse," Thorn said, and levelled her gun.

Ovidiu held up his palms to her. "No, please wait. Let me at least have a good drink before I die. You might as well try some," he said, and scuttled over to a cabinet and popped the cork on a bottle of blood. He grabbed five glasses and poured out the blood. He passed one over to Thorn, who sighed and lowered her gun. Ruby aimed hers at him. "Just keeping him covered," she said.

Ovidiu passed a glass to Rip, Cassius and me. He held his glass by the stem and swirled the blood around the glass, leaving a red mark around the sides.

He lifted it to his nose and breathed in. "Such sweet aromas. This is the blood of the local girl on the day she became a woman. It has a delicate balance. The harvesting has to be perfect." We all watched as he took a mouthful and drank it back. "The blood is fine. Please drink up. It is no trick."

Rip held it to his nose and sucked in the aromas. Cassius stuck his nose into the glass and shook his head.

Thorn took a big gulp with an air of indifference, then raised her eyebrows and licked her lips. "Hmm. Sweet at first with mature after tones. This is good," Thorn said and took another drink.

Rip took a sip and worked the blood around his mouth, leaving his teeth stained red. "Yes. That is a delight." He tipped back a mouthful. Cassius followed suit and nodded in appreciation.

"Drink up, young sir," Ovidiu said and took another gulp.

I was a fully transformed Dragan, so the blood would easily go down. But the talk of the person it was taken from felt weird. Rip clasped my shoulder. "Just give it a sip. You need to learn to feed when you can."

Ruby glared at me, and I looked away and sipped the blood. The blood rolled over my tongue and tasted like raspberries, then slid down the back of my throat to give a sour taste at the end. The blood absorbed into my stomach and delivered a kick to my powers, my sphere of magic pulsating as it hit. Saliva washed into my mouth, and I took another gulp of blood, enjoying the sweetness to a hint of sour and the resulting rush of power.

"You all enjoy?" Ovidiu asked.

I nodded my head.

"More." Rip held out his glass.

"Of course," Ovidiu said and refilled his glass.

"We still have to kill you," Thorn said.

"No, you don't. I could come with you and bring my supply of blood. I could also help in the war. After all, I am a Turned General. Who do you think has been working on the strategies and advising Bramel? I know of the plans to fight the Dragans and Humans. I know what Bramel intends."

"You would work against your own?"

"I owe Bramel nothing. He took my army and my title from me. He held us back when we could have been ruling. I have waited hundreds of years for revenge. What better way than to join the Dragans? Especially if you believe it was South, a Dragan, controlling us all along."

"But you believe in vampire rule? Not co-existence," I said.

"At my age, I just believe in peace and quiet and a good bottle of blood. It is Bramel that now believes in vampire rule. He is fed up with living in the shadows and deferring to humans. There must be a change, but he still believes an all out war is un-winnable for either side, hence the alliance with the Hunters. A hybrid solution. You should understand that concept, V. Bramel believes it is time to reveal our existence to the world, so he can take his rightful place of power at the head of this union."

We huddled together, sipping our blood and speaking psychically to one another.

'Surely, he is just saying anything to survive. He could be a Turned double agent,' I said.

'Of course, but this is nice blood. Much better than that sanitised rubbish MI5-S gives us. He also knows his wines. I have seen some excellent vintages,' Rip said.

'We can't trust him. He was the first-ever Turned to rebel against us. Regardless of what he says, it looks like Bramel has treated him well,' Thorn said.

"Arggh," Ovidiu shouted, and a glass shattered on the floor, exploding blood across our feet.

We all turned around. He clutched his chest as the fire rippled from his wound.

"No," he shouted again, grabbed the bottle of blood and gulped it down. The lava in his veins pumped around his body and broke into his muscles. His body erupted on fire until it reached a critical mass and exploded to ash. The bottle smashed to the ground, splattering its red contents up our legs.

The ash settled to give us sight of Ruby holding a silver stake in her hand. "Mission completed."

Chapter Three

My stomach ached, and I stretched my legs under the blankets and rolled over towards Thorn. Her closed eyes flicked back and forth underneath her eyelids. I watched her dream and wondered what delights or nightmares she would engage in. The thought crossed my mind of invading her dreams, using my psychic powers. I had never tried it before, but I guessed it must be possible, just like a noise or movement in the real world weaving into your dream world.

We had agreed never to read each other's thoughts without permission, and only to communicate psychically when necessary. Although these weren't her thoughts; these were her dreams. I was sure this didn't count. It would be a useful experiment either way. A possible tool in the war.

I closed my eyes, silenced my thoughts for a moment, and reached out. It had only been a couple of days since the trip to Argentina, so my full Dragan state remained. I pushed my thoughts into her mind, but I met resistance and chaos. I needed more power to break into her subconscious. This wasn't like reading a person's conscious thoughts. This went deeper and would take more energy.

I imagined my sphere pulsating magic, letting my emotions draw in power from outside. I focused on my psychic ability and directed my mind into Thorn's dreams. A fog surrounding her thoughts drifted away, and the images and feelings sharpened up. I would find out what dark thoughts lay in her mind. What evil she may truly be capable of, if left to her desires.

In the dream, Thorn sat outside her chateau on a stone bench under a full moon. In her arms was a baby wrapped in swaddling, wriggling and crying.

I felt sick. I didn't think Thorn would feed on a baby. I pulled my thoughts out, not wishing to see the horror. But Thorn's emotions swept through me. She stared up at the moon and sang a lullaby.

"Shush now, little baby, don't you cry. Mummy gonna kill you a vampire. Shush, little baby, don't you cry, mummy's gonna kill all vampires."

She looked down and love enveloped her. The baby lay still, giggled and eyes tinted red.

I lost my focus and the fog drifted back across the scene. I snapped my senses back and rolled out of bed.

"Where are you going?" Thorn said.

I jumped, surprised by her voice. "It's night. I am going to get some breakfast, as we have the de-brief soon."

"Is it? That is a shame. I was having a lovely dream."

"Really?"

"Yes. Come back to bed. We didn't get the chance to celebrate our first successful mission in the new alliance." Thorn pulled back the blankets to reveal her body and beckoned me over.

I wasn't in the mood after invading her dreams and seeing her mothering a baby. I stood resistant to her charms and stared.

"What is wrong with you?"

"Nothing. Just not sure I am in the mood."

Thorn leapt out of bed, wrapped her arms around me and squeezed her warm flesh against mine. "You have never said that before. Is something wrong? Don't you find me beautiful anymore? Is Ruby distracting you?"

"No. No and No. Of course, you are still beautiful. Of course, I still want you. Can't I just not be in the mood for once?"

"No. You can't. You are still in your Dragan form. You should always be in the mood. Don't worry, I can fix it."

Thorn kissed me and ran her hands down my body. She was right. She could fix it, and I followed her back into bed. Being with her was as wonderful as usual. But seeing her dreams had left me shaken. It was the last thing I expected.

Afterwards, Thorn lay with her head on my chest and then kissed my cheek and rolled out of bed. She pulled her clothes on, black leggings and vest top, with heavy-soled boots tighten around her calf muscles. She tied back her raven hair and applied liner to her sky blue eyes. "Let's go. I fancy trying some of the blood Rip brought back from Argentina."

I pulled on my jeans and t-shirt and followed her out of our small grey military barracks room. We walked down the grey corridors and into the briefing room. The room had several rows of chairs facing a big blank monitor and a desk with a laptop.

Ruby stood behind the desk with Mary sat at the side. Bradders sat at the back with Dunk and Smash, all dressed in green and brown camouflage clothes. Cassius sat on the other side, opposite Bradders, having turned his chair around to monitor the exit and our human buddies.

I walked in and nodded to Ruby, who returned it with a smile until Thorn walked in behind me, and then she returned to her laptop. We joined Cassius at the side of the room, pulling chairs around to keep an eye on everyone.

"We are just waiting on Rip, as per normal," Ruby said.

"He is on the way. I just asked him to bring refreshments," Thorn said.

Rip walked in, holding four glasses and a bottle of blood tucked under his arm. He walked over, handed us each a glass and poured out the blood.

Rip had dressed casually like the rest of the Dragans, the opposite of our human buddies, who dressed in standard-issue camouflage clothing.

"Do you have to drink that stuff now, with us in the room?" Ruby asked.

"Yes. It will make this de-briefing more bearable," Rip said and took a seat with us.

"Okay. I will make this quick as not to bore you. After that, Mary has an update for us."

The screen behind Ruby flickered into life, dividing it into eight squares, showing eight body cameras, one for each of us during the raid.

"The mission was an overall success. Everyone wing suited correctly and covered the ground at the right time. Parachute deployment good. Rip, you left it very late to open. It may be something to watch in the future."

Rip raised his glass. "Yes, ma'am."

"Jon, your landing was too close to the rest of us. Luckily, Bradders steered you away."

"Okay. Can we go over it later?"

"Of course," Ruby said. "Next, we followed the plan and surrounded the vineyard correctly. We evaluated the situation and took an alternative course of action as required. The use of psychic comms and other Dragan abilities gave us a clear advantage in coordinating our tactics and keeping the Turned in the dark."

"What about the failure of the intelligence, about the numbers at the vineyard?" Thorn said.

"Yes. This is something we will investigate. No intelligence is one hundred percent, but we had alternative plans. This secondary plan worked well in causing a diversion for the attack from behind. Rip, you left yourself open in your charge through their rear lines and jumping down onto the porch."

Rip wagged his finger. "No. I knew V and Thorn were on the way through. I could sense the numbers and weighed up the odds. It was a small risk, but I was having so much fun."

"The only part to discuss is the finding of the Original," Ruby said.

"You mean how you killed him without our approval," Thorn said.

"No. I mean the fact you even delayed."

"Regardless, the agreement was to make joint decisions. You broke that agreement?"

"The mission assignment was clear. Eliminate The Original. He talked of switching sides, but it was obviously just to stay alive. I don't believe he meant it; after all, he led the Turned rebellion against the Dragan's. At best, he would have told us just enough to stay alive. At worst, he would have been a double agent. The mission was clear, kill the first-gen Turned to prevent future generations from being created. It was you that went off mission."

"These things may be true, but it wasn't your choice to make alone."

"We were running out of time. He had probably sent a distress call, and the extraction didn't have room for another body."

"I don't care. Next time talk to us. Tell us what you're thinking. I will act fast."

Mary stood up and walked into the centre of the room. "Anyway, this isn't the only off-mission point we should be discussing. I want to know why Jon took the vampire formula."

"For starters, how many times must I re-iterate that his name is V. Jon Harper is no more. Secondly, the agreement was not to take the formula while at the base. He wasn't on the base when he injected."

"That is not what we said. I said no using the formula while working with us."

"No, you said no using the formula on the base."

Mary shook her head. "I knew we should have written this down and signed it."

"Yes. Then maybe you would have remembered about taking joint decisions."

Mary closed her eyes, took a deep breath, and turned back to the front of the room.

"You can't change the mission," Ruby shouted.

Thorn bolted out of her chair and I grabbed her hand. Ruby pulled her pistol from the holster. Dunk and Smash leapt to their feet, scattering the chairs across the room. Cassius rose from his chair. Rip drank more blood, and Bradders scratched his chin.

Mary spun around and held out her hands towards Ruby and Thorn. "Calm down, everyone. We obviously have some ironing out in the relationship. The mission was a massive success. We killed The Original and a whole load of second and third generation Turned. You also worked incredibly well together in the field. Let us not forget those facts."

I tugged on Thorn's hand. "Mary is right. No point in us fighting over a success. I would hate to see what would have happened if the mission had failed." Thorn sat back down and Cassius followed. Ruby re-holstered her gun, and Dunk and Smash put the chairs back and sat down again. Rip poured more blood. Bradders sighed.

Mary walked to the desk and worked the laptop, and Ruby sat down at the side. The screen changed from the video capture of our mission to different CCTV footage.

"I am glad we have that out in the open because we have more pressing demands. This is CCTV footage from our secure facility."

Black and white night vision CCTV showed a floodlit barbed wire fence. Lights flashed through it and a bus hurtled in, tearing a hole in the wall, ripping the metal posts out of the ground. A swarm of figures rushed the fence and pulled apart the wire links, letting another group of armed men dressed in full body armour invade the facility. A few soldiers stood guarding the broken fence as the rest rushed in.

The CCTV change to another camera angle, showing the soldiers shooting at the building. Retaliatory gunfire blasted back, knocking down the invaders. The door to the building opened and the group rushed in.

The camera changed again to show a man stood in the middle of a prison cell staring at a door. He was dressed in an all in one boiler suit. The door opened, an invader entered and handed over a machine gun. They exchanged words and Cyrus, the prisoner, followed them out.

The CCTV footage switched back to the main gate, where a tall man clothed all in black stood with his arms crossed behind his back. Cyrus followed the Hunters through the hole in the fence and stood in front of Bramel. They stood opposite one another for a few seconds, and then Bramel extended his hand and Cyrus shook it. After that, they all left and the footage stopped.

"As I said, we have more pressing demands. Bramel has released Cyrus and they are working together."

"They always have been. Surely this confirms beyond any reasonable doubt that Cyrus is South," I said.

Mary weakly smiled and nodded. "It would seem while we were chasing down The Original, the Turned were freeing their true master."

"This is unlucky. If we were still in the country, we might have been able to go after them."

Rip stood up and drank down his blood. "This is no coincidence that we were in another country while they freed Cyrus. This was intentional."

"You think they sacrificed the Original to get us looking the other way?"

Thorn asked.

"Of course. As Ovidiu said, there is no love lost between him and Bramel. With the true identity of South known as Cyrus, who is really next in line? Cyrus's own creation, the leader of his armies or Bramel, the vampire he fought against? Bramel sacrificed the Original to get rid of a political rival and along with it, destroyed the majority of a rival faction."

"I don't understand," I said.

"The Turned are divided into two factions. Those that fought for Cyrus and led by the Original, and those that fought for Thorn and led by Bramel. The majority of second-gen and third-gen Turned come from either Ovidiu or Bramel. The reason Bramel never killed Ovidiu when taking the title of King, was that it would alienate half the Turned. So he let him live in a subservient role. With Cyrus being outed as South, Ovidiu may have a stronger claim to the title of King of the Turned with the aid of his Dragan master. Bramel has killed off a rival and secured the friendship of South all in one move."

The room was silent as we all reasoned it through. "But we don't know how Cyrus controlled the Turned. He must have been doing it through Bramel. And Ovidiu betrayed Cyrus in the first place. So your theory does not convince me," Mary said.

"This is also true while South remained in the shadows. He needed to work with the strongest of the Turned. But now visible, he could choose his own right-hand man. He could have replaced Bramel as wouldn't need the strongest Turned as the King. It may even suit him to have a weak vampire in place, one that was bound to him by the blood bond," Rip said.

"Just a minute. If bound to him by the blood bond, how did the Turned ever rebel?" Bradders asked. We all turned around and stared in surprise. "What? It is a perfectly reasonable question."

"We know, Bradders, but it is the first intelligent thing you have ever said," Ruby responded.

"Haha. I am always thinking. You just don't pay me for my thoughts."

Thorn stood up. "This is a good question. One we have thought about for some time. We believe they broke the bond because of the overriding instinct to survive. The first Turned rebelled against Cyrus as they were losing the war. Cyrus's Turned army was decimated. He wouldn't surrender and kept sending them against us. The fear of the true death and the need to survive bound them all together. This joint bond between the Turned was stronger than the connection to their creators. It had replaced that bond with another amongst themselves, and Cyrus's army left him."

"But what about your army?" Mary asked.

"Same thing but different circumstances. I had won and no longer needed a vampire army. The vampires no longer had any goal or purpose. I claimed some lands and gold, but having such a big army to feed soon became a problem. We were attracting all the wrong attention. I thinned the pack. At night, Cassius and I would pick off vampires and kill them. The disappearances were noted, and we put it down to desertion. But the army was too large for us to deplete it by killing a few a night, so I created a death squad from the vampire ranks, offered them money and power.

"One night of hunting, the death squad got caught by a group of vampires who had started their own secret vigilante squad to protect each other. The truth soon came out and the vampires bound together to survive. Bramel knew of the death squad and saved his skin by leading the revolt and killing the death squad. We had to go on the run. Bramel led his Turned army to find Ovidiu's army, and there was a battle for King of the Turned. Bramel won but had to keep Ovidiu alive and onside to make peace and cement his leadership."

"So, basically, the Turned replaced the blood bond to their creators with a bond amongst themselves. But Cyrus would probably have preferred Ovidiu to Bramel. Hence, why Bramel sacrificed Ovidiu to remove a rival and gain a powerful ally," Mary said.

"Yes. But Cyrus is now free and in charge of the Turned and Hunter army."

"Will the Turned accept him?" Mary asked.

"If Bramel says it is okay, then I would imagine so. But it would be interesting to see the reaction of the Turned when finding out they have been under the control of a Dragan all along," Thorn said.

"With Cyrus released and aligned with the Turned and Hunters, we need to speed up our plans." Mary clicked a button on the laptop, and the screen changed again to show pictures of two young women, identical in features and clothing, talking to alone young man sat at a cafe table. One sat opposite and the other to his side with the chair moved around to face him. Both women smiled up to their sky-blue eyes, and a white cloth band swept back their dark hair.

"Ladies and gentlemen, these are the Twins. I expect they caught this young man in their rapture and probably provided them with a good feed. These two Dragans are highly dangerous. You have probably heard us discuss them before. We know where they are, but we have been reluctant to contact them due to their unique abilities. But if Cyrus is out, he will be looking for them."

Rip shifted in his seat, poured himself more blood, and looked away from the screen. This was the first time I had seen a picture of them, and they looked familiar.

Bradders raised his hand. "They are Dragans but what is so special about them?"

"They have abilities and a past that doesn't align with our own goals," Mary said.

Thorn stood up again. "Let me explain. I know them better than anyone else." Mary deferred and Thorn took centre stage, looking at us all as she spoke. "The Twins are Dragan, as you know. They have the normal abilities of speed, strength and psychic powers. But it is these psychic powers that make them stand out. You have heard of human twins having a strong connection, an almost psychic connection. All Dragans have a psychic connection if we wish, but as these two are identical twins, that psychic connection makes their minds as one. To put it simply, when together, they have twice the psychic power of a normal Dragan. Two normal Dragans can't meld their minds together to create this same level of psychic force."

"What does that mean? What can they do?" Bradders asked.

Thorn looked at Rip and bit her lip. He downed his blood. "I will tell you as I have suffered first hand. Their powers are strong, even against another Dragan. For example, they can double the Dragan power to seduce through their connection and identical scent. They can delve into your mind and discover your hidden secrets and desires. They can direct their thoughts into your mind and make you see and feel things that aren't real. Yes, they did this to me, and as a result, Cyrus's Turned army killed Thorn's family."

"So it is an assassination mission. I have my sniper rifle at the ready," Bradders said.

Thorn snarled and eyes misted red. "NO. We do not harm these girls. Do you understand?"

Bradders jumped back in his chair and it hit against the wall. He held his hands out in surrender. "Of course, whatever you say. It just sounded like you wanted to remove the threat."

Her eyes reverted to normal. Ruby took her hand off her pistol. Thorn continued. "You are partly right. Yes, we want to remove the threat, and this means getting to them and recruiting them before Cyrus does."

"They worked for Cyrus before then?" Ruby said.

"Yes. Cyrus had formed a connection with them while I was in Union with him. I thought it was over when he left, just a schoolgirl crush. But they became hostile from the events and fled. Cyrus was waiting for them and they formed a Union."

"The Twins are responsible for the death of your son?" I asked.

Thorn closed her eyes for a moment and took a deep breath. "They didn't kill him. The Turned did. I don't know if that is what they wanted, but they were an integral part of the attack that night."

"Now, Cyrus is free. He will go after them and use them against us. What makes you think we can recruit them instead?" I asked.

"Because they don't realise that Cyrus is South."

"How can you be sure? Maybe they are part of it, using their powers to control the Turned."

"Not that many in one go, even they have limits."

"It is a big risk trying to recruit them, considering their background and powers," I said.

"It is either recruit or imprison. Either way, we must keep them from Cyrus," Thorn said, and returned to her seat. Mary handed over the laptop to Ruby.

"The next mission is to capture the Twins, Isabella and Marcella. This will be a Dragan led mission as the Twins could too easily overpower us. We will tag along for background support only." Ruby sat down, and Rip stood up and walked to the laptop to face us all. "V and Cassius are going to retrieve the Twins. They will speak with them first."

I sank back in my chair. "Why me? You just said they are extremely dangerous. I am not even a full Dragan."

"You are still in your transformed state. It will last another couple of nights as you near the end of your evolution and you can accelerate your powers. Unfortunately, if they sense Thorn or me, they will run. You, on the other hand, are a curiosity. They will want to meet you for sure. They have probably heard of you already, just as The Original had. The human boy who became King of the Dragans, in Union with Thorn, and can transform into full dragon state. They won't be able to resist."

"Oh, great. I am bait, yet again. Just like with Rip. Why is it always me?"

"It wouldn't work with anyone else," Thorn said.

"Talk to them. We will listen in on hidden microphones, but we can't risk being too near without them detecting our psychic patterns. Tell them Cyrus is South. Tell them your story. Get them to agree to meet with Thorn on neutral ground," Ruby said.

"Thorn, I don't like this at all. They could kill me."

"Trust me."

I examined the picture of the Twins again. There was definitely something familiar about them. I couldn't shake that feeling we had already met. My thoughts struggled in my mind to unveil the truth, but every time my thoughts cleared, darkness descended. "There is something you aren't telling me. I know these girls from somewhere."

Rip coughed. Thorn gave me a cold hard stare. "You are right; there is something I am not telling you. I won't tell you else the plan won't work. Do as I ask without question. You must trust me one hundred percent."

I grabbed the bottle of blood from Rip's seat and poured a glass. "Will you ever tell me?"

"Of course, I will. You will need to know once the Twins have joined us."

I took a sip of blood. Usually it left me feeling sick, but since my last two transformations, the blood had an appeal. "It doesn't sound like I have a choice."

Mary shut the laptop lid. "Good, grab your gear. We are heading to Rome tonight, and soon we could have two new allies or two new prisoners."

Chapter Four

We grabbed our equipment and clothes and made for two waiting helicopters in the parade ground at the training centre. We flew out under cover of darkness, a short half hour skip across the treetops till we reached an airstrip and a sleek white private jet sat at the start of the runway. The helicopters landed next to it, and we ran out from under the whirling blades, up the stairs and into the jet.

The stairways rolled away as the air stewardess closed the jet door and clamped it shut. The jet had about twenty big leather seats and tables in front of each pair. Thorn and I buckled in next to one another. I watched as the two helicopters took off, peeled away and landed next to an aircraft hangar set back from the runway.

The plane rolled forward and the stewardess went through the safety briefing as we trundled down the runway. She finished and went into the cockpit. The plane lurched forward and pinned us back into our seats, its wheels rumbling down the concrete and engines roaring in stereo to propel us forward.

The plane tipped back, and the rumbling of the tyres on the concrete stopped as the aircraft lifted off the ground and rocketed up into the night. We banked around, tilting to view the ground, and then, after a few minutes, it levelled off.

Rip unbuckled and shouted to the cockpit. "Any complimentary drinks?"

The flight attendant re-appeared and pulled out a small trolley at the back of the plane and wheeled it to Rip. "I heard, sir, might want some red wine." She passed him a small bottle of red wine and a plastic cup.

Rip turned to Mary, who sat a few seats back with Ruby. "I am beginning to like you."

Mary smiled. "No problem. We have to look after our allies."

Rip winked back and opened his red wine.

Thorn nudged me with her elbow and whispered. "I think romance is in the air."

I looked from Rip to Mary and then whispered back to Thorn. "Those two?"

Thorn just smiled and held her hand up to get the stewardess's attention. "Two more red wines here, please."

We opened our small bottles and drank. "Is this for training?" I asked.

Thorn took a sip and shook her head. "No. I have just developed a taste for it."

"These Twins, who are they? What is it you are hiding from me?" I said, hoping a quick, direct question might catch her off guard.

Thorn placed her red wine down and held my hand. "V, I said, don't ask. You have to trust me."

I thought of the Twins again and looked at Thorn. Something was falling into place, and then it darkened over again. I couldn't quite put the pieces together. I blinked my eyes and scanned around the cabin to clear my mind. Rip and Cassius both laid back in their seats with their eyes closed.

"V, look at me," Thorn said.

I spun back. "It is on the edge of my thoughts. I just need some peace and quiet, and it will come to me. I know it."

"Trust me and stop trying to work it out. The plan requires your ignorance. So, please accept this explanation and all will become clear at the end. When you meet the Twins, you can ask them yourself, or they will probably tell you straight away."

"How can you expect me to go in there without knowing the truth?"

"We do lots of things without knowing the actual reasons why? Can you explain why you rescued me from prison?"

"I felt drawn to you because of the blood bond in the formula."

"That is the cause of your feelings that you discovered later. But at the time, why did you rescue me?"

"I just had to see you again."

"See. We do things without really understanding them. The reasons only become clear later on."

"I suppose," I said.

"Let us think of something else. Let me tell you of the time I fought the devil."

"What the..?"

"Yes. Drink up and I will tell all." Thorn signalled to the stewardess for more red wine.

Thorn told me the most fantastic story. The devil had noticed her due to the Dragan Civil War and tried to recruit her with the offer of great power. She had refused, to which the Devil didn't take kindly and they fought. She still had the Devil's red sword stored away in her chateau. The story sounded true, but as usual with Thorn, there were missing details. True or not, it had the effect hoped for, as I had forgotten about the strange familiarity of the

Twins.

After a couple of hours, we landed outside Rome and a group of black cars drove us into the city centre. I looked out the car window for the top quality hotel we would stay in and thought of the view from the penthouse.

The car whizzed past several high-class establishments with sweeping driveways and bright illuminated entrances and awaiting hotel staff. But we pulled down a side road and halted behind a row of scooters. We had stopped outside a grey concrete building that went up three levels, with fewer rooms on each level as it stepped up to one grey block and window at the top.

Inside, a man waited for us and we all followed him up the dingy stairs, with suitcases and backpacks in tow. On each level, he handed out keys until we reached the top with just Thorn and I left.

The room was on the top floor, but I wouldn't have described it as a penthouse. The room was basic, with a double bed, standard desk and cupboard and TV hung on the wall. There was a small terrace outside big enough for a small round table and two chairs. It looked onto the surrounding buildings, but no grand view of Rome.

I flung the suitcase onto the bed and sighed. "This isn't our usual standard."

"No. I didn't book it. We are here on a mission, so it is best to keep a low profile. Leave the suitcase. We are too late to find the Twins. Tomorrow, we will go over the plan early evening, and you and Cassius will head out. In the meantime, let us take a stroll in the night."

"Are you looking for a feed?"

"I wish. It may attract unwanted attention. It is bad enough with us arriving in the dead of night and staying inside all day. I just want to take in the air and get my bearings."

We wandered out into the night for a stroll, and Rip and Cassius went in the opposite direction to a late-night wine bar. We walked through the maze of narrow cobbled streets, lined with little shops and cafes, with customers drinking and puffing out smoke. The three-storey buildings, which overshadowed the customers, had rough stonework and plants crawling over the archways and windows. The streets led into even narrower side streets with parked scooters and overflowing bins.

The side streets popped out into a market square with wandering groups of people and onto larger modern roads, carrying a flurry of traffic, connecting to the old historic streets of Rome.

Thorn grabbed my hand. "Last time I walked these streets, Cassius and I were looking for Cyrus and the Twins. We both wore flared trousers and platform boots. It was the seventies, 1974, I think. I had left London and changed my identity from Tessa Horn to Tracey Horn. I had given Marcy ownership of the shelter. And I couldn't return for a few years to allow my new identity to settle in and appear at the right age. I had stayed too long as Tessa Horn. People were wondering how I remained so young, but I had to stay until Marcy was old enough to look after herself.

Anyway, we hunted around for Cyrus for about two weeks with no luck. This was before the information technology boom. We had no CCTV and no phones or internet to find people. We just relied on the printed press and word of mouth."

"What made you think they were here?"

"In exchange for helping the British secret service during the second world war, they were keeping an eye out for any intelligence that could lead to other Dragans. There had been a pattern of disappearances in Rome and a few stories of people with supernatural powers. We hunted around the areas mentioned and spoke with the people involved. But I think Cyrus and the Twins had already left the area."

"But you think they have returned?"

"It is not far away that we located Cyrus last year. They probably rotate their living arrangements to avoid uncomfortable questions about their lack of ageing. I do the same. Move from place to place to avoid any suspicions. They probably have houses across the world. Remember, Max met Cyrus in America and he was heading into Canada following a lead on us?"

"That was probably because of our skiing holiday. Those fights and feeding on the tourists and locals must have attracted attention."

"Most likely. Cyrus worked for the Nazis in the second world war, and the Americans inherited his service afterwards. He probably got the info from them," Thorn said.

We headed back after an hour of wandering the streets and rested up during the daylight. As the light faded into the night again, Thorn woke up and pulled on jeans and a black vest top. I stretched out under the covers and held out my hand to her. "Why so quick to get up? The mission doesn't start for a few hours, as we need to wait for them to go out hunting. We could spend some time together first."

She smiled and tied her hair into a ponytail. "Not tonight. I want to make sure we have everything ready for confronting the Twins. We need our minds on the game."

I sat bolt upright in the bed. "Is everything okay?"

Thorn sat down and pulled on a pair of black leather boots. "I am fine. It will all be okay if we follow the plan. I don't want to make any mistakes. I want to focus on the mission at hand."

"What better way to focus than to make sure any distractions are taken care of," I said and reached out my hand again.

Thorn kissed me. "Get up and get ready. You will need all your energy tonight," she said and then walked out the door. It was unlike her to be so tense. The Twins must be dangerous.

I put on jeans, a plain white t-shirt and then followed her downstairs. The others weren't up yet, so we waited in the cafe next door, drinking coffee. Once everyone was awake, Mary arranged a few cars to take us to the briefing location.

We arrived at a construction site. She undid the padlock to the gates, ducked under the scaffolding and prised open the chipboard panels into a shell of a new building.

Flood lamps in the corners focused onto a central spot where four tables had been set up. One table had two human operators with two computers running . One laptop had a map of Rome and streamed CCTV pictures from the cafe quarters.

Another two tables had weapons laid out, machine guns, pistols, shotguns, knives, and swords. The last table had a fridge by the side attached to a generator, which also supplied the lights. On the table were bottles of water and blood, and flasks of tea and coffee, and a tray of cakes.

I picked up a doughnut and devoured it in a few bites, licking the sugar off my fingers. Mary went to speak to the two men at the computers. Rip and Cassius headed for the blood, and Thorn went through the weapons on the table.

Mary walked back with one of the computer operators. "George is going to fit you with a hidden camera and GPS unit, so we can follow your movements."

George placed a bag on the floor. He clipped a wallet-sized device onto my jeans and pinned the camera onto my chest; it looked like a football badge. He clicked a button on the device. "They are paired together. The device on your jeans is the transmitter. Without it, we can't get the images and your location."

Thorn walked over, holding out a knife and ankle strap. "Take this," she said and knelt, pulled up my jeans leg and strapped it around my calf muscle.

George walked back to the computer. “Everything is working okay,” he said, and I could see the image of Thorn as she stood up in front of me.

“They will listen to every word you say. So be careful what you talk about,” she said and tapped a finger to her head. *‘We can still communicate psychically for a while, but you will go out of my range else the Twins will pick it up with their enhanced powers.’*

‘I shouldn’t accidentally give away our secrets then.’

‘Exactly. Keep your mind on the mission only. Don’t let anything slip. We shouldn’t trust the MI5-S unit.’

“Okay, you two, have you finished your psychic chat? Are you ready to start?” Mary said.

“Ready,” we both said together.

Mary led us outside to an awaiting car and van. Thorn, Rip, Mary and George, carrying his laptop, climbed into the black van. “Good luck. We will be watching,” Thorn said, as she pulled the van door shut. Cassius and I got in the back of the car.

The car weaved through the back streets and then joined the crowd of cars hurtling along the roads, horns tooting and people shouting and gesticulating out the windows at perceived slights. I was concerned we wouldn’t even make it to the drop off point. The traffic in Rome was hectic. I couldn’t work out how anyone drove through these streets. There was obviously some unseen order to the chaos that I couldn’t figure out. The van followed but dropped back into the traffic until it was lost in the flow and stream of headlights.

The car stopped at the edge of a pedestrian area. We got out and the car re-joined the flow of traffic, with a blaring of horns and flashing lights from the other road users. The driver gave a hand signal to show his appreciation.

“Follow me, little one. I have been briefed on the areas to scout out to find the Twins,” Cassius said.

“You know your way around?”

“Of course, Thorn and I visited Rome a few times. We got different reports of Cyrus and the Twins in the area but never found them. I suspect the Twins always stayed one step ahead of us. They always sensed us coming.”

“What is different this time?”

“You, for a start. They will have heard of the infamous V. Plus, we have MI5-S tracing them as well.”

“Would that not alert them?”

“The use of technology means they don’t have to get so close. Hacking their accounts, flying drones and using bugs helped track them down and kept them under surveillance without triggering their senses."

"But as we approach, they will sense us and run away," I said.

"There are lots of people around. Psychic clutter," he said as we joined in the crowds. "Plus, Rip has taught us a trick or two. We need to use our magic to dull our Dragan selves, shut off the psychic abilities, hold back the Dragan scent and heat. It should be enough in amongst the crowds to cover our identities. We can get close enough before they realise who we are."

The heat of the day had dissipated, but it remained warm enough for people to stay dressed in lightweight and shorter clothes. The cooler air freed up everyone's energy and groups gathered, and we navigated our way in between the milling crowds.

Cassius took us into the middle of the crowd and checked his phone. A map showed two red pinpoints slowly moving around and us as a blue arrow on the screen. We were only a ten-minute walk away.

"I guess that is them," I said, pointing at the two red pinpoints.

"Yes. We have hacked their phones and been tracing them." Another screen popped up in the corner, showing images of them scanning the crowds at a flood lit cafe area. "We have the cooperation of the local authorities as well. They gave MI5-S access to the CCTV cameras in the area. "

"The Twins are looking for someone," I said.

"Their latest feed. The intelligence states it has been a couple of days. This area is perfect for them. Lots of tourists who get too drunk to remember what happened, or too embarrassed to say they went with twins, or they can't remember due to the Twins overwriting their memories. Also, a lot of temporary working staff who aren't recorded or not wanting to get involved."

"So, what's next? Do we stop them?"

Cassius held a finger to his ear. "Message from Mary and Thorn. Let the Twins engage and focus on a victim. That way, they will be pre-occupied. Then we will get a little closer, so we can be ready to move in."

We walked on for five minutes through the wandering groups of tourists and locals enjoying at night out. We stopped and watched the CCTV stream as the Twins circled the cafes, looking for a target. They both dressed exactly the same to maximise the effect, a short black skirt and white vest top to reveal as much flesh as possible, but still looking elegant.

Eventually, Marcella walked over to a lone man drinking coffee at a table. She showed him something on her phone, and he offered her a seat. Marcella waved over to Isabella, who wandered through the other occupied tables to join them. She called over a waiter. The two women sat on either side of the lone man at a white metal table. They laughed, flashed their sky-blue eyes and flicked back their dark brown hair as they talked.

The camera changed to a picture of the man. He grinned as he talked and the Twins laughed. Marcella reached out and held his hand, and Isabella stroked her hand across his beard.

Cassius held his finger to his ear and nodded his head. "Time to go. They are making their move; we only have a few minutes before they whisk him away. You go straight ahead. I will take the right. You approach them from the front, and I will cover in from behind."

Cassius walked off to the right, and I walked straight ahead to the cafe. I walked through a cluster of tables, keeping the Twins in sight, who were still gazing into the man's eyes. Marcella smiled, flicked her dark brown hair back and glanced around. She looked straight at me and then looked away again. Her face frowned and she looked back. I smiled back at her and walked directly towards them.

Isabella's head spun around and she glared at me. Marcella let go of the man's hand and stood up. Her eyes narrowed and I felt a twinge in my forehead. I had been using my magic to cover up my Dragan aura, but now I let the magic go and pushed it into my mind to stop her from invading.

Isabella leapt up and said something to the lone man, who stood up and approached me. "Leave these women alone. They have told me how you beat them," he shouted.

He held his hands up to block me. I grabbed his hand, twisted his arm around and forced him to the floor, yowling in pain. I let go and marched on.

The Twins turned away straight into Cassius. "Hello, Ladies. Where are you going?"

They snarled at him and turned back to where I stood in front of them.

"So you are Isabella and you are Marcella," I said, pointing to them.

"No, she is Isabella," Isabella said, pointing at Marcella.

"And she is Marcella," Marcella said, pointing at Isabella.

"Hilarious. And I am V."

"The infamous V," Isabella said.

"The special one, mummy's little boy," Marcella said.

"Not this again. Why does everyone think I am missing a mother and that Thorn is a substitute?"

The Twins looked at each other and laughed. "He doesn't know," they both said.

"Know what?"

"Not very bright either," Isabella said.

My attack on the lone man had attracted some attention, and a group of waiters had formed behind me.

"This man causing you any problems, ladies. We saw him knock over your friend."

They both stared at me and smiled. "No, he is no problem," said Marcella.

"He is a special thing to play with. That man he knocked over was trying to sell us drugs. Our friend is protecting us," Isabella said.

The waiters turned away and ushered the man out of the cafe area, with a lot of colourful language.

"We need to talk," Cassius said.

"Why not," Isabella replied.

"Yes, I think we would enjoy that," Marcella confirmed.

I was more confused than ever and followed them out of the cafe area across the plaza. It sounded like Thorn's plan worked. My ignorance was indeed vital to get them to talk to us. But now, my curiosity was burning. What on earth was it I didn't know? And why did that so intrigue the Twins enough to put their own safety at risk?

As we walked away into the open space, three men walked towards us. They looked to their sides. I looked to my side and back as two women closed in from behind, another two men from the left and a man and woman from the right. This wasn't just random crowd movements. The circle closed in on us in a directed effort. I sensed no psychic thoughts from them, but they looked and smelt normal, like normal humans. They must have just fed to blend in so well. The Twins stopped and Cassius scanned the new arrivals.

"It's a trap," Cassius said.

"Just keep moving. They won't attack with all these people around," Isabella said.

They pushed in closer, forcing us to stop dead in our tracks. Cassius and the Twins snarled.

One woman stepped a little closer to the Twins. "Come with us. No need to make a scene."

"No. I don't work with the Turned," Isabella said.

"You did once. Cyrus has sent us to protect you against these people until he arrives."

"Never. Cyrus is a Dragan. He would never align himself with the Turned," Marcella said.

"He created us, remember? Now come quietly and leave these two."

"No. I don't believe your lies. Out of our way," Isabella replied, and Marcella front kicked the woman into the other Turned. The other Turned held her up. The woman's eyes changed and thin yellow claws ripped through her fingers. Her skin wrinkled up and decayed, and a foul odour of rotting meat released from her body. The other Turned all snarled and forced on the change, with bodies reverting to their real vampire state of decaying flesh, black eyes and yellow claws.

The confrontation had already attracted the attention of the people in the plaza. The transformation into vampires sent screams echoing around us and the scattering of people, knocking over tables and chairs, smashing glasses and plates to the stone slab floor.

The Turned woman leapt at Isabella, who ducked out of the way, and Marcella punched into the space to hit her. Cassius charged forward with a double fist hammer blow to the skull of a snarling Turned, breaking its neck and it flopping to the floor like a rag doll.

As I reached down to my ankle for the silver knife, a Turned jumped on my back and hauled me upwards. I twisted to the side and threw him over my shoulder. I went for the knife again, but two Turned tackled me to the ground.

One scrambled onto my chest and the other clawed into my stomach. The pain gripped my body and fuelled my magic. I focused it into my legs and kneed upwards, pitching the Turned off and away from slashing at my flesh.

I thrust my hand forwards, my claws ripping straight into the vampire's throat. He clutched at the wound and fell away. I rolled back onto my shoulders and flipped to my feet in time to launch a roundhouse kick into an attacking Turned. I ducked the next punch and rolled out of the way into space, reaching down to my ankle and withdrawing the silver knife.

The Twins fought side by side as the Turned attacked in either direction. Isabella blocked a punch and counterattacked with a roundhouse kick that was way off target. Marcella did the same on her side. Both vampires launched into the space to attack while the Twins spun around with their backs facing them.

The Turned dived into the space and into the undefended backs of the Twins. But both Twins kept spinning and moving backwards, and then jumped up and kicked out behind them into each other's attackers, hitting the attackers full-on as they charged in. They smacked both the Turned off their feet, who cracked onto the stone.

Other Turned rushed in. The Twins stood back to back, blocking the onslaught. Isabella swung in a spinning back fist, which the Turned ducked.

But Isabella spun around and hit an opponent attacking Marcella, who had already dipped, twisted in the other direction to punch the Turned escaping from Isabella.

I watched fascinated as they fought as one person, with four eyes, four legs, four arms, with four sets of claws and fists. They moved in synchronous, balletic movements, covering each other's attacks, altering the direction to evade and surprise the enemy. I understood how dangerous they were, not just the psychic abilities for mind control, but to coordinate their fighting movements as if controlled by one mind.

A Turned ran from the Twins to attack me. I blocked its fist and stabbed in the silver knife. It staggered back, burning blood flowing out from the stab wound until it flamed all over and exploded to ash.

Sirens rang into the plaza, and it wouldn't be long before we would be cornered. The Twins knocked their last attacker down. The fallen vampires scrambled to their feet and ran off, and the Twins sprinted away from the sirens.

"After them," Cassius shouted as he fought the last remaining vampire.

I concealed the knife back into the ankle holder and sprinted after them. For once, there being two of them was a disadvantage. When I couldn't see what direction they had run in, the people they passed stared after them and gave off a psychic surprise at seeing two beautiful identical twins sprinting through the streets. I just followed the path of psychic shock and used my magic to accelerate after them.

I chased until I was a few footsteps away. They slowed to a walk and opened the door to a block of flats.

"You might as well come in," Isabella said.

"Doesn't look like we can shake you off," Marcella said.

"Good, I have some questions."

They walked into the apartment block, and I followed them up three flights of stairs. I assumed Thorn would still get the images and location from my device. Hopefully, I could keep them occupied for long enough or even talk them around in time for Thorn's arrival.

They unlocked the door and walked into their apartment. It opened up into the main living area of polished wooden floors and white painted walls. Two large beige sofas sat at right angles in the middle, with a glass coffee table in between. On either side of the short hallway was a door. One was open into a bedroom with twin beds and mirrors along the walls.

The Twins sat side by side on a sofa and offered me a seat on the other sofa. As I walked around to join them, I viewed the spotless kitchen to the side. I guess they hardly ever used it. Then stopped and pulled back the curtains to look through the folding glass doors onto a balcony. The view looked straight into the apartment across the narrow street.

"Please, sit down," Isabella said.

I took a seat on the other sofa. They sat mirroring each other's pose. I looked at both of them and that feeling of similarity came back again. It wasn't just the way they looked. But it was also the way they talked and moved. Surely, I must have met them both before.

"You have questions?" Isabella said.

Where to start? I had so many, but the obvious one seemed the best place.

"Have we met before?"

They both laughed and tossed their hair back at the same time. "No."

"But I recognise you. There is something strangely familiar about you."

The Twins looked at each other.

"He really..." Isabella said.

"Doesn't know." Marcella continued.

"How sad…"

"That she didn't tell him."

"She knows how much we like to take her things."

"Maybe it is a gift."

"To bring us back?"

"No."

"Then why?"

"She likes her secrets."

"She knew we would be interested."

"But he's lost his babysitter."

"And now he is…."

"All alone with the wicked women," they both said together and giggled.

The constant starting and finishing of each other's sentences had my head spinning. It was hard to keep up.

"Okay. You are obviously dying to tell me. So please get to the point."

"Ah. Mummy's little boy is getting frustrated."

"I told you. Thorn isn't a mother substitute."

They smiled and Isabella sat forward. "I never said she was. You are interpreting the wording as a phrase and not applying the correct English to it. We said, mummy's little boy. As in, our mother's little boy."

My stomach cramped and mind rocked as the information made sense. I sunk back into the chair and stared at the two women. Their features, dark hair, sky-blue eyes, and their sick sense of humour and flirtatious manner. No wonder they seemed familiar.

"You are Thorn's daughters?"

They nodded.

I could see it now. As I looked closer, the similarities stood out. The facial structure and shape of their nose. As I stared at their features, comparing the similarities, their light olive skin faded.

"You had an affair with Cyrus, and helped him kill Thorn's parents, your grandparents, your baby brother and Thorn's husband."

"Our father, you mean. After the failed Union with Cyrus, mummy and daddy got back together to make more Dragan babies. They knew it would work."

"But why did you kill them all?"

"Thorn wasn't much of a mother. To interested in her place in the realm as the princess and heir to the Dragan throne. Although I am sure we were gorgeous babies and the talk of the realm. But as we grew up, we presented a problem, which one of us would be in line to the throne."

"The eldest, I assume."

Isabella shook her head. As she shook, her straight hair kinked into waves of raven black hair.

"Not that easy. They never recorded which of us came first. Secondly, I think you can see we are of one mind. How could we ever be separated?"

"So two queens. But is it such a problem? Thorn's parents and Thorn are immortal. You would be waiting a long time."

"Not immortal. Just very hard to kill and with an undiscovered lifespan. However, it seemed our grandparents weren't as resilient. They were clearly ageing, even if at a slower rate. The transformation had weighed heavily upon them. But not so for Thorn, as she was born a Dragan. She would become the queen one day and live for a very long time."

Marcella stood up and walked over. "Come and sit with us. It will be easier to talk." As she walked over, her body stretched out, and her curves slimmed down. She reached out her hand and her olive skin continued to fade to a pale white. I gazed up into sky-blue eyes and a breeze curled her newly raven tinted hair.

Thorn stood before me. I placed my hand in hers, and she helped me off the chair and guided me back to the sofa. Isabella patted the sofa with her pale white hand. She smiled, and her sky-blue eyes lit up and raven hair blew in a supernatural wind.

"Sit in-between us."

I took the seat and gazed into Isabella's eyes, Thorn's eyes. Her body had changed as well, and I looked back and forth between Isabella and Marcella. But I was wrong. I sat between Thorn and Thorn. One Thorn placed her hand on my knee and the other on my shoulder and guided me into the sofa. "Just relax. We got you," the Thorn's said.

"Let me tell you the rest," Thorn said, where Isabella had been.

"Yes, Thorn," I replied, and they smiled at one another.

"Isabella and Marcella couldn't be the heirs to the throne, as being twins caused an issue. But also their special powers had manifested. The rest of the Dragans feared them. So I had to keep them out of the way. I spent very little time with them. Instead, I focused on having another baby with Cyrus. A child that could be my true heir," the first Thorn said.

"Cyrus couldn't manage the job, so I looked elsewhere. I suppose inevitably, my wonderful daughters and Cyrus found each other. Two of my cast-offs. But when I found out, I flew into a terrible rage, threw Cyrus out, and held my daughters captive. They eventually escaped as well. Luckily, Cyrus was there to comfort them," the second Thorn said.

"You locked up your own daughters?" I asked.

"Yes, and I had been just as bad, having an affair with Rip. With Cyrus gone, I contacted the Twins' father to try again for another baby, a new heir. Of course, he accepted the position to become the Dragan King. We had another baby and replaced the Twins."

Both the Thorns shuffled in closer. One placed her hands on my shoulder and forearm. The other on my thigh and tucked her arm around my back. The supernatural breeze blew back their hair and a mist rose to my knees. Their touch electrified my skin.

"Cyrus returned with an army. They took control and liberated the Dragans from my cruel reign. If my parents were dead, I was dead, and my husband and son were dead, they would have the best claim to the throne, being my first born. Cyrus arranged a Union with them both and having been the potential Dragan King once, he had the right birth line. He would become King of the Dragans."

"So they attacked and started the civil war," I asked.

"Yes, but now you know the full history of events, you can understand why they did it. I am a terrible mother. If only I had paid them more attention. Understood their unique nature, then we could have avoided all of this."

I nodded along as their hands stroked over my body and mist tentacles rose out of the ground, wrapping around my stomach, tingling against my flesh. The mist spiralled up my nose, releasing my tension and overflowing it with desire.

"I am and was a terrible mother. But I am a terrific lover," they both said and leant in and kissed my cheeks. One Thorn rubbed her hands under my shirt and against my chest. The other stroked my inner thigh.

A voice in the dark shouted out that something was wrong. It felt like my voice, but locked in a box and thrown into a dark dungeon. I tried to focus on the voice, but I only felt her hands and the mist twisting around my torso and exhilarating my senses.

I leant back into the sofa and wrapped my arms around each of the Thorns. I closed my eyes and let myself go. Lips pressed against mine and kissed my stomach. I copied their movements to search them out as her hands worked at undoing my belt and trousers.

A loud cracking of wood stopped my enjoyment. Their lips and hands released from my lips and body. I heard faint voices as my mind fought to awaken. The voice in the box had been released and screamed out until it lit up my thoughts. I jolted upright on the sofa, my eyes sprung open and body tensed. The mist had gone and Isabella and Marcella stood up, staring at the door. My Thorns had disappeared.

"Hello, mom."

"Girls. I see you are amusing yourselves."

"Of course, another one of your men we are claiming. Just like Cyrus and Rip."

"Looks like I got here just in time."

They both snarled at Thorn and extended their claws and fangs. I scrambled away from the sofa towards Thorn. "I..I.."

"Don't worry. Just stand out of the way."

"We will see you later," the Twins said and turned to the window when the curtains blew back as the windows flung open, and Cassius climbed through.

"Not this time. You have to stay and face the consequences," he said.

"Don't run. We need to talk to you about Cyrus," Thorn said.

"What have you done with him? We haven't heard from him in months."

"He came to join us, but he betrayed us again. Cyrus is South."

"Never. South is just a story."

"We have proof. After he attacked V, he was locked away, but the Turned rescued him. Today at the plaza, Cyrus sent the Turned for you."

"Lies. Cyrus is done with the Turned. He couldn't be behind them. I would have sensed it."

"We have evidence we can show you. But you must trust us and come back to our base."

"Never." They closed their eyes, and my head tingled.

"Take them down," Thorn shouted and Cassius rugby tackled Isabella to the floor. Marcella attacked Cassius, kicking him off Isabella. Thorn charged in and punched Marcella, then Isabella kicked through Thorn's legs and upended her onto the floor.

Marcella staggered back and recovered. Isabella flipped onto her feet. Cassius scrambled back up and stood in front of the window. They turned to the door. Thorn rolled out of their way and they sprinted for the exit.

Rip appeared in the doorway and fired two darts into Isabella, who jolted back and yanked them out. She went to run but her legs buckled. Marcella slung Isabella onto her shoulder, but her eyes rolled. She staggered forward and Rip front kicked her back into the apartment. She tripped over and slammed to the floor, with her sister on top.

Rip walked over and stood above them. "The thing I worked out while waiting to meet again is that your psychic link is also your greatest weakness. You only have to beat one of you, and the other follows. You feel each other's pain and pleasure."

He fired two more darts into Marcella and they both fell asleep.

Chapter Five

The Twins lay asleep on the floor. Rip held out his hand to Thorn and pulled her to her feet.

"They always look so peaceful and harmless when sleeping," Thorn said.

"They are out for the count. Come and get them," Rip said to the MI5-S soldiers crammed in the doorway.

The soldiers walked in carrying big black bags. They knelt next to the Twins and rolled them onto their fronts. Next, they pulled back their hands and zip tied them together. Then wrapped gags and blindfolds on the Twins, and then a set of earphones from which I could hear heavy metal music pounding out.

I couldn't look at Thorn after what she had seen. I felt embarrassed to have been caught in the act with her daughters.

"V, you okay?" Thorn asked.

"Yeah. What is with the headsets?" I asked, trying to avoid the uncomfortable questions.

"Loud music will make it hard for them to concentrate. The blindfolds and gags will disorientate them as well. Should stop them using their powers between the drugs wearing off and us administering a fresh dose."

The men carried Isabella and Marcella out.

"Follow us. We have vehicles waiting downstairs to take us somewhere more secluded to have a proper talk with my wayward daughters."

Thorn took my hand as I headed to the door and held it as we walked downstairs. I still couldn't look her in the eye. But she seemed to be okay. It didn't make sense.

A van opened up its back doors, and they placed the Twins inside along with the soldiers, Rip and Cassius. Thorn got in the driver's side of a black Mercedes. I joined her in the car, just the two of us. The van drove off and we followed.

"So, you are not talking?" Thorn said.

"I don't know what to say."

"Say whatever comes to mind. I arranged for us to drive alone, as I knew you would have questions?"

I felt too confused in the immediate aftermath of Thorn discovering us to think straight. I couldn't believe she wasn't screaming and shouting at me.

"Why are you okay?" I asked.

"Me. Why shouldn't I be? The plan worked perfectly, sort of. We had to adapt a little after the Turned attacked. But otherwise, we succeeded in our mission."

"So you are okay after seeing the Twins and me together. In a few more minutes, things would have gone too far."

"No. I am not alright about it. We got there just in time. I don't think I could have forgiven myself if it had gone any further."

"Forgiven yourself! You forgive me then?"

Thorn stared at the road and remained silent for a minute.

"Of course, I forgive you. I think you are still a bit confused. This isn't the first question I expected. Remember, I said you had to trust me, that I hadn't told you everything? That it was vital to the plan."

I sat in silence for a few minutes, my memory replaying our previous conversations.

"You didn't tell me they were your daughters. You didn't tell me, so they would take an interest. You knew they would try to seduce me."

"Correct. While they were taking an interest, we made our move."

"I was bait?"

"A lovely handsome bait, but yes, you were bait. This is why I had to keep it a secret. Your prior knowledge of the Twins' true identity would have made you less appealing. They would have found it funny that you didn't know they were my daughters. They would have liked the idea of corrupting you to get at me."

I stopped staring at the floor and glared at Thorn. My muscles tensed and face flushed. "You used me. You put me in danger."

"Danger! Unlikely, you seemed pretty relaxed when I found you."

My anger faded to embarrassment again, and I looked out the window. But it wasn't my fault. I spun back again, fangs snarling. "I thought it was you. I couldn't stop them."

"Calm yourself. This is why I am not angry. You can scream, shout, and curse at me all you like. But I kept my word. You are safe and the Twins are captive. They revealed all when you met them. I never lied about having a secret. The entire plan hinged on you not knowing. I was surprised you didn't know because I referred to them as my girls when we argued with Cyrus at the forest lodge. I thought you must have known."

"I didn't hear it or make the connection. A lot happened that day."

"With us fighting the Turned and werewolves?"

"Exactly. I was a bit preoccupied trying not to get killed. But, regardless, how couldn't I see it before? The similarities between you and the Twins?"

"So, there is more to tell. Rip, Cassius, and I all had to block you from working it out. I know we said no mind-reading, but you were going to work it out otherwise."

"The clouding over in my mind every time I thought I had the answer. That was you three?"

"Yes. We had to tap into the magic and combine our psychic thoughts, a bit like the Twins but not as powerful, to block you from discovering."

I stared out the window, not sure what to say next. I had been used, but she hadn't lied about it.

"You have some making up to me?" I said.

"Why? I told you I was keeping a secret and you had to trust me for the plan to work."

"Really! How would you feel if it was the other way around?"

"I would have punched you in the face."

"Exactly."

"Okay. I will think of something."

"It best be good. Even looking at you now, I can't get the images of them appearing like you out of my head. It is going to be difficult to relax together."

"Those girls. Why is it always me they imitate?"

"They copied you before?"

"They taunted me with it. This is how they seduced Rip and let in the Turned. I suspect they have done this with Cyrus as well."

"They really don't like you. They told me their history when speaking as you."

Thorn raised her eyebrows. "You might as well tell me."

"They said it was all your fault. You are a terrible mother. You ignored them and kept them away from people who feared their powers and that they couldn't take the throne as Twins. That you had a baby to replace them as heir to the throne?"

Thorn wiped her hand across her eyes and swallowed hard. She drove on and fidgeted with the radio, trying to find some music. I grabbed her hand and switched the radio off.

"Are you going to say anything to defend yourself?" I asked.

She shook her head.

"What are you saying, that it is true?"

She cleared her throat and wiped her eyes again. "Some of it is true. Yes, others feared their powers and questioned if they could take the throne. I allowed myself to be swayed by them. I did have another baby, but he was never meant to replace them. However, I think other people had the idea he would make a better ruler after I had gone."

"So you used to ignore them and keep them out of the way?"

"I was a spoilt princess. Other people raised them for me. I got other Dragans to bring us food. It is true. I was a terrible mother. Something that I will always regret."

"Maybe you could patch things up?"

Thorn snorted and glared at me. "Maybe we can form a temporary alliance. But patch things up! It has been hundreds of years. They helped kill my son, their father and grandparents, and I was at war with them for years. It seems beyond patching up."

"True. And they would say the same. Both ignored and pushed aside for a new son. They never got the love they craved."

"I will talk with them. We might not even get them to join the alliance, let alone become friends. We take it one step at a time."

We followed the van out of the main city centre for an hour before turning into an industrial estate and drove up to an electrical components storefront with a warehouse at the back. Someone had already parked another black van outside, and the other pulled alongside it. The windows wound down, a brief conversation between the drivers took place, and then the van with the Twins drove off to the back of the warehouse.

Mary got out of the parked van at the front and pointed at the customer parking bays. She wore a black suit and sunglasses. We parked up, and Thorn grabbed my hand as I got out of the car.

"Mary and I will talk to the Twins alone. It is safer that way."

I nodded. Rip and I were probably too susceptible to their powers.

We greeted Mary and her four guards, our human training buddies. "It all went according to plan?" Mary asked.

"Yes, if the plan was to mess up my head, then it was perfect," I said, and scowled at Thorn.

"That well. I guess you know everything now. You probably need to rest up. Rip wants to talk to you and will help with your recovery," Mary said.

"The Twins?" Thorn asked.

"We have taken them into the warehouse around the back," Mary said. "We can walk through the shop front and into the back. The others will meet us inside."

A guard unlocked the shutters on the shop front and opened the door. We walked through, passed the shelves stocked with tools, catalogues and wiring, through a staff-only door, then behind the counter and into the warehouse. The warehouse had rows of metal shelves stacked with pallets and boxes. A forklift truck parked in the corner and a sliding ladder rested next to it.

"There is a staff room over to the side. Rip will come and talk to you. Help yourself to coffee and cakes," Mary said.

Thorn and Mary walked through a door at the side of a closed metal shutter about the size of the van. They held the door open, and Cassius and Rip walked through from the other side, along with the MI5-S soldiers.

I entered the staff room, grabbed a glass from a cupboard and pushed it against a water dispenser. I drank down the water in one go and filled up the glass again. Then took a seat on one of the two brown sofas set at right angles to one another up against the wall and placed my drink on the small coffee table strewn with magazines.

Rip walked in, shut the door, and took a seat on the other sofa. He leaned back, arm across the top and one leg bent on top of his other knee.

"How are you after your experience?" he asked.

"Confused and angry."

"It is to be expected."

"Thorn said I had to speak with you while she negotiated with the Twins. I don't understand why," I said.

"Why do you think?"

"Rip, now is not the time for the wise mentor routine of answering my questions with a question. I just what a straight answer."

Rip nodded and sat forward with elbows on his knees. "Because I went through the same thing. Those girls got inside my head. Made me see things and do things that led to the death of Thorn's family. I understand what it is like. I can help you come to peace with it."

I stood up and drunk down my water and then refilled my glass again. My hand shook as I held the glass and stood in front of Rip. "That was hundreds of years ago. And my experience was different. Thorn set me up. You and Cassius blocked my mind from finding the truth. The betrayal is worse than what the Twins did."

"You have every right to be angry. We did a strange thing. But we never lied. We told you there was a secret that you couldn't know about for the plan to work. We asked for your trust and you gave it. Nothing bad happened to you. Thorn and I were monitoring you the whole time."

"Nothing bad! The Twins made me think they were both Thorn. Even though I knew it couldn't be true. They suppressed the voice of reason."

"Yes. But that isn't the worse part of it, is it?"

"What do you mean?"

"They did a similar thing to me. Although, only one of them pretended to be Thorn, while the other opened the gates. But the worse thing I have had to live with for hundreds of years is the fact I enjoyed it. Part of me wishes to experience it again."

I stared at him and drunk down the rest of the water and placed the glass in the sink.

"No, it isn't the same."

"No! Weren't you wrapped up with desire? I can't imagine how it must have felt with both of them, and you are in love with Thorn and in Union. But at least no one died when it happened, not like when they tricked me."

I gripped the side of the sink and tensed my muscles.

"I should be grateful then and just have enjoyed the experience?"

"You should not feel guilty about having enjoyed it. You need to let go and focus on the here and now. Don't keep re-visiting it. Accept it as something that has happened and learn from it."

"What do I learn from that?"

"That you love Thorn. That you don't allow yourself to be alone with the Twins. That you can trust us, but war is difficult and sacrifices have to be made. It means doing as you're asked without question for the greater good."

I squeezed the side of the sink, trying to force out my anger and not let it take control. The wood and metal warped under the pressure.

"I learnt you lie to me. The Twins violated me as revenge against their mother, and I would have enjoyed every moment."

"You need some closure with the Twins and us, but it will have to wait until the right time."

I picked the glass out of the sink, spun around and threw it. Rip ducked, and it shattered on the wall. "No. I want answers now."

I ran out of the room to the door by the shutter. Two guards stepped forward, one held out his hand. "No entry." I twisted it over and flung him into the other guard, knocking them both down. I opened the door to find the Twins tied to chairs side by side, with the gags and blindfolds removed. Thorn stood in front and Mary was behind them. I slammed the door shut and bent the handle up to prevent anyone from following.

"Jon, get out," Mary shouted.

Thorn turned around and placed her hands on my shoulders. "You can't be here. Your mind is still open to them. Go back and rest up."

I brushed her arms away and marched towards the Twins. "I want answers."

The Twins glanced at each other and smiled. "Of course, we can give you what you want."

"Why couldn't I stop you? It is obvious there aren't two Thorns."

"Because you didn't want us to stop. You love her. The idea of two of her was too exciting," Isabella said.

"Are you saying I wanted it?" I said, and my vision blurred for a second.

"Jon, help us. Thorn has tricked you and she will kill us," Marcella said, but her hair was sparkling and turning red. Freckles popped up across her nose and skin paled.

"Scarlett?"

"That is right. Thorn captured Amber and me. She and her Dragan friends made you think we were someone else. She wants to kill us," she said.

I looked back to where the other twin sat, only to see Amber in the chair wrestling against her bonds. "Jon, my saviour, my prince of darkness. You came to rescue me again."

Something grabbed my shoulders and flung me back to the door. "V, get out. They are in your mind again."

"Why do you have Scarlett and Amber?"

"I don't. It is another trick. Scarlett is dead, remember? Amber is in America. Max can confirm it," Thorn said.

The door rattled but remained stuck, and the shutters at the side rolled up.

Thorn stood in front of me and looked at the shutters as Rip's head poked underneath.

I pushed her arms away and ran to the captives. I wanted to look closer at Scarlett and Amber or the Twins.

"Cyrus, get away from them," Thorn shouted.

I twisted back. Thorn's eyes had gone red and claws grew through her finger ends and fangs jutted out of her mouth.

"It is me, V," I said.

"Get away from my girls."

"They are playing with your mind. Ask me a question that only V would know the answer to."

She growled and stepped forward. "Answer quickly, so there is no chance they are reading your mind. Where did we spend our first night together?"

"In a loft. In an empty house."

She stared a bit longer. "What is the name of the pet dog we had in

London?"

"We didn't have a pet dog," I answered quickly.

Her fangs retracted and eyes reverted. Rip and Cassius ducked underneath the rising shutter. They ran over and stood on either side of Scarlett and Amber and closed their eyes. "Thorn, remember the training. We perform as practised," Rip said, and Thorn closed her eyes as well.

Scarlett struggled in her chair. "Jon, help me. They are hurting us. They are attacking our minds."

"Jon, join them to be one mind against the Twins," Mary said.

I could only stare at Scarlett and Amber fighting in their chairs, wishing that Scarlett could be alive. Then I could apologise to her and protect her.

"Jon, this isn't Scarlett. Let me prove it to you. Scarlett, what was the name of the nightclub we were leaving when we saw Jon again?" Mary asked.

Scarlett and Amber stared at her. "It's a lie. You don't know Scarlett. Just like they had no pet dog."

"Guess again. There is no way you could have known Mary and Scarlett were friends," I said. I closed my eyes and sought out Thorn's thoughts. In moments, I found a mass of psychic powers breaking the Twins hold.

Cassius's and Rip's psychic thoughts all directed into Thorn's mind, amplifying her one thought aimed at the Twins, . I linked into Thorn and added my voice to the one mind. With my psychic abilities added, the power ramped up and the Twins minds buckled. I opened my eyes as Scarlett and Amber's faces faded back to the Twins, their eyes closing and heads dropping.

"It worked. Well done, everyone," Rip said, opening his eyes.

Thorn crouched by the Twins and held their faces in each hand.

"Why didn't I know about this plan to psychically link up?" I asked.

"Because it would have given away too much of what we planned. The fact we clouded your thoughts earlier. We knew you would pick it up and be able to join in quickly if we ever had to use it," Rip said.

"This is the same technique you used on me, to stop me from realising the truth about the Twins before the meeting."

"Yes. I promise we won't do it again. But it helped to practise on you in readiness for tackling the Twins. Now we have a way of stopping their powers, but it takes at least three of us to slow them down. A fourth to beat them. It is essential for us all to recognise when they are using their powers and to enact the one mind quickly."

Thorn stroked their faces. "Wake up, girls. We haven't finished yet."

Their heads shook and eyes popped open. They sat upright and twisted in their bonds. "What did you do to us?"

"What you do to everyone else. We took over your mind," Thorn said.

They jumped up and down in the chairs and screamed.

"Let us out."

"I will, but I want you to do something for me."

"What?"

"I want you to read my mind and let me read yours."

"This is a trick. Why would you let us do that?"

"I want you to relive my memories and feel my real emotions. I want you to understand me. To know I am not your enemy, that I am your mother and still love you. I want to see your memories to understand you and realise how I drove you to such actions. I think it is the only way we can ever trust one another again. What we find could help us come to terms with the way we acted."

"And what if we don't find anything good? What happens if we can't reconcile?"

"We find somewhere for you to sit out the war until it is completed."

"You trust us not to hurt you?" Marcella said.

"What you find will surprise you, and I hope you won't want to hurt me. Anyway, I have Rip, Cassius and V watching in case anything happens."

"It looks like we have no choice," Isabella said.

Mary untied them, and the Twins rubbed their wrists and ankles. Thorn sat cross-legged on the floor and held out her hands. The Twins sat down and held a hand of Thorn and each other's hand to form a circle.

"I will open my mind first. You tell me what you need to experience, and then it is my turn," Thorn said.

The Twins closed their eyes and steadied their breathing. Thorn smiled at me. "This may take some time. Make sure we stay safe." She closed her eyes and her breathing slowed down.

Mary and her soldiers went back under the shutter and closed it. Cassius, Rip, and I stood in a circle around Thorn and the Twins. We watched in silence, exchanging messages psychically between us as not to disturb their focus.

We had been watching for ten minutes when red wells appeared under the eyes of the Twins. I stepped in closer and crouched down. The red wells broke free and tears lined their faces. They didn't absorb back into their skin, but just stained their cheeks and dripped onto their white vest tops.

After another ten minutes, red tears streamed down Thorn's face. They all opened their eyes. Thorn knelt forwards and held her arms open. The Twins knelt up and dived into her embrace, their heads on either shoulder and red tears rolling down onto Thorn's shoulders.

I stood up to give them space. Thorn smiled up at me, red tears streaming out.

"You boys can leave us. I need to spend some time alone with my daughters."

Chapter Six

After a couple of days, we all flew back to England into a new base just outside London. Events were happening fast and a base closer to the main travel links was important. We had lost time travelling from our headquarters in Wales to get to Rome and Argentina.

On the journey back, Thorn spent most of her time with Marcella and Isabella. I had to get used to sharing her on a full-time basis, but I knew better than anyone what family meant. I wouldn't deprive them of time with their mother. But it all seemed too easy. After years of conflict, they had resolved it by sharing their memories, making each other see it from their own point of view. I wouldn't be so easily convinced.

The new base was more comfortable. The rooms were bigger, with an en-suite and painted a light yellow, which made a change from military grey. Our building was a student hall of residence for MI5 agents and had a shared kitchen isolated to a floor and wing of each building. The other buildings had conference and classrooms, a shooting range in the basement, and a full gym and swimming pool.

I woke up on the first night back to find Thorn gone from our double bedroom. I put on some clothes and wandered down the hallway towards the sound of talking. Thorn sat at the kitchen table with the Twins, sharing a bottle of blood. Isabella and Marcella laughed as I walked in, and I scowled at them and went over to put the kettle on. The room went quiet. "V, I was just telling them your vampire joke."

"Which joke?"

"No, not a witch joke, a vampire joke. Sorry, you know the one. What do you call an asthmatic vampire?"

"Vlad the inhaler," the Twins said and laughed again.

"Ah. Yes. I remember now," I said and turned back to making a coffee.

"Stop being grumpy," Marcella said.

"I am not grumpy," I said, pouring in hot water and facing the other way.

"Come and talk to us," Isabella said.

I stared at them. Marcella smiled and Isabella pulled out a chair from the long wooden table.

"Really. Just like that, it is all forgotten what you tried to do to me, what you did to your mother."

"Scolding us, are you? Just because you are in Union with our mother doesn't make you our father."

"I should hope not after what you tried to do."

"V, stop being childish," Thorn said.

"Childish! These two tricked my mind and were going to have their wicked way."

"I know. Things happened between all of us. We also tricked them and invaded their minds. I have made peace with them."

"And us with her," Isabella said.

"After everything that has happened. We are all laughter and smiles?" I said.

"What do you want, us ripping each other's hair out and constantly blaming each other? We shared our memories. I felt what they felt. I understand how isolated and lonely they became and how it drove them to an alliance with Cyrus. That was my fault. I saw they didn't kill my family. They didn't know that would happen when they invaded the castle. It seems to have been on Cyrus' instructions. They argued with him about it. But once the war had started, they had nowhere else to go. They had made their bed and had to lie in it."

"Likewise, we experienced mum's memories. We feel her regret for what happened. She has always loved us. We understand why she went to war with us afterwards. We saw what happened with Cyrus. And from the Turned attacking us and what they said, we believe Cyrus is South. We want to end the war and take our revenge on Cyrus. He tricked us into working for him and killing our family. We were just pawns in his games to get the throne. Because of him, we lost everything."

"And what about what you did to me?"

"It hardly compares to what we three have been through," Thorn said.

"No, mum. He has a point. How can he trust us in the future? Let us talk with him alone."

Thorn looked back and forth between us. "V, are you willing to talk with them alone? Can I trust you?"

"Trust me. What do you mean? That I might carry on where I left off in the flat in Rome."

"No, that you will listen to them and be reasonable. You won't seek violent revenge for what happened. Keep that dragon within you under check."

I took a deep breath and then sunk back the rest of my coffee. "Okay, let's go for a walk outside. I need some air and will feel safer in an open space."

Both the Twins finished their glasses of blood and stood up. "Let's go."

"Behave you three. Take your time and listen to each other."

I headed out of the building with the Twins following. The five-storey building was one of three that formed a courtyard in between them. Four roads intersected the courtyard to a large roundabout with a helicopter pad which we had landed on the other night. Behind us, the lights in the three buildings were turned off apart from a few in our building. They had emptied the base for us.

I strode ahead of the Twins, not sure what to say.

"Let's get out of the base," Isabella said.

"Yeah. There is a town nearby. We could go to the pub. I haven't been to a pub in years," Marcella said.

"Is that a good idea?" I asked.

"Yes. We will have fun, a bit of bonding. We can talk on the way," Isabella replied.

"Why not?" I said and walked to the gatehouse. The guard came out and lifted the barrier. Fencing, security lights and CCTV ringed the rest of the base. It kept outsiders from poking around, and it also kept an eye on us.

We left the base behind and walked along the edge of the road towards the town.

"You best spit it out, V. Or do you want us to start," Marcella said, them both walking either side, hooking their arms through mine.

"I don't know what to discuss first."

"Let us start. You are annoyed about us tricking your mind into seeing two Thorns. But mostly annoyed that it wasn't real and didn't get to finish it."

"No. It is not that at all."

"So you aren't annoyed about seeing two Thorns?"

"Yes, but not about it being left unfinished. It would be hard to live with afterwards if we had gone all the way."

"But, regardless, you would have liked to have experienced it."

"No."

"You wouldn't want to be with two of Thorn, if it were possible. If they were both really her."

"Don't be silly. It is not possible, so it is a pointless question."

"Well. It is possible. As a gift to you, a way of saying sorry and giving you closure, we could place a hypnotic trigger in your mind. The next time you and Thorn are together, you could activate this trigger, and it would make you see and feel double. You wouldn't be cheating on her, maybe cheating with her instead."

I stopped and the Twins stood in front. For a moment, I stared at them. "I am not letting you in my head again."

"But the offer is appealing?"

"Let's just walk and talk about something else. Tell me about Rip. What are you going to do to make it up to him?"

"Okay. I will tell you about Rip, but the offer stands. Once you learn to trust us, maybe you will have a change of heart," Isabella said. They both hooked their arms in mine again and we walked on.

"We will have words with Rip and find a way of making it up to him. However, he doesn't realise that we saved his life that day," Marcella said.

"How wouldn't he know that?"

"I had seduced him while Marcella opened the gates to let in the Turned Army."

"I thought you used your powers on him?"

"We did. Marcella was still connected into my mind, amplifying the illusion to Rip. Once they entered the castle, Cyrus sent the main group after Thorn and her family, and left four Turned to kill Rip. They told us to move out of the way so they could kill him. I thought we were taking everyone captive, keeping them in the dungeons so we could parade our victory in front of them. I never wanted to kill my family. I just wanted what was rightfully ours. I realised my mistake. We killed the Turned and smuggled Rip out of the castle and set him free into the night."

"Why doesn't Rip remember?"

"The psychic illusions still hazed his mind. Did you ever wonder how he survived?"

"I assumed he just fought his way out."

"We had him subdued. He couldn't have fought against us. We freed him. After that, we raced back into the castle to stop the others from being killed. We were too late. We saw the last battle. My grandparents had transformed into their dragon forms to fight the Turned and to allow Thorn to escape. They sacrificed their own lives. The dragon form burnt through their life force, and they knew it would kill them," Marcella said.

"But they threw down their lives so that Thorn could survive. I saw them kill wave after wave of Turned. Cyrus watched as his new army destroyed itself against them. But eventually, their dragon form took its toll, and they both fell to the onslaught. They died from exhaustion caused by their dragon state and not by the strength of the Turned," Isabella said.

"But you stayed with Cyrus afterwards."

"We had nowhere else to go. Thorn raised an army and hunted us down.

We needed protection."

"Does Thorn know all of this?"

"We shared this memory, along with memories of our childhood and events just before and after the battle. For some time, Thorn believed we were behind all of it. That we had seduced Cyrus and convinced him to attack and kill them. She thought we were South."

"And now she has seen the truth and everything is okay?"

"We are all willing to move on. Nothing was as it appeared to be. Thorn knows we didn't plan it and weren't involved in the murders. She knows we saved Rip. And we know she never meant for us to be isolated. Our brother was never a replacement. She argued with others that suggested a replacement. The Dragan that originally suggested they replace us was Cyrus when they first started their Union. He wanted his child to be the next in line. But, of course, they had none, which changed his opinion. Instead, with Thorn out of the way, a Union with us would legitimise his rule. This is why he had them killed."

"It all seems plausible. But how do we know this isn't just another lie? That you haven't created false memories and faked it to Thorn."

"So un-trusting. It would be almost impossible to fake memories to that level of detail. Thorn would tell the difference. Memories are too vivid compared to faked images. They have emotions and senses attached. It is impossible to fake everything. Plus, she has her own accounts of what happened, and these would back up our memories."

"Well, it seems you have us all convinced. I am not sure there is anything else to discuss, so we might as well head back to the base."

I stopped, but the Twins dragged me along. "You promised to take us to the pub. I have something I want to show you."

"Okay, one drink. I could do with a change of scenery. Some normality. What do you have in store? I don't want any surprises," I said and allowed myself to be escorted into town.

"Well. I understand Thorn has taught you to fight. Cassius has explained our history. Rip has taught you how to control your magic, which I hope someone will show us. We are going to teach you how to use your psychic powers to their full potential," Isabella said, taking over the conversation from Marcella.

"I can already use them."

"You are all barely scratching the surface. You use them to communicate and implant suggestions into humans. But there is more," Marcella said.

"We used them to good effect the other day in making you sleep."

Their arms tensed around mine and they strode on. "Yes. But I understand that was a first. A trick Cassius thought of based on our capabilities. I am going to show you other possibilities."

"Like what?"

"It is easier to show than to tell. Look, there is a nightclub with a queue of people outside. Seems very popular. It would make for a much better demo than a pub."

The Twins changed direction to the nightclub. The club had a glowing sign above the door, "Venom", and disco lights flashing on the pavement. Two black-clothed men stood guard at the door and controlled access via a red rope barrier. A queue snaked back of twenty people, all smartly dressed, no jeans or t-shirts. They chatted to one another or impatiently flicked through their phones.

We had left the base in casual gear. I wore jeans and a t-shirt, and the Twins dressed in identical skinny jeans, heels and a white top, baring one shoulder. We wouldn't meet the dress code.

The Twins strolled us to the front of the queue. The awaiting customers glared at us and the security guard blocked our path. "Sorry, but..." His eyes glazed over for a second. "I didn't recognise you for a moment. Go through," he said and unclipped the red rope on a metal pole. He waved us through. "These three have VIP access. Hand them the wristbands."

We walked through to the angry shouts of the queuing people. Inside, a woman sat inside a glass booth, with another security guard watching CCTV monitors. "What are your names?"

"Isabella, Marcella and V. We are at the top of your list," Isabella said.

The woman looked at the list. "Any ID?"

Marcella put forward her palm.

"Looks all in order. No payment required," the woman said.

Isabella nudged my ribs. "Look at the CCTV monitors."

The screens all went static, and the guard tapped them and pressed the keyboard in front of him. "The screens are on the blink again," he said.

"Try turning them off and on," the woman in the booth said, and then handed us three red wrist bands marked VIP.

"Thank you," Marcella said. "Can you tell us where the VIP area is?"

"Up the stairs to the 2nd floor."

The Twins hooked their arms in mine and we climbed the stairs. The first level opened to a packed dance floor, euro trash music blaring and lights flashing, people two deep at the bar. Other customers pushed through the crowd to and from the full dance floor.

We carried on to the second floor. At the top of the stairs, two security guards barred the way to a set of white double doors. We flashed our wrist bands and they pushed open the doors.

The room looked smaller than the one downstairs, but the decor was better, the sound quality was cleaner, and the lighting classier. Near the door was a long bar with waiters running back and forth, collecting trays of drinks and depositing trays of empty bottles and glasses. At the other end of the room, a dance floor encircled by chrome railings with customers leant against it.

Along the walls, inset leather seating curved around circular tables. Tall tables occupied the rest of the space where people stood around and placed their drinks. Plenty of room to walkabout. The air was not as hot and sweaty as the room downstairs, and the customers were better dressed.

"I will get the drinks," I said.

"I will get those in a moment. Did you see the screens go static downstairs?" Isabella asked.

"Yes. Was that you? I assume you used your powers to get us in as well."

"Of course, it was me that got us in. As for the static, psychic powers work by creating or reading the electrical impulses in your mind. This means we can create electrical impulses in any electrical system. We can't communicate with electronics, but we can disrupt them. It's useful to block out cameras or break computers. There is one above the bar so they can watch the far end of the room. Try and force a psychic thought onto it. We usually find a scream works best."

I focused on the CCTV monitor above the bar, where a barman watched it while waiting for the next order. I pretended the monitor was a brain and focused my psychic thoughts as a scream. The picture on the screen flickered for a few seconds.

"More. Think of something that makes you angry. Like when we had tricked you back in Rome."

The anger flooded in, and the picture turned to black and white fuzzy lines.

"Well done. Remember how that worked. You may need to do it again soon. Now let's get that drink. You stay here with Isabella while I scout out a good place to get a drink."

"The bar is behind us," I said.

“We have plans to show you our other skills.”

Marcella scouted the room, checking the people on the dance floor, drinking at the tall tables, and those who sat in the plush leather semi-circular sofas down the sides of the room.

Isabella squeezed my arm. “I got you all by myself.”

“Okay. What does that mean?”

“Stop panicking. I want to hear about your history. I heard snippets from other people, but how did you end up with Thorn?”

“Did she not tell you?”

“From her point of view. I want to know yours. I have a keen interest in psychology. I like to understand the difference between how people think they reacted based on their experiences compared to the real reason that I can detect.”

“Oh. So you like to see if they are lying to themselves about their actions?”

“Exactly.”

“So, the story from my point of view. I wanted vengeance on those that hurt me, and I was attracted to Thorn. It was the perfect package.”

“Can I listen to your mind as you talk to see if it is the truth? It would be valuable insight for yourself as well.”

“I know why I did it. Those are the reasons, so feel free to listen in.”

“Repeat it.”

“I wanted vengeance, and I was attracted to Thorn.”

“More than attraction!”

“Okay. She enthralled me.”

“Yes. So rare for someone to have that honest understanding of their own emotions.”

“Can you check something for me? Everyone says that I am attracted to her as she is older than me, as a mother substitute. Is that true?”

She closed her eyes for a second and held my hands. “No. You had no idea how much older. Her being older than you is a point of attraction, but not as a substitute. Her power meant she could protect you and her age gave her authority, someone you could trust and believe in.”

“You mean like a mother?”

“No. Unless your mother was a seven hundred-year-old Dragan. Don’t buy into that labelling of relationships based on your childhood. I can see into people’s minds. Nothing is that simple. Everything is layered and complex. No one thing defines us.”

"But aren't your actions based on your childhood?"

"Clever. Yes, but not all of it. As I said, it is more complex. It definitely had a foundation effect. But I also chose my actions as well. Just as I choose to re-build that relationship with Thorn and accept you as the Dragan King."

"Thank you. I wasn't aware there was a problem."

"Technically, I am still next in line, but now Thorn is in Union with you, our claim will be diminished if you and Thorn have a baby. But we are relinquishing any claim to the throne anyway, so it makes no odds."

"Baby! It is unlikely. There is a fertility issue."

"Yes. One that Thorn hopes your transformation can unlock. The science that enables the change could resolve it."

"I know about that, but there is a war to win. Afterwards, they can research my transformation to find the answer. Then, maybe you could have children?"

She smirked and patted my arm. "Silly boy."

I frowned and thought about what that could mean.

"Marcella has found us some drinks over the far side. Let's go," Isabella said and held my hand and guided me around the groups drinking at the high tables, around the side of the dance floor with people leaning on the chrome barriers, to stand next to Marcella who was looking over the dance floor.

"I don't see any drinks?"

Marcella stepped away from the dance floor and looked to one of the semi-circle leather sofas where a group of five men sat. They all wore black shirts. The man in the middle wore a gold watch, bracelet and gold necklace. He put a gold vape machine to his mouth and blew out a stream of vanilla flavoured smoke. He grinned to show a flash of golden teeth.

On the table, three bottles of champagne and a cluster of empty and half-filled glasses. Two men in black suits stood in front of the sofa, holding back a queue of people. The man wearing gold sat in the centre of the group, spoke to the guy next to him, who spoke to the next man, who then tapped one of the black-suited men on the arm. The black suited guard leaned over the man at the front of the queue and ushered him forward to the table.

I had been in enough places with Thorn to recognise the setup. The group was a gang, the top-level generals. In the centre of the group, the gold man was the boss. The men in suits were bodyguards controlling the queue of people who had come to plea for mercy or ask a favour. The night club meant they couldn't be overheard.

"Let me guess. This criminal gang has our drinks."

"Correct. A bottle of champagne each on that table belongs to us," Marcella said.

"You are just like your mother."

"I will take that as a compliment. You think we are going to attack them?"

"Yeah. It's what Thorn would do. A training test. Is it really necessary? You know I could beat them. All it will do is draw attention to us."

"Oh, please. I have something more interesting in mind. I am showing you the true potential of your psychic powers. Now, to start with, can you knock out that camera embedded in the ceiling?"

The dome camera pointed at the gang. I focused my magic and imagined psychic thoughts burning into the electronics. The energy built until it filled my magic sphere, and I fired it out as a psychic scream into the camera. I held the scream, firing into the black dome. The camera sparked, and the lens dropped and spun away from the corner. At the bar end of the nightclub, a staff member pressed the remote and tapped the screen.

"Impressive. I assume that was with your magic? You really must show us how to do that," Isabella said.

"Yes, it was magic. What next?"

"Stand back a little and watch the show. Just take care of anyone disturbing us."

Isabella and Marcella stepped in front of the men in suits, cutting into the queue of people.

"Go to the back, ladies," he said and ushered them back.

"We have VIP passes. It is fine for us to go next," Isabella said and waved her wrist at him.

He stared blankly for a second. The woman at the front of the queue grabbed her wrist. "These are just for this room. Go to the back of the queue."

"No, these are for anything I like. You need to run to the toilet." The woman crossed her legs and hurried away.

The bodyguard turned to the gang, who had their latest victim sat in between them. The leader had his arm around him, talking into his ear. One of the crew grabbed the victim's hand and held it on the table. Another pulled out a small hammer.

"Excuse me, sirs. This lady is next," the guard said.

"What! Can't you see we are busy?"

Isabella stepped around the guard and waved. "Hello. There seems to have been a mistake. You have our drinks. If you just hand them over, I won't have to kill you all."

"Are you out of your fricking mind? Mitch, get rid of her now," the gang leader said.

The guard placed a hand on her shoulder.

"Mitch, they are about to kill your father," Isabella said.

The guard looked at the victim. "Dad!"

The other guard stepped in front. "Mitch, your dad died years ago. You killed him. That isn't your dad."

Mitch looked again, rubbed his eyes, and shook his head. "You are right."

"Bad choice. It happens. If the suggestion can't possibly be true and not desired, the psychic spell can be broken," Marcella said to me. "We will have to improvise."

"I think you need some fresh air. Clear your mind," I said to the guard.

"Yeah. Good idea. I will take him outside. Boss, we need five minutes," the other guard said, took his friend's arm and walked him down the nightclub. The guard rubbed his eyes and shook his head and muttered to his friend. "I was sure it was him."

"Clever. You are getting the hang of it. You are far more interesting than we originally realised. I can see why she likes you," Isabella said.

I grinned and watched as the guards walked out.

The gang leader stood up and shouted. "Where are you going? What on earth is wrong with you?"

"You still have our drinks. Hand them over," Isabella repeated.

"You want the drinks, then come and get them," he said and waved us on, and sat down.

"No. You need to apologise for taking my drinks and give them to me on your knees."

"Are you flipping serious? Get lost before you get hurt."

"Isabella, he will need some encouragement," Marcella said.

Isabella turned to the queue, who were staring at her in disbelief. A couple of people secretly filming on their camera phones. "This is the person you are afraid of. Go home and tell your friends he is scared of a woman. Your fear in him and his gang is misplaced. They have no balls."

She turned back to the gang. The leader stared.

"I ain't falling for this. It is a trick. No one is that stupid. Someone is watching. Someone is waiting for us to make a move."

"What is wrong with you? I just called you out as a coward in front of your gang and your subjects. Have you no pride. These people will go away tonight and tell everyone you are scared."

“I ain’t scared or stupid enough to fall for this bullshit,” he nudged the man next to him, “Fetch the club security and get this woman removed. Get them to check the camera as well. They should have been here by now.”

“Yes, boss,” the man said and stood up, but rocked on his feet for a moment and leaned on the table. He grabbed a champagne bottle by the neck and pulled it level with his chest.

“Good idea. Get more drinks as well,” the leader said.

The gang member swung it down and back into the leader’s face, smashing glass across his forehead and spraying champagne across the group. Blood streamed down his face, and he screamed, clutching his head. The others jumped out of their seats and tackled the attacker. In the melee, the potential victim crawled out from under the table and ran off past the queue, who were filming the brawl.

The attacker curled up into a ball as the gang members reigned in blows. Then one of them twisted his punch at the last moment and hit one of the other gang members, who rolled back and started fighting him instead, despite his protests that it was an accident.

The gang leader squeezed through the mayhem and under the table. He wiped the blood off his face and picked up a bottle, climbed onto the table and smashed it over the head of his attacker, and then stabbed in the broken glass. The attacker’s body went limp. The two other gang members still fought, and the leader jumped down into the seats and pulled them apart.

“Stop fighting,” he shouted.

One of them checked the original attacker. “You killed him. My brother.”

He pulled out a knife and slammed it into the back of the leader. The gang member, on the other side, pulled the leader away.

The man with the knife turned to us. “My brother worked for you. He is dead and it is your fault.” He charged at us and stabbed the knife at Isabella, who stepped to the side, grabbed the knife and twisted it around in the man’s hands and let his momentum stab himself in the gut.

“Never met him,” she said and shoved him to the floor where he clutched the protruding knife, blood slickening his dark shirt.

Isabella turned around. “With the proper use of power, you hardly need to fight at all. Just the right thought at the right time can make all the difference. Now it is your turn. The security guards are on their way and want to talk to you.”

“To me. Why me?”

Isabella just smiled and looked over my shoulder. I spun around as four club security guards ran across the floor. I stood back to let them through, but they altered their direction. "Stay there," the one at the front shouted and pointed at me.

Isabella and Marcella smiled.

I stepped away and held out my hands towards the security guard. "Hey, this is nothing to do with me. I just happen to be standing here."

He kept running and swung in a fist. I ducked underneath and fired in an uppercut, rattling his jaw and pitching him off his feet. The next guard tackled me and bowled us over into a group of onlookers, who toppled over in a heap, spilling drinks over us.

I whipped in an elbow to his face and rolled his unconscious body out the way. Another guard threw in a kick. I grabbed it in one hand and pivoted around on the floor to kick through his supporting leg. He crashed to the floor, and I rolled on top and punched him twice in the face, splitting open his nose.

An arm throttled my throat and pulled me upright. I stamped my heel down onto his foot, dropped into a crouch, held his arm and flipped him over my head, onto the bodies of the other guards.

"Well done, but you're still not using the one muscle that counts," Marcella said and tapped her finger against her head. "You need more practice."

"This must be your fault," the remaining gang member shouted and clambered over the table. He charged and I pushed my thoughts into his mind, making him step wider than he wanted and tripped over Isabella's leg. He fell flat on his face, grabbed his nose and rolled around.

One of the security guards staggered to his feet. I focused my mind into his mind.

"What did you call me?" he barked at Marcella.

"What?" she said, and I grinned at her. "Oh, good. You have finally picked it up," she said.

"A fat pig!" she shouted at the guard, and he reached out and Marcella kicked his groin. He dropped to his knees, holding his injured parts, yowling in pain.

"Let's go," Isabella said and grabbed the two bottles left on the table. She thrust one into my stomach and took a swig from the other. "Congratulations. Training completed and you passed the exam."

Chapter Seven

A few days after our field trip to the nightclub, the Twins gathered the Dragans in the kitchen. We sat at the long kitchen table, and Rip fetched out bottles of red wine and blood. He liked to alternate between the two.

Rip did the honours and served everyone their choice of red wine or blood. I had only just woken and chose coffee instead. I sat next to Thorn. The Twins sat together on her other side. Rip and Cassius took the seats opposite.

Once everyone settled and took a drink, Isabella knocked on the table and waited for silence.

"We want to share our knowledge of psychic powers as part of the healing process between us. Over the last few days, we have tried to spend time with everyone. We took V nightclubbing. I am sure he has shared his experience. We have talked with Rip about the events of the castle raid and start of the civil war," she said.

Rip raised his glass. "We have. Although I am not one hundred percent happy, the information and shared memories give this a new perspective. All these years, I never understood how I escaped that night. I just assumed it was the haze of battle. To find out you saved my life has weakened my anger. I will share our ability to channel magic. We have to trust each other."

Marcella smiled and raised her glass to Rip. "Thank you, Rip. We are all a lot older and wiser. We have spent time with Cassius and talked about the past. We discussed the battles between us during the civil war and have documented it for historical keeping. We hope to repair our relationships with you all."

"It is a start. I must also bear some of the blame. I mistreated you," Thorn said. "A toast to new friendships." We all raised a glass and exchanged a clink of cups in the middle of the table.

"Now, to prove our loyalty to the group, we are going to share our psychic knowledge and send you off to do some homework," Isabella said.

"Good. I have homework for you as well," Rip said, and pushed over a bottle of red wine. "V will teach you, as he has done his psychic training."

"This won't take long. Your recent mind merging shows a good understanding. Let us start with electrical disruption and then onto mind nudging. Above us is a camera hidden within the smoke alarm. Once you practise, you can detect electrical signals and distinguish between them. Your MI5-S friends are eavesdropping."

"What a surprise. I shall have words with Mary," Thorn said.

"I need a volunteer. Thank you, Cassius. Look up at the smoke alarm and think of it as someone's mind. Try to connect," Isabella said.

"I sense just a buzzing."

"That is right. It won't make any sense. Is it one or two buzzes?"

"Two. I guess one is the alarm and the other a camera."

"Good. With practice, you may distinguish one from the other and be able to recognise the signals. Pick one and focus your thoughts as if psychically screaming into someone's mind."

Cassius closed his eyes and then stared up, face frowning. The red light on the smoke alarm flashed rapidly, and then the alarm wailed. The other alarms in the hallways and bedrooms joined in moments later. Cassius screwed up his face, muscles tensing until the kitchen alarm stopped. The others stopped as well.

"Excellent. Obviously, that one was the smoke alarm. Now do the same to the other signal while we prepare for our visitors."

Cassius focused again and a tiny spark fizzled out from the smoke alarm.

"Excellent. Just in time for our keepers to arrive," Marcella said as the door to our section banged back and feet thumped down the hallway into the kitchen.

"Who burnt the toast?" Ruby said as she skidded into the kitchen. Dunk and Smash stood behind her.

Thorn laughed aloud and the rest of us held it back.

Ruby sniffed the air. "What is happening here?"

"Nothing. We are just having a drink and sharing stories," Isabella said.

Smash whispered to Ruby. She looked up at the smoke alarm. "It looks like we a have a wiring issue. I will send the electrician down to look at it."

"Can we borrow the training rooms in the basement to go through the room clearances with the Twins?" Thorn asked.

"Of course, just let me know the time and I will book it in. I will see you all later," she said and looked around at us again and frowned. We fought back our laughter with hands over our mouths and eyes watering.

We waited until the section door closed and burst into laughter. Isabella and Marcella smiled at each other and tapped their drinks together.

"Lesson one completed. Now go and search for any other suspicious signals. We will help isolate any more bugs and short them out. But this only work on implanted bugs. We can't detect hijacked cameras or spy software. In the meantime, I think V is going to start our magic training," Marcella said.

The others took one last drink and set off into the rest of our section, checking the bedrooms and the communal living room. I grabbed a glass, poured in red wine, and topped up the Twins' glasses.

"So, how do we train?" Isabella asked.

"You drink and you answer my questions? Let me give a demonstration," I said, and flicked out a claw and cut my arm. I focused my magic on blocking the healing. The blood stayed on my arm.

"But I want to heal," Isabella said.

"It is just a demonstration of how we can control our bodies. We can use it to block healing, accelerate healing and enhance other existing abilities."

"We can run faster, hit harder and enhance our psychic powers?" Marcella asked.

"Absolutely."

"This is what you all did to amplify your psychic powers?"

"Yes."

"So, how is it done? Can you show me rather than tell me? Let me feel what you are feeling. It will save time."

"Of course, we used the same trick to learn from our human buddies and them from us. I will run through the blocking of our healing and then the acceleration of our healing."

We closed our eyes and their hands grabbed mine. I opened up, letting the feeling take hold in my thoughts, consciously thinking through each action. I pictured the sphere of magic and used my emotions to draw in the magic from outside. I used the recent laughter as the catalyst to open the gateway.

As I stepped through each stage, they asked questions and I answered. Then, I moved onto accelerating the healing.

I let go of their hands and opened my eyes. The wound on my arm had healed up.

"Your turn," I said.

They cut into each other's arms and closed their eyes. The blood welled up and stayed on the surface.

"Good. Now open your eyes and start drinking. Use your magic to stop your healing from burning off the alcohol."

They opened their eyes, stared at the cuts, grabbed a glass, and slugged back the red wine.

"Enjoy the taste of your wine. Don't just gulp it down," I said and realised I sounded just like Rip. "Now, while drinking, let us talk. You need to learn to control the magic at a subconscious level. So I will try to distract you."

"Go ahead. We are ready," Isabella responded.

"Tell me about Thorn. I keep hearing she was a spoilt princess. I would love to hear the tales."

"She wouldn't be happy if we told you. But I think you should know what she used to be like. For starters, Thorn isn't her actual name. Just like Vengeance isn't your real name. We take on new names depending on the circumstances. Immortality is a long time to have the same name. I will let you ask Thorn about her real name. But behind her back, everyone used to call her Precious, as she used to be very sensitive about everything."

"Precious. That is hilarious. Carry on."

"Princess Precious to give her the full title. She was fussy about her food. She would often send back whatever human had been brought: too old, too fat, too skinny. She liked free range organic even before it became a thing. Instead, she liked her blood from country folk, who had plenty of exercise, clean air and lived on a fresh diet. She hated food from the city. Declaring it sluggish and tasting of the sewers."

I laughed at the thought. "Did she know of her nickname?"

"We believe some unfortunate said it once by mistake. She got Rip to punish them. She would never dirty her own hands to touch a commoner."

"What else?"

"Her wardrobe was huge. She loved clothes. This proved to be a nightmare to move around. She would have dresses imported from all over Europe. She insisted no one could talk to her directly or look her in the eye. They would have to talk via people like Rip and Cassius, who would pass the messages on. She would never train to practise her fighting and feeding. She didn't feel the need as she had people to do it for her."

"Really. It is hard to believe."

"It is all true. Hence, when the war started, she had no idea what to do. She had to flee and needed her parents to protect her, as they had always done. On the other hand, we spent plenty of time training with Cassius and learned to look after ourselves. As you heard already, Princess Precious was too busy to bring up children," the Twins said and faces hardened, the blood soaking in.

"Focus. Use that rage to fuel your magic, block your healing," I said. They both looked at their arms and the blood stopped absorbing into the wound.

"Anything else you want to know?"

"Rip? Is that his real name?"

"No. Thorn's father gave it to him. Rip as he ripped people to pieces."

"You two don't have other names?"

"Yes. We are the Twins. But no individual alter ego names, nor do Cassius or Cyrus. It isn't mandatory."

Thorn walked back into the kitchen. "We have found a few suspect signals."

"Excellent, well done, my precious," I said and smirked.

Her eyes narrowed and she glared at the Twins. "What have you told him?"

They both shrugged and took a drink of red wine.

She dragged back a chair and took her drink. "I will tell you the rest to make sure there is no misunderstanding. Yes, they used to call me Princess Precious. Anyway, once the war started, I wanted revenge. Death of my parents, baby, Union partner and loss of my daughters will do that to you.

The persona of Princess Precious was the idea of my parents. They believed for us to be a royal dynasty; we had to act like other royals. I had to appear more refined than anyone else. I had to act in a particular way to be seen to be above ordinary matters. When possible, I secretly trained with my mother and father.

After the attack, Cassius stepped up my training and we worked on our plans for revenge. After a few years of being on the run from Cyrus's army, we built our own army and hit back. It was Cassius that helped rename me. Precious was dead, and Thorn was born. The name Thorn is a reminder. If they touch me, they bleed."

"Your real name?"

"Is irrelevant. I am Thorn. Let's take out these electronic bugs, then the Twins can teach us the next part."

Isabella and Marcella split up and helped the team to disable the bugs. It didn't take long for the electrician to turn up with Mary and MI5-S soldiers as an escort.

I met them at the door. "Jon, can you let us in, please? We have detected multiple electrical faults."

"Hold out your hands," I said. She opened them and I tipped in the handful of bugs we had found in our accommodation. "Don't bug us again." I shut the door and locked it.

We continued with the training. First, the Twins showed everyone the rest of the psychic skills demonstrated in the nightclub. The ability to make people hear or see things. Later, we ran through the room clearance exercise with the Twins, who quickly picked up the squad tactics. Afterwards, we settled down in the kitchen to practice channelling our magic.

Rip opened the kitchen cupboards and fetched out the glasses and two bottles of red wine. "Now we have a drink and practise a little. But don't forget to savour the wine, enjoy the cherry undertones and oaky subtleties."

"Or just swill it down," Cassius said and took a big gulp.

The Twins took a full glass each and sipped at it. "Could we not have champagne or even prosecco?"

"You need to put your order in with the management. Speak with Mary," Rip said.

"Her. I don't like her much. She tricked us. She prefers you, Rip. If you ask her, then we will get it," Isabella said.

"Meaning?"

"You know. She likes you."

"You shouldn't be reading her mind."

"We don't need to. We can tell by the way she looks at you."

Cassius spluttered on his wine and I looked away.

"I am glad you all know," Rip said. "All have a good laugh."

"Sorry, Rip. Remember who she works for and that relationships with humans rarely last," Thorn said.

"I am sure I will cope. Now practise controlling your magic. Use it to hold back your healing powers. Let the wine take hold and relax your body."

"Speak of the devil. We have a visitor," Marcella said.

The door to the kitchen opened and Mary stepped in. "We need you all in the briefing room. Drink up and make your way over," Mary said, glanced at Rip and left the room.

The Twins laughed and I couldn't help but giggle as well. We finished our drinks and walked across the helipad into the next identical building in the triangle and into the main lecture theatre, the briefing room. The lecture theatre had a fire exit onto the central area between the three buildings and had been opened up for us to walk straight in. The room would have held the main classes each day for the MI5 students. It banked upwards in rows of seats and held about two hundred people.

Inside, Mary stood at the front with Ruby. The rest of our human buddies were already scattered across the first two rows of seating. I sat down in the front row and the Twins sat on either side of me. Thorn frowned at them, and Isabella got up and walked around to sit next to Marcella. Thorn took her seat next to me and patted my knee.

Rip and Cassius sat a few rows back and put their feet up on the backs of the chairs in front.

"Thank you for joining us. Rip, Cassius, put your feet down, please. Have some respect for our facilities," Mary said.

"Yes, Miss. Sorry, Miss," Cassius said and Rip nudged him in the ribs.

Mary clicked a button on a laptop rested on the podium at the front. The white projector screen at the front lit up, and it showed CCTV of the Twins and me, going into the nightclub. She pressed another button and the picture fast-forwarded until police cars and ambulances turned up. A few moments later, the Twins and I exited the building, each carrying a bottle of champagne. A policeman talked to Isabella but suddenly got distracted and walked off.

Mary paused the image. "I don't know what happened inside, as the CCTV cameras seemed to all malfunction. But there were multiple injuries to the security guards. A group of friends appeared to turn on one another, resulting in two fatalities. All this happened the same time you three were inside."

"We saw nothing," Marcella said.

"Yes. We can't help it. These things happen in night clubs. I think they were a criminal gang. Probably an argument over drugs," Isabella said.

"Well. Some people recorded it on their phones," Mary said, and the screen changed again. The images played of the gang member standing up and smashing the bottle into the leader's face. The recordings replayed the ensuing mayhem. Including my fight with the security guards and Isabella stabbing the gang member in the gut.

"It was all self-defence. The film shows the guards attacking V, and Isabella defending herself against the knife man. We didn't start any fight," Marcella said.

"I am sure you did something. Provoked them somehow. Used that psychic power to get them to attack each other. Anyway, I have cleared it all up. Don't let it happen again. If you want to find someone to fight or practice your powers against, we can provide suitable targets and discrete locations. Please don't draw attention to yourselves."

Ruby looked at her phone and disappeared outside.

"Are we done? Can we go back to our red wine? It is important Dragan training," Thorn said.

"Yes. If you wish," Mary said and shook her head.

Ruby returned and showed Mary her phone. They turned away and whispered. Thorn was listening to them. She tilted her head around and forehead frowned in concentration.

Rip and Cassius started to walk out of the room. Ruby walked to the door and shut it. "Sorry, we have received a tip off on some unusual activities in a research centre and our AI has picked up a pattern indicating a vampire cell. Looks like we will need to divide up our forces for a while."

Rip and Cassius sat back down while Ruby went to operate the laptop. A picture flashed up of a glass and metal four storey square building with the words - BioRebirth - in huge white letters on the front.

"This is a research centre in Scotland. According to the company's mission statement, it is investigating ways of extending and enhancing life. The Hunter organisation is using it as a parallel research arm. We shut down all their government funded labs, but they appear to have significant funding invested elsewhere. I would imagine this money has come from the Turned organisation, embedded in organised crime. We need a team to head to Scotland, infiltrate the research centre and find out the truth. We can't all go as we have another mission, which I will discuss in a moment."

The Twins raised their hands. "Infiltration and intelligence gathering is our speciality. So I think we go and V comes with us," Isabella said.

"Wait a minute. We should hear what both the missions are first. Plus, V should stay with me. He might not want to be left alone with you two," Thorn said.

"Mum, don't you trust us?"

She glared at them. "What do you think?"

"We never hurt him the other night. Instead, we showed him our skills and trained him," Marcella replied.

"I know, but you could have gotten him hurt."

"Really! You have never put him in danger. Like when he was used as bait to find us."

"Please. I was not far away. He is always safe."

"We will always be around to look after him as well. We wouldn't let anyone hurt mummy's boy."

I watched the conversation bounce back and forth, amused at the tug of war.

"Enough," Mary shouted. "I think one thing we can all agree on is that Jon can look after himself. Secondly, it doesn't make sense to have both Thorn and Jon together. They are two of our strongest warriors and the King and Queen of the Dragans. For the sake of resiliency, it makes sense if you two go on separate missions and it stops you both from getting distracted."

Thorn grunted and the Twins smiled.

I put my hand up. "Hello. Do I get a say?"

"No," Rip said and laughed.

"Ha ha. Let's hear both missions and then we can decide. But I will do whatever is best for the team. Just don't decide for me," I said.

Acknowledging nods and mutters sounded around the room.

"Let me tell you about the other mission. We have found an extensive vampire cell in the criminal underworld. Hence, where the research money has come from. We have proof the Albanians, Mafia, and Russians are being controlled by someone else. The vampire cell via the organised crime syndicates are buying up weapons: guns, swords, knives and large amounts of silver. We propose Thorn uses her contacts to set up a massive sale to the vampire cell, big enough to lure them out of hiding. We close in and take them down," Ruby said.

"Pardon. I don't have organised crime contacts?" Thorn said, looking indignant.

Everyone burst into laughter.

"Come'on, Thorn. You have contacts everywhere. We are hardly going to arrest you," Mary said, half laughing still as she spoke.

"Okay. You can all stop laughing. Of course, I have contacts. So it looks like I am on team two luring out the vampire cell. The Twins have to be team one to investigate the research centre. I think V should go to team one as well. My contacts may detect something unusual about him. I will take Cassius. Therefore, Rip to go with V and the Twins. Does everyone agree?"

"Sounds sensible to me. As long as you can cope without me," I said.

"I have coped for hundreds of years before. So I will be okay."

"Our team will split based on the buddy system. I will go with Jon. Bradders will join us. Smash and Dunk go with Thorn and Cassius," Ruby said.

"That will work. I can pretend they are hired muscle. Their backgrounds will check out," Thorn said.

"Good. Team one leaves in half an hour for Scotland. Get your things ready," Ruby said.

"One hour," Thorn stated, jumped out of her seat, dragging me after her hand in hand. She slammed open the fire exit door and marched across the courtyard between the three buildings.

"Wait, there is more to discuss," Mary shouted out, but we kept walking.

The other Dragans followed and went back to the kitchen to finish the red wine and blood.

We returned to our bedroom and Thorn locked the door. I guess she wanted to say a special goodbye. She grabbed my rucksack out of the cupboard and started pulling my clothes out of the drawers.

"It will be cold in Scotland. Make sure you pack plenty of warm clothes. Listen to the others and work as a team. Keep an eye on my daughters. I am sure Rip will help keep them in line. Don't let the humans boss you around."

I grabbed Thorn by the waist as she fussed around my clothes. "You will be counting out my underpants next. I am old enough to pack. This isn't why we came back to the room and asked for an hour."

She twisted around in my hands and wrapped her arms around me. "Of course not. Just thought we should get the boring bit done first," she said.

"Are you worried about me?"

She pursed her lips together and blinked a few times. "Always. It is just that every time you go away without me, something terrible happens. I guess I feel guilty. But I couldn't insist that you stay with me. It would undermine your position. You need to do this without me and prove it was just bad luck on other missions. At least this time, you are not alone."

"You are talking about my tortures and fights with Giles. Thanks for the reminder. But as you said, I am not alone this time. I have the Twins and Rip. I will be fine. Leave my clothes and say goodbye properly."

She smiled and we kissed.

Chapter Eight

We flew up to a Scottish military base and slept in regular, standard basic rooms with a heavy lick of dull grey paint. Ruby woke us at midday to go through the plans in the briefing room. It was the typical box room with rows of chairs, a TV screen, and a whiteboard at the front. Almost identical to the one in Wales.

Ruby commanded the briefing from the front of the room. We took seats and settled down while Ruby drew on a whiteboard. "The plan is simple. We park outside in our vans, and the Twins try to scan as many minds as possible, looking for someone who may know the secrets inside. If they identify someone, our tracking systems can work out their identity as they leave for home." She had drawn a block building and two cars outside.

"In the daytime?" Isabella asked.

"Yes. Not everyone lives at night. You will be protected in the van and you can bring whatever coverings you want."

"When?"

"We leave in twenty minutes. Meet here. We could be camped out for a few hours, so be prepared."

Twenty minutes later, we had gathered back in the briefing room. The Twins and Rip had both dressed head to toe in special black combat suits, which Thorn had designed. They had built-in hoods that covered the face completely. The sleeves had gloves rolled up into an extra compartment. They wore normal clothes over the top so they wouldn't stand out. The rest of us dressed in casual civilian clothes.

Ruby led us to a garage containing two white road maintenance vans with yellow chequered hazard signs and orange lights on top. "Twins and Rip in this one with me. There is an operator inside who will run the tracking kit. Jon, you are in the other one with Bradders and another operator. Sorry, not enough room for all of us in one van. We can always swap over when stopped."

I jumped into the back of the van with Bradders. The Twins and Rip went in with Ruby. I heard the garage door rise and the vans drove off. We followed the other van, and after a forty-minute drive, we stopped outside the research centre on the grass verge opposite the entrance.

The entrance and exit to the research centre had red barrier poles that blocked the way. A white booth sat on the entrance side with a guard sat inside monitoring cameras. Through the gates, the road split up onto a roundabout. The visitor's car park was next to the reception. The employees had parked everywhere else in the car park that encircled the building.

Green metal fences bordered the area, and hedges and trees camouflaged the fences to diminish the harshness of the security. Bushes and small trees sectioned off different blocks of the car park. Every block had CCTV swivelling around, sweeping the perimeter. The security guards could keep a watchful eye on every section of the property.

The company had plenty of money for such a plush office and extensive security to protect it. We couldn't just walk inside.

The building had four levels of glass and metal framework. The main section curved in and around, and the entrance curved outwards in contrast to the rest of the building, making it stand out. Across the reception area, giant white letters spelt out 'BioRebirth'. Underneath, visitors pushed through the double rotating glass doors.

I sat next to the operator and watched the images streaming back from the cameras built into the orange lights on top of the van. As cars drove in and out, the computer software isolated the licence plate numbers and ran traces. Details of the owner and the history of the car flashed on the other monitor. A red light in the corner showed it was recording.

A person rode out on a bike, their face was captured, and social media accounts flashed up on the next screen.

"This is cool. MI5 keeps all that info on each person?"

The operator laughed. "They do, but people mostly do it for us now with their social media accounts. They tell us of their relationship statuses, job, location, political and religious beliefs. What teams they support, and when and where they go on holiday. It is amazing that everyone gives up so much personal info about themselves."

"I guess you don't have any social media accounts?"

"I do. If you don't have one, it is abnormal. However, my one is full of fake info. Let me connect us to the other van so we can speak with them." He pressed a few buttons, and I heard the voices of the Twins coming through.

"This would be easier with V in the van with us. The four of us could connect as one mind, and I could use Rip and V's powers to amplify my own. Just as they did together against us," Isabella said.

"There isn't room," Ruby said.

"Well, get out," Rip said.

"I need to keep an eye on you three," Ruby stated.

"I will come over," I said through the microphone and jumped out of the van. Ruby flung open her van doors, jumped out, and quickly shut them.

She walked over and grabbed my arms. "Get back in. I can't leave you four guys alone with just the operator."

"We are supposed to be allies. Do you trust me?"

She tilted her head. "Yes. I trust you. But the Twins, I am not so sure about."

"You can hear everything from the other van. The mission is all that counts. We are hardly going to kill him."

She sighed. "Okay. I am trusting you. Make sure our agent is protected. I told them they would be safe."

"Of course. We aren't suddenly going to break the alliance just to feed on one person."

Ruby nodded in acknowledgement and headed to the other van. I knocked on the van door and the operator opened it. The Twins and Rip sat at the other end, shielding from the sunlight.

The operator took his seat back at the computer and replaced his headset. His monitor screen showed the same tracking information, picking up cars and faces, and displaying personal details.

"V sit down and hold our hands," Isabella said as she sat on the floor with Marcella opposite and Rip to her side. Isabella held Rip's hand and offered her other hand to me. I placed my other hand in Marcella's, so we formed a circle.

"Rip and V. Just open your minds to us and channel your magic. You don't need to do anything else. We can draw power from you and amplify our thoughts. You will hear and see whatever we hear and see when searching through the minds of those inside."

We opened our minds and the Twins connected. The Twins dived into the mind of the operator and we viewed him watching the monitor. We jumped out again and into Ruby's mind. *'Let's see what secrets she is hiding,'* Isabella said.

'No, leave her alone. Go into the employees in the building,' I said.

'Spoil sport,' Marcella replied, and we jumped out and into the security guard, who was watching the vans and noting down the licence plate numbers. We hopped into the receptionist, who was balancing phone calls and a line of impatient visitors. On again to the next mind we could find, hopping from mind to mind, looking for anything unusual.

After some time, we found people drinking coffee and gossiping about a secret project in the basement. We jumped from person to person, looking for our way down into the depths of the building. We found a few scientists writing up and reviewing reports. However, none of us understood the formulae or the writing. We kept in the same area, hoping something obvious would occur.

Nothing was happening, so we took a break to recover our energy and refocus our magic. Once refreshed after half an hour, we jumped back in again and quickly found ourselves in the basement. We caught the right person as they knocked on an office door.

"Come in."

"Dr Holland, I have the report you requested."

A woman with greying hair sat at a desk with a keyboard and monitor screen. "Thank you. I will review it later."

The person handed over the report and left the office, and we jumped into the mind of the grey haired woman. She sent off some emails and her signature revealed her to be the Chief Scientist of Project XV. The numbering of the projects using the same Roman numeral systems as the data we recovered from my dad's old workplace. We broke off again to rest up.

The entrance's red barriers raised and cars streamed out. Daylight had gone and the Twins and Rip relaxed. We gave the operator the name of the chief scientist in the basement, Dr Olive Holland, and he searched up the details. The van opened up and Ruby and Bradders squeezed in and we had to stand up to make room. Ruby squeezed through us to the operator and read off the computer screen.

"Dr Olive Holland has worked at BioRebirth for the last three years. Gained her doctorate at Sterling University in biology. She is fifty years old, has two boys of seventeen and fifteen. Husband, Gerry, 48, is a medical doctor. She regularly donates to cancer research, having lost her mother to breast cancer at seventeen. She rarely goes on holiday and then only in the UK as concerned about the environmental impact of international travel. According to the traffic cameras, she used to work late most nights and went in early every day. But recently, she has had a few days absent and been leaving for home earlier and arriving later. A recent report in the employee database shows an official warning. So what do you all think?"

"I think that is a surprising amount of info you can get on someone in a brief space of time. What does mine say?" I asked.

"You don't want to know. Let's just stick to the task at hand. Sounds like she is the person to speak to. Obviously, there have been some issues at work recently, as she received a warning and has spent less time at work. I suggest we talk to her. I think Jon could use his boyish charms and Dragan seduction powers to get her to talk," Ruby said.

"I am closer to her age. I am also very charming," Rip said.

Ruby rolled her eyes. "Maybe your charm works on some people, but you are an acquired taste. I have my orders that it has to be Jon if a female target and one of the Twins if a male target. You best speak to Mary if you disagree."

"No worries. I am sure V can handle it," Rip said.

"So, what is the plan?" I asked.

"We wait for her to come out of work and follow her home. Work out her route. Then we plan a way of getting you alone with her."

"I have to seduce her and sleep with her. Are you sure Rip isn't better suited to the task?"

"You are an attractive, handsome young man. How could she possibly refuse? We will need to work on your story, create an emotional connection. You can use the Dragan scent and psychic abilities to implant suggestions," Ruby said.

"We can help with that. If V focuses on his seduction scent, we can implant ideas into her mind, make her see exactly what she needs to see and feel in order to take the bait," Isabella said.

"Good. In the meantime, can you two track her inside and let us know when she is leaving? The software should alert us when her car leaves."

We waited in the van until it reached 5:30pm and then a stream of cars left. At 6:00pm, the Twins gave us the nod that the target was on the way, having let the first rush get out of the car park. Her silver Volvo pulled out the gate and she waved goodbye to the security guard.

I went back to the army base in a van with Rip. Ruby and the Twins took the other van and followed Dr Holland. Two identical vans following her would have been suspicious.

Back at base, Rip and I got two bottles of red wine and waited for the others to return. We sat in my room at a small square table. Rip poured the wine and took a gulp, his body relaxing as it went down.

"So Mary doesn't want it to be you to seduce the woman," I said.

"Who knows? Could be she doesn't want it to be me or could be they would like it to be you."

"Why would they prefer it to be me?"

"They are always encouraging a conflict between you and Thorn. Ruby, your red haired buddy, is to remind you of Scarlett. They were happy to use you as bait for the Twins. Then offering you the reverse formula and now this plan for you to seduce another woman. All of it is to create conflict."

"I thought it was just that Mary fancied you and didn't like the idea of you with someone else."

Rip shrugged. "You are right. She does like me, and I also like her, but it makes no difference. Relationships between Dragans and Humans never last long. We don't grow old, they do. We only live at night and we drink blood. These things drive a wedge between us."

"Have you had a relationship with a human before?"

"Several times. But eventually, the differences are too great. They try to change you. 'Don't drink human blood. Can you be awake in the day but just stay indoors? Don't use your powers'. You get what I mean. They love the excitement to start with but cannot maintain the levels of energy and desire of a Dragan. Such relationships are always doomed to failure."

"What about a Dragan and a Turned? Does that work?"

"I have never turned anyone, so I wouldn't know. Whenever I met a Turned, I killed them. You should talk with the others. But I suspect it would not last. One is inherently more powerful than the other. If it was someone they turned, they would be more like a pet. And have you seen any of our fellow Dragans with a Turned lover?"

"I guess not. So you and Mary aren't getting together?"

"It would be fun for some time. We shall see how things work out. But I will be clear to her about the likely outcome. However, this usually only seems to encourage people. It is like a challenge."

We continued to drink red wine and discuss our relationships. About two hours later, the Twins found us.

"Come on you two, stop your gossiping. We need you in the briefing room. We have a plan."

Chapter Nine

The next evening, we had parked our yellow Volkswagen beetle in a small layby on a country road. Next to the road was a hillside of slate held back by thick metal wiring. The other edge was a slope covered in pine trees to the winding road below that led up the hill.

Light rain splattered the windscreen and the road ahead misted in water. I sat in the front passenger seat next to Isabella, and Marcella sat in the back. We awaited the phone call from Ruby to say the target, Dr Holland, was on the move.

I sensed psychic chatter bouncing back and forth between Isabella and Marcella, but I didn't join in or try to listen. Not that I could, anyway. They could easily block it. I drummed my fingers on the side of the door and looked down at my phone. Then I pulled down the sun visor and flicked back the plastic to look in the mirror to check my hair and skin complexion.

"Don't worry. You look handsome enough. Have you tried your seduction powers recently?" Isabella said.

"Rip made me try it in the canteen last night."

"And?"

"I got the attention of two women. It worked fine."

"Did you enjoy yourself?"

"No. Nothing happened. I turned them away. I slept alone."

"Thorn wouldn't have minded. It would have been good practice."

"Is this the same Thorn we are talking about? She would have minded. I would have minded as well. I should only use those powers when absolutely necessary. It wouldn't have been fair on those women."

"You may have the body and powers of a Dragan, but your mind will always be human. No Dragan would have let an opportunity slip."

"You say that as if it is a bad thing?"

"It is a strange thing. The whole nurture vs nature topic takes on a whole new perspective if someone changes their nature. The nurture, the way you were brought up, is still a strong part of your identity even though your nature has changed."

"Maybe you should speak to my human friends; they would argue it has changed me. Whereas you are saying, it hasn't."

"It is a curious thing. Probably both are true. You have adapted where necessary, but we can only see the bad sides from our point of view."

"Maybe it is a good thing to hang on to my humanity. I can bring peace and balance between Dragans and Humans in the long term."

"Live in both worlds but not fully integrated into either. This will cause you a lot of dissonance. You would be better off choosing one and fully embracing it," Isabella said.

"I am not sure I have a choice. I may have the body of a Dragan but a soul of a human."

I rechecked my phone and waited. A phone rang in the back of the car and Marcella answered.

"Okay... right... we will be watching... Yes, we will let you know once we engage. One of us will text you," Marcella said and hung up. "She is on her way. It will take about ten minutes to reach us."

I checked my hair once again and flicked back the sun visor. Isabella started the car, and Marcella opened up her bag, pulled out a remote and switched it on.

We waited for a few more minutes and I turned around in my seat to watch out the back window. Dr Holland's silver Volvo curved around the corner and drove past. Isabella pulled out and followed on, being careful to keep some distance.

"Do you have the signal?" I asked Marcella.

She watched the red light on the remote. "Not yet."

I alternated from looking ahead at the silver car to the remote on Marcella's lap.

"We will lose the opportunity if we don't do it soon. Isabella, drive a little closer."

The car surged forward and the light flicked to green. "Press it," I said.

Marcella pressed the button, and suddenly the silver Volvo decreased in power.

"Slow down, hang back a little," I said.

"Do you want to drive?" Isabella snapped.

"She has put on her hazard lights and is pulling over. Follow her in and park behind."

"Yes, sir," Isabella replied and parked behind the silver Volvo on the verge of the road. I pressed the hazard lights on the dashboard.

"Okay, do you remember the script?" I asked Isabella.

"Of course, stop being such a nag. Let's go. Follow my lead," she said and got out of the car. We walked over, the light rain dampening our clothes.

The silver car's starter motor crunched, but the engine didn't turn over. I walked behind Isabella, who tapped on the driver's window. The window buzzed down, and a grey-haired woman with a grim face stared out.

"Hi, is everything okay? We were driving behind when we noticed the engine stop and your hazards go on," Isabella said and smiled.

"I don't know what is going on. The car was only serviced a week ago. I will be fine. I will just call the recovery people."

"Okay, we will wait until you have spoken with them, so we know you will be alright."

"I am sure there is no need. I will be fine. You should get back in your car. It is raining," she said and buzzed the window shut.

Isabella shouted to be heard through the glass. "We will wait. Just to be sure."

"Come on, Jon, let's just step onto the verge and wait."

"It won't take her long before she realises there is no service on her phone," I said.

The car door opened and Dr Holland got out. "I can't get a signal. Do you mind if I borrow your phone?"

Isabella fetched out her phone. "You could, but I am getting a 'no service' sign." She tilted her phone to Dr Holland, who put on her glasses. "Damn. I am stuck."

"We can give you a lift. Our hotel is only ten minutes away. I am sure you can get a signal there. We have made calls from our rooms."

"I shouldn't really leave my car."

"It is dark already, raining and it will get cold out here, and you have no way of making a call. Please let us give you a lift. I couldn't bear to think of you left out here at night by yourself."

Dr Holland looked back to her car, zipped up her coat, and looked up into the cloudy night sky as her breath froze before her. "Who are you?"

"I am Isabella. This is Jon, my cousin, and in the car is my twin sister, Marcella. We are staying up here for a wedding at the weekend."

"Are you from Italy?"

"Yes. Rome."

"Really. I love Rome. I shouldn't really take a lift, but I have a good feeling about you. Let me get my bag and put up a temporary warning sign. My name is Olive," Dr Holland said.

I knew Marcella was psychically broadcasting that good feeling from the back seat of the car. Olive fetched her work bag from the car boot, unfolded a red reflective triangle and placed it behind her car. I walked around to the back passenger side and opened it up for her. Isabella and I returned to our seats, and we drove away.

Olive introduced herself to Marcella. "You are identical Twins. That is very interesting. I work in genetic engineering. This is my field of interest. Can you two sense each other's thoughts and feelings?"

"Most definitely," Marcella replied.

"Oh, interesting. Do you mind if I ask you a few other questions?"

"Go ahead," they both answered at the same time.

We drove on, with Olive fascinated about the Twins. This wasn't how the conversation was supposed to go, but I didn't want to interrupt. She had agreed to come with us, and I didn't want to abruptly break the conversation.

We drove into the car park of the four-storey hotel in which we had booked a couple of rooms for the night. The hotel was a few miles outside of town, halfway up the hillside. The road we were on wound back down the hill into the nearby town.

"We are here. I will try my phone again and call the recovery team," Olive said.

We sat in the car waiting.

'Jon, you need to talk to her,' Marcella said psychically.

'I can't get a word in edgeways.'

'We will get her into the restaurant area and grab some coffees while she waits. We will find an excuse to give you some time alone to work your charm.'

'Cheers. But I think she would prefer to talk with you two.'

Olive hung up on the phone. "As I am in a safe, warm place in public view, I am no longer a priority. It will be up to three hours before they arrive and take me back to the car."

We knew that would be the answer; MI5-S was intercepting the call. Just as we knew, there would be no signal, as we had turned off the phone masts. And the night before, we had installed the device that knocked out her engine.

"At least it is warm and dry here. Let us buy you a coffee. I am going to start university next year and I am thinking of studying genetics. Maybe you could offer me some advice," I said, smiled, and released the seduction scent and thoughts towards her. Her eyes narrowed as if it was the first time she had really looked at me. "Let me buy the coffee. It is the least I can do after being rescued."

We went into the modern hotel reception and then through to the restaurant area. The room had blocks of dark wooden fabricated tables and chairs lined up and arranged identically in rows. We took a seat at a table for four people, but the Twins didn't sit down. "Can you excuse us please, Olive? We are having a meal out tonight with the Bride to be. We need to get ready. But Jon would love a coffee and a chat."

"Of course. I will answer Jon's questions. Thank you for the lift."

The Twins left for their room, and the waiter took an order for two coffees. Once back in their room, they would assist with their psychic powers, and I would continue to use my magic to release the biochemical triggers.

"It is hot in here," Olive said and removed her coat. I stared at her, not sure what to say. It was one thing chatting up a young woman or Thorn, but this woman was old enough to be my mother. I wasn't used to talking to older women.

"So you had questions. What is it you want to know?"

"Ah yes. What is the best University for genetic engineering degrees?"

Olive answered, but I wasn't really listening, too busy trying to think of what to say next and how to steer the conversation around to going to my room.

"Jon! Jon, did you hear me? What grades did you get?" Olive asked.

'V, for goodness' sake, try to relax and talk to her,' Marcella said.

'Sorry, but I am not used to talking to such an older woman. I don't know what to say.'

'Lies. Thorn is much older than this woman. She just doesn't look it. She is just a person. Get her to talk about herself.'

"Sorry. I got A grades, so I have my pick. Where did you go to Uni and what did you study?"

She started talking about university, and I just asked more questions about her life, career, and current job. It seemed to work. Plus, I could detect a rising in body heat. Her hormones were kicking in, and the Twins were assisting and opening her mind to the possibility.

"Enough about me. I feel like I just told you my life story. I wouldn't normally be so open with a complete stranger. Tell me about yourself. Do you have a girlfriend? Do you have any interests?"

"No girlfriend. I find most women my age too immature. They are only concerned with their social media profile or the latest reality TV shows. I have always liked women a little older and more experienced in the real world," I said and blushed a little. Olive sipped her coffee down fast and her heart raced. I carried on. "I like to keep fit by training in martial arts. I hope to work in the same sort of job you are doing, so I would really like to hear more."

"That would be nice. But I am sure the recovery people will be here soon," Olive said and looked out the window at the car park.

"It has only been one hour. It is at least another two hours before they arrive. We can't sit in the restaurant the whole time. People will want the tables soon for evening meals. Why don't you come up to my room? I have a kettle and a minibar if you prefer something a little stronger."

She smiled and looked at her phone screen with a picture of her two sons and then looked out the window and back at her phone again. She took a deep breath and placed her screen face down on the table. "Jon, have you ever seen one of those films when a gorgeous young woman chats up the middle-aged old man in a bar and then they go back to his hotel room, only for her to rob him or kill him?"

"I think so."

"Do you never watch them and think, why does he not realise it is a honey trap? She is far too beautiful and young for him. This would never happen in real life, and it is far too good to be true. Anyone would see through it. Are we supposed to believe it because men only think of one thing and would fall for such a trick?"

"I am not sure I follow."

"You are an attractive young man. I am a fifty-year-old woman with grey hair and I have had two kids. I would love to think you are truly attracted to me, but it is far too good to be true. So, unlike the men in those films, I am afraid I cannot accept this offer. I will not make the same mistake."

I stared in silence. I got no messages of help from the Twins. "It isn't like that. I just thought it would be nice to talk in my room."

"You weren't going to try and get me into bed and then spring your trap. You really do prefer older women?"

"I can say, without a doubt, I prefer older women."

"You are a good actor. That sounded as if you meant it. I wish this were all real. My body is going crazy, aching to do something. I haven't felt like this for years. But my head is stronger than my desires. Something is not right here. Which company do you work for? What did they put in my coffee?"

"There is nothing in your coffee. I don't work for any company."

"Please. I drove past you on that road, and then my car breaks down and I have no phone signal. You turn up to rescue me. A safe ride back to a hotel to wait for three hours while you work your charm. I don't know how you are doing this, but please stop it at once."

I sat back in the chair and stared at Olive. She smiled back, face flushed and eyes dilated, but arms folded.

"Well. This is interesting. I'm pleased you worked it out. I see this isn't going to work, so I might as well come clean."

'Jon, no,' Isabella screamed into my mind.

"This isn't industrial espionage. But I want to know what happens in that basement. What experiments are you up to?" I asked.

"Why on earth should I tell you?"

"You aren't happy with your job and what you are researching. Every time I mentioned it, you tense up."

"Who are you really?

"I work for MI5. We got a tip-off that something wasn't right with BioRebirth."

Her eyes widened, and she looked around the restaurant.

"Sounds like an excellent cover. That is what a spy would say?"

"But it is true."

"You wouldn't believe me even if I told you the truth. You would think I was mad," she said. As she spoke, images of a vampire flashed in her mind. One strapped to a table and given injections.

"I think I would. I can prove it?"

"Go on."

I leant across the table and held a hand to the side of my face so no one but Olive could see. She leant in, so our eyes were only a hand's length apart. I flashed my eyes red and jutted out the tips of my fangs. She jumped back and banged her knees into the bottom of the table, forcing the empty coffee cups to jump off the table and topple over. She sat bolt upright and scanned frantically around the room.

"Relax," I said, "if I wanted to kill you and drink your blood, I could have done it at the side of the road. I just want answers. We are the good guys. We are trying to stop the experiments and whatever it is you are working on."

"Maybe we should go to your room after all," she said, "not sure we should talk about this in the open."

She stood up and grabbed her coat. I jumped up and led the way to my room where the Twins were waiting. I opened the door and showed the way in.

Olive grabbed the chair at the desk, turned it around and sat down. The Twins and I sat on the bed.

"Are you all vampires?" she asked.

"We are not vampires," I replied.

Her face drained, and she opened up a bag and fished around until she found a blue inhaler. She pushed it into her mouth and pumped in two bursts of chemicals. She breathed out long and slow.

"You are the source?"

"The source? I am not sure what you mean. But we are the ones that can create vampires."

"Yes. The source of the vampire power. You are the original creatures. Was it your blood that has been supplied to complete the research?"

"Maybe, I dare say the blood samples taken from me have been used," I said, thinking back to the samples taken when imprisoned and tortured.

"Recently, we have received more than just samples. We received a whole pint of blood. From it, we have been able to advance our research and test new formulae. We had only a few tissue and blood samples before from some hybrid creature. But this pint of blood was from a fully formed vampire, more powerful than the ones we experiment on."

"That will be Cyrus's blood," Isabella said.

"Cyrus. Who is he?"

"Probably be easier if I start from the beginning."

I told her the history of the Dragans and Turned, including events up to the present day and the reason for our subterfuge. Halfway through the story, she gave into the minibar and poured herself a gin. I finished with our meeting and reasons for wanting to know about the experiments.

She opened another small bottle and drunk directly from it. "Well. This is turning out to be one hell of a day. It was me that sent the tip off. I was getting concerned about the work we were doing, and the fact the results and the trial formulae were being sent away. I was told to keep secret about the creatures we worked on and the test materials, the blood samples. I thought they would use it for medical treatments. But I soon became concerned it was being weaponised."

"Good. We are getting somewhere. What can you tell us about the formula?"

"The vampires taking it have their strength increased for a few hours."

"By how much?"

"Thirty percent on average."

"Thirty percent is an entire generation shift," Isabella said.

"Pardon?" Olive replied.

"A Turned can create another Turned, but they can only go to three generations. A third generation Turned can't create a fourth generation

Turned. The difference in strength between a first and second, and a second and third gen, is about thirty percent. Any third-gen Turned taking this formula would have the power of a second-gen. Any second-gen would have the power of a first-gen."

"And what if a first-gen took this formula?" she asked.

"Then I guess a first-gen Turned could have the same strengths as a Dragan," I answered.

"Would this tip the balance of power?" Olive asked.

"Yes. All those third-gen Turned becoming second-gen, even for only a few hours, would cause mayhem. Is there any way to prevent it?"

"The first batch of a hundred doses has already gone. Also, the details on how to create it. They should be able to synthesise more. However, I know the work and have started building a formula that could reverse the effects. I didn't want my work used as a weapon. I have all the details at home."

"We have to get that research and make sure you are safe. Let's take you home," I said.

Chapter Ten

The Twins called Ruby and gave her the update. We brought Olive down to meet her, and they spoke privately in the back of the van with no Dragans present. However, the Twins were listening in the whole time. Ruby opened the back and summoned us to the door to talk.

"We drive to Dr Holland's house. We will relocate her family to a safe house until we can come up with a solution. Dr Holland will hand over the research and has offered to help us complete it. We have already been working on a reverse formula to the vampire formula Jon takes. If we combine our research, it will accelerate results."

We agreed to the plan. Rip joined us in the car and we followed the two vans back to Dr Holland's house. Everything seemed to be working out.

As we approached, Marcella fidgeted in her seat and frowned. She closed her eyes and then shouted out. "We are too late. Get them to stop." Isabella flashed her lights and beeped her horn. The vans pulled over and my phone rang.

"What is the problem, Jon? It is literally just around the corner. I have an evacuation team on route that should be here in twenty minutes. And a Chinook helicopter to take you south as quickly as possible," Ruby said.

I pressed the speakerphone button and held it in the palm of my hand in the middle of the car.

Marcella leant into the microphone. "Other people are already at her house. Security from the research centre. Plus, Hunters, and I would guess a few Turned as well."

"Damn... Okay, we tool up and go in. This is a rescue mission. Bradders find a position to give sniper cover. Twins scan the area and give us intel. Rip, Jon and me will go in."

Bradders jumped out the back of the van, with a long black bag over his shoulder. He ran off around the corner. We popped open the boot and unzipped the bags and boxes inside. I pulled on a bulletproof jacket, strapped on a pistol and silver knife around my waist, and a sword across my back. I grabbed a submachine gun with a silencer. Rip pulled on a bulletproof vest and wrapped around his waist a belt of silver knives and placed a pair of short silver swords on his back. Ruby joined us and had dressed in a bulletproof jacket, helmet, dual pistols strapped to her sides and held a silenced machine gun.

"We ready? Any more intel?" Ruby asked.

"They are keeping her family locked in one bedroom. They plan to threaten them to get her to cooperate," Isabella said. Marcella had stayed in the car, her mind scouring the humans inside with Isabella's assistance.

"How do they know?"

"Yesterday, the security guard became suspicious of the vans. Then her husband called BioRebirth to find out if they had seen her, as he had received a call from a neighbour that spotted her abandoned car on the hillside."

"What is the best route in?" Ruby asked.

"The bedroom is at the back of the house on the second floor. If someone can get in and take out the guards," Isabella said.

"I have backup on the way. I suggest two teams. One hits the front as a distraction. The other around the back to free the family," Ruby said.

"I agree. But we will need the Twins as well. They can throw in some psychic confusion as well as lend extra firepower," I said.

"Agreed. I suggest you and I take the back of the house. Rip and the Twins hit the front," Ruby said.

"The bedroom is on the second floor. I can climb up and in through the window. I doubt you can do that as stealthily and as quickly as Rip and I."

"Fine, you and Rip take the back, and I will coordinate from the front with Bradders and the Twins, and distract them," Ruby said.

Everyone agreed. Marcella joined Isabella at the back of the car and loaded up on weapons.

Rip tapped my shoulder. "Let's go. We will need to loop around and then hit fast before they detect us."

Dr Holland's house was on a small exclusive housing complex,with only ten big three-storey houses. It seemed being the Chief Scientist at BioRebirth paid well. Her house was easy to spot, as it had four cars parked outside. The lights were all on, and the neighbours twitched their curtains to look at the unfolding spectacle.

We sprinted down the pine tree and hedge lined road into the exclusive estate. Ahead, Bradders hid behind a hedge, his rifle nestling through the branches and aiming at the front of the house. Rip diverted us to Bradders, and we lay down at his side, peering through the leaves.

"Her house is in the middle. There is a woodland out the back, which the gardens link onto. You enter from the woodland," Bradders said, "I can get a shot on the cars and take out the tyres. Stop any escapes if required."

"Sounds good. Thanks, Bradders," I said, and we sprinted around the back, leaping a high fence into the woodland and took a wide arc around to halt at the back fence of Dr Holland's long garden, mostly a mowed lawn and flower beds. I jumped on top of the fence and viewed the second-floor windows of two rooms. A figure moved past one window and the other window was dark.

Rip jumped up beside me and pointed at the back wall light. "There is a motion detection light on the back of the house that will go off as soon as we get about halfway across the garden. We will have to move fast."

Ruby's voice emitted over the radio. "Jon, the Twins and I are in place next to Bradders. What do you need?"

"Create some noise, but be careful, other people live in these houses. I don't want any collateral damage," I said.

"Bradders take out the cars," Ruby said. "That should get some attention."

The ping of bullets hit the cars outside. "Keep it going to cover our assault," I said.

Rip and I jumped off the fence, sprinted across the lawn, ran up the walls, using the window sills for leverage, and jumped onto the roof. The lights in the garden flashed on. Rip held my legs as I swung down and forced open the window to the dark room.

Rip released my legs and I twisted and swung in through the gap. I held the bedroom door shut as Rip swung in, and then he grabbed a knife in each hand. I opened the door and slipped through onto the landing.

A guard stood outside of the other door. "H..." he shouted, as Rip's knife smacked into his neck and he dropped to the floor. Rip checked the stairwell to see if anyone had heard. There was no noise. No one had heard from downstairs. We stood on either side of the door to the room holding Dr Holland's family. Rip opened it and let it creak.

"What is it? What was that noise?" someone said.

We stayed silent.

"Stop messing around. Go and check it," a man said from inside the bedroom.

A man pulled the door wide open. Rip stepped in and rammed a knife into his stomach and threw the body against the wall. I stepped around the doorframe into the room. An armed man stood over Dr Holland's husband and two teenage sons, who sat on the floor with their hands tied and mouths gagged. He raised his gun and I fired into his head. The body catapulted backwards, blood spraying up the window and then slumped to the floor. I entered the room and checked the corners. No one else in the bedroom. The corners crammed with wardrobes and bedside tables either side of a double bed. Rip dragged in the other body and shut the door. With the room secured, I untied the captives.

"What the hell is going on?" the husband shouted.

"Shh. Keep your voice down. We are here to help. People are after your wife because of her research. We are here to get you out of danger and somewhere safe. How many in the house? Anything we should know?"

"I called her work to say she hadn't come home and that her car had been abandoned. They sent around security people straight away and said they would call the police for us. I let them in and then they pointed guns and brought us upstairs. They took photos and sent them to Olive."

"Your wife is safe, sir. How many downstairs?"

"Originally, it was four people, but then other cars turned up and they have been searching the entire house."

I opened up the radio comms. "Hostages safe. What's next?"

"They have sent out scouts to find us after the sniper fire. The best way to get the family to safety is to eliminate the threat. We might be able to keep a few for questioning. I doubt they were expecting us," Ruby said.

"Okay, we will work our way downstairs. If you tackle them from the front, we can hit them in a pincher movement."

"Good. Let's clean up," Ruby said.

Rip and I discussed a plan. I crouched down with the family. "We are going to secure the house. Stay here and keep quiet."

I stood by the door. Rip opened it and I took point in the hallway. We reached the top of the stairs, and I switched to my pistol and carefully stepped down. I sensed no one on the first floor, and then guns fired outside.

We moved onto the first floor and checked each room, which were already wide open and contents of drawers turned out onto the floor and mattresses flipped over. We reached the top of the next stairs. On the ground floor, a group of soldiers ran back in and slammed the door shut. The sound of smashing glass followed and movement of furniture.

"They are coming. It's the Dragans," someone shouted.

Rip held another two knives in hand. He sneaked down the stairs into the hallway. I followed on covering his back. The bottom of the stairway led into a large entrance hall with rooms on either side. A soldier peered through the peephole on the front door to view the attack. Rip sneaked up, grabbed his head and twisted it. The soldier's neck snapped, and he dropped to the floor. I went to the left and Rip to the right, taking a room each.

I peered around into the room where three soldiers had over turned a dining table and rammed it up against the window. Plates, cutlery, and food were scattered on the floor. I opened fire across their unprotected legs, ripping into their thighs and twisting them in pain. I stepped in, punched them out and removed their guns. I preferred not to kill. Shouts ran out as a flaming figure ran past the doorway, and then ash burst back into the room. I guess Rip got the room with the vampires.

"Room cleared," Rip said.

"Room cleared," I replied, and we met back in the hallway and opened the front door. We moved to secure the back of the house as Ruby and the Twins entered. We opened the kitchen door and bullets splintered the wood. I slammed it shut, and we crouched down to the sides of the doorway.

"Give up," I shouted. "We have the place surrounded. I am giving you the chance to live."

There were a few voices and then gunshots, but no damage to the door and then blood trickled underneath. I stood back from the door and Rip pulled it wide open. I ran in, rifle at the ready. A man lay dead on the floor, a bullet wound in the back and a woman held up her hands with a gun in it.

"Gun down," I shouted.

"You can have it. I am not dying for them," she said and dropped it to the tiled floor.

I scanned the rest of the room and Rip entered.

"Kitchen secured. One prisoner," Rip said. The Twins and Ruby checked the other rooms.

"All clear," Ruby said and walked into the room. She looked at the woman and shouted. "Sit down." The woman sat on a barstool at the kitchen counter, and the Twins entered the room.

"Well done, everyone. The Chinook helicopter is nearly here with reinforcements. Once they disembark, you can climb aboard and it will take you to Thorn. The arms sale is happening tonight. I will take care of everything here."

The sounds of the engine and whirling blades approached. "Okay. Where will the Chinook land?" I asked.

"Who said anything about landing?" Ruby said and looked out the glass patio doors at the rear of the kitchen.

The windows of the house vibrated as the helicopter flew overhead. The cutlery on the side, shaking back into the sink and rattling around.

The garden lights flashed on and four black combat figures stood at the folding glass doors. Footsteps thumped down the hall and another four soldiers stood to attention at the door.

Ruby folded back the glass doors and the soldiers entered. Behind them, four ropes hung in the garden from the helicopter.

"Your ride waits, ladies and gentlemen. Send Thorn my regards," Ruby said.

Rip ran out, jumped on the rope, and started climbing. The Twins jumped on the other two ropes.

"I suppose I should go. I only knocked out the guards in the front room. You probably need to restrain them," I said.

"Of course, off you go. Your girlfriend needs your help," she said and stepped out of the way.

I ran outside and watched Rip and the Twins hauling themselves hand over hand into the helicopter, its blades buffeting the garden furniture over and piling it into the corner of the fence. The surrounding trees bending against the wind.

I grabbed the rope, pulling myself up, hand over hand, flying up the rope and into the helicopter. The soldier inside wound in the ropes and shut the doors as the helicopter rose, banked around and sped away.

The others had placed on big green headsets with microphones. Rip signalled to a pair on the hook behind my seat. I stuck them on. "Okay. Is someone going to fill us in?" I asked.

"Of course," Thorn said over the radio, "we have had some luck and set up a big arms deal tonight. Big enough to warrant the leader of the vampire cell to attend. We are heading there now, a remote part of the countryside just outside of Birmingham. You should reach us in time to gatecrash the party. I have been told you should arrive in about one and a half hours. It all happened a bit quicker than expected."

"We are on the way and already armed. Let us know what to do," I said.

"I will fill you in on the way. And you can tell us later what happened in Scotland."

"We will. So what happened?" I asked as the helicopter raced over the countryside, crossing over motorways and towns.

"I contacted my friends, who were already trying to put together a large arms deal. They needed some help, as had issues smuggling in the arms and moving such large quantities. Mary followed up on the lead and it trailed back to an unknown group. Cassius and I scouted them out and detected vampires. We agreed to get the weapons into the country as long as the group's leader attended. We upped the ante a little with even more enticing weapons and sent proof, courtesy of MI5-S. The meet is arranged for tonight."

"So you actually have the weapons for them?"

"No, we just sent samples and photos. Cassius and I will be hidden and our scent covered as the meet goes down. MI5-S will have the area surrounded and ready to spring the trap once we have established vampires are on site."

"That was lucky."

"Not sure if it is luck or not. Just goes to prove the Turned are preparing for a full-scale war. They are moving their agenda forward at an increased pace. They are taking risks."

"This will be Cyrus's doing," I said,

"I agree. He has always been very impatient, which is unusual for a Dragan."

As the helicopter darted across the country, I reloaded my guns and checked my knives and sword. We still had time left, so I closed my eyes and focused my thoughts. I relaxed and used the magic to replace my energy levels and repair any wounds. I must have relaxed too much, and the vibrations of the helicopter somehow soothing, as Rip nudged me awake.

"Five minutes out, V," Rip said, "clip onto the rope. The party has already started, so we are going in hot."

"What do you mean, going in hot?" I said, rubbing the sleep from my eyes.

Rip laughed. "You will see."

I stood up, pulled on a harness and clipped it onto one of the four ropes inside the helicopter. At the back of the helicopter, the Twins did the same thing. The soldier pulled back the doors, and we leant out the sides. The air pressure from the blades pushed us down and the speed of the helicopter pushed us back. I tensed up to hold my position and stared ahead.

In the distance, tiny bursts of gunfire lit up a field. Two groups exchanged bullets and fought at close quarters. A group of soldiers took cover behind a row of cars and held off successive charges from vampires.

Rip pushed off and sailed down the rope. The Twins did the same. I leant out, removed my feet and loosened off the clamp. I sailed down the rope and swung around underneath.

The helicopter dropped until we were skimming over the hedges. The bursts of gunfire grew louder. Our feet were only a meter above the ground as the helicopter lowered again.

Ahead, a gun battle blazed, and I detected the differing glows of Dragan and Vampire, firing at each other. Rip and the Twins fired into the melee of vampires, and then unclasped and hit the ground running. I released the clasp from the rope and dropped in next to them at full speed.

I fired in burst after burst, killing the Turned, ash exploding out and blinding the others. In the confusion, I charged in and threw the empty machine gun into the face of a vampire. I unsheathed my sword, jumped and horizontally spun in the air, hacking down as I landed. The vampire's head sliced in half. I roared as I yanked out the blade embedded in its neck bone.

Rip unloaded his knives into the Turned and switched to his short blades. The Twins hacked away towards the centre, twisting and turning around each other, protecting and counterattacking while cutting into the middle of the mayhem.

Thorn and Cassius stood in the middle of the battle, demolishing a stream of Turned. Thorn blocked and ducked, then cut away legs before jumping up into a series of slicing and hacking movements. Cassius arched his huge broad sword back and forth, swotting away the Turned, smashing through their defences. I charged into the attackers, cutting through the rotten bodies, fighting my way to Thorn.

Rip and the Twins stormed the breach, breaking the attacking formation of the mass of vampires. The MI5-S soldiers behind the row of cars unloaded their guns, picking off the enemies as they scattered from the onslaught.

The Turned retreated, regrouped and charged on mass. We formed a lined and focused our magic into our speed. We darted into their ranks, metal ripping into their flesh, strewing body parts across the bloody field until ash rained down to soak it up.

I picked out the enhanced glow of a second gen Turned directing the vampire troops, but he had a group of third gen Turned protecting him. It made sense as a second gen Turned could add more to their numbers. He held a samurai sword and wore grunge clothing, and had piercings in his ears, nose, cheeks and forehead.

I psychically signalled to Thorn and Cassius.

'This is the one. The cell leader,' Thorn replied. *'Surround him. V, head around the back to block his escape. Cassius smash through the middle, and I will cut in from the side. Rip, Twins, keep the rest of them busy. Show no mercy. No one can escape.'*

I fought sideways through the throng and arched around. A protective bubble of vampires enveloped the second gen Turned. Cassius squared up to the front while Thorn slipped around the side, waiting for a gap. Rip and the

Twins provided a distraction and prevented any reinforcements.

Cassius coiled back his broad sword. He lifted it above his head and roared to gain their attention. He charged in and swiped down. The third gen Turned stepped in to parry the below, but it scythed through them, smashing through swords and cutting through flesh.

"Run," the second gen screamed, and I hit from the back, halting their escape.

In the moment of hesitation, Thorn cut through the middle of the blocking Turned and thrust her sword into the temple of the cell leader. His eyes rolled and blood poured. The protecting Turned panicked and ran.

The MI5-S agents had circled behind and blazed in a rain of bullets, mowing down the escaping vampires. There was no one left to fight. The only evidence of battle were bullets sown into the ash-caked mud.

We sheathed our swords. Thorn flung her arms around me and squeezed tight, lifting me off the ground. "Good timing," she said and kissed me hard.

Chapter Eleven

The helicopter had flown around and landed after the battle had finished. We climbed aboard and took off to beat the oncoming dawn.

Thorn and I kissed and held each other all the way back.

"Get a room, you two," Rip shouted above the noise.

"Leave them alone. We won. We should celebrate. Would you like a kiss?" Isabella said, and puckered her lips and held out her arms.

"I am not sure I am ready to revisit that place. A nice bottle of blood and wine will be enough," Rip said. "I still have a special vintage from Argentina."

We landed in the middle of the three buildings and ran into our accommodation block as daylight clipped the horizon. The Twins shut the blackout curtains, and Rip headed to the kitchen to open the bottles. Thorn led me to our room, but Cassius blocked the way.

"Later, you two. We should all celebrate together first. We all want to know about Scotland."

Thorn rolled her eyes. "You're right. We should celebrate as a team. Lead the way."

She held me back for a moment and whispered into my ear. "Later. You don't escape that easily." Then playfully bit my ear.

We stood around the long kitchen table and took a glass of blood. "To Victory," Thorn toasted.

"To Victory," we responded and raised our glasses and clinked them together.

The Twins turned on the stereo in the living room, and it pumped out loud heavy metal music vibrating the speaker. Through the hammering guitars, we heard our doorbell ring, and Thorn and I answered. Bradders stood at the door holding a stack of pizza boxes. Smash and Dunk held packs of beer. "Anyone invited to the party? We have our own supplies," Bradders said, holding them up.

"Of course," Thorn said, and waved them in.

They set up in the kitchen, and Rip hid the blood away and poured out the red wine.

Dunk shoved a cold beer into my hand, and Bradders opened the pizza boxes. I grabbed a slice of meat feast to go with my beer.

Ruby arrived next and grabbed a cold beer. "To the alliance," she shouted.

"To the alliance," everyone yelled and thrust their drinks into the air, it sloshing out the sides and then downing a mouthful.

Ruby joined the Twins in the living room and pushed back the sofas and coffee tables to make a bigger dance floor.

Smash and Dunk stayed in the kitchen and hammered back the beers in a rush to get drunk.

"We should join them. Let the alcohol take effect," Thorn said. I agreed and activated my magic to keep the alcohol circulating.

We drank back and danced in the living room. We moved around the accommodation wing, chatting to each other, Humans and Dragans, sharing stories from our missions. Just one big happy family.

"Mum, you should have seen V trying to seduce Dr Holland. She totally rumbled him," Marcella said and laughed.

"I don't know if I should be happy or sad about that," Thorn said.

"Give him a break. He did great on the raid at her house afterwards," Rip said, rescuing my ego.

A few hours later, Mary arrived with other soldiers from the battle. We were well into our drink and feeling fuzzy. She arrived with a cold bag full of prosecco for the Twins, who quickly opened a bottle each. The soldiers carried in more beer and food. Mary grabbed a drink and toured the partygoers, listening to all the stories.

Word of the Twins abilities circulated the room, and they performed party tricks on willing subjects like a hypnotist. She had one soldier acting like a chicken. Some of the MI5-S soldiers tried to chat them up but with no luck.

Mary stood on a chair in the middle of the dance floor to grab our attention. Isabella turned down the music, and the others joined us from the rest of the accommodation section.

Mary waited for everyone to arrive. "Everyone listen in. A great night for us. We have struck a massive blow to the Turned and Hunters. We have found out about the new formula and have their Chief Scientist helping to make an antidote. We have dismantled a criminal vampire cell gathering weapons for the war effort. We have worked together well. Enjoy tonight. But the training starts again tomorrow."

We all cheered and slugged back our drinks. The Twins took to the dance floor and men encircled them, trying to join in.

Rip sat by the window in the kitchen, smoking a cigarette and whispering with Mary. We drank, danced and talked to everyone well into the afternoon.

I talked with Dunk, Smash, and Bradders over a few beers and pizza. Afterwards, I found Ruby dancing with the Twins. I danced with them for a while and then asked to speak with Ruby.

"What is it?" she asked as we found a quiet spot in the corridor to talk.

"I just wanted to thank you for the training. I never had much of a family. Just my dad and me. He was always working. You guys have accepted me and been so nice. I never had that before. You and the Dragans are my family," I said, and gave her a hug.

She smiled. "Thank you, Jon. I appreciate it. But I think you may have had a little too much to drink. I didn't think alcohol affected Dragans."

"We've been practising. Just because I am a bit drunk, doesn't mean I don't mean it," I said and laughed.

"I get it. The army is my family. See you later. Go and find Thorn. I don't want to get in her bad books," she said, and gave me a hug and left.

We rejoined the dance room. A few minutes later, Thorn dragged me away and on the way out, she used her psychic skills to muddle up Ruby's feet, tripping her into Isabella's arms. They smiled at each other, and Isabella helped her up and they carried on dancing together.

"Don't pick on Ruby. We all know you admire her, really," I said in a drunken slur.

Thorn squeezed her lips together. "Says who?"

"Obvious, she is the leader of the special forces team. You admire her determination to get the job."

"Whatever. She is right; it is time you sobered up a little else the party will be over."

"You were listening in?" I said.

"Of course."

"I don't want it to end. It's a party. I don't think I have ever been to a proper party before."

"It will end soon, anyway. Rip and Mary left hours ago. The beer and wine are running out. Everyone is drunk. Let's go back to our room to celebrate. I have waited long enough."

I grinned and nodded. She slid her arm around my waist, and we staggered back into our bedroom and locked the door. She flung herself at me. We ripped at each other's clothes, and Thorn's eyes blazed red and fangs jutted out. She picked me up and flung me on the bed and crawled on afterwards, fangs out and growling. She crawled in between my legs and over my body, kissing my chest and stopping at my neck. I gripped at the sheets.

A sharp cut hit my neck and she sucked hard. I wrapped my arms around her as she pumped down the blood. Thorn withdrew and stared down with blazing red eyes. She smiled, revealing her stained fangs and a mouthful of blood oozing through her teeth. She tossed her head to the side and pulled back her hair. I flipped her onto the bed, bit her neck, and drank in her life force.

I pulled back, the blood lingering in my mouth and smeared across my lips. She kept the blood in her mouth, staining her lips. She dived into a kiss. Her tongue searching for her own blood, exchanging mine for hers, re-enacting our Union ritual. We didn't go to sleep until late evening.

We spent the next couple of days recovering from our battle and post-battle celebration. I had to wear a high collar shirt to hide the bite marks Thorn had left. I should have just washed them out and healed them over, but I enjoyed seeing and feeling them. Thorn wore hers with pride.

Rumours circulated about what happened after the party. Rip and Mary's location couldn't be established. The Twins split apart for individual entertainment. Our human buddies remained in their accommodation for a couple of days to recover.

Eventually, Ruby called a debrief meeting in the lecture theatre. We all assembled and waited while Mary set up the laptop. Ruby's phone rang and she left the room.

"I thought I would give you all a couple of days to relax. We have been following up on the aftermath of the mission. I am pleased to say Dr Holland and her family are safe. She is already sharing her research with us and it looks extremely promising. We may have something in a few days.

"The vampire cell is broken. This has left a power vacuum, with different groups in London looking to take over. We may have accidentally started a gang war. However, this is not our concern. If we are lucky, they will just kill each other. Ruby will go over the detailed actions looking for improvements, but overall, it was a success. As such, I want to give all our Dragan colleagues MI5 identity cards. These will help you get assistance from other departments," Mary said and walked around the room, handing them out.

Ruby stormed back into the room. "You will all want to see this."

The pictures on the screen changed to a scene outside of a pub. The time in the corner showed it to be only half an hour ago. Three black vans skidded to a halt, slamming into the curb. The back doors flung open and out streamed several people. They kicked aside a sign saying Private Party and knocked out the security guards controlling the entrance.

The cameras switched to follow them inside. The invaders brandished guns and forced the partygoers outside into the back of the vans. A tall man with a white beard fought back, but a vampire jumped on his back and sunk in their fangs. Another man threw a chair at a vampire attacker, but they parried it away, smashing it into a window. A vampire slashed her claws across his chest. A woman tried to help him, but they dragged her to the vans by her hair. The vampires loaded up the vans with warm bodies, and then the vehicles screeched away, leaving rubber and blood marks on the road.

"This was half an hour ago. The police are trying to locate the vans. But it appears the Turned has kidnapped at least thirty people and killed a dozen in the process. There are a few survivors that we should speak with. We need to go right now. I have four cars coming around the front," Ruby said, and looked at Thorn and Mary.

"You heard the lady, training time is over. It looks like the war has started," Thorn shouted. "V ride with me."

"Thorn, can Jon and I take a separate car? I want to talk with him in private," Mary said, jumping in between us as we headed for the cars.

"No. Can't it wait?"

"Prefer it not to."

"Thorn, it will be fine. There isn't much we can prepare for until we have more info. Let me catch up with Mary."

She nodded and caught up with Ruby to discuss plans. The rest followed on, and Mary and I walked out last. They jumped into the three queued black range rovers with tinted windows. A black Mercedes drove around the corner, and Mary and I got in the back seats.

Sirens and lights flashed on the headlights of all the vehicles, and they accelerated away in a convoy, snaking out the campus, through the barriers and pushing the traffic apart on the main roads.

I held on to the side of the car and buckled my seat belt across my chest and lap.

"ETA?" Mary asked.

"Twenty minutes," the driver said. Mary pressed a button and a black screen rose between the driver and us.

"Some privacy for our chat," Mary said.

"Okay, so what is so important that we must speak alone?"

"Jon, I want to talk to you as a friend, not as the representative of MI5. I am worried about your behaviour."

"What behaviour?"

"The incident at the nightclub. You killed and hurt innocent people."

"Let me set you straight. I didn't kill anyone. They killed each other and

Isabella defended herself when attacked."

"You are splitting hairs. You may not have done the deed directly, but you did nothing to stop it. People got hurt when the Twins played their party trick."

I shrugged. "But they weren't innocent people. That was a drugs gang in the corner."

"It is not your choice who is innocent and who isn't. We have laws and courts for this type of thing."

"Laws and courts. Huh. I can tell you one hundred percent they weren't innocent. We can read minds. I know what things they did. I knew why people were queued up to speak with them. We did everyone a favour."

"What about the night club security? Had they done anything wrong? What about the other nightclub customers that got hurt in the mayhem? Had they done something wrong?"

I looked out the window as we chased after the black range rovers and squeezed past the regular traffic letting us through. "They didn't die. They will survive."

"This is my worry. You have lost all sense of humanity. I don't care for drug dealers, and if you lot want to hurt people, we can arrange suitable targets, but in suitable places."

"So as long as we kill for you, then it is okay? You're a hypocrite."

"Maybe. I have to walk a fine line. But it is your total disregard for other people that worries me. You no longer see yourself as human."

"Funny. The Dragans think I carry too much human sentiment around. It seems I can't please anyone. The transformation is ninety-five percent complete. Just one more injection will make it permanent. We shall see then what type of person I become."

Mary grabbed my hand. "Jon, please reconsider the reverse formula. We can try to change you back again."

I tried to remove my hand. "There is no going back. I look forward to the day of completing my transformation and fulfilling my destiny."

She held my hand tighter and shifted around in her seat. "What do you think Scarlett would say if she were here? I will tell you. She would ask you not to carry on this path. To remember, you are human and to remember all the good things about being human."

I shifted around in my seat and looked Mary straight in the eyes. "Scarlett is dead. Killed by the Turned. That only convinces me it is the right decision to avenge her and my father."

"Avenging them is fine. But you don't need to complete your transformation. At least hold off with the last injection."

"I will think about it," I said, but truth be told, I had no intention of holding off the final transformation. I enjoyed having powers. I enjoyed being stronger than humans. We both settled back into our seats. Mary clicked away on her phone and I stared out the window.

We followed the range rovers, cutting down back streets and whizzing past cars as they parted the way. The car stopped, the sirens went quiet and lights turned off. Thorn and Ruby were already negotiating past the police, who were controlling a small crowd of onlookers outside the pub, The Queen's Head.

The front of the pub appeared normal at first glance. The hanging flowers were in bloom and signs painted on the windows. But the blue lights of the ambulance and police vehicles, reflecting off the blood splattered windows, gave away the grim reality.

I got out and the Twins were waiting for me. Cassius and Rip walked through the police barricade. At the same time, Bradders and Smash showed badges to the police officers, who were keeping the crowds behind the blue taped line. Mary ushered us through the line while talking to the police officers.

We passed a smartly dressed policewoman talking on the radio, and two paramedics dragged out a trolley from the back of an ambulance.

"Follow the paramedics inside. I want to talk to the deputy chief constable about crowd control and press releases," Mary said and headed over to the woman talking on the radio. The policewoman glanced up at Mary and turned off her radio. "I should have known you would be involved. This is getting to be a regular occurrence. It's not that crazy red woman again, is it?"

"Not this time."

The ambulance crew wheeled in the trolley and a policeman ran out and vomited on the curb. A colleague crouched by their side and rubbed their back. I clenched my teeth and steeled myself for the show inside.

Piles of black body bags crowded the entrance. Body outlines in white tape on the floor and numbers at the side while people in white paper suits and masks snapped with cameras, lights flashing all around me. A tall man with white hair and a beard lay on a bench, slash marks across his chest and throat cut. We stepped around two dead bodies of men with their throats ripped out and blood splattered across the floor.

"V, this way. We have a survivor at the back," Thorn shouted.

We walked around the upturn tables and crunched on the broken glass till we reached an open door onto a balcony used for smokers. A couple coated in ash sat near the railings. The man and woman both held bottles of beer, their hands shaking. A policewoman sat in front, quietly asking questions while taking notes.

"Can you speak to them? You are best at talking to humans," Thorn asked.

I walked over and the policewoman offered a chair after I showed her my MI5 badge. "Hi, I am Jon. What are your names?" I asked the shaken couple.

"Emma and Russell," the woman said.

"Tell me what happened."

Russell scratched his beard and Emma tucked her blonde hair behind her ears and started talking fast. "It's a works party, and we came out on the balcony to have a smoke and escape the crowds. There was no one else out here, and we started kissing. Then there was a noise inside, but we decided it was best to stay out of trouble. Probably Mark got too drunk and started an argument or a fight had started. We rarely get out as we have a three-year-old daughter, so we wanted to make the most of it."

She took a swig of beer and took a deep breath.

"You are doing fine, Emma. Please carry on," I said.

"You look young for a policeman, about the same age as my oldest daughter. Is your colleague the senior officer?"

Thorn stood at my shoulder. "He is a fast track, but don't worry, he is good at his job and I am listening in as well."

"We were kissing. Some guy comes onto the balcony and shouts at us to go back inside. There is plenty of time left in the night and no one said the balcony was out of bounds, so we just ignored him. He shouted again, grabbed my shoulder, and pulled me away. I spun around and slapped him across the face, and then his face it..." Emma closed her eyes, held her head in her hands and took another drink.

Russell took over. "His face was disfigured. His skin was rotten, teeth yellow and eyes black. I thought it was some homeless drunk or druggie that had gatecrashed the party. I told him to get lost. He pushed Emma to the floor and went to grab me. I stepped back into the railings and he lurched forward, but Emma tripped him up and he fell onto the spikes on the railings, straight over his heart. We were in shock and thought we had just killed someone. The man writhed on the spiked railings, and claws and fangs appeared. Then he burst into ash. How is that possible?"

"Someone will explain about that later, but for now, we need to know every detail. What happened next?" I asked.

"I ran back to the door, but at the last moment, I suddenly thought about what was inside. I opened the door a crack and everyone was being forced out. There was blood everywhere and bodies on the floor. One of them looked like Mark, his throat cut and chest slashed to pieces. So I shut the door and shoved a chair under the handle to stop it from opening," Emma said.

"I was calling the police," Russell said.

"And that was it. You had no more interaction with them. You didn't hear where they might take them?"

"No, I didn't, but a couple of the guys in the team are well known for drinking too much, so they turn on their phone's GPS, so we can make sure they have got home safely or work out where they have gone or went that night. You could probably track them down via the app," she said, and fished her phone out of her pocket, opened up the app and handed it over.

"That is brilliant," I said and handed it to Thorn, who took it away.

"I want that phone back at some point. Make sure you get them home safely."

"Whose phones does it track too?"

"John and Christian's phones," she said.

"Thank you. That info is great. We will track them down quickly. Someone will be along in a minute to talk with you," I said and stood up.

"But who and what are they?" she said and stood up at the same time.

"Someone will explain. I have to go."

"You owe us an explanation. If I didn't know any better, I would have said they were vampires."

I smiled weakly, unsure what else to say. "And if they were vampires, would you expect me to tell you that?"

She glared up at me. "Why not? We should know the truth."

"People will come over and tell you the truth, but it is not my department. I have to get your friends back. That is my job," I said and walked away. Two MI5-S agents walked over to her as I left, trying to placate her exploding rant while Russell drank back his bottle of beer.

I went back inside, looking for the others. Thorn and Ruby sat at the back of the pub. They crowded around a laptop screen on a table covered in beer bottles.

"Hi Jon, looks like the app stayed on and it agrees with traffic cameras on the direction of the vans. We know where they are," Ruby said.

"So we saddle up and ride into action?"

"I am not so sure," Thorn said.

"You have to be joking. They will kill them or turn them."

"Yes. But why do it in such big numbers? I have never seen them take so many before. It is always one or two people. This is different. Something has changed."

"Ovidiu told us when the civil war started, he and Cyrus turned large numbers," Ruby said.

"That is what worries me. Feels like they are building an army and they don't care if we see it."

"Maybe. It sounds like the war has picked up a level. But they wouldn't know we have tracked them so quickly. We can't leave innocent people to die."

Ruby shut the laptop lid. "He is right. My team is going regardless. It would be good if you could join us."

Thorn stood up. "Very well. This day was inevitable. It had to escalate at some point. Our recent victories have probably forced on the pace. Gather the troops and bring the weapons. We are going to war."

Chapter Twelve

The black range rovers set off again in a screaming convey of flashing lights and sirens. I sat in the back with Thorn on one side and Mary on the other. Rip sat in the front and the rest followed in the other cars.

"Where are we going?" I asked.

"The Turned have the humans in abandoned steelworks near the docks. We have sent a unit in to secure the area and perform recon," Mary said.

"What's the plan? What are they going to do with them?" I asked.

"The plan is to meet our unit and find out what they have seen. We decide from there. I can only think of two reasons for taking people. Either they are going to turn them into vampires or feed on them," Mary said.

"Probably fifty-fifty. Half will be turned and the other half fed to the new vampires. Either way, we need to stop them. This is a dangerous acceleration of their plans," Thorn said.

The cars whipped through the streets. The traffic ahead moved to one side, and we squeezed through the gaps and shot across red lights. We skidded around a corner and I braced myself against the door to avoid squashing Mary. Thorn held onto the inside door handle. We righted up and surged forward, sirens blasting our ears, and blue lights flashing off the passing vehicles. The other drivers and passengers stared and then followed in our wake.

We cut off the main roads and blasted down sidestreets. Rain splattered across the windscreen, and wipers flicked back and forth in a fury. The lead car turned off its lights and sirens, and the rest copied to stop announcing our presence to the Turned.

Up ahead, the side street ended by a wire fence that had been smashed apart. We parked up near two black vans inside the perimeter and got out. One of the vans' back doors opened, and a woman in a pink tracksuit held up their hand and summoned us over. Mary, Thorn, Ruby and I all climbed inside the van while the others assembled at the back, trying to shelter from the rain.

Inside the van, two operators sat at either end, busying themselves on computers streaming information through the monitors.

"Hi, I am June. Sorry for my clothes and smell. I got called out of the gym," the woman said. "In the other van is a drone operator who is flying around the perimeter to get us a better sight of the situation. The images are being streamed to this monitor," she said and pointed at the green night-vision images of an old building with two massive chimneys on top. The screen switch to a heat vision filter and faint outlines of people glowed from inside.

"We can't see as much as we would like. This was a steelworks, so the walls were extra thick to contain it. The heat camera doesn't get out as much as normal. However, we can confirm people are inside."

"Do you have anything that will help us?" Thorn asked.

June looked around at the other computer operator. "They are bringing up the blueprints of the building and google images to see if we can find a good way in."

"We can't wait. Those people are in danger. We need to go in now," I said. "We just arm up and smash our way in."

Thorn grabbed my arm as I headed out of the van. "Hold your horses. A couple of victories and you have turned into Rambo. I have spent a long time teaching you military strategy, and now you want to go full-frontal attack. I have told you before, only four percent of all documented battles have been won from a full-frontal assault. Strategies and tactics win. A moment of planning can save a lifetime on the battlefield. Engage your brain for a second. Think of our strengths and their weaknesses. What is their plan?" Thorn said.

I didn't want to stand by and do nothing, but she was right. I just wanted to dive in, not only to save the people being held, but this was the real beginning of the war.

I flung open the van doors to take a breather. I stepped out and looked toward the old steelworks, but other wrecked buildings blocked my view.

The brickwork had given away on the other buildings, revealing the metal skeleton framework, and material flapped in the wind like loose skin. Rain lashed into the holes, deteriorating more of the structure, forcing moisture inside and breaking away the walls. The brickwork had chipped off and crashed down into mounds of rubble growing around the base of the buildings. Like a castle wall broken from a siege.

Old twisted wrecks of London's industrial past filled the landscape. The ground was a composite of broken concrete, muddy gravel, and weeds. A haven for criminals and the homeless, where the police would not venture into without backup. A big wooden sign stated the purchase of the land and forthcoming redevelopment into a shopping mall and flats.

The Twins walked to either side and rested their hands on my arms. "You okay?"

"Yeah. Just trying to think of a plan. Thorn said to think about our strengths and weakness, but my thoughts are a mess. I can only think of the people inside. They must be scared and in pain. I need to calm myself."

"You just need to focus. Think of one thing that could help and then the next will come. You don't need to solve the problem in one go, just a step at a time. All you need to do is take the first step."

"Why are you two so wise?"

"We told you. Psychology is a speciality of ours. When you can see into other people's minds, you learn how people work. You discover the best ways people think and feel. The best ways to cope with your emotions and drive high performance. We have observed many people in high-pressure situations."

I turned around to look at them both. "You two are one of our strengths. Could you reach out to a human inside and talk to them?"

"Possibly. We may need to get closer first, but it may bring us into the detection range of the Turned senses. The range limit is similar."

"What if we place you downwind?" I said.

"Should be enough to give us the advantage. But what do you want me to tell them?" Isabella asked.

"I want to know how many Turned are inside? How many humans? Are they ready to escape if we attack?"

"Good. The first idea. What next?"

"The drone gives us additional info, but they will know the layout better. However, we have found them quicker than expected because of the tracking app."

"Good. Let's talk to Ruby and Thorn."

I climbed into the back of the van and the Twins followed. "So, do we have any ideas?" I asked.

"Yeah. We can attack from different entry points. Attacking on multiple fronts is our best option. Dragans in first and humans mop up. Back up is on the way, but we need to act quickly. Looks like they are sorting the groups into two halves, just as Thorn mentioned," Mary said.

"The Twins could contact the humans and find out what is happening inside," I said.

Thorn frowned. "Don't you think it would freak them out? Someone talking in their head."

"I suspect they are already freaked out. Plus, they can just read the scene through their eyes. But it will be best if we can get them onside ready for our assault. How can we get the Twins close enough without being detected?"

"I can get them on a boat. The smell of the river and being downwind will get them in closer," Mary said.

"Agreed. We split into two groups of four as the main raiding parties. Split the rest of the soldiers between us. We go in for a group each and when the backup arrives, they can re-enforce where necessary," Thorn said.

The operator brought up a blueprint on the screen. Ruby pointed at the two different sides of the building. "Jon, Cassius, Smash and I on this side. Thorn, Bradders, Rip and Dunk on the other side. The Twins will be on the river trying to make contact and can join in when ready."

"Don't worry. Once contact is made and the shooting starts, we will join the fun," Isabella said.

"Good. Let's go. Weapons are in the back of the cars," Ruby said.

The drivers had already flipped open the car boots. We went around the back, and the driver handed us bulletproof jackets and took a step back. Inside the boot were opened cases with weapons inside. I strapped on a pistol and knife around my waist and thighs. I grabbed a submachine gun and slung it around my chest. The others did the same, picking up their weapons of choice. I had chosen close-quarter weapons. Ruby and the other humans picked longer range weapons to pick off the Turned and Hunters from a distance.

The Twins disappeared off with Mary, and we split into our two groups with four soldiers providing additional firepower. I followed Ruby around the left-hand side of the waste ground, keeping a distance to the steelworks with other buildings in-between, as not to let the Turned sense our arrival.

"Let us know once you detect anything," Ruby said.

I focused my senses on the building. "I do not get much. It isn't like in Argentina. The conditions there were perfect. These thick walls and smell of the area are covering everything up. The wind is blowing in the wrong direction. Cassius, are you having any luck?"

He closed his eyes for a second and shook his head. "Same here. It smells of the river. The building is disused and damp. The walls are too thick to pick up any heat signatures of the humans. I don't like it. The place is too well hidden from us."

"Okay. We wait for the signal from the Twins. Then we go straight ahead. There should be a fire exit door. But we don't know the conditions of the entrances. They could be hanging off or boarded up. We might not get in without making a noise," Ruby said.

"Don't worry. They will have already detected us by then. I suggest V and I make an opening. You guys provide us with covering fire when it kicks off," Cassius said.

We waited for the signal. I tried to reach out with my psychic skills but to no effect. The voices were too distant, jumbled and drunk. I could enhance it with my magic, but I was saving it up for the assault. Hopefully, the Twins would have better luck.

Ruby and Thorn exchanged messages on the headsets. We were all in position and waiting to go.

Our headsets crackled into life. "Isabella here. We made contact. There are about forty human captives held by about twenty Turned. Ten guards hold each group of twenty humans. Also, Cyrus and Bramel are on site. This is serious. I am sorry, but I think Cyrus detected me in a human mind."

There was silence. No one spoke for a minute, letting the understanding between us settle.

"It doesn't matter. We have to go in," I said.

"V, we all know we must go in. But if those two are here, it is important to them, which means I suspect it is heavily guarded," Thorn said.

"Or they have made a mistake?" I replied.

"Think about it. Why would Bramel and Cyrus oversee the kidnapping of humans to be turned? Surely any of the Turned or Hunters could accomplish such a mission."

"Maybe we should think about it. Wait for backup?" Ruby said.

The radio crackled again. "Guys, hate to stop the debate. But it looks like they are preparing to start the transformations. Both groups are being prepared. They are ripping off their shirts and jackets to get access. They are lining them up and creating spaces on the floor for them to transform."

"Decision made, we go in," Ruby said.

"Don't panic. Unless they have an army of 2nd gen Turned, it will take ages to turn them all," Thorn said.

"Something else is happening. Cyrus just told them we are here and to start the conversions. They have all pulled out a needle and they are injecting themselves. Bramel and Cyrus as well. He definitely detected me."

"What! We need to attack before whatever they are taking works. It could be the formula from BioRebirth. If it is, they will all get a power boost," I shouted and jumped up and ran into the desolate landscape, rain stinging against my face.

I ran to the first fallen down building and crept around the edge. Ahead, across the patchwork of concrete, gravel and weeds, lay the steelworks. The building showed a similar level of disrepair to the others. The walls breached, the roof destroyed, piles of debris around the edge like a besieged castle that had seen better days. It wasn't a safe place to be inside; the walls could tumble down at any moment.

"Jon, come back," Ruby shouted.

I sprinted on again, picking my way carefully across the uneven terrain, trying to minimise the sound of my footsteps. Luckily, the noise of the wind blasting rain across the landscape provided enough cover.

I kicked down a boarded-up door and charged inside. Cassius appeared at my shoulder. Gunfire sprayed across us, and I dived behind blocks of rubble. Cassius dived the other way. I peaked over as the vampires grabbed the humans. A couple of people fought back but were hit unconscious and laid down. One woman vomited all over a vampire and collapsed to the floor. The vampires crouched over them, clamping fangs to their throats. The others screamed and wept as the vampires bit into their necks. They punched and kicked to no effect. The Turned locked on and drained them of life.

As the humans succumbed to the attack, they were laid down. Gunfire erupted over the other side as Thorn and co crashed the party.

I couldn't just fire over the top without checking first. I could hit the humans we were trying to rescue. At the broken doorway, Ruby released a volley of bullets. The other MI5-S agents ripped the boards off the windows, fired through the openings, and ducked down again. Bullets hailed back, but the thick walls offered plenty of protection.

"They are turning all the humans," the Twins shouted down the radio.

The bullets sprayed over ahead. "It is not possible. They are only third-gen Turned. The copies will never take," I said.

I crawled along the wet, dirty floor to look around the side. Rubble and old metal posts from the debris of the building had been used to barricade the way. We would be out in the open for too long if we attacked head-on. There had to be another way.

"We will never get to them in time, not save them anyway. We can only ensure a quick death," Thorn said on the radio. I assumed her side was the same.

"We should retreat and pin them in until backup arrives. Then we kill all of them. It is the sensible and strategic thing to do," Ruby said.

The soldiers firing through the windows shouted and dropped to the floor. Bullets ripped against the walls outside and through the open door. Ruby and Smash dived inside to join us. "We are surrounded. It's a trap," she shouted.

"Hunters are closing in from outside. They just eliminated our operators in the van. Our backup is still ten minutes away," Mary said over the radio.

Bullets fired in from either side, with vampires to our front and Hunters to our back. We were caught in the crossfire with no way out. The bullets hit either side, and we tucked in tight to the walls and rubble for protection.

"Hey, V. Get out of this one. You must think we are stupid to let you find us. Guess you realise the truth now," Cyrus shouted in a lull of bullets. I peaked the submachine gun over the rubble and fired a wave of bullets to shut him up.

"Is that the best you've got? Those people you tried to rescue will soon scrabble over those rocks to tear your heart out!" he shouted as the bullets ended.

I fired over the rubble again, but bullets hit back all around us. "Stop. You are giving away our position. Do nothing," Ruby shouted.

Bullets peppered the walls, dusting us in concrete and stones. I wiped it off my face.

I pressed the headset. "Any ideas? I don't think we can wait this out. If those humans do all transform into vampires, they will overrun us."

"You're right. The injection must enable it. The boost in strength must allow the third-gen Turned to transform humans. We need to escape and fight another day," Thorn replied.

"V, come out and face me like a man," Cyrus shouted.

I kept quiet.

"Not such a big man without all your friends surrounding you. Not willing to fight now that I have the same strengths as you. I always said you were just a boy."

I went to shout, but Ruby grabbed my mouth. "No. He is just trying to provoke you into showing your face. Don't be a fool."

I hunched into the barricade and tried to ignore his barbs.

"Are you a chicken? Silly little boy realises he is out of his depth. You were lucky last time. I won't make the same mistakes again."

I bit my lip and let the anger grow.

"V, let's shut this idiot up. It is time to show them what we did in the nightclub. I can reach the Hunters pressing in on Thorn's group. You and Cassius take on the others. Your escape route will be clear," the Twins said over the radio.

"Agreed," I said. "Cassius and I will reach out and try to confuse them. You can take the opportunity to gun them down," I said to Ruby and Smash.

"The gunfire from inside will make it impossible for us to get a shot in without being hit ourselves," Ruby said as more bullets sprayed the rubble barriers.

"True. I will take care of the gunfire. Just be ready. In the meantime, hold them back."

Cassius had already tucked himself down into a corner and closed his eyes. I shut my eyes and reached out with my thoughts. Gunfire exploded beside us as Ruby and Smash returned fire inside the building.

I reached into a Hunter's mind who was shooting at us, and I twisted his body sharply around, so his bullets went wide of the target. There were yells from his colleagues. I focused my thoughts once again, imagining my sphere of magic and released it into my intentions. I flashed the image of Thorn onto the head of the gunman next to him. He turned and shot. Cassius mentally nudged a guard to fire back. The gunfire from outside stopped and re-directed upon itself.

"Cassius, keep up the momentum. I will take care of the group inside."

"V, the Twins have worked their magic and our route out is clear, but we are taking too much gunfire to escape. We will have to go for a full assault," Thorn radioed in.

"Just wait a moment. I will buy you some time," I said.

I placed the gun on the floor and shouted over the gunfire and barricades. "Cyrus, we both know that just killing me will not give you satisfaction. You want to prove yourself first. Your new friends know I beat you. I am the reason you got captured and locked away. I discovered you are South."

The gunfire stopped and there was silence for a moment. "I told you before I am not South. The Turned and I have a common enemy. We worked together once and do so again."

"Do your new friends respect you after being beaten by a mere boy?"

"You want to fight, then so be it. Show yourself."

"Cyrus, no. He is just buying time," Bramel shouted.

"V, you have until our latest additions are born. So I would make it quick," he shouted. I looked over the barrier where Cyrus stood on top of a concrete block, the rain pouring through the holes in the roof, plastering his blond hair to his face.

I took off my weapons and bulletproof vest and climbed onto another concrete block, wiping the rain from my eyes. "Let's take this outside where there is more room."

Cyrus snarled and jumped off his platform onto another rock and punched. I swayed out of the way and my feet danced over the wet rocks. He balanced on the rocks, with feet on two different pieces. He sidestepped across and flung in a kick.

I blocked it with my shin, but misplaced my landing foot, slipped on the wet rocks and toppled over. Cyrus stamped down, and I rolled across the broken brickwork ripping at my back.

He jumped across, stamping at my body as I tumbled across the rubble and flipped back onto my feet. Blood poured down my chest and back from the jagged bricks and rocks that carpeted the ground.

He attacked again. I jumped out of the way and circled, feet skipping over the large debris.

"Come and fight me. We are even this time as I have had an injection as well," Cyrus shouted, brandishing his claws.

I moved around him, looking for an opening.

"Time is ticking, V. You either fight or my new friends will attack."

I focused on what magic I had and jumped forward, placing my feet on separate pieces of the broken building. One wobbled underneath, and I skipped to the next one. I forced my magic into my body to make up for the few percent of human remaining. My eyes tinted red and fangs cut through. I swung in two lefts and a right. He blocked the first two and then ducked and kicked through my leg, which sent me toppling over on the unstable platform, and I smashed my face on the rocks.

I went blank for a few seconds until I heard a cry of victory in my ear. I twisted around and whipped back an elbow, catching Cyrus on the jaw. He stumbled back but regained his footing on the wobbling rocks.

I hauled myself up and we faced off again. My legs shook on the rocky ground, and the icy rain soaked through to my flesh, diluting the flowing blood to a red stream.

The humans had been bitten, laid down and were being fed blood from the third-gen Turned. It was only a matter of minutes before they arose from their deathbeds, ready to kill. There were twenty on each side of the building. I realised it wasn't me stalling Cyrus. He was diverting us from a full-scale assault, so his new army could be born.

I charged in again, knowing I had to break him and get through to take out the Turned and the new recruits. I drained my magic into my attack, flashing a flurry of punches at Cyrus. He blocked and skipped back. I chased again. He blocked and counter punched onto my nose. I staggered back and wiped the tears from my eyes.

I pushed forward again. He blocked and trapped an arm and then punched through the joint, breaking it. I screamed and dropped to my knees. He recoiled both fists back as one and released a hammer blow onto my head. My head spun around and the world went sideways as I crashed in between the rubble.

I struggled to grab at the rocks and pull myself on top. Cyrus's face loomed into view. I could make out small scales on his skin, and his eyes had taken on a yellow tint. He had the markings of the dragon transformation. "No escape this time, little boy King. I won't make the same mistake you did. I will kill you."

He grabbed my throat and hoisted me into the air.

"Just in time to see my victory," he said, as the bodies of the dead humans awoke, claws and fangs appeared, eyes and skin discoloured as their flesh decayed. They jumped to their feet, foaming at the mouth and heads jerking around scouting out their first meal. "My new soldiers. There is food for you," he shouted and pointed over the rubble to where Ruby, Smash and the other MI5-S soldiers took cover.

My friends bolted out from their cover and through the exit. Cassius stood up, gun at the ready to cover their escape. The newly created vampires scrambled over the rocks. Cassius fired into them, but only caught a few before they attacked him at the same time. He fought against the group; the others streamed past and ran into the night, running like primates, hands and feet motoring along the ground.

Cyrus stopped one of the new vampires from running past. "Look at my new creation, V. A fourth-gen Turned. They have tiny brains and can't even pass as humans, but they make up for it in their thirst for blood."

He pushed the vampire away, and it joined the attack on Cassius, who had three vampires on top of him. He rammed his body into a wall to shake them off. Three fell to the floor, but others jumped on top, claws and fangs slashing into his flesh.

Cyrus squeezed, restricting my breath. I kicked out at his legs and thrashed around with my fists on his chokehold. He increased the pressure and grinned. The blackness closed in, and my mind reached out for help.

The noises of a helicopter above distracted Cyrus for a moment, allowing me to breathe and push away the enveloping darkness. Four ropes dropped out of the sky and two figures slid down, landing with knees bent and hands out to keep their balance. The rubble kicked up from their landing, and they simultaneously stood up next to one another.

"My special girls have arrived. It is a shame you chose the wrong side. We could have ruled together as planned."

They both smiled. Cyrus released his grip, and I hit the wet rocks.

"Who said we had chosen any side? We were just biding our time until we were back together. Why do you think I let you detect us in your captives' minds? We knew you would sense us, and it would be a warning that we were coming. I had no choice but to play along with Thorn's game until the right moment. Else I would have been locked away or killed."

"Splendid," he said and opened his arms. They both stepped into his embrace. Marcella looked over his shoulder and grinned. Isabella bent her neck up and Cyrus leant down so their lips met. Marcella smiled as her hands run over Cyrus's body.

Another four figures rappelled down the ropes and landed in the rubble. They wore black and carried guns. Cyrus broke off the reunion. "Werewolves," he shouted.

He screamed and doubled over with his hands clutching his groin. Marcella pushed him to the floor, and Isabella wiped her lips and spat on the ground.

"You really think we would want you back after all the lies you told? You killed our father, brother, and grandparents. You trapped us and turned our family against us. And we thought you did it for us."

One of the black-dressed figures ran over and helped me up.

"Need some help, old friend," Giles said, "didn't Mary tell you backup was on the way?"

"Giles. Max. And?"

"We have new recruits. Let's talk later. Can you walk?"

"I can walk and fight. Even with just one arm."

My body was naturally healing. However, I had a lot to heal and I didn't want to force it in case I needed the strength to fight.

The other three human werewolves ripped off the vampires smothering Cassius, and flung them away, nailing them with bursts of gunfire. Cyrus kicked out at Isabella and flipped onto his feet. He snarled and sprinted out the door.

"Let's go. We have a small window to escape before they regroup and attack again. Thorn has led her group out the back. We eliminated all the Hunters trapping them in," Marcella said.

I jumped off the rocks and followed Isabella and Marcella out, and Giles covered the escape. The newly turned vampires had attacked the incoming Hunters, ripping them to pieces, only wanting to feed on the nearest humans.

There was no sign of Ruby, Smash and the other MI5-S soldiers. We ran around the corner of the building towards the docks. The fourth-gen Turned had slaughtered the Hunters and noticed our escape. They gave chase, running with hands and feet along the concrete ground, sniffing and growling after us. Giles, Max and the other two werewolves laid down suppressive gunfire to hold them back. But as we reached the docks, the Turned caught up. We had nowhere left to run.

"I'm out of bullets," Giles shouted.

"Same here," the others replied. With our backs to the water, we stood firm. Giles, Max and the other two, a man and a woman, lay down their guns, preparing to make the change into a full werewolf monster. The group of twenty Turned, both new and old, stormed forward.

Bullets ripped into them. Ruby, Smash and the other MI5-S soldiers appeared from around a mountain of wooden pallets. Then another volley of gunfire joined from the other side as Thorn, Rip and others opened fire from around the corner of the building. The Turned jerked about in the barrage of bullets, and a few exploded to ash. The others sprinted off to find easier prey.

"Quick, onto the boat. It won't be long before they come back. Cyrus and Bramel are still out there," Mary shouted from the dock.

We ran over and climbed aboard a police riverboat. We crammed people into every available space on board, standing room only. It reversed out of the dock and powered off down the River Thames.

Chapter Thirteen

As the boat took us to safety, I sat in silence, nursing my broken arm, watching the waves on the side of the boat and the wake spreading out across the river. Everyone remained silent, doing their best to shield themselves from the battering rain. My body should have been healing fast, but somehow it was being blocked.

Ruby took a headcount. Dunk, Thorn's human buddy, hadn't made it to the boat. The MI5-S soldiers recounted the deaths of five of their unit.

It was my fault. I had charged in against advice and committed our forces into the trap. My stomach rolled along with the movement of the boat, and I swallowed hard to keep down the acid creeping up my throat.

Giles perched next to me. "Hey, buddy. How is the arm?" he said.

"Broken."

"It will fix."

"It doesn't seem to be."

"Is Cyrus's Dragan DNA caught in you, blocking the healing, just like when we fought?"

"No, I don't think so. He mostly just punched and kicked me."

"I am sure it will recover. Maybe you just need a rest after the fight."

I nodded and stared at the waves.

"So, how is America?" I asked, trying to keep my mind off vomiting.

"Good. Well. I haven't been in America for the last month. We have been in England at a training camp."

"Pardon. Where? How come we didn't know?"

"You best talk to Mary. But Max and I flew over and joined Ian and Dawn in the training camp."

I looked at the middle-aged couple sat on the edge of the boat. They were holding hands and looking out at the river's edge. "The other two werewolves. The other backup."

"Yeah. They were changed some years ago while on a camping trip to Wales. Mary's unit offered them a job, trained them up and connected us with them a month ago."

"Why the secrecy?"

"I think we were Plan B, or she was unsure if we were ready. We have only had a month to train together. Although we have all been trained beforehand."

"You had some time in America with Max to learn about being a werewolf."

"Yeah. He is an excellent teacher. I have learnt a different point of view."

"Cool. And you met Amber and Eleanor."

Giles scratched his neck. "Hmm. Something I need to tell you. Amber and I have become good friends."

"You mean you're dating."

Giles blushed and nodded.

"Good luck to you both."

"Cool. I understand you and Amber had a thing for a while."

"We did," I said, but I didn't know what else to say, considering what Max had previously told me. Amber hated me for what happened between us. The fact I had used my powers of seduction on her, the chemical scent from my Dragan body enhancing her desires. Thorn had picked out Amber as a training exercise. After I had gone on the run from Thorn, I sought out Amber and lived with her until I arranged a plane ticket. I decided it would be best to stay quiet on the subject. I had essentially used Amber on both occasions, coerced her into sleeping with me, and I had got her into trouble with a local gang.

Rip stood in front of us. "V, how is the arm?"

"Not healing."

Giles stood up and offered Rip his seat and then joined Max in conversation.

Rip sat on the edge of the cramped boat.

"Not healing. No fragments lodged that could be blocking it," Rip said.

I shook my head, too numb with cold and pain to speak.

"You're not purposefully blocking it?"

I shook my head again. "Why would I do that?"

"A chance to feel something. Even if it is pain. Are you punishing yourself for not beating Cyrus?"

I glared at him. "Cheers."

"Do you know how I discovered the ability to channel magic? Did I ever tell you?"

I shook my head again.

"Well, you don't look in the mood for a long story, so I will keep it short. Thorn's father had taught us we could use our rage to fuel our fighting. We had some basic understanding, but not to the level of mind-body connection we have now. I was living with this lovely woman called Belinda on a small farm in America, during the wild west era." Rip looked up into the night sky, smiled and rubbed his eye. "Anyway, I had been into town for provisions and got into an argument with an unsavoury group of men. It turned into a gunfight and I killed them. But when my back was turned, I was shotgunned by one of them that had been enjoying the company of a young woman and hadn't been in the fight.

"The preacher rushed to my side and started delivering the last rites. Obviously, I didn't die. The blood-soaked in and the flesh re-grew. He ran and locked himself in the church, shouting to everyone that I was the devil. Others joined him upon seeing me rise from the dead. I tried to talk to them, but they had taken refuge in the church and barricaded it. So I rode back home to see Belinda.

"While I slept during the day in an underground room in the house, the preacher and a mob descended and burnt the house down with Belinda in it. I was trapped underground with the house burning down on top. It was three days before I clawed my way out and found her charred skeleton. I went to town, killed them all, but got shot a few times for my troubles. However, the wounds didn't heal normally like they should for a Dragan.

"I stumbled away into the dark with bleeding wounds. Although they gradually healed, it took too long. After that, any cut or bruise would take time to heal. The same time as if I was a human. I had to be more careful. It wasn't until I met the lovely Sarah in a saloon bar in Washington, did things change. I had fallen in love again and I had talked through the events before. She told me it sounded like I was unconsciously punishing myself for the death of Belinda. I made the connection between mind and body. I was somehow preventing my body from healing. I think you are doing the same. Afterwards, I sought out ancient masters and studied the control of the spirit. What do you think?"

"You get through a lot of women."

"Not that part. About why you are not healing."

"I am unconsciously stopping myself from healing. So if I know this is possible, then I should heal?" I said.

"You have to move on and accept what has happened. Think of something that will lift your spirits. Look to the future."

"But to forget it so easily. I made a mistake and people paid for it with their lives."

"Maybe. But we don't know what the alternative could have been. If we hadn't attacked, then we wouldn't have fully understood the effects of this new formula. We wouldn't have killed so many of this new fourth-gen

Turned. They could have been left to rampage across London, killing even more people. Cyrus has played his strategic advantage and we now know of its existence. In the next battle, we will be ready to counter it. The whole incident was a trap meant to kill us all. We survived and learnt from it, so we should count it as a success. Things are progressing at a rapid rate. There are always casualties in war."

Rip stood up, slapped my good shoulder, and walked away. Thorn sat down and kissed my cheek. "How are you feeling?"

"Better," I said and gazed into her sky blue eyes. I clenched and unclenched my fist on my broken arm and felt the healing accelerate. Her presence was enough to lift my spirits.

"Good. I have something to help the healing when we return to base," she said.

The boat pulled alongside a wooden pier next to a car park, and a row of black jeeps waited for us. They drove us back to the base. I didn't talk on the way back; no one did. I just sat in the back next to Thorn, holding hands.

We arrived back at the base and split up into our rooms. Giles and the others had rooms on the next floor up and their kit was being moved over. Mary would call us, if any news, else we would meet the next night for a de-brief.

Thorn and I went to our room. She fetched out a black case from a safe and opened it to reveal the final needle inside.

"It is time we finish your transformation. The battle tonight shows you need to be at the height of your powers if you are to fight Cyrus. It will help fix your arm as well," she said.

I nodded, but closed the box and passed it back. "I agree, but not tonight. I am not in the mood to go through that. Plus, I thought we agreed not to take it while in the MI5-S base."

"We agreed for you not to take it while at the base in Wales. We never agreed not to take it while at any other base. V, this is the final transformation. We will need you at your full power if taking on enhanced Turned and Dragan."

"I know. It is what I want, but just not tonight. Let me have one more day and night, partly human. All I want to do is go to sleep."

Thorn put the box back into the safe, and we went to bed saying nothing else. I lay in bed, with Thorn cuddled behind me, knowing this was my last night as part Human. I felt I couldn't say human, because at some point, which I couldn't remember, I became more Dragan than Human. It happened with no fanfare. The final injection didn't hold that much significance to me, just the last step of an inevitable journey.

Chapter Fourteen

I slept for short periods throughout the night. Each time I drifted off to sleep, the pain of the fight returned and my loss at Cyrus's hands rattled me from my slumber.

The last time I woke, the smell of bacon dragged me out of bed. No one normally cooked in our kitchen. It was only Dragans in this section. I got dressed and left Thorn asleep, wrapped up in the duvet.

I shuffled down the hallway and into the kitchen area. Max stood over the hob, frying up some sausages, bacon and eggs. Giles sat at the table, pouring tomato sauce onto his breakfast and then coffee into a mug.

"Evening," I said.

"Just in time. I was hoping the smell of food would stir you. Maybe we could talk before the others get up," Max said and dished up the food onto two plates. He passed over a plate and took the other and sat next to Giles.

I took the other seat at the long wooden table in the middle of the kitchen, opposite them both. We all tucked away a few mouthfuls before Giles spoke. "How is the arm?"

"Good. Rip helped me fix it. How are you two after last night?"

"We are fine. Luckily for you, we happened to be heading to the base, anyway."

"Why is that?"

"Mary had asked us to move into the base and join in with the training. She was concerned that you were losing touch with humanity. Too much time around just Dragans. Plus, it was time we combined our skills."

"Sounds about right. Thanks for coming."

We carried on eating and soon the others arrived, helping themselves to coffee, and blood from the fridge. They chatted amongst themselves. Thorn took a seat. Rip talked with the Twins. Cassius chatted to Max. Then Ruby entered the kitchen. "Briefing room in five minutes," she bellowed to get our attention.

I chewed and swallowed the last slice of sausage and washed it down with the dregs of my coffee. Everyone finished their food and drinks and chatted as they headed to the lecture theatre. Thorn grabbed my hand and led the way across the courtyard into the next building.

In the lecture room, the Dragans and humans mixed together. Rip chatted to Bradders, Cassius to Smash. Ian and Dawn were talking to the Twins, and Giles and Max sat together. Ruby stood at the front with Mary. Then I remembered there was no Dunk, Thorn's human buddy. Thorn and I took seats by the Twins and Rip.

Mary waited for the talking to die down. "I don't want to go over the failures of last night. We learnt a lot from last night. But we should discuss how to improve for next time. Unfortunately, next time could be tomorrow night, so we need to focus on that instead. Ruby will continue the briefing," Mary said and left the room.

Ruby scanned the team. "As you all know, the Turned have a formula that increases their powers. It allows the third-generation Turned to create another vampire, a fourth-gen Turned. It increases the power of the second generation close to that of the first-gen. A first-gen near the power of a Dragan. For Cyrus, it gave him Dragon powers, like V. The fourth-gen vampires are blood thirsty monsters that only want to feed. They even attacked the human Hunters. Other units spent most of the night mopping up after these vampires as they randomly attacked people. It appears their creators have little control over them. They probably aren't a viable weapon in the long term. They can only destroy and disrupt. However, the power the formula affords to the other Turned generations will take away our advantage of Dragan numbers."

Mary walked back through the door with an older gentleman, white-haired and ruddy complexion, wearing black trousers and a white shirt. He smiled and stood next to Mary on the stage. Ruby stood down from the stage and gave a slight deferring nod to the man, who raised a hand back.

"Everyone, this is the boss, Sir Allan. He would like to talk to you all," Mary said.

"Your boss?" Thorn asked.

"No. Higher than that. So much higher, I don't know his position."

The man stepped forward and spoke in a soft Scottish accent. "It doesn't really matter who I am and what is my position. I have come with news. This conflict has reached a critical point, so I have called in a major asset to help us," he said and turned to the door. "Come in. No need to be afraid."

The door pushed open, and another man walked in wearing jeans and a black jacket. He had white hair as well, but it was scruffy and he sported a day's growth on his chin. I recognised the man, but I had never seen him looking so dishevelled.

Thorn jumped out of her seat. "Gabriel. What the hell is he doing here? He experimented on me."

Sir Allan waved his hands down to motion Thorn to sit. "Yes, Yes. I know. To you, he is the enemy. The man leading the experiments on you. But to me, he is an old school friend that has stayed undercover until the moment was right to switch sides and bring with him critical information. Now is that time, so please listen to him."

Gabriel gave a weak smile and cleared his throat. "I know you don't trust me."

"Really? You had me tortured and nearly dissected," I said.

He stood up straight. "I think you'll find those orders never came from me. I wasn't even at the base when they ordered your dissection. Those orders came from Bramel and whoever he used to talk with."

"You mean South."

Gabriel looked back to Sir Allan, who answered. "Let's carry on."

"So I couldn't intervene, as it would have blown my cover. I had to hope other plans were in place to get you out," Gabriel said.

"You led the experiments on me as well," Thorn said.

"I just managed the unit. I didn't perform the experiments. Anyway, you survived with little harm done. So do you want to hear my news? Why I came in from the cold?"

"Continue," Sir Allan said.

"You know of this new formula. The data gathered from their experiments on Thorn and V, were enough to create this boost. With the material from Cyrus, the people at BioRebirth have made a huge batch. The formula only lasts a few hours, but it has devastating effects. Their army could double in a few minutes by creating new Turned. The others all get a major boost, enough to tackle a unit of Dragans. The plan was to lure you in and kill off the main opposition. They failed. Although you may think you lost that fight, it ruined their plans."

"What plans?" I asked.

"After cutting the head off the snake, which is you lot. They were going to perform a full takeover. They would use the formula to create an army of fourth-gen Turned to set loose on London. In the chaos, they would select strategic personnel to be transformed by first and second Generation Turned. These new members of the army would give them access to higher-level personnel and help control the reaction of the security forces."

"So similar to how Cyrus and The Original created the first Turned army," I said.

"Yes, but on a bigger scale. They would have to hit quick and hard before anyone realises what is going on. The plan is to get to the highest levels. With their failure to kill off the Dragans and their strategic advantage revealed, they are bringing the plans forward a couple of weeks. The vampire takeover will take place in a couple of days. With me leaving, they may accelerate it further."

"Tomorrow?"

"Could be. They have summoned the rest of the Turned and Hunter army to London."

"How many?"

"They have been arriving in England over the last few weeks. Gathering weapons and training. As your recent destruction of the vampire crime cell is evidence."

Sir Allan stepped forward. "Don't panic. They have been tracked, but we may not have got them all. We will stop the majority of them, but allow a few through in order to follow. We have to be ready to fight at any moment. Now, Mary has other news."

All eyes fixed on Mary. "Ever since we have been fighting the Turned and Hunters, we have been in a biological arms race. We have the formula that Jon uses. They have a formula for turning humans into Turned temporarily, the werewolf formula and now a vampire boosting formula. As I have mentioned to Jon, we have a reversing formula under development. This was meant to reverse the Vampire formula that Jon takes and restore his human DNA."

Thorn took a deep breath of disapproval. Mary glanced over before continuing. "However, with the help of Dr Holland, it should also work against this new boosting formula, counteracting the boost it gives the taker. But we have limited stocks and haven't tested on these fourth-gen vampires."

"So it may not work?"

"Might not, but we are creating a supply. The MI5-S team are the core of a new Hunters org to replace the corrupted one. They are travelling down to join us."

"So we have a plan?" Thorn said.

"Yes, but it needs work. We need to put our heads together and think this through. Once they gather for the push, we will get little warning. Everyone needs to be ready and geared up, with positions and playbook understood," Mary said.

Thorn stood up. "I suggest we give everyone a couple of hours to get their stuff in order and come back in combat gear. But we stay on high alert, ready to go at any moment. On our return, we go through the scenarios and work out strategies," Thorn said, grabbed my hand and walked out the room, pulling me behind her. We walked past Gabriel and glared. He stepped back behind Sir Allan. The other Dragans followed.

"I haven't finished," Mary shouted, but we kept on walking.

Thorn and I walked back through the courtyard and into the accommodation block. "Mary still had something to say?"

"They always have something to say. At some point, they stopped talking to us and started telling us what to do. Hopefully, we can end this alliance soon. Anyway, we have important work to do before any battle starts," Thorn said, and winked at me. She led us into our bedroom, shut the door and stripped off her top. "Come on, get your clothes off."

I pulled off my t-shirt and unbuttoned my trousers, letting them drop to the floor. Thorn removed the rest of her clothes. I quickly followed and then sat on the bed while Thorn opened the safe and fetched out the final vampire formula needle.

"Take your last injection, complete the transformation, so you are fully ready, fully transformed once and for all. We might as well celebrate your lasting change. Plus, who knows if we will be together again?"

I went to take it, but she snatched it back. "Let me do it. Your last one has significance, and it means we will always be together."

"Sure."

She beamed, pushed me back onto the bed and straddled over me. She took off the lid of the needle and held it in one hand. Then flicked her hair to the side and dived into a long, deep kiss. "Our last kiss with you as a human," she said and grinned.

She bent over my arm and placed the tip of the needle against the skin. Then pushed it in and squeezed down the plunger. She sat up, eyes wide and smiled. I felt the warmth of the vampire formula coursing into my blood, seeking out the last remaining parts of my human DNA to change forever.

Thorn kissed my lips and worked down to my neck and chest, her hand caressing my hot and twitching muscles. She sat upright, moving along with my tensing, twitching body, and placed a hand on my accelerating heart rate. The pressure built and muscles vibrated. I was reaching the point of transformation, but no temporary death, no white light and vision of my departed parents. I didn't have to go that far anymore.

My heart spasmed and muscles clenched one last time. A surge of strength raced along every sinew as my vision sharpened and hearing increased. My eyes burnt red, and fangs erupted out. I was complete. I was human no more. Forever a Dragan.

We locked in a kiss to seal the deal. We could be together forever. Both the same; both Dragans. I could now truly be King. With the excess energy circulating my system, I wrapped my arms around her and spun her around. We embraced and kissed, and I didn't want it to stop. By the end, I was exhausted from the final transformation and our passion, and I drifted off into a short sleep.

Something brushed my face, and I opened my eyes. Thorn's hand was lightly stroking my cheeks and brushing back my hair. She smiled and muttered in almost a whisper. "Sorry, I had to wake you up sleepy head. We need to talk."

"Sorry, I didn't mean to. The transformation is tiring."

"It's not a problem. I enjoy watching you sleep. You are so adorable."

I couldn't think of anything to say. Although I knew it was a compliment, it made me feel like her pet. I just smiled back instead.

Thorn stroked my face again. "Before we get ready, I need to tell you something."

"Of course, you can tell me anything," I said, matching her whispered voice.

"I may not say it very often, but it is important that you know, as everything will change after this battle. If we lose, then who knows what condition we will be in? If we win, then our mission will be complete and we will need a new purpose."

"I understand ..."

"Shhh. Just let me speak for now," Thorn said and stroked my face again.

She composed herself and took a deep breath. "I need you to know. That whatever happens during the battle or after the battle. No matter what happens from this day on. I.. I.. I love you. More than I have ever loved anyone else in my seven hundred years. I am crazy about you."

I smiled back and my eyes tingled. "I know you love me. You have shown it with your actions many times."

"But now I am saying it to you, without the heat of the moment to fuel my actions or voice. Just us tucked up in bed, naked and alone together. I love you."

My throat choked up. Although experiencing her love through her actions was a wonderful feeling, like when she was prepared to give away her title to Cyrus to save my life, her telling me with no extenuating circumstances carried a stronger weight. She didn't need to tell me. She didn't have to open up about her feelings. But she chose to say it.

Thorn stared back at me as I soaked in her statement. I smiled back again while I thought of something to say.

Thorn raised her eyebrows. "You can speak now."

"I know," I said and took a deep breath and rubbed the back of my fingers across Thorn's cheek. "I. I know you love me."

"Pardon," she said.

I tried to reply with the right words again. I gazed into her sky-blue eyes framed by her raven hair. My heart pounded, but the words just got stuck in my throat. "I.. also feel the same."

She glared and pulled back from my arms. "You are just an emotionally stunted teenager."

"Sorry. I find it hard to say. When I look at you, I know how I feel, but I get too scared to say it."

"Scared of me, still?"

"Not scared in that way, but of my own emotions."

She sucked her lips together and looked down. "Well. Okay. I suppose we should just get ready for battle," she said and went to get out of bed.

I placed my hand on her arm. "Wait. There is something I need to tell you. Something I need to tell my best friend. But you have to bear with me for a moment and let me whisper it into your ear."

She lay back in the bed. "Ok, go ahead."

"I need you to hug me," I said.

"My pleasure," she said, and shuffled in closer and wrapped her arms around me, and I slipped my arms around her and held her tight. Her heart pounded against my chest. I knew she could feel my heart hammering away as well. I just held her for a moment, enjoying the touch of her skin and the warmth of her body.

I lifted my mouth to her ear and kissed it. She quivered and her heart pulsed for a moment, and she squeezed tighter.

"A couple of years ago, I met the most wonderful woman in the world," I whispered, and the tips of her claws touched my skin. "Her name is Thorn." The claws retracted. I didn't realise how that might sound. "You would like her. I have never met a person like her. She is stunningly beautiful. She has hypnotic, sky-blue eyes. I could drown in those eyes. Her hair is as dark as a raven's feather and complexion is flawless. Her body is to die for, and I have many times. But these beautiful things aren't even her best qualities."

She gulped and her hand stroked my back.

I took a breath and whispered again. "She is courageous and independent. She is strong and fierce, but also caring and soft. Although others would disagree with that last statement, she actually protects people in her own special way. She only takes what she needs. She protects the weak and punishes the wicked.

"I once made the mistake of leaving her. Although I have never told her this, while apart, I missed her. I felt a void in my heart. What I felt for her was real and not just a reaction to her seduction powers. I missed all the things I just said: her eyes and body, her strength and caring. But I missed the everyday things most of all. A simple hug and kiss. Training together. Learning from her. Playing computer games. Watching films. Her explaining the history of the world. I love her stories most of all."

I paused a moment and took a breath and kissed her neck. "In human relationship terms, she is one hundred percent pure psycho girlfriend." Her claws indented my skin again, but I was ready for it this time. "She gets insanely jealous, although she tries her best to act calm. She gets violent and sometimes fatally so when things don't go her way." The claws dug in a little deeper.

"But you can't judge her on human terms. She isn't human. She is a mythical being of immense supernatural power. The blood that pumps around her body is magic. It runs hot with passion." The claws withdrew again.

"She is only one of a handful in her race. She can not make relationships easily. There is no online dating or friendship group app for her kind. She needs to find others to trust and this takes time. So, she fully commits to those few relationships she can make. She invests her time and her heart into them. It is no wonder she is so protective of them and reacts passionately when they are under threat."

She sniffed and kissed my shoulder.

"In the beginning, I may have found these qualities scary. They are now comforting to me. I know how much of her heart she has invested in me. I know she will always watch out for me. This is no fling. This is the real thing. She just told me she loves me. But I couldn't say it back to her face, as it is too scary to admit. But I do love her. I am crazy in love with her. I will change for her, and I have literally changed already. I think I finally understand her."

"Yes," Thorn murmured.

I whispered again into her ear. "Although I can't tell my amazing girlfriend that I love her. I can tell you, my best friend, that I am in love with her."

Her body quivered again and she held me tight.

I drew a breath and whispered. "No matter what happens. I love her. I will always love her."

I relaxed my hold of her and drew back my head to gaze upon her face.

Her eyes had red tears welling up. I felt my own and tried to blink them back.

"I love you," I said, and smiled, and her tears rolled forth.

I wiped a finger across her cheeks to remove the red lines.

"Leave them," she said, her voice croaking.

My own tears wanted to break free, so I let them go.

She smiled and placed her hand on the side of my face. My red tears collecting on her fingertips. She stared into my eyes and I slipped into a trance, staring back at her.

"You bastard," she said. I rocked back, but she held me in her grip. "We are about to fight the biggest battle of our lives, and you have reduced me to a blubbering wreck. My heart has melted and streaming out tears of joy. No one has ever weakened me this way. And no one has strengthened me as much. And all at the same time."

"Sorry."

"Don't apologise. It is the most wonderful thing anyone has ever said to me. I don't know if I will ever be as happy as I am now."

"I will try to always make you this happy."

"Thank you. It is a shame it has taken this event for us to talk openly, and I wish we could stay here and enjoy the moment, but people are waiting for us," she said.

"I know. I guess we should go."

"When this is all over, we need to talk. I know I can fully trust you. We are soulmates. Bonded together through love and blood. There are other things about me you should know."

"Like what."

"Like...," Thorn said, closed her eyes and took a deep breath, "like it can wait. It's been a couple of hours. We should get back. We have a war to fight." She kissed me, and her red tears absorbed into her skin. She rolled out of bed, and I gathered my thoughts.

"I agree. We need to spend more time alone," I said, and got dressed.

"Don't worry. We will have all the time in the world," she said, pulling on her black combat gear and left the room.

"I know, but we should spend time together. Live like a normal couple for a few months."

"We will never be normal. Once the war is won, we will have other concerns about rebuilding the Dragan empire."

"I know, but it would be good to take timeout and reflect on what has happened."

"Of course, we will deserve a holiday. We can talk properly, and I will give you my full life story and the full history of the Dragans, which will take some time. There is a lot to tell," Thorn said, and grinned to herself as we dressed in our combat gear.

We walked out of the accommodation block into the floodlit triangle courtyard between the three buildings. A snake of headlights swept around the corner, and a convoy of cars and army trucks crisscrossed the courtyard and parked. Combat ready troops jumped out and opened up sliding panels at the base of the buildings to reveal storage areas. The other soldiers unloaded equipment from the trucks, forming a chain of people passing it into several storage lockers at the base of each building.

We crossed the courtyard as two people carriers drove up. The doors slid back, and out stepped a group of entirely black-clothed people, with face covers, black goggles, and helmets. They had hid their entire bodies under the covering of black combat gear.

The group unloaded bags and crates from the back. A couple of soldiers stopped in their tracks and stared at us, and I stopped and stared back. I detected a familiar odour. The staring soldiers moved away and helped with the bags. Thorn clasped my hand and led the way into the lecture theatre.

"Why are they staring at us?" I asked.

"We are famous. You best get used to it. Let's find Mary and Ruby before they make all the decisions without us."

"I sense you have had enough of them."

"They don't include us in everything. But I get it, they have a huge number of reports coming into them, and they need to decide which ones to share. They are also awake at different times of the day, so we might miss out on some of the incoming intel."

"When do they sleep? They work in the day and are awake with us at night."

"I sleep only about six hours a day. Unlike you Dragans, you are worse than my cat." We spun around and Mary stood behind us, holding a paper cup of coffee.

"Hi, how did we not sense you?"

"I think your minds have been elsewhere. I was trying to send someone to get you two out of your room, but no one wanted to accept such a dangerous mission."

I gave a wry smile. "We are here now. Who were those guys all dressed in black?"

"This is our squad of tranquillizer gun specialists. We have put them together in the last few days to fire in the reverse formula. Firing a tranquillizer gun differs from a normal one. So, we had to find experts in the area, especially when we have so few rounds of ammo, every one has to count."

"And why are they hiding?"

"It is for everyone's benefit. They don't want their identities revealed in case the battle is lost. This team will be last on the battlefield and first out. I will only engage them if it is safe to do so. They are not combat trained to fight vampires." It made sense and I nodded along.

"So what plans have you cooked up while we were away? Have you found any other paranormal forces that can help us?" Thorn asked.

"None at the moment. No one we can trust."

"But I have heard rumours of witches and demons ever since magic started returning to the world."

Mary shook her head and frowned at the question. "Thorn, I found out the truth. I visited the paranormal investigation unit and saw your portrait on the wall, Countess Tabitha Horn, the founder of the unit. Two hundred years ago. I guess you have seen all the reports. You know witches were casting people to hell and about the demonic forces it unleashed. I can't believe we didn't realise the connection to you earlier. However, none of these forces are under our control yet, as you know."

Thorn smirked. "You would be surprised where I have influence still undiscovered."

"Yes. You have had plenty of time to work your way into the foundations of government. Hundreds of years and stacks of money to weave your influence into the fabric of society. I am sure you have many more places that you wield control. It is because of this, we want you to consider a permanent alliance. Once the Turned are dealt with, there may be other forces to control, such as witches and demonic forces. The gates of Hell may be opening. The unleashing of magic has made everything very complicated. Who better than the Queen of the Dragans to control it."

"I will think about it. After all, we don't want the Turned meeting up with these other forces and becoming friends. They are bad enough by themselves."

"Too late. It has happened once already, but it was taken care of. That is a discussion for another day."

"Don't worry, I already know. In the meantime, what plans do we have in place for our current threat?" Thorn asked.

"Speak with Ruby; she can fill you in on the plans. But can Jon stay and talk to me for a moment?"

Thorn and I exchanged a quick psychic conversation. She let go of my hand and went to find Ruby. Mary pulled me to one side into the corner of the entrance as troops marched in and out to get orders.

"Have you taken the formula?" she asked.

"Yes. How do you know?"

"Your eyes are still tinged red. I thought we agreed for you not to take anymore until the war is won."

"No, we didn't. But don't worry, I won't be taking it again. This was the last one. I will complete my transformation and just in time by the looks of it."

"We have the reversing formula."

"No. It is done. When the formula wears off in three to four days, I will remain a Dragan. It is what I want. Please, just accept it and realise I need my power for the upcoming battle."

"Fine. Let's do it your way," she shouted and stormed into the lecture theatre.

It sounded like a threat, but I had no time to consider it. I went into the lecture theatre to a mass of green combat clothed personnel. They had set up extra desks at the front to accommodate the computers and weapons. I found Ruby and Thorn stood at a table with a row of sub-machine guns, silver knives, pistols, and a couple of swords. Thorn picked up a sub-machine gun and slapped in a magazine of bullets. Ruby grabbed two knives and spun them around in each hand. Thorn raised her eyebrows and smiled. "Nice."

At the side of the room by the stairs leading up to the rows of seats, the Twins stood on either side of Giles, touching his arms and chest. He stared at them like a cornered, startled rabbit.

"Hi Giles, are Marcella and Isabella looking after you?" I asked.

"Of course, we are looking after him. We will take excellent care of him," they said together.

"I am sure he appreciates your special attention. But can you please be on your best behaviour?"

"That is what we intend."

"Not that type of best behaviour. He is a friend of mine. He is on our side."

"And? We won't hurt him. We won't hurt you, Giles. Just a little pre-battle relaxation."

Giles laughed nervously, looking back and forth at the Twins. "I am not sure what is going on here."

"No, not with Giles. He is taken. I am sure there are plenty of other people to choose from," I said.

I grabbed Giles by the arm and climbed the stairs to the top of the lecture theatre. "Spoil sport," Isabella said, and they joined Thorn at the weapons table.

We reached the top and looked down at the mass of people swirling around. Soldiers marched in and spoke to commanding officers, who gave them their orders or conferred with the operators sat in the first few rows of the lecture theatre. They would check the info and talk to colleagues or make phone calls to give updates or get answers.

Phones rang out and people took the calls outside. Keyboards clattered and commanding officers gave the soldiers' orders. They would then update Mary or Ruby about the current situation. It looked like chaos, but there was a pattern to the behaviour, a clear command structure in place.

"Thanks, Jon. I wasn't really sure of what was happening. It was hard to keep up with their conversation."

"No problem. Just be careful of those two. Have MI5 given you orders?"

"Yeah. I am to stick with Max. We will join the battle if it goes hand to hand to provide impact. Else we will form the rearguard."

"Good. I wouldn't want you stuck in the middle. I have to get you back to Amber in one piece."

"That would be nice. She wasn't impressed with Max and I joining you."

"I bet. Don't worry. You will be fine."

"And you?"

"I haven't heard the plans yet. I guess I will be where ever Thorn is."

"Which will be in the thick of it?"

I nodded. "Of course. This is my war. I have a few scores to settle."

Ruby marched up the stairs. "Hi Giles, Max is looking for you."

Giles walked down the stairs, where Max and the other two werewolves waited.

Ruby ushered us to the seats, and we sat down next to one another. "It's been a while since we talked. I am still your operational buddy. Although I realise we are no longer in training. I just wanted to talk to you about what will happen when the battle starts," Ruby said.

"It's okay; I have been in battles before."

She smiled weakly and shook her head. "They were skirmishes. This will be a battle. There will be hundreds of people. Bullets flying in all directions. Noise, smoke, blood and panic. It will be hard to know who is who, especially as we are fighting at night."

"Maybe I will have the advantage. My night vision is excellent, and I can tell the difference between Turned, Human and Dragan because of my enhanced senses."

"Maybe, but they have humans fighting for them as well, and one of their side is also a Dragan. Basically, I'm just trying to say is stick together, follow orders and remember your training. You are a good kid. I don't know how you got mixed up in this mess, but I have a duty to get you through it. I might not see you on the battlefield or afterwards. In case we don't meet again, I just wanted to say good luck and make your own path in life. I hope once this is done, you get the peace you are looking for."

Chapter Fifteen

We worked until the sunlight touched the windows and then raced back to our dorm block to rest during the daylight hours. I slept fitfully, thinking of the coming battle, facing Cyrus and Bramel once again. Hopefully, for the last time.

The sun reached its full arc and daylight dwindled. I was relieved to leave my bed and get back to work. Doing anything was better than worrying. I left Thorn in bed, sleeping as if she had no cares in the world. I guess she had been in battles and wars before. This was nothing new to her.

I returned to the lecture theatre, grabbed a coffee and pastry served from a long wooden table just inside the door. Agents sat on the student seats with laptops perched on the small desks. They typed and scrolled away while conferring information. On the main screen, a map of London with numerous red dots flickering across it, and a group of people, including Mary and Ruby, were studying it.

I bit into the cinnamon swirl and slugged back the coffee as Mary and Ruby talked.

"They are definitely on the move. The algorithm shows them moving into London, a few have gathered in Hyde Park," Ruby said.

"Just the ones we have trackers on," Mary said.

"The ones being followed as well. Sir Allan's team have reported they started moving at dusk. They are on the way."

"So this is it," I said.

Mary turned around. Ruby just carried on. "Looks like it. We have teams following them, and trackers and phone locations on others. Also, we have satellite and CCTV permissions on everything available. And we have anti-terrorist units and the new Hunter org following suspects."

"So, how many?"

"We are tracking about sixty. But I suspect we have only picked up about half the number, so we have to prepare for over one hundred."

"Are these just the Turned or Hunters as well?"

"Both. But with their new ability to replicate, they could double numbers again with fourth-generation Turned. So we have called in the police and army units to help contain their numbers."

"Sounds easy with your resources. Do you even need our help to kill them?"

"The Dragans caused this problem; they can clean it up. And yes, we would need your help. We have the numbers and firepower. But with the vampire speed, strength and healing powers, they would get inside our ranks and rip us apart at close quarters and then turn our people into more vampires. We need something to neutralise the threat. Someone to sense humans from vampires. Someone to negate their powers."

"Well, I am glad we still have our uses. I best get the others up."

"If you could. It will still take a couple of hours for the Turned and Hunters to assemble all in one place. But we need to be ready to move at a moment's notice."

I scoffed down the rest of the swirl and slugged back the coffee as I walked to the accommodation block. Night had taken over, and the lights were on in all the buildings and lit up the courtyard and roadway in-between. It illuminated figures in the windows of rooms previously dark at night. The army packed the entire base to capacity.

Soldiers exited the buildings, carrying helmets and backpacks. The panels at the base of the buildings had slid back to open the storerooms, and soldiers had set up desks and computers at the front. Other soldiers queued at the desks, and the store masters ticked off names, handed out rifles, packs of bullets and bayonets. Each soldier had to place a fingerprint on a machine to verify receipt.

"Remember, unused bullets must be returned and can be verified on rounds shot. These bullets are silver, so we want them back. The bayonets are silver as well. We are counting out and in," the store master shouted to the queue of soldiers forming up at the desk.

The soldiers chatted in the queue and a few stared over. I was famous. I felt like I should say words of encouragement or at least introduce myself as we would be fighting together. But the thoughts of the soldiers weren't friendly. Some thoughts of wonder and others of distrust or outright resentment that they were fighting a battle with us. I sensed the anticipation of the battle to come from all the soldiers.

I went back to our rooms and awoke the other Dragans with the news of the Turned convergence. I swapped my clothes over to black combat gear, flak jacket, and boots. The other Dragans wore the same to protect themselves against silver bullets. Their black clothing could extend to cover their skin from head to toe if required to stop a UV attack. We gathered up our guns and did a check through, loaded up the bullets and packed the extras into ammo belts around our waists. I swung a sword around my back, pistol and knife around my waist and strapped to my thighs.

Thorn pulled her hair into a ponytail and then looped it into a tight knot to keep it out of the way. Rip sat on the floor cross-legged with his eyes closed, focusing on his magic. Cassius chatted to Max and Giles, who had arrived during our preparation with the other two werewolves. They wore loose black clothing, a backpack of spare clothes, and held a semi-automatic rifle. We talked tactics and checked over each other's weapons and gear.

Once everyone had geared up, we tramped down to join the rest of the troops to find out the latest news. We crossed the packed courtyard, and the lights shone down on the waiting groups of soldiers. They sat in their units on the floor in square formations, rifles across their laps, bags next to them, and helmets on the bags. A couple of units had full-length metal riot shields. They talked together, played cards and smoked, just filling time until the killing started.

A few soldiers looked over as we crossed the courtyard into the lecture theatre, the operations centre. Mary stared at the map on the main screen; the few red dots had multiplied into a converging mass of red, all centred within Hyde Park, in the middle of London. We stood next to her and stared at the map.

"How many?" Thorn asked.

"One hundred and seventy-eight so far. There are more on the way. Our units are stopping them with fake traffic offences and other outstanding warrants against their names. But it is more than we expected already."

"But you have the power of the UK government and the army behind you. Just call in more troops."

"I am. But they will take time, and it may be too late. I have drafted in the police, armed response and any available operatives in the area. The police will create an envelope around Hyde Park, create a lot of noise to drive them towards us," she said and waved an arc behind the red dots and line in front.

"Maybe it's another trap?" I said.

"Doesn't matter if it is or isn't. We can't leave them unrestrained. They would tear into the city. We have to stop them," Mary said.

I took a deep breath and slowly let it out. There would be no choice. We had to fight.

Ruby walked in front of us. "Everyone is ready to go. I am going to send in the main infantry now. The police are assembling and cordoning off the area. The tranquilliser unit will follow on in ten minutes. Just us to go. I have a helicopter that will fly us straight in, so we can finish any strategy discussions on the move."

"Thank you. I will relay over any more info from the team," Mary said, glancing behind her at the group of ten agents sat in lines in the seats behind us. "I have satellite images, reports coming in from the field of tracking units, police, and your units. We will coordinate."

"Yes, ma'am. The units are leaving now, and the helicopter will land once the courtyard is empty. We have some good news. Dunk has survived and is meeting us on site."

"Excellent, we can get the whole team back together," Mary said and looked over to Bradders and Smash as they entered the room.

The trucks rolled into the courtyard, and then an eruption of footsteps, doors slamming and sergeants shouting as the soldiers loaded up and drove off. We took seats behind the line of ten communication operatives and watched the infrared satellite images of the vampires gathering in London.

The last army truck drove out of the courtyard, and we watched the CCTV of tracked cars driving into London and followed people exiting the tube at Hyde Park station. Some comms bounced around on chat channels, co-ordinating with other units. The operators all wore headsets and would suddenly talk to some unknown operative or a commander in the field of operations.

After about thirty minutes, a buzz of helicopter blades descended into the courtyard, buffeting wind through the open door. The maps on the tables fluttered about and sets of notes flew off. We jumped out of our seats and hurried into the helicopter.

"Good luck," Mary shouted and waved us off, as the downdraft from the blades flapped about her clothes and hair.

The helicopter flew up over the base and nearby town. I just about recognised the nightclub the Twins and I visited.

The helicopter cut across the country, over the main motorway of vehicles streaming in and out of London, and over the sprawl of the city.

The landscape changed to never-ending blocks of high-rise buildings and snarled up traffic. The constant lights of unaware humanity below us as we skimmed through the air to our final destination to confront the Turned. They sat in their cars moaning about the traffic as we flew overhead to fight for their lives. If we won, they would never know how close they came to extinction. If we lost, they would find out soon enough.

"We will go straight to the park and rappel in. The Turned are already on the move, and the police have pushed them towards us," Ruby relayed to us over our radios. She stood up, fixed her gear on the rope, and flung it out the side. Bradders and Smash did the same. They turned around and hung off the edge of the helicopter as it descended.

Lights shone around the park and shouts erupted. Below us, soldiers carrying the big full-length metal shields lined up across the park. The rest stood behind the shield wall, with guns levelled towards a mass of charging figures.

Ruby, Smash and Bradders leant off the helicopter and let go, letting their weight slide them down the rope where a group of soldiers waited for them. The werewolves clipped on next and went down. The rest of us followed, with Thorn and me arriving last.

Ruby directed her troops to line up behind the infantry gunmen and the werewolves to hang back until called. Rip, Cassius and the Twins joined Ruby's unit, but Thorn grabbed my hand and hauled me back.

"This is it, V. Chance to live up to your name. Everything we have worked towards. All the training. All the fear and pain. This is our chance to take revenge for all the wrongs done to us. Tonight, you are the living embodiment of Vengeance."

"We will have our vengeance tonight. Then we can have a normal life. Or whatever passes for normal with us," I said.

She smiled, grabbed either side of my face and kissed my lips. We sprinted down behind the infantry and shield wall. In front of the wall, a mass of creatures charged through the park. We stood in a line of Dragans. Thorn and I, Cassius, Rip and the Twins.

"Shield wall ready," Ruby shouted.

The line at the front planted their metal shields in the ground and braced themselves behind it. The Turned stopped their charge and let loose a hail of bullets. Thorn grabbed my arm and pulled me down. The wave of bullets thundered into the metal wall and whizzed overhead. Occasionally, a soldier in the wall went down, only for the wall to close up and the infantry behind to drag the soldier to safety. The wave of bullets stopped.

"Return fire," Ruby shouted, and the infantry stood up and fired back over the shields into the front lines of the vampires, felling rows of the rotting creatures. "Stop," Ruby shouted again, and the soldiers ducked behind the shields once more as a wave of fire returned, crashing into the metal wall in front. The noise of bullets on metal deafened us and the air filled with the smoke of gunfire. The bullets stopped.

"Fire!" Ruby shouted, and units jumped up in a line and fired back in bursts of gunfire. Bullets fired back to hit a few soldiers, sending them to the ground. "Stop!" Ruby shouted again, and the soldiers took cover.

"They are charging," a soldier in the wall shouted.

"Prepare for close combat. Shield wall part on my command," Ruby yelled.

That meant it was time. We couldn't let the vampires attack the humans as they would rip them to pieces and start converting them. The infantry split in half to leave us a pathway.

Thorn unsheathed her sword and slashed the air twice. I locked and loaded my machine gun. Cassius drew out a huge, two-handed broadsword and rested the flat on his shoulder. Rip held two small swords and spun them around. Marcella held a submachine gun, and Isabella aimed her dual pistols ahead.

Behind us, the werewolves moved into position, awaiting their orders. I winked at Giles. "Good to have you here, buddy. Keep safe."

"Ruby, they are charging in fast. They must have already taken the boost formula. Be ready," Thorn said.

"Okay, shield wall on my mark. Infantry on the mark," Ruby shouted.

I looked to Thorn, who had huddled all the other Dragans together. I squeezed in next to Thorn and Cassius.

"Let's show them who they are messing with," she said, and her face changed to the sick, grey contorted skin, burning red eyes, fangs jutting out, and claws slicing through her finger-ends. Cassius' face followed suit, and then Rip and the Twins, all the way around to me. I smiled and let the beast within take over.

"Shields part. Infantry fire," Ruby shouted.

The shield wall parted in the middle, and the infantry stepped into the gap and released a hail of bullets. Other soldiers fired over the top into the on rushing vampire army, mowing down the front line, which the next row charged over in seconds. The soldiers blocking our way stepped back. Thorn sprinted into the gap, sword flashing in her hand. The infantry guns ceased fire as she screamed past. I fired at either side of her, killing the Turned with armour piercing silver bullets. Rip and Cassius flanked us, with swords coiled back for first contact.

Thorn dropped to her knees and skidded along the wet grass, slicing around the blade and severing two vampires to ash. She jumped up and shoulder barged into the next group, bowling them over into the ranks behind.

The vampire line swung around to enclose her. I let the bullets fly. Cassius triggered the arc of his broadsword, hacking the rotten bodies of the Turned into the air and raining down ash on their replacements.

Rip hit the other side, his two blades taking turns to slice and dice the enemy. The Twins stood back to back with Thorn, preventing the vampires from swinging around and attacking from behind.

The vampires focused on us, Thorn parrying and hacking back. Cassius deftly pivoting his giant sword around by the flick of his wrists. Rip's twin blades working in perfect tandem. And the Twins fighting as one person, blocking, countering and killing in perfect harmony. Behind us, Ruby, Bradders, Smash and Dunk picked off the vampires intent on fighting us.

We waded into the never-ending bodies of the enhanced third-generation Turned, the wet ground soaking up the falling ash and turning the ground into a mud bath. A series of howls raised our spirits. The Turned backed off for a second and scanned around.

"Keep fighting," a vampire commander shouted from the back. They attacked again. A group of vampires detached and went for the human backup. A unit of infantry had joined in and free-fire blazed from their guns, but the vampires dodged and covered the ground, losing a small number in the blanket of gunfire.

The vampires hit into the group. Ruby flung her gun away and pulled out two silver knives. She stepped into the first swipe of claws, double arm blocked, and slipped a knife through its guard into its chest. Bradders ordered the infantry into a line while Smash and Dunk fought off the vampires.

"Forwards and stab," shouted Bradders. The infantry rushed up as one line and stabbed forward with their rifles. The silver bayonets plunged into the vampire flesh. Recoiling from the pain, the wounded vampires staggered back. The silver cuts not enough to kill them outright but enough to injure them and take them out of the fight.

But for each successful stab, a vampire hit its attacker, its claws raking against the soldiers' body armour. The blows hard enough to knock the soldiers down, and followed by a killing bite or slash into an unprotected part of the flesh. Screams from downed soldiers rang out. The Turned hacked into the humans, breaking bones and necks, surgically cutting into the meat across the jugular.

Four huge shapes slammed into the sides of the vampires, knocking bodies into the air. The werewolves stood up, towering over their prey, claws slicing through the vampires' bodies, giving them the ultimate death. The fear glowed brightly in the vampires under the onslaught of the werewolf beasts.

Some vampires fled back into the darkness. The panic spread and our combatants turned from the fight and fled with them. The infantry gave chasing, shooting them in the back, setting off mini-explosions of ash in the retreating army. I chased after them, pressing home our advantage.

"V, come back. Wait for the orders," Thorn shouted through the radio. I skidded to a halt and jogged back, checking behind every few paces.

"Everyone gather around. The battle isn't over yet. That was just an exploratory attack. Did you notice it was only third-generation Turned? Cyrus, Bramel and the other higher generation vampires haven't joined yet. They are waiting for news on our numbers and capability," Thorn said.

"Of course, they will return with the entire army. What do we do next?" I asked.

Ruby held her hand up for us to pause and cupped her hand over her ear. "Bad news. The police penning in the Turned have been compromised. They were already Turned and Hunters in their ranks. Those not already on their side have been turned into fourth-gen vampires. Our skirmish was more than scouting out our capability; it was a distraction. Satellite images show them joining up together, and we have reports from a few survivors to confirm our data. The Turned army has doubled in size."

Chapter Sixteen

No one said anything. We all just looked at one another, letting the news sink in. We had forced back a small group of third-gen Turned, but that number had joined the main army and doubled in size, and they were coming back with second and first-gen Turned and Cyrus and Bramel. They vastly outnumbered us. We only had a handful of Dragans and werewolves; everyone else was human. This would be a slaughter.

"Do we retreat and fight another day?" Bradders said.

"We can't. That many Turned would overrun this city. We have to stop them. Or at least slow them down until there is more back up," I said.

"There is no more backup. We can call in the army. But the time they would take to respond would be too late, and once they arrived, the Turned would have infiltrated the senior ranks or have swelled their numbers and spread far and wide," Ruby said.

"Why didn't we have a full army in the first place?"

"Politics. No one wants to expose a supernatural problem. The existence of vampires and werewolves and god knows what else. We were to deal with it as quietly as possible," Ruby said.

"They will all know about it soon enough when they are tied up in blood farms," I said.

"They are coming. We can argue the rights and wrongs of this another time. Now we have to think of a way to stop them," Thorn said.

"We make a stand. All-out attack. Go down in a blaze of glory," Bradders answered.

"Do you know how many victories are won from a full-scale front assault against overwhelming numbers?" I asked. Bradders shrugged. "None," I replied.

"So, military genius, what is the best strategy against an overwhelming force?"

I stared at him for a moment. All the military campaigns and battles Thorn had made me study cycled through my mind. I looked at Thorn, Cassius and the Twins. Our thoughts connected to the memories of the vampire civil war battles replayed over between us. Each of the Dragans had been a military commander, and I had studied all the battles they had fought against each other.

"This isn't the first time a Turned army has been beaten. Know your enemy was the key to Thorn's victories. The Turned have powers, but they rely on their creators for leadership and direction. The further down the Turned generations, they are less powerful and have less intelligence and only have the instinct to survive. We saw that the other night. The fourth-gen Turned are easily spooked if the battle goes against them."

"And? What does that mean for us?" Ruby said.

"We spook them. They fear Dragans and they fear werewolves, and they panic if they lose their leaders. We give them something to fear."

"We could channel our inner Dragons. If we bring those features to our faces and claws, it will help. V, we need to tap into your memories of the Dragon change to see if we can replicate it," Thorn said.

I nodded. "But just the features. We can show the full red eyes, talons, double fangs and a few scales. If we take on the full power, it will damage us."

"What can we werewolves do?" Giles asked.

"I am thinking of cavalry. Your circle around and hit from the back like cavalry harassing the infantry. Once they are engaged against our shield wall, keep charging over and over. But don't stop to fight as they will overwhelm you. Just charge through thinning down their numbers and spreading fear in the back lines."

The werewolf group nodded.

Ruby coughed. "We have something that might help. Don't get cross, but we have a helicopter with a bank of UV lights."

Thorn glared. "I knew it."

"It isn't what you think. We know everyone would cover up once the UV hit. It would only slow the vampires down for a few moments. But this is perfect. This will throw them into chaos and pain for a few moments while the troops move in," Ruby said.

Thorn's eyes flashed red. "Actually, that is a good idea. If we can herd them into a big group, a direct UV blast would give us an opening, as long as we were ready and covered up."

"What about the tranq squad? Can they come with us to attack from the back?" I asked.

"It is too dangerous for them. Plus, at close quarters, it wouldn't make any difference. These guys work best at a distance."

"Can we just take the tranq darts and stab them in during close combat?"

"Yeah. I have some. Take a few of these each. The unit will still be useful in picking out targets at a longer range. Night vision goggles will help them detect high generation Turned as they give off a stronger heat signal," Ruby said, and held out two handfuls of darts.

"Good. We can use them to even up the odds."

"So we have a plan. Anyone got anything else to add because they are on the way," Ruby said. No one said anything. "Good, I will coordinate the shield wall defence. Thorn, the Dragan and werewolf unit is yours to command."

"I know it is. Hold the vampires in place and let us know when the UV will be ready to light up. We will give the command."

"Of course, good luck everyone," Ruby said and placed her fist in the middle of the circle, and we all held in ours as well.

Ruby jumped out of the circle and shouted orders to the soldiers.

Thorn held us in the circle. "Max, take your werewolves around the back and get ready to attack. Shepherd the vampires into a group against the shield wall. V, go with Cassius and Rip around to the right. The Twins and I will go the other side."

"See you on the field," I replied and followed the werewolves bounding off into the dark and circling around the back. We sprinted after them, leaving alone the human army of infantry, shield wall and new Hunters to hold back the vampire army and protect the whole of London.

We sprinted through the trees and around the side of a lake, and then across the water and through the trees. On the other side of the water, the vampire army charged in the opposite direction towards the human defences. The shield wall was in place; the infantry at the ready. Ahead of us, the werewolves crossed back over a bridge and crept down the tree line, taking position behind the vampire army. We followed their route but held back.

I crouched down and watched the massive glow of vampire bodies charging toward the shield wall. Gunfire rang out as the infantry let loose into the frenzy of bloodthirsty creatures. Rows of vampires fell, but an endless sea of claws and fangs replaced them, sensing a sizable meal only meters away.

"Time to show us your game face," Rip said.

"Okay. Everyone link into my mind and follow my lead. Only need to change our features to Dragon at the moment," I said to Rip and Cassius and broadcasted a psychic message to Thorn and the Twins.

Each Dragan entered my thoughts. I took a deep breath and cast my memories back to the last time I transformed into a Dragon when I fought and beat Cyrus. The trigger had been him hitting Thorn and humiliating her in front of everyone. I felt the rage open up a channel to the magic all around us. The energy streamed in, captured within my sphere of magical power I held at the centre of my being.

I tensed up, squeezing the magic back. I listened in to the others, coaching them along, getting them to find their own memory of uncontrollable rage.

For Thorn, it was the death of her son. Rip, the betrayal of the Twins. Cassius, the attack by Cyrus at the Castle. For the Twins, the discovery that Cyrus had used them.

I waited for us all to reach the critical point of our magic bursting out of the containing spheres. I pictured my magic streaming out, my fangs extending from top and bottom, eyes filling with a blood-red rage and tinting my sight.

I released the barriers. The magic exploded out, ripping down the created pathways. My eyes burnt and I gritted my teeth, but the growing fangs forced my mouth open. To fight through the pain, I dug my claws into the ground and held them in the mud. Rip and Cassius' eyes blazed red. And I saw the images from Thorn's and the Twin's eyes. Everyone had changed. But I could also feel it burn through our energy. We couldn't stay like this for long without causing severe damage to ourselves.

Metal clanged and screams echoed down the park, and then bursts of gunfire interspersed with mini-explosions. I connected into the mind of a human. The shields held firm. The infantry stabbed their silver bayonets through the gaps and fired in rounds of bullets when possible. Vampires exploded to ash on critical hits, buffeting the wall back and the next line of ash-coated vampires rammed into the spaces. The humans wouldn't last forever.

Overhead, the blades of a helicopter vibrated the air. The werewolves looked back, and I pointed into the battle. They sat down on their hind legs and howled up to the full moon overhead. I hadn't noticed it before, a bit of luck giving the werewolves their full power.

The vampires ramming against the shield wall froze for a moment, then I heard the familiar shouts of Cyrus and Bramel urging them on. The vampires surged forward again, fear driving their renewed attacked. Fear of the werewolves and fear of their own commanders.

The werewolves bounded off, swooping in from the side, sweeping around to the back of the vampire army. They charged across the rear, claws slashing the back-line, toppling a row of vampires, who fell screaming to the floor. The werewolf DNA burning within their rotten flesh.

The back lines panicked and spun around. As the vampires checked back, the pressure on the shield wall lessened. The humans shoved the shield wall forward a step, and the infantry poured in a volley of bullets.

"Attack. I will kill the wolves," Cyrus shouted. Good. He was moving to the rear of the battle. Easier for me to find.

The sound of the helicopter drew closer. The heat of its engine glowed in the night. It was only a couple of minutes away.

Rip and Cassius pulled up their hoods, tied them tight, and put on gloves. Thorn had already covered up and charged in from the other side. We charged down the field to join her in battle. I swung my machine gun level. The werewolves circled and raked against the vampire bodies. In the confusion, Thorn and the Twins blasted in a round of fire. The werewolves wheeled around again as I squeezed the trigger and let loose a hail of silver bullets into the vampire ranks.

We hit and moved away, not stopping in one place long enough for them to mount a counter-offensive. Bramel and Cyrus forced their way to the front of the back-line.

"Form a rearguard. Protect the front lines," Cyrus shouted.

The back three lines turned around and held swords out in front, creating a spiked line neatly containing the vampires into one place. We could no longer hit and run from the back. But we had forced them into one area. I held up my fist.

"Stop. We have them in place," I said over the radio link.

The air rippled down from the helicopter blades. Cyrus's hair flapped about in the down breeze. The werewolves circled and waited behind us.

Thorn spoke over the radio. "Ruby, let there be light."

"And there was light," Ruby responded.

A few moments passed and then the light glared down from above, shining its rays into the mass of the vampire army. The creatures collectively screamed and skin smoked. They dropped to the ground, grappling with clothing to block out the scorching UV rays. The fourth-gen Turned had no coverings. The recently turned police and soldiers, burning up and scrambling for cover. They fought each other to hide, burying themselves under each other's bodies for shelter. The perfect moment of confusion.

Thorn and the Twins let loose, bullets ripping into the undefended ranks. The shield wall dropped to their knees so the infantry could unload everything they had into the crowded vampire bodies. Cassius and Rip opened fire into the burning piles of flesh. I squeezed the trigger down, spraying the toxic bullets into as many vampires as possible to slow them down. The werewolves waited at our side.

The Turned pulled on their coverings and returned fire. The confusion had passed.

"Lights off," Thorn said, and a few moments later, the UV stopped.

Our gunfire stopped. The shield wall arose, and the infantry took shelter once again, preparing to time their attacks. With the lights turning off, the vampires ceased fire.

In the momentary pause, a sound of whizzing and then the vampires clutched their bodies. The tranquilliser unit had joined the fight and darts fired in, sounding like a hundred flies darting through the night air. The vampires collapsed, the reversing formula taking effect and reverting them to normal. A couple of darts hit fourth-generation turned vampires, and they dropped to the ground, writhed around and ceased. I guess it had been enough to kill them.

"Tranq unit withdraw," Ruby said over the radio.

Thorn and the Twins charged at the vampire ranks, who had shot randomly into the dark to find the source of the darts.

The werewolves swung along the line, raking their claws in a cavalry charge. I flung my gun to the floor and drew my sword as I charged in, following the wave of destruction. Cassius hacked the giant broad sword in an arc, dispatching three vampires to ash at a time. Rip twisted and turned, his swords a blur, slicing through the vamps and disintegrating them into ash.

I surged into the vampire ranks, hacking my way through, searching for the glow of the higher generation Turned to sever its leadership. I cut apart a fourth-gen vampire in a police uniform and slashed apart two vampires in army uniforms. The majority of the crazed and frenzied fourth-gen Turned in police or army uniforms. The higher Turned vampires dressed in black combat gear.

I spotted a deep glow, a second-gen Turned. To my side, I parried the frenzied claws of a fourth-gen attacker and slashed back, decapitating it. I slipped under the blade of a third-gen and spun around, whipping my sword around in a circle, slicing the legs off three vampires, felling them to the ground. The momentum swung the blade up and through the chest and head of the next attacker.

The second-gen Turned stood in front. I roared through my dragon double fangs. At that moment, I saw my opponent lose hope. I swung the sword in. They blocked but couldn't counter the heavy blows as I waded in, swinging side to side.

They fought hard, bringing the sword back and forth to stop the impacts from the side and above. I faked another blow. They flung the blade to the side to block. I twisted my wrist, slipping the tip of the blade underneath their defence and stabbed it through their heart. I drove it in and ripped it out to defend against another attack. The second-gen Turned dropped to its knees, clutching its chest and then exploded to ash.

The death of a second-gen Turned impacted the surrounding vampires. They stepped back and brushed the ash off themselves, gripped their swords, and launched a screaming attack. The death had enraged them, but they were swinging wildly.

The Turned had re-grouped and re-focused, surrounding us. Cassius and Rip fought to my side, defending and attacking in a triangle, back to back. A series of barks and the group surrounding us burst apart, and the four werewolf monsters rammed through, catapulting Turned bodies into the air.

The Turned were in disarray again. Cassius cut a determined path through to a first-gen Turned as Rip protected his back. At the same time, the werewolves scattered bodies across the muddy ground. The acrobatic Twins worked their blades in tandem. I sensed Thorn fighting by their side.

The Turned parted and a first and second-gen Turned took centre stage, swords held up in front of their faces. Their auras glowed higher than the other Turned, revealing they had taken the boosted formula. The normal Turned stepped away to let them fight against me.

I circled around. The pair held their swords at the ready and stepped to either side to split up my defence. I had to force them back together to defend one at a time.

The first-gen Turned, a woman with long silver hair, attacked from the right. I parried and twisted away as the second-gen Turned, a tall, slender man, slashed from the left. My dragon features didn't scare them, so I re-directed my magic to supercharge my muscles. I returned my features to normal.

They attacked again from either side. I ducked and rolled out of the way and met a circle of third-gen Turned hemming me in. They snarled and thrust their swords to drive me back into the ring. They wanted to see a Dragan killed. But likewise, if I killed these two, I would break their confidence.

The silver vampire attacked with a two-handed thrust. I parried and slashed back. She swung the sword up, blocked and cut back, catching the edge of my arm. She smiled and licked her lips at the sight of blood. Her speed and strength were nearly that of a Dragan. The boosted formula had lifted her up a generation of power. My cut healed over and the blood flow stopped. Her smile turned into a grimace. Obviously, no one told her I was immune to silver.

I pressed in on her moment of hesitation; thrust, uppercut and back; short, sharp, quick movements, pivoting off the speed in my wrists. She kept the blade moving to deflect each blow. However, it was at the edge of her ability.

The second-gen vampire attacked from the other side as her defence crumbled. I spun on my heel, deflected the blow and counter stabbed, cutting into his side. He grabbed his stomach and whipped the blade around. I slid out of the way, pirouetting around to kick him in the back and into the silver-haired vampire. She held him up and pushed him back onto his feet. He didn't have the same immunity to silver and the wound hissed.

They roared together and charged as one. I stepped back, slashing the sword back and forth to deter the blows. One of them I could defeat, but both blades were raining in. I couldn't keep it up. The silver vampire slipped past and stabbed my side. I jumped back and the blade only penetrated an inch. The vampires at the edge of the circle stabbed their blades into my back to prod me forward. I sprinted around the edge of the circle, slid onto my knees, and slashed through a row of vampire legs.

The circle broke apart. The vampire stepped away from the burning bodies. I grabbed one and threw it across at the two chasing attackers. They dodged out of the way, but I had thrown another two at their feet. The injured vampire bodies flushed a deep red, their faces tensed and teeth gritted as the temperature rose within. The attackers stumbled over the burning lumps.

The injured vampires exploded, hazing the air with ash, knocking my attackers over. I focused my energy on healing to even the odds.

The cloud of ash drifted to the floor, and the two vampires regained their stance, waiting with swords at the ready. They screamed with fangs out and eyes black and leapt into the air, hacking down. I dived under their attack, rolled up and attacked the silver vampire. She twisted around and parried my blow, but it forced her sideways across the second-gen Turned's line of attack. We fought blades slashing back and forth, and I kept her body in the pathway of the second-gen Turned. He moved side to side but couldn't find a path through.

I let her attack slip through and caught the flat of her blade between my arm and body. I slammed a fist onto her chin, jerking her head back. Then I opened my fist, holding a tranquillizer dart, and drove it into her throat. She gagged and loosened the hilt of the sword. She sunk to her knees, ripping out the protruding dart. The man swung from the side, and I ducked and sidestepped away from the writhing silver-haired vamp. She clutched her throat and shook all over. The formula was reversing the boost effects. I guessed taking power away was much like receiving it. Her system was reverting to normal, which caused her pain.

The man swiped back, and I twisted around to block. He stepped away from his fallen friend, whose shaking had slowed down and she gasped for breath. I attacked, and he retreated against the swift blows, until he reached the edge of the vampire ring. They growled and he counterattacked. I blocked and flicked around my blade, wrenching his sword from his hand. He stepped back with hands up.

"Cheat. Can you not fight someone of the same power?" the silver vampire shouted from behind. I twisted around and jabbed the sword back, under my shoulder, into the second-gen Turned, feeling the blade temporally resist against his flesh until it pierced. I thrust it in and yanked it out. The heat on my back built up as I strode forwards into the next fight. The dying vamp exploded to ash, spraying around me into her eyes. She flinched and blinked. I jumped and spun, flicking out my blade edge, slicing her head in half.

The ash cleared in time for the surrounding vampires to watch her head slide apart and body melt to lava and ash. I shielded my eyes from the second wave of ash. The circle of vamps wavered. Those at the back stepped away.

"Who's next?" I shouted.

The vampires backed off and some ran. A sword hammered into them. "Stay and fight, you cowards." The shouting figure pushed through the crumbling ring of vampires.

"I'm next," Bramel said, dressed in his typical black goth clothing and wielding a black blade with silver runes.

I waved him away. "Go away. Bring me Cyrus. I want a proper competition."

"How dare you? You've never beaten me before."

"You're right. But back then, you always had the power. I am a full Dragan now. You don't stand a chance. Bring me a proper Dragan."

"I have my own formula. I am equal to your power, and I have years of experience you don't possess."

"Have it your way," I said and then shouted over the ring of vamps. "Cyrus, South, once I have beaten your lackey, then you're next."

Bramel's face compressed in anger. "He is not my leader. I am the King of the Turned."

"Please. He is South. It was you that told me about him."

"My enemies' enemy is my friend. This doesn't make him South. You have no idea."

"Then tell me."

"No. You don't get to know the truth," he shouted and drove forward, swinging the sword up to the side and then thrust at my chest. I deflected and front kicked, but he twisted out of the way and swung the blade around. I ducked and stepped inside his attacking arc, but his trailing back leg whipped around, hitting my chest, knocking me to the ground, sword skidding from my grip.

He laughed and jumped into a downward hack. I rolled backward into a handstand, grabbed my sword and flipped to my feet. His blade hit the dirt.

"It will not be that easy," I said, spinning the sword around in my wrist.

"I have your power and I have greater combat skills. She is a fool to think you could be King," he said.

"Let me guess. You should be King of the Dragans."

"Why not? It would make sense. There would be no need for this war then. Our Union would combine two great forces."

"I will tell you what I told Cyrus. The position is already taken."

"Then I will make an opening," he said, and attacked again. I parried away the blows and spun around. I replayed our previous encounters. When he fought me in the gym in front of all the Hunters, he quickly punched me to the floor and allowed the Hunters to get revenge as well. In the forest, after I defeated Norris, the fight had already weakened me and Bramel knocked me down again. He gloated during my tortures and when they discussed my pending vivisection.

I didn't have this amount of power in our previous battles. I would avenge those losses. As I circled around and defended against his attacks, I let the anger grow, ready to fuel me.

"Come on, V, fight me. You are supposed to be the all-powerful King of the Dragan's. But now we are the same, and you are scared. One day, I will find out how to make this change permanent."

"You are not the same. Being a Dragan isn't just a physical thing."

"Show me," he shouted back and charged in with a three-pronged attack, slashing left, twisting into an uppercut and stabbing at my face. I swayed back and whacked his sword away. The anger opened up the channels for the magic to flood in. I let his attacks come and for his grinning, smug face to fuel the sphere inside.

"Look, everyone. The Dragan is not a threat. I will defeat him and we will take this city, and then this country. Vampires will rise up across the world and we will take what is ours."

He came again, his blade edge blurring in the dark air. But arrogance had a price, a loss of control and I could foresee his attack. I released the sphere, and its power took over, guiding my movements, my blade flicking out and pinging his sword to the side and then stabbing into his shoulder. He dropped his sword and crashed to the floor. I stood over him, blade held high, and hacked it down to his head.

The blade's edge sparked against metal. Another sword barred its way.

"Go, Bramel. V is mine, remember. Go and capture Thorn," Cyrus said and pushed back against my sword. I jumped away as Cyrus stood in between Bramel and me.

Cyrus swept back his blood splattered hair with a scaled hand. His black clothing sprayed with blood. "From our last battle, I would say it is all square, one victory each. How about a decider?"

"Fine by me. To the death," I said and swung the sword up, so the edge lined up between my eyes.

"To the death," he said and copied my stance.

The crowd moved back, and Bramel scrambled out of the vampire ring. Cyrus held the sword in front and glared at me. I took the ready position, sword held in front, and stared back. I didn't flinch or circle around. It was a battle of wills.

I twisted my front foot into the ground. He shifted his weight to his back leg. I breathed in and out through my nose, keeping my breathing steady and core solid. His hands repositioned on the sword hilt, the blade quivering in the air.

I relaxed my wrists and gripped my toes into the ground. His red eyes blinked several times. I held my gaze calm and focused on his eyes, studying his brightly glowing aura flickering in spikes of heat. The boosted formula had changed him.

His red eyes twitched and he launched off his back foot. I twisted around, spinning my wrists to knock his sword to the side. I stepped back and waited again, staying calm and steady. The nervous schoolboy scared of the creatures in the night had gone, and I had become the thing to be feared.

Cyrus emitted a low growl and paced side-to-side, occasionally faking an attack, lurching forward and jumping back. I stayed still, eyes on the prize, not willing to be intimidated.

"He is scared. He won't fight," he shouted to the crowd, playing up to his audience. Perfect.

He turned again and shouted. "Fight me." He lowered his sword for a split second as he screamed in frustrated rage. I released the magic within, pushed off my toes, and sliced diagonally across him. He swung two hands up in a desperate measure, the defending blow overbalancing him. He fell to the floor. I hacked down and he held the sword up to block the blows. I switched it around, swiped my sword underneath, and whipped his sword out of his hands, and it flew off and stuck into the ground a few yards away.

I slashed back, but he had already rolled out of the way. He grabbed a watching vamp, flung them into me as he ran around the edge of the ring and picked up his sword.

I stabbed the vamp through the chest and shoved him back into the crowd. I faced Cyrus again.

"Bramel underestimated you. He didn't believe how strong you had become, as he had always beaten you before. But I know differently. I have seen you at full power. Your aura is on fire. You are channelling the Dragon again."

"And you are boosted, just as you were the other night to gain Dragon powers. The full red eyes and scales give it away."

"True, but this makes us even. Now we can fight man to man."

I reached into my pocket for a tranq dart.

"You are going to cheat. I saw the others use those darts on the Turned. Have you no honour?"

"There is only winning. There is no place for honour in death."

"So you will let all the vampires know you are afraid to fight me properly. That you couldn't win in an even battle. You are weak."

I withdrew my hand. The point of defeating Cyrus was to place fear in the hearts of all vampires. I had to ensure our victory today and all future victories by proving that we couldn't be beaten.

I scanned around at the Turned as they watched our argument. I had the chance to turn his audience against him. "You are revealed as South, their true leader, a Dragan. What do they think of you now?"

"I will say this one last time. I am not South. I am working with the Turned. Bramel offered me a deal. We kill you. He gets Thorn. I become King of the Dragans and bring us together again. War with humans is inevitable. MI5's actions have proved it. They seek only to kill us. But together, we can defeat them and work with the Hunters to create a new sustainable world order."

"More lies. You want nothing but power," I shouted.

"It is you that lies, little boy."

I gripped my sword and sprinted into an attack. Cyrus blocked and our blades jammed against one another. Our body weight and arms pushed the blades together, sparks flying from the scraping metal. Our eyes on either side of the steel cross formed by the swords. I gritted my teeth and dug in my feet. Cyrus' eyes burnt a deeper red, and his face tensed up and scales formed up his neck.

I released the pressure a little and he lurched forward. I used the shift in momentum to tense up and release the renewed energy to shove him back, and I leapt back with the counterforce.

We both skidded on the muddy ground and then stormed back. Our swords clashed again. Cyrus blows, firing in from every angle. I matched his boosted power with my channelled magic, fuelling my reflexes to deflect, block and parry until he hesitated, and I went on the attack. My blade spun around, slashing left to right, circling around, cutting up, and hacking down. But he matched my attacks, dodging and glancing the blows away.

I focused my energy on the movement of the blade, firing in attacks at an increasing rate of knots. The swords clashed, sparks raining around us, the constant impact vibrating the sword hilt and numbing my hands. I summoned up my strength for one big hit, and Cyrus swung with equal force to block. The clash of steel sung out, and the shockwave flung us both to the ground. The Turned rocked and staggered back. We scrambled up to face off again.

"You can't beat me. We are evenly matched," Cyrus said, panting.

"And you can't beat me either," I said, forcing air into my lungs.

"I don't need to. I just need to keep you busy. Stop you from slaughtering my vampire army."

I looked beyond the circle to the other Dragans fighting. Thorn faced Bramel and a handful of Turned. Rip fought three second-gen Turned. Cassius encircled by a large group of third-gen Turned, who constantly moved out of his way and attacked his back. A group of Turned vampires had formed a line blocking off the werewolf cavalry. The Twins had been split up and faced their own groups of vampires.

"Stalemate then?" I said.

"No. We are keeping you busy while the rest of my army breaks that pathetic shield wall and turns them all into vampires."

"Your army, so you admit to being South at last."

He shook his head. "I am not South. We have a common enemy, the vampires and I."

"Lies."

"I don't care what you think. You are beaten. My forces will overwhelm your human friends and your once allies will return to kill you. Until then, it is stalemate."

I watched the Twins fighting, split apart from one another, not using their psychic link. I flashed back to our adventure in the nightclub, manipulating everyone's thoughts. But the Turned surrounded me. There was no psychic connection possible to the Turned. Only psychic connections to humans and Dragans worked. Cyrus grinned as he watched my despair. I smiled back.

"You are wrong. It isn't stalemate. I will win," I said.

He laughed. "Never. We are physically matched."

"As I told Bramel, there is much more to being a Dragan than pure physical strength."

I pulled out a silver dagger from my belt and held the sword in just one hand. Cyrus pointed the tip of the blade at me and jumped forward, raising his sword above his head, ready for a downward slash. I redirected my magic into my thoughts and screamed them into his mind, an image of a dark figure attacking from his side. He glanced around. His sword hesitated, ready to redirect against the unknown assailant.

I stepped in, tilting up my blade horizontally to block his delayed hack. The momentary hesitation passed, and his entire force redirected into the blow. The metal blades rang out on impact, and I drove the silver dagger underneath our clashing swords into his stomach.

His eyes went wide and reverted to normal. I ripped the dagger upwards, gutting him, spurting a line of blood across both our faces. I released the silver dagger and wrenched his sword out of his grip.

He slumped to his knees, hands around the gaping wound. Blood and guts poured from his stomach, pooling around his legs. I stepped around his back and pulled my sword up with the tip pointing down.

"It is over," I shouted and plunged the sword down, execution-style, through his shoulder, into his heart and sticking out of his chest. He tried to scream, but the blade had shredded through his lungs and nothing came out. His mouth gaped open, expelling a hiss of air. I yanked the blade out, and his body dropped into the ash and blood caked mud. I held the bloody sword aloft and shouted. "Cyrus is dead. South is dead."

The ring of Turned looked to one another for help and then fled. The sight of the escaping Turned and Cyrus's dead body at my feet spread to the other groups fighting the werewolves and Dragans. Panic ensued and the vampires darted away in all directions. The group around Cassius paused, but he did not and hacked through, scattering them to the wind. More ran and the fear spread like a virus.

The Twins fought back to one another, linking their fighting together again and dispatched their group to ash. Rip spun around, isolated one of the second-gen vampires, and cut them down. Thorn killed the few remaining Turned, leaving her facing Bramel alone.

They fought for a short time until Thorn disarmed him. Bramel dropped to his knees and she hoisted her sword up. He held out his hands and screamed. "No, my Queen. I am sorry I betrayed you. I only wish to serve you."

The sword lashed sideways, cutting through his outstretched hands, and slitting his throat open. His hands splashed to the ground, and his bloody stumps clamped to his throat. His eyes closed and his lifeless body slumped to the ground. Thorn walked away as his body heated up, melted to lava and smoked to ash.

The Turned had fled and the human infantry ran past, chasing down the escaping army, unloading silver bullets to ensure their destruction and the safety of London.

I waited for Thorn's arrival and our victory embrace. No one could ever part us again. She sheathed her sword and walked over, smiling with arms open. I awaited our moment of triumph as she sent images of her plans for our private celebration. I thought the celebration against the vampire cell had been wild. This was nothing compared to the thoughts we exchanged. It would be a night to remember, free of the Turned/Hunter threat, free of the need for vengeance. Free to live again.

At last, I had a family, the Dragans and MI5-S. I was part of something bigger. No longer alone and isolated. I had a new life ahead of me: Cyrus and Bramel were dead, the Turned defeated, the Hunters broken and London saved.

I had completed my last transformation. From this night on, I would always be a Dragan. Everything we worked through had come to fruition. The mission completed.

The tranq unit sprinted past and stopped, and I got that familiar feeling again, a scent. I scanned the group and felt drawn to a person with red hair poking out of their helmet.

"Ruby. Is that you?" I asked, stepping towards the red-haired figure.

"I am behind you."

I spun around to find her stood at my shoulder and the shield wall soldiers encircling us, blocking the entrance to Thorn.

"What the hell is happening?" I said.

One of the tranq soldiers took off their mask and helmet. "Jon, stay calm. We won, but I need you to take the reverse formula to stop your transformation," Mary said.

"No way."

Thorn, Rip, Cassius and the Twins approached the shield wall.

"Let him go. He doesn't belong to you," Thorn shouted.

"He needs to know the truth," Mary shouted back.

"What truth," I yelled.

The figure, with the fragment of red hair, dragged off their goggles to reveal green eyes. Their flame red hair cascaded down as they removed their helmet. They dropped it and then reached around their head to unclasp their mask. They flung the last of the coverings away. She smiled, her emerald eyes wrinkling up in pleasure. "This truth," Scarlett said.

My knees buckled and I dropped my sword into the mud. A sharp pain stabbed into my neck. I twisted around and pulled out three tranq darts.

"Sorry, Jon. It's for your own good," Ruby said.

The reversing formula streamed in, a creeping cold disseminating into my blood. My hands faded blue and joints weakened. I folded up onto my knees, body trembling, arms wrapping around myself as the reverse formula fought the effects of the Dragan transformation.

I violently shook as my blood ran cold, circulating around my body and slamming home at my heart. The cold paralysed my arms and legs, and I toppled face first into the mud. My body fitted and face rubbed into the dirt, limiting my sight to a flickering of light.

Screams and shouts buzzed in my ears, but the muffled voices made no sense. I couldn't tell who was who. Footsteps thumped about as another wave of pain washed through me. The voices drifted away. The flickering of light diminished to total darkness.

Chapter Seventeen

Thorn smiled. 'I told you they would betray us.'

Low voices approached, a Latin chant grew louder. I could only see Thorn's face. Everything else was black. I tried to look around but everywhere was just Thorn's face, which drifted away as the chanting grew louder. Her sky blue eyes blinked as they washed away, followed by lights tearing in at the corners and then a slit across my vision as my eyes fully opened. Bright lights forced them to shut again and I blinked a few times. The bright lights diminished on each blink to bring contrast and sharpness to my whereabouts.

Suspended white tiles hung from a ceiling, connecting to glass half-height walls and solid white brick underneath. Directly in front was a glass door with a pass card pad. The room was transparent for outside observation, and cameras hung from all four corners of the room. Every angle covered. I was being watched.

I lifted myself up, but restraints held me back. Brown leather straps fastened across my arms, wrists, waist, knees and ankles. They had dressed me in grey tracksuit bottoms and a white vest.

The chanting sounded to my side, and a white-haired woman dressed in light white clothes held a candle in her hands and placed it on the floor.

"Hello, where am I? Who are you?" I said, but my mouth didn't move. Something glued it together.

She glanced up and walked around the trolley bed I was strapped to. The chanting sounded from the other side; a brunette stood up and walked as she continued the Latin chant.

She continued circling the bed and chanting. I scanned the rest of the room. It looked like a lab. Only three of the walls were half-height glass to observe from the outside. The one behind was solid white concrete blocks. Workbenches and lab equipment ran along the walls and other equipment sat on trolleys and pushed to the sides. I lay strapped to a trolley bed in the middle of the room.

I focused my psychic thoughts onto the chanting women but felt a fog in my head. I couldn't concentrate enough and only sensed the same fogginess bouncing back.

Two figures appeared by the glass doorway, Mary and Scarlett. I had almost forgotten I saw her earlier, thinking it may have been a dream. They talked to one another, but again, I couldn't detect their thoughts.

The two chanting women stood in front, turned to each other, held each other's hands, closed their eyes, and shouted a few last words. They both turned away, and Mary opened the glass door.

"It is completed," the white clothed woman said. They walked through the open door and disappeared into the darkness behind it. Mary shut the door, and Scarlett lent into Mary's ear and whispered something.

Mary nodded and opened the door. They both entered. Mary shut the glass door and walked over, her black boot heels clicking on the white-tiled floor. She wore a black trouser suit and a white shirt open to her chest. The sleeves on the jacket rolled up.

Scarlett grabbed a trolley ladened with medical instruments and pushed it over. She had braided her flame red hair, and her mud splattered camouflage clothes looked as if she just left a training exercise. They stopped on either side of the bed.

"Morning, Jon. How are you today?" Mary asked in a low, soft voice.

I tried to answer, but only muffled sounds came from my mouth.

"Silly me, of course you can't talk. We taped your mouth over. It will have to remain that way for a while. I want you to listen and keep those nasty fangs at bay."

I tried to speak again and struggled against my straps.

"Hey, hey, calm down, wriggle worm. You're not going anywhere. Best relax. It will go easier on you that way."

I frowned and tried to connect psychically to them both.

Mary shook her head. "I can see your forehead frowning, trying the psychic link. It won't work. Those two ladies have cast a spell over this lab. It prevents psychic interactions and your seduction abilities. We are also wearing talismans to protect ourselves against you and any of the other Dragans searching for you," she said, and pulled out a strip of leather string around her neck with a circular symbol hanging on it. "I told you we were working on countermeasures."

I just stared and waited for her to talk.

"I guess you have questions. But as you can't speak, let me tell you what is happening."

I nodded.

"Congratulations on winning the battle. Obviously, we kidnapped you at the end of the battle. We drugged you and loaded you into a helicopter. We brought you to the depths of a research lab on a military base. Even if I took off your tape, no one would hear you scream. And even if they did, they expect to hear screams from this room anyway," Mary said.

"Hey, don't cry. We will not hurt you," Scarlett said, and placed a hand on my arm. I wasn't aware I was crying. But I was still feeling drowsy from the drugs, so it was hard to tell. The mention of a research lab didn't fill me with joy.

"I know you don't have pleasant experiences from being kidnapped and being strapped to a bed in a medical research lab. But this is for your own good. We did this to protect you," Scarlett said.

I stared at her wide eyed and back to Mary and back again.

"You realise that sounds crazy, right?" Mary said to her.

"But it is true. We kidnapped him for his own safety. We care for you, Jon. It was an intervention. These restraints are for our protection until you see things our way."

"I know. But it makes us sound like psychos," Mary said.

"He will understand once he hears the full story. Should we continue with the medical exam?" Scarlett answered.

"Go ahead. We need to make sure he is lucid and well enough to have the talk."

Scarlett pulled on a pair of purple latex gloves. She opened a notebook and scribbled at the top of the page. "We need to do a few tests," she said and picked up a light pen. "I need you to follow the light with your eyes while I move it left to right and up and down."

She moved it around and I just stared straight ahead.

"Don't be difficult. We are trying to make sure you are well. It is just following the pen light with your eyes. The quicker you comply. The quicker we can remove the tape and we can explain why you are here."

She moved the pen light again. "Well done. That wasn't so bad, was it?"

She scribbled down into the book. "Now I am going to check the pupils in each eye. Hold still. Stop shaking your head around," Scarlett said.

"Jon, behave yourself," Mary said.

Scarlett glared at me again. "I don't think you appreciate the effort spent bringing you here and making you safe. Is this all the thanks we get?"

Appreciate being kidnapped! They had gone crazy.

"We had to keep it secret that I was still alive. I had to arrange all the plans without Ruby's and Mary's knowledge so they couldn't reveal anything. The medical lab needed to be cleared for use. A nice comfy room for you with a tv, games console and music you like is waiting. I have set up three decoy prisoners on other bases across the country to keep your friends busy. Some appreciation wouldn't go amiss," Scarlett said, and crossed her arms.

Mary stared at her, raised her eyebrows again, and looked back at me. "As you can see, Scarlett went to a lot of trouble to make sure you were looked after. You wouldn't want to upset her. Some people in the government just wanted to kill you. Hey, calm down. Don't cry. You are safe. We will look after you," Mary said. I couldn't deny my reaction this time.

Mary continued. "So, stop being a wriggle worm and hold still. Then you will get to hear the full story and understand why we had to take such drastic measures."

I couldn't be bothered to fight anymore. There was no point. I nodded my head.

"Okay. Open your eyes wide," Scarlett said, and shone the light on each one and then scribbled into her book again. "Blood pressure next." She wrapped the cuff around my arm and pumped it up and then let it deflate and recorded the measurement in her book.

"Let's test your temperature." She pointed a temperature gun at my forehead and then scribbled again.

"Your touch." She ran her finger across my forearm and my arm flinched.

"Good. Now your ears." She picked up a small instrument and crouched down by each ear to look inside. Her face was up close and her breath tingled my skin. The small hairs on my neck stood up.

"All done. His vitals are all good," Scarlet said.

"I will have that talk with him now. Go and get him a drink. I am sure he is thirsty."

"Okay. I will be back, Jon. And then we can have our own little chat," she said and left the room.

Mary picked up a long metal stick. "This is a cattle prod. Produces a huge electric shock."

I struggled against my bonds again.

"Relax. I will not use it unless you make me. I am going to take off the tape. Behave or I will go zap. Keep those fangs out of sight."

I nodded, and she grabbed the tape and tore it away. I flexed my mouth around and licked my lips.

"So. You're not going to cut me open?" I asked.

"Of course not. These restraints are for our safety. Not to hold you in. We are your friends."

"Friends don't drug and kidnap each other. How long have I been here?"

"Well, we had to hit you hard with the drugs and keep you sedated while transferring, clearing the base and setting up your room. Convincing our bosses not to kill you. I would say about two weeks."

"What!"

"Like we said, it was for your own protection. You are a killer. I had to ensure the safety of everyone involved. Obviously, you need an explanation. It is a long story. It is hard to know where to start. But I think there is one truth you should hear first. Everything else comes afterwards."

"More lies. What is so important that you couldn't just tell me without all the drama? What couldn't wait until after our victory celebration?"

"First, I needed to stop you fully transforming. The first needles we injected you with were the reversing formula. You need to hear the truth first before you decide to transform fully," Mary said.

"Just spit it out."

"You aren't going to like this and probably won't believe me either, but I have the proof, which I can supply once you have settled down."

"Tell me already," I shouted, straining at my bonds.

She placed her hand on mine. I tried to pull it away, but she added the other one on top.

"Thorn is South."

An involuntary laugh exploded out of my lungs, and I rocked back into the bed. "Is that the best you can come up with? Thorn is South. I killed South. Cyrus was South. You agreed with us."

Mary shook her head. "I can prove it. But for the moment, just listen to me."

"No, it is lies. You are trying to turn me against her. Why? So I will go back to Scarlett. I am pleased she is alive and well, but I made a choice, and it isn't safe for her with me."

"No, it is the truth. Keep quiet for a moment and let me explain. The leader of the Turned is South and is the opposite of Thorn, the leader of the Dragans. The opposite of south is north. North is an anagram for Thorn. You know how she likes to hide in the open. This is typical Thorn behaviour. She named her alter ego the opposite of her own name. South is the leader of the Turned. North/Thorn, the leader of the Dragans."

I stared blankly as I re-arranged the letters of north into Thorn. "It is just a coincidence."

"No. I can prove it. We have intercepted communications and can trace them all back to her locations. I told you that a call came from your group before the Turned attacked in the forest. You all jumped to the conclusion it was Cyrus. I couldn't say it was Thorn."

"So you have known the whole time?"

"More or less. We had to play out the game."

"Game! What game?"

"There is a reason Thorn has been South this whole time, playing both sides against one another. We can only theorise the motivation, but this is what we think," Mary said, and paused for a moment and took a deep breath.

She looked me straight in the eye and continued. "If we go back to the beginning, the start of the Dragan civil war. We think everything she told us was true up to the point Bramel ran off with the Turned to join the Original's army. The facts from the other Dragans would back up this story. However, we believe it was Thorn that sent Bramel off with the Turned to take over. She and Bramel were working together the whole time."

"But why? What good was it to her?"

"She realised that the Turned would leave anyway and join the other army. So she took control of the new vampire army instead by installing her own person in charge and controlling the agenda they followed. If you follow the history of the Turned and the Dragans, you can spot some interesting facts. For instance, only Thorn gained lots of power and money. Most of the other Dragans were hunted, driven on from place to place and assets seized. Cyrus had little money even after all these years. Thorn, on the other hand, was always one step ahead of the Turned.

"Also, Bramel faced a few threats to take his position of King. These threats often fell foul to the hands of the Dragans, usually Thorn and Cassius. The other Turned marked this down to bad luck. The number of vampires were also kept low. Bramel didn't believe in expanding. He didn't want to draw attention to their kind. They could live below the radar, which kept the Dragans safe as well."

"Wait. This doesn't make sense. She let Bramel take control of the Turned and conspired with him to control their numbers and use them as her own army by proxy to hunt down her enemies. Then why was she captured and experimented on by them?" I asked.

"Good question. The status quo remained for some time. Turned, Dragans and Hunters. The Hunters came for both of them originally, keeping the numbers in check. Then, in the last twenty years, DNA sequencing and genetic engineering meant everything changed. You know the story of how the Hunters and Turned worked together and formed an alliance. But it was Thorn behind this alliance. She wanted the secrets of her DNA unlocked to cure the fertility issue, and even with her money, this wasn't possible. Too many questions would be asked in a public company, but a secret government research project would be fine and it would be free."

"So Thorn allowed herself to be captured and experimented on. Kept prisoner for over a year."

"Yes. We believe so. One year to Thorn is a drop in the ocean. They only took samples of flesh and blood. There was no continuous torture beyond the initial breaking in. There wasn't any dissection planned. Plus, doesn't it seem strange they could capture and keep her a prisoner and got her to cooperate? This is Thorn we are talking about."

A memory, a conversation with Carmella, flashed back. She had said Thorn broke to their tortures quickly and then complied. Carmella had been disappointed in her lack of resistance as it meant the end of the UV tortures. She had questioned Thorn's powers. But what if it had been on purpose? Just enough to give a show of being a broken prisoner to let them take the samples. No rescue attempt from Cassius and no solo prison breaks. It did seem weird in hindsight.

"But how would she have controlled things from inside?"

"Her psychic powers. Bramel used to visit and we think there was a Hunter also working for her, probably Gabriel."

"I thought he worked for MI5."

"A double agent, we believe."

"But you can block psychic powers?"

"Back then, we couldn't. It wasn't until the portal opened and magic returned to the world that we have been able to cast spells. It has only been in the last few months we have reached that level of competency to block psychic abilities."

"Let me get this straight. Thorn controls the Turned via Bramel. Allowed herself to be experimented on to find the cause of the Dragan infertility or a way of getting around it," I said, and Mary nodded. "So Thorn had them torture me and set up all the battles. Controlled every bad thing that has ever happened to me."

"We are unsure of how much she ordered directly and how much was done by Bramel. He would have had to keep up appearances with his followers and the Hunters. It would have drawn suspicion if he just let you go. Moreover, Bramel didn't like you much. You had what he desired."

"But the war. Our battle in the park. Why now?"

"War was inevitable once genetic engineering meant they could unlock the Dragan secrets. Bramel couldn't hold them back forever. Thorn wanted the war as well. It was the final stage of her plan. To destroy all her enemies in one go."

"She planned the war?"

"Think who benefits the most from this war. From the victory."

I couldn't think straight and just stared at Mary, hoping she would answer.

"Let me explain. Cyrus is dead. The Turned are defeated. The Dragans reunited under one ruler. Her daughters are back. The Hunter's organisation is beaten and broken up. An alliance agreed with the new Hunter organisation, providing the Dragans with peace and prosperity."

"Thorn. She gets everything she wants."

"Nearly. She didn't get you. The key to the genetic research. The potential solution to the Dragan fertility problem. The continuation and expansion of her race and empire. We had to stop her from getting this last thing. The most important thing. The key to her new empire."

"Okay. Let's pretend it is true. She has played us all. Why did you let her?"

"Because our goals aligned. The Turned and corrupted Hunters defeated. The Dragans together under one ruler is easier to manage and they can help us with the increase in supernatural activity. But we drew the line at Thorn having you. A limited number of Dragans is fine, but a reproducing race of Dragans is a disaster. What if the next set of Dragans starts another civil war, wanting to replace Thorn? They re-create the Turned and start this entire cycle all over again. No. We can't allow that to happen. The handful of Dragans left is controllable, and after their history, they would be unlikely to create the Turned again."

My head hurt from all the info. I lay back on the bed and closed my eyes. "How do I find out the truth? Most of this is a theory."

"Only Thorn knows the whole truth, and she would never reveal it," Mary said.

"You expect me to believe these lies?"

"I expect you to read our proof and then decide for yourself."

"In the meantime, am I free to leave?"

Mary pursed her lips together. "No. Sorry. We got you a comfy room, but you must remain here until you have read the evidence. We need to give you a health check after taking the reverse formula as well. Then we can start on further treatments once you are ready."

"I am a prisoner."

"It is best to be honest. Yes, you are my prisoner. Now don't sulk; it is for your own good."

I looked back at Scarlett, who was watching intently from the door. "How did Scarlett end up with you? Is she a double agent, after all?"

"I will let Scarlett tell you her own story. Shall I send her in?"

"Yes."

"Okay. Just listen to what she has to say. Afterwards, we will move you to your own room," Mary said and tapped the top of my hand and left. She spoke with Scarlett outside the glass door for a couple of minutes.

Scarlett buzzed open the door and walked over, her white trainers squeaking on the tiles while avoiding eye contact. She held the glass up to my mouth, and I sucked on the straw to drink back the water. She put the glass down on top of a heart monitor.

She finally looked up and gave a half-smile. "So, we can now both talk. It is not how I wanted us to meet again. But I guess you have questions like how am I alive?"

"Yes. Let me say first. It is good to see you alive and well. But who are you?"

"You think I am one of them?" she said, pointing over her shoulder. "I am not a spy or an agent. I am the person you know. I am Scarlett. It is a simple story. After the ambush at the car park, when I escaped and they killed your dad and captured you, I called Mary for help. Little did I know she was actually MI5-S. She was in the area tracking us down. I called and she turned up in a blacked-out range rover with four burly guards. I nearly didn't get in, but Mary was with them and I was scared the vampires were chasing."

"Mary took you in and looked after you."

"Yeah. We realised I couldn't go home without the Dragans, Hunters or Turned finding me. We faked my death instead. Since then, I have remained with MI5-S and they are training me as an agent."

"Strange. I had a conversation with Bramel about who would most benefit from your death. He was pointing the finger at Thorn. When, in fact, you would gain the most from your own death. It gave you the chance to be free again."

"It isn't ideal. I have left my family behind. Severed all links. I might be able to return now the war is over."

"And you are staying with MI5-S to get me to swap sides. A prize for my loyalty."

She slapped my face. "How dare you? I am not a consolation prize. I am not here to win you back now the truth about Thorn is out. I am not some stupid teenager in love with a vampire. Even if you swap sides and believe the truth, I am not sure I want you back. You are dangerous."

"So, why are you here?"

"I am here as a friend, a familiar face to help you through this change. If you want me back, you will have to regain my trust and show me you are committed to your old life. Then maybe, just maybe, I will reconsider. At the moment, you are more Dragan than Human. If you were ever more Human than Dragan, it could be possible. Else there would be no future for us anyway."

"You talk about trust. I am the one who has been kidnapped and strapped to a bed. I am the one who went to your funeral. I am the one who cried their eyes raw when I heard of your death. I have a few trust issues as well," I said and yanked at the straps, but they held firm.

Scarlett stepped back. "I did what I had to in order to survive."

"So did I."

We both remained silent for a moment.

"More water?"

I nodded and sucked it down.

"We start from scratch then. You read the evidence, and I will be here for someone to talk to," Scarlett said, leaned over me and kissed my forehead. I couldn't help breathing in her scent as she draw close, it rekindling old happy memories of us cuddled together.

"That would be nice," I replied. But I couldn't help thinking this was another means of control. However, it would do no good to call it out. I would read the fake evidence and gain their trust, but no one would hold me prisoner.

Suddenly, my eyes drifted and head rocked back.

"You feeling sleepy?" she asked.

"Yeah," I said, my muscle relaxing and focus fading.

"Must be something in the water," she said and giggled. "Don't worry. It's just so we can move you."

Chapter Eighteen

I pressed play on the video again, starting it from the beginning.

The video showed two men holding me at the side of a gym floor and a man in beige karate clothes in the middle. Around the sprung gym floor edges, men lined up dressed in similar beige martial arts clothes. The man in the middle bowed to Bramel, Carmella and Gabriel, who sat in chairs at the edge of the gym floor. The lead Hunter, Patrick, who had killed my dad and tortured me, made a speech, pointing me out as the man who had killed his friend in Vegas and killed others when rescuing Thorn. Those around the edges shouted and stamped their feet, vibrating the gym floor.

Patrick shouted out "One", and the instructor took a fighting stance in the middle of the gym floor. The two guards shoved me into the middle and the instructor attacked. I easily defeated him, to my surprise at the time.

Patrick shouted "Two", and I beat them both. This carried on until we reached "Eight". I was looking bruised and battered but still winning. Bramel halted the proceedings and stepped forward. He engaged me in one on one combat. I was already hurting and only about twenty-five percent Dragan at the time, and I didn't have the vampire formula coursing through my blood. Bramel won and let loose the remaining Hunters to beat me unconscious. Bramel bowed to the video and the filming stopped.

This had happened when I was captured by the Turned and Hunters. My Dad, Scarlett and I, had broken into their base and stolen sensitive data. They had tracked us down and killed my Dad, but Scarlett had escaped the car park after I killed her pursuer. Mary had presented this video as evidence that Thorn was South. They had intercepted the video being sent to her from Bramel. They had internet records of the transaction, server names, IP addresses, and date stamps.

I always knew it was filmed for someone. I had assumed it was to be studied later by the Hunters and Turned. But Bramel's bow at the end indicated it was meant for a person. I never saw that at the time as being beaten unconscious. The evidence was damning if true, but anything could be faked. Why would she want to see me beaten to a pulp?

I lay back in my bed in the cell, which was decorated as if it was inside a perfectly normal family home. They had painted the walls yellow and put up music and film posters to hide the black painted runes underneath to block out psychic messages. I had a stereo, TV, and games console. The bed had crisp black and white chequered sheets. A light grey, thick carpet that you could bury your toes in covered the floor. A shower room and toilet were en-suite. The only giveaway to it being a prison cell was the black metal locked door with a hatch underneath to pass through food and other items, such as the video evidence.

Although a prisoner, I had been treated well. They let me out twice a day to exercise in the gym. But four armed guards escorted me and I wore a restraining collar that dealt an electric shock if I misbehaved. I gave them no reason ever to use it. Scarlett and Mary visited, and we would talk about the latest round of evidence, or they would tell me about what was happening in the world. At least it was a change of pace after the last few crazy years. I took the opportunity to rest. I had no other choice.

A knock rang on the metal door and the eye hatch slid back.

"Hi Jon, do you have time for a chat?" Scarlett asked.

"Yeah. I have room in my schedule," I said and laughed. I walked over to the door and the security guard handed over the restraining collar.

"Stand back and put it on," he said.

"I know the drill," I replied and wrapped the white plastic and metal collar around my throat and stood with my back against the door. The guard reached in, clipped the ends together, and initiated the device on my neck. It beeped and a light flashed from green to red.

"He is ready for you, Miss," the guard said.

"The name is Scarlett."

The guard unlocked the door, and Scarlett walked in carrying her medical bag and took a seat on the blue sofa opposite the bed. I sat on the bed facing her.

"First, I need to do the daily tests," she said, undid the bag and put on her purple latex gloves.

"Of course," I replied. I wasn't convinced this was needed anymore. They only did it as a means of psychological conditioning. They got me to comply with small unobtrusive commands each day, conditioning me to comply with their requests, so when the major commands were asked, I was used to saying yes.

"Okay, eyes first," Scarlett said, and sat next to me on the bed, holding a light pen.

I played along, as it was the most personal attention I received all day. It could be the only human interaction I would have on some days.

"Blood pressure."

I held out my arm. She took the reading and scribbled it in her book.

"Reflexes."

"Temperature."

"Finally, let's check your ears," she said and squatted close up on either side of my face to check. I could feel her hot breath each time, and the hairs on my neck tingled.

She packed away her gear and finished writing up her notes. "All done. What shall we discuss today?"

"Is this collar still needed? It has been three weeks since I was brought in. At what point will you trust me?"

"Not my decision. It is Mary's and the other MI5-S agents monitoring you."

"Can you tell them it isn't needed anymore?"

"So you agree to start the treatment to reverse your Dragan DNA. You believe our version of events."

I scratched around the collar resting on my neck. "Your proof is very compelling. This latest video is very revealing."

"She ordered that beating and asked them to film it. She ordered your tortures, your Dad's death, and all the original attacks in Leeds and London. You can see that she is evil. Surely, you don't want to be like her, a Dragan."

Everything Scarlett said sounded compelling. But the evidence never supplied a smoking gun, it was all circumstantial or could be faked. There wasn't evidence Thorn had ordered any of the attacks or tortures, just proof phone calls had been made between her locations and those of Bramel. They had no recordings of phone calls or direct messages between them. I wasn't sold on the idea that Thorn was South. But I hadn't discounted it either. A lot of it made sense. Bramel was in love with Thorn and would have done anything she asked. His plea before she killed him, "No, my Queen. I am sorry I betrayed you. I only wish to serve you." Tied into this theory of Thorn being South.

When captive, I had heard him on the phone, taking orders from someone. There was no doubt in my mind that South existed. However, their identity couldn't be proved to Thorn with such flimsy evidence. But I also realised nothing proved it to be Cyrus either. This is what I wanted to say but couldn't. I had to play the game.

"You are right. There is no doubt Thorn is South. But I can't take the reversing formula. I need to confront her with the truth. I need to keep my powers if I am going to have my revenge."

She shook her head. "There is no point. She would never admit to being

South. Anyway, they don't want you to find her. They agreed for her to be left in peace and reign as the Dragan Queen. In return, she would help them with supernatural matters, but you are to remain in our custody. If you go after her and kill her, who will rule the Dragans? Who will help us control the supernatural threats?"

"I could. I am the King of the Dragans."

"They don't like that idea. None of the outcomes work for them. Either you kill her and they lose an ally, or she seduces you again and the alliance will be broken, or she kills you and the alliance would be broken. It is best for everyone that you never see her again."

"Okay. I get it. You never want me to see her again. But I am no good to this organisation as a human. I have powers that can help them. You wouldn't need to rely on Thorn and her friends. I could provide all the support you need."

"I will speak to Mary."

"Thank you."

"How is everything else? You got everything you need?"

"Can I get some drawing equipment? Just pencils and paper."

"Of course, that should be easy to get. Anything else?"

"I would like to go outside the base. It would be nice to see the real world."

"Again, that is Mary's decision."

"How can I show you I can be trusted without you trusting me first? I can't prove myself otherwise."

"Fine. I will bring it up with her. Anything else?"

"Do you want to stay and have dinner with me? It is takeaway night. I thought we could have pizza and play a couple of computer games together."

She smiled. "Yes. But just the pizza. I will bring it in and we can eat together."

"Thank you. It would be nice to have some company."

Chapter Nineteen

At the exit of the building, I stood next to Scarlett. I had no idea of our location, and no one would answer questions on the subject. I didn't know if this was a military base or a research centre.

One of the accompanying security guards wrapped a red tartan scarf around my neck to conceal the restraining collar. "Okay, Miss, your pooch is ready for his walkies," he said and handed the remote to Scarlett.

"You are under my control now, Jon," Scarlett said, holding up the controller.

"Just like old times," I replied and laughed.

The guard opened the door and walked towards a waiting black saloon car. He got in the driver's side and his colleague opened the door at the back. Scarlett and I climbed in and he got in the front. The car drove off, and I looked around at the base.

We had left the building through a side door, a fire exit. As we drove around towards the gate and wire fence, I craned my neck around to get a glance at the front entrance, which had double glass sliding doors. The building behind was one of many built on top of each other. Its central part was a three-storey white building with four large square windows on each level. Connecting over it was a domed roof over to a tower block building with a large satellite receiver on the top, and three single-level buildings branched off the sides like spokes. A helicopter pad sat in an open area and car park to its side, linking around to the road we drove on towards the gate.

Army guards hailed us to slow down. The driver wound down the window and passed over a slip of paper. The guard waved to the controller in a booth, who operated the large metal gate, which mechanically trundled back, allowing us to drive out.

We drove through the gate and down a tree tunnelled two-track road. The forest area extended around the base and secluded it from passing traffic. The road led straight to another wire fence topped with curled barbed wire, which stretched along the perimeter. We reached a gate, which automatically swung open. On top of the gateposts were two cameras, one facing in and one facing out. The driver waved at the camera, and we drove through to a connecting road as the gate swung closed.

Soon, other traffic merged in on the same road and we took our place in the flow. I watched out for road signs to give a clue to our location. I watched the road signs to remember the direction we were travelling in from and would do the same on the way back to triangulate my position.

We passed another welcome sign of a town and turned onto local roads. We carried on to the edge of the town, past a green park with kids flinging themselves around a concrete skate park. Drove past a small supermarket with cars queued up to find spaces and then parked on the second floor of a multi-storey car park.

The driver turned off the engine and the guard in the passenger seat swivelled around. "You two have one hour. We will be following. Don't try anything stupid."

"Don't worry, I will ensure he behaves," Scarlett said.

"Good. You can take your dog for a walk. Make sure to clean up after him," he said, and the driver laughed. I would wipe that smirk off his face.

Scarlett held my hand and led the way down the stairs and through an alleyway onto a bustling pedestrian high street. I had lost track of the days of the week in prison, but I guessed from all the kids in the park, the crammed supermarket and the packed town centre that it must have been Saturday.

"What would you like to do first?" she asked.

"Coffee. The stuff in prison is horrible."

She scowled. "It isn't a prison."

I raised my eyebrows. "Am I being kept against my will? Imprisoned by MI5-S."

"Let's not argue. Please don't call it a prison while we are out in public; it causes unnecessary attention. There is a coffee shop just down the street."

We walked on and noted the two guards following us. We went inside and got two drinks and cakes. I guided us towards two available seats in a busy area, right at the back, crammed between two other occupied tables. The escorting guards would have to sit further away from us.

I sipped the black coffee and bit into my chocolate brownie. Scarlett spooned off the whipped cream on her hot chocolate. I looked around at all the different people enjoying their everyday lives. It felt strange sat in the middle of humanity but not hearing their thoughts. I felt the blocking talisman through my shirt. I could yank it off, drop it to the floor, and kick it away. But they would check again on my return, and I would lose any trust I had built.

I watched all the normal people doing normal things. Being outside the base gave me a chance to experience real life, a normal life. I scoffed down my brownie and emptied my coffee cup.

"You enjoying yourself?" Scarlett asked.

"Yes. It is nice to be out. Would be nice to be less restrained," I said and re-positioned the scarf.

"All in good time. We have to be sure you can be trusted."

"Eventually, you will have to trust me and let me out on my own."

"We shouldn't be talking about this in public. However, I said the same to Mary, but she said they have kept dangerous people as prisoners all their lives when necessary. Let's change the subject," she said and glanced around at the other customers, who looked away. They had clearly overheard our conversation.

I looked across at the young couple sitting next to us. Although my psychic senses were impeded, my other enhanced senses were operating normally. Stuck in prison, this was of little use, but in the middle of the coffee shop, I was soaking in the sights, sounds and smells of everyone.

The man at the next table was watching a conspiracy theory video about wireless communications. The belief that governments used it for mind control. His girlfriend tapped the table impatiently as she tried to talk to him quietly. "Put that phone down. We need to talk about money. Rent is due. They will kick us out."

He grunted in response, pushing up his baseball cap. "Laters. I need to visit my mates. It's poker night. I'll win it back."

"What! That is how we are short of money in the first place."

In front, a group of women with prams circled a big table and exchanged stories about their kids. Two men behind discussed the football results from the premier league. The machines behind the counter ground the coffee down and jetted hot water through it. The smell of coffee permeated the air and the toasting of bread drifted along with it. Prison, in contrast, was very stale; it had the same old smells and sights every day. I felt like my senses had been starved.

The man watching the video stood up and pulled down his baseball cap as he pocketed his phone. "Need the loo." He walked to the aisle and through the doors to the toilets.

"Scarlett. That coffee has gone straight through me. I will just be two ticks," I said and stood up and followed the baseball capped man. A guard put his coffee down and followed. I hurried through the doors and caught up with the man as he entered the toilets.

"Mate, hold up. Take this piece of paper and contact the people on it. Pass on the message. They will pay you well," I said, forcing a square of paper into his hand.

"What. Don't talk stupid."

"Quick. I need help. The government is holding me prisoner. My guard will walk in any second. I know the truth about radio signals and mind control," I said and pulled back the scarf to show the electronic collar. "I am being controlled."

On cue, the MI5-S guard opened the door. "Jon, what are you doing?"

I looked at the baseball cap guy and back at the guard. "Going for a pee. Is that allowed?"

"Go then. I will wait here."

The baseball cap guy's eyes widened, and he pocketed the paper and went into a cubicle. I didn't need to be psychic to know the guard's intervention had sealed my story. Once I used the toilet, the guard escorted me out. I sat back with Scarlett and the guard leant down to my ear.

"You walk off again. Then we are going straight back. Do you understand me, dog," he said and gripped a hand on my electronic collar.

He straightened up and stared down. I glared up and let the anger rise to flash my eyes Dragan red. "I am sure we have an understanding."

He jerked back and his body temperature increased, sweat droplets appearing on his forehead. "Good," he said and strode off.

"Don't do that?" Scarlett said, "not all of them know what you are."

"Not my problem."

"Jon, behave."

I gritted my teeth. "You tell Mary about their attitude and I will behave."

"I will report back. What shall we do next?" she said, finishing her coffee.

"Shopping. Maybe I can convince you to buy me the new star wars game. I have completed the others."

"Of course, I have been given some spending money. Let's go."

As we stood up, the baseball cap guy returned from the toilets. He placed his phone on the table with the screen opened on the text messages. A list of messages between him and the phone number I had given him, the number for Miss Jones, who ran the homeless shelter in London, Thorn's friend.

I left the coffee shop in high spirits, which were further lifted after Scarlett bought the computer game to play. We got back in the car, but Scarlett received a phone call from Mary before we left. She got out of the car and walked away. The driver switched on the radio, and I couldn't overhear the conversation. She called out the two guards, who left the car and locked me in. They talked and looked over at me.

The driver made a call and after another conversation, they all returned to the car. We pulled out of the car park but headed off in a different direction than the one we arrived in.

"What is going on?" I asked.

The driver glared in the rear-view mirror. "Your handler can tell you. But for your information, I don't agree."

"My handler?"

"That is me," Scarlett said. "That was Mary on the phone. As you know, we defeated the main Turned army, but some escaped and some never attended the Hyde Park battle. As such, there are still vampire cells operating, and MI5-S have been cleaning them up. One such cell has been detected nearby, but we don't have enough resources to tackle it tonight, so they would likely kill more people. Mary has asked if we could swing by and eradicate the problem. Explicitly, could you go in and kill them all."

"Me? I am a prisoner. Why the hell would I help you?"

"Not for us, but for the poor innocent humans that would die tonight. However, Mary has authorised me to present you with a deal. You kill these vampires and we will remove the collar permanently and allow limited access around the base."

"And what is stopping me from just taking off instead?"

"Trust. We build trust between each other. You do us this favour and we trust you more. We only ever took you as a prisoner to help you. It is an intervention, not imprisonment. We want to show you that Thorn had deceived and used you. It has always been our goal for you to join us of your own free will. This would be that first step."

"I get weapons and to fight?"

"Limited weapons. No guns, just blades. And yes, you get to kill vampires."

"It would relieve the boredom and get this stupid collar off. I will do it."

"Good. We hoped that would be the answer. We are heading to the nest now. If you had said no, we would have gone in without you," Scarlett said.

"You were going in?"

"Yes. What do you think I have been training for this whole time in MI5-S. I killed a couple of vamps at the Hyde Park battle."

"I only do this on the promise you stay outside and keep safe. I couldn't bear for you to die again."

"If it keeps you happy. But I will go on hunts in the future whether you like it or not."

"Not today. If you are going to hunt, I should train you."

"No need. Ruby has taken personal charge of my training. Assuming you taught her properly, then I should be fine."

The car drove to the edge of the town and through side streets until we pulled into a long road with a grass park in between the two sides of the street. A burnt out car sat in the middle of the grass and kids threw bricks at it. Another group of young men had gathered in a circle and passed around a long rolled-up smoke while music echoed out of a phone.

The men spotted our nicely polished and clean car and immediately ran off. A few curtains twitched, and the kids ran over to the side of the park. "Get lost, coppers."

"There goes our surprise assault," the driver said.

"Vampires often set up bases in rough areas. It is not unusual for people to stay indoors all day and only go out at night. The state of their skin is put down to drug use. They always feed away from their own doorsteps. Plus, like now, any strangers scouting around are always spotted and warnings are given," I said.

The driver pulled the car to the kerb. "So they will be expecting you. Should we abandon the mission?"

"No. They will be listening out. But they won't be expecting a Dragan," I said.

"What about the locals?" the guard said as the kids spat on the windows.

"I will take care of them as well. Just be ready to pick off any escaping vampires. It is getting dark, so they will risk an exit. Right, where are the weapons?" I asked.

"In the boot. I will flip it open."

The guard opened the back door and I got out. The kids shouted over. "Get away, police. We know who you are?"

I stepped out and crouched down. "Kids, can I ask a favour?"

"What?" they said and hesitantly stepped forward.

The Dragan inside let rip, eyes filling blood red and fangs cutting through my mouth. My voice deepened and I growled. "Get lost."

The kids scattered, running into one another and tripping over, screaming all the way home.

"Subtle. We will have their parents out in a minute complaining we have scared their children," the driver said.

"That is your problem. I have a vampire nest to terminate."

We walked around to the boot of the car, which had unlocked. The driver pulled back a false layer of the boot to reveal a few metal cases. He reached in and opened one box. Inside the box, my sword lay in encased in black foam.

He grabbed it and handed it over.

"House number 3, with the overgrown front lawn and broken gate. Turn around and let me take off the collar and the blocking talisman. Okay, you are now free to use all your powers. Please hurry up before we have a mob of angry locals asking about the crazy guy with a sword and fangs," the guard said.

"We will cover the exits," Scarlett added.

"I will see you in a minute," I responded and twisted the sword around in my hand as I walked towards the target. It felt good to have my blade again. The last time I used it was to kill Cyrus.

I smiled as I walked, flexing my wrist around to cut the air. An old woman peered out between her curtains and then pulled them back to hide. I didn't care if I was seen. If the police came, then MI5-S could take care of it and earn their keep.

I kicked the waist high gate off its last remaining hinges. It scudded across the concrete path and thudded into the door. I listened out and took a big sniff of the foul-smelling air of rotten flesh. Definitely vamps inside. I heard about five different areas of movement inside and different scents competing. They would soon pick up my scent and know I wasn't human or a vampire. They may have never met a Dragan before, but I was sure they would quickly work it out.

I punched the lock through and the door swung open.

"Hello. Didn't anyone tell you we won the war? You are supposed to be dead already," I shouted inside as I walked in with the sword held out in front. A shotgun blasted through the thin walls. I dived and ducked out of the way, a few fragments catching my back. I shrugged the wound off and barged through the door.

The vamp turned and fired again. I ducked behind a sofa and then vaulted the chair, thrusting the sword into his throat. I took the pump-action shotgun, reloaded it with one hand and walked back out. The room exploded in ash as I stepped into the hallway.

Footsteps ran down the stairs, and I shoved the nuzzle through the wooden bannisters and fired. Blooded legs gave way, and the vamp tumbled down to a heap on the ground. I ran up the stairs, digging the sword into the vamp as I went, killing it off for good.

The next one burst out a door with an axe and swiped down. I slashed up and cut off its hands, and the axe and hands fell to the floor. I pumped the shotgun again and unloaded it into the head of the screaming vamp.

Movement at the far end of the hallway. I dropped the shotgun, picked up the axe, and threw it at the door at the far end. The door opened and a vampire attacked. The axe hammered in-between her eyes and she stumbled to the carpet. I charged in and pierced the sword through her heart, causing a spasm of muscles and a gasp of air. I stepped over and burst into the room as the hallway behind redecorated in ash.

Downstairs, a vampire fled out the front door. I ripped off the boards over the windows and leapt down into the overgrown garden.

The smoking vamp ran towards Scarlett and the guards. The sunlight had not quite gone. Scarlett stepped forward, holding a silver stake in her hand. The vampire snarled and charged, claws hacking down. Scarlett dodged the initial blow and punched the vamp in the face.

Claws slashed back and Scarlett ducked, stepped in and hammered the silver stake into its chest. The vampire jerked away, clutching its glowing wound. The two guards pulled Scarlett back as the vampire exploded. A small crowd making its way across the park fled back inside their houses.

I strolled over and sniffed the air. "They are all gone. Nice moves by the way."

"Thank you. Are you getting back in the car, or do we have a problem?" she said, gripping the silver stake and glaring into my red-tinted eyes.

"As promised," I said, and held the hilt of the sword out. I could escape but not without a fight. A fight I didn't want to have.

Scarlett took the blade. "Good choice."

Chapter Twenty

I sat up in bed playing the star wars fighter pilot game, idling away the day as usual, hoping I would hear from the Dragans, hoping I would regain my freedom.

The day out had been great, going for a coffee and getting a message to Thorn's friends. The detour to the vampire cell had been a great distraction and won some trust with MI5-S. However, I was still stuck in the cell, killing time and virtual baddies on the computer.

I had blitzed through the game levels already. My increased reactions made a huge difference to every game. I wished they would have let me play online against other people, as I would have become a gaming legend.

A knock echoed into the room three times and the eye slot scraped back. I paused the game. "Hi, can I help you?"

"Hi, Jon. It's Mary. Stay seated. We are coming in," she said.

The eye slot scraped back and the multiple locks clicked out of the holes in the door frame. It swung open and Mary and Scarlett walked through, backed up by five soldiers, two with shields, three with electronic batons that could deliver huge shocks.

I stood up to greet them, and the two soldiers with the shields rushed to the front. I raised my hands in the air. "Hey, chill out. Just trying to say hello."

Mary waved them back and signalled for me to sit back down. She stood in front of me with Scarlett at her side, holding a birthday gift bag.

"Considering your actions in terminating the vampire cell, we will keep to our side of the bargain, starting from today. So here are some presents," Mary said, and Scarlett handed over the gift bag.

Inside the bag were an access card and lanyard, and an ankle tag. I tipped them out onto the bed.

"The card will give you limited access around the base to the canteen and gym. The ankle tag is to make sure you don't stray outside those areas by tailgating unwitting members of staff. If you pull up your trouser leg, Scarlett will fit it."

I pulled up my trouser leg and Scarlett clipped the grey plastic around.

"Excellent. Now follow us and we will give you the tour," Mary said and spun around.

Scarlett smiled and held out her hand. I took it and she helped me off the bed. "See. I told you we could be trusted. We keep to our word. Grab your access card, as you will need to try it out." I pulled on the lanyard and the access card hung around my neck.

Mary stepped outside the cell and ordered the soldiers to remain but to be ready for her call. She waved us to follow and guided us down the corridor.

"There are only four cells in this building. They are generally not used. Some have been used for temporary storage. You are the first prisoner here for ten years. Just at the end of the corridor is the exit out of the cellblock. Please try your card."

I stepped up to the access pad and held my card against it. The light turned green, the latch clicked, and the door opened. Mary strode through the grey corridors and I tried my card on each access pad. The last door opened into a room with rows of tables and benches on either side. At the far end, a counter with trays of hot food, drinks machines, and fridges.

"We will no longer bring meals to your room. The access card also has money on it. Enough to pay for all your meals and snacks every day. You can explore the canteen at your own leisure. I have more to show you."

Mary walked through the canteen and I eyed the big plates of breakfast being devoured. We followed her through another set of corridors.

"Try this door," Mary asked. The light turned red. "Good. This is as far as you can go. If you follow me back this way, the last door we passed takes you to the gym."

The access card opened the door into a large room with running machines, free weights in front of mirrors and out the back a boxing ring and punch bags.

"For both the canteen and gym, the access card works until 9pm at night and starts from 7am every morning. If not in your room at these times, the alarm will sound."

"I got it. This is great. Anything else?" I said.

"Yes. As we speak, gym gear and other clothes are being put in your room. Washing will be collected daily at 8am. Please leave it in the basket inside your room. The cell will be cleaned every Friday at 10am, so please ensure you are out of the room," Mary said.

"Excellent. Almost like a normal life. At least you aren't cutting me open."

"We are your friends, Jon. I know it may not seem like it, but this is for your own benefit. Have you had any more thoughts on the evidence we have shown you about Thorn being South?"

I gritted my teeth and glared. "It doesn't look good. But I would need to speak with Thorn myself."

"I appreciate that, but it can't happen. We can't risk the fragile alliance between us. Things are strained enough."

"So, where does this leave us?" I asked.

"Until you accept the evidence and take the reverse formula, you will have to stay as our guest."

"You mean prisoner?"

"As a compromise, let us call you a reluctant visitor. There are still other vampire nests to be eradicated, and our teams need training. Ruby and the team can only train so many people at a time. A real life Dragan would be of tremendous benefit to the setting up of the new Hunter organisation. If you help us, then we can expand your privileges."

"Internet access? More days out?"

"It is possible. But if you try to escape, you will lose every privilege and remain locked in the cell."

"So I work for MI5-S or stay a prisoner."

Mary sighed. "Unfortunately, yes. Orders from the very top. We can't have you running around as a free agent. You are far too dangerous," Mary said.

Scarlett still had hold of my hand and she clutched it with the other one as well.

"Just consider it, Jon. We can have a life here. We can be your family. I can never go back to my normal life and neither can you. MI5-S are offering us the only chance we can have of a normal life and we can do so much good. We can help control the supernatural forces. We can save people's lives."

I stared into Scarlett's green eyes. If I had been offered the chance of a normal life with Scarlet years ago, I would have snatched at the opportunity. Now it felt hollow. Not really a choice. Just the lesser of two evils, but it would gain their trust and relieve the boredom.

"Okay. I will try. I don't think I have much choice."

"Good. You won't regret it, Jon. Now let's go for breakfast. You can pay," Mary said.

Chapter Twenty-One

I thought I had cracked it with the baseball cap guy in the coffee shop, having contacted Miss Jones. However, three months had passed, and I had no sign that any rescue plans were in place. In the meantime, I acted the perfect prisoner and was granted more freedoms within the base, as per our agreement. I could now leave the room, but my card pass limited my access around the base. I could go to the gym and canteen, but I had to be back in my room by 9 pm every night and I had to wear an ankle tag.

I continued to have days out with Scarlett for social and work reasons. There were a few more vampire nests that I eliminated. I also visited other parts of the base and other military locations to train the new Hunter organisation. I had enjoyed seeing Ruby again, who had let the dye grow out to her normal brown hair. She now went by the name of Amanda, her real name.

On the social days out, they changed the location every time. I guessed this was why I couldn't be found. All the time, they presented me with evidence of Thorn's betrayal and asked if I would take more of the reversing formula, which I refused. They took regular blood samples to see if my Dragan to Human DNA had altered, but it hadn't gone back any further beyond the first dose. I remained about ninety-six percent Dragan still. The reversing formula had only reverted one injection.

To take my model prisoner role to the next stage, I requested Mary's permission to ask Scarlett on a night out. I wanted to take her to an Italian restaurant in the first town we had visited. Mary had agreed to the request, and Scarlett smiled at my invite out. She was pleased and still attracted to me. Although I didn't have my psychic senses, I could detect other clear signals from her behaviour. Her eyes had dilated, body temperature rose and scent changed. Her micro gestures betrayed her true feelings, the glimpse of a smile and the straightening of her posture.

I felt a pang of guilt at the offer. I was trading on her feelings. But it wasn't the only reason I had invited her. During the last few months, the love I had for her returned. It had never really gone. I dare say she could read my signals as well.

However, I knew our relationship couldn't move forward until I answered the question that was driving me mad. Who was lying? If Thorn was South, then Scarlett had rescued me and I owed her my life. If Mary and Scarlett were lying, then they were as bad as the Turned and Hunters, and Thorn and I would take our revenge. Either way, the answer to the question didn't exist in a prison cell.

Date night came around and the car dropped us off in the same town again as our first outing. I had convinced them to return to the same place as it was closest to the base and would let us have more time together.

Our two guards followed us a few yards back, and I had booked us into the same restaurant but a few tables apart. I had picked a local independent Italian restaurant with excellent reviews in the middle of the high street. I hoped if anyone were still looking for me, then this central location would give me the best chance of being spotted.

We sat across the table from each other and the guards sat behind us, a few tables away. I was glad not to see them but only to view Scarlett, who looked gorgeous in a black dress and heels. She wore her flame red hair down, touching her bare shoulders. She had put in the effort for our date night. I had ordered some smarter clothes and got a basic haircut.

Sitting across from one another in the restaurant felt like nothing and everything had changed. We never went for proper meals when together before. We didn't have the money. But now Scarlett received a wage from MI5-S, and I had the money my father had left me, which was a considerable amount with the sale of the house, life insurance, and savings.

Yet, looking across the table at her beautiful flame-red hair and green eyes, I felt like I had never been away. However, time and events had changed us. She had lost some of her enthusiasm for life. Her let's give it a go mentality had been replaced with a more cautious attitude or maybe it was just around me.

We ordered pizzas, a bottle of red wine and shared some garlic bread for starters. I focused my magic to hold back my healing and let the alcohol take effect, enough to mirror Scarlett.

I held up my glass. "To old friends."

She smiled and clinked her glass with mine. "Old friends."

We both sipped and the pizzas arrived.

"These look delicious. It is so good to get out and spend time together, almost alone," I said and glanced behind at the guards.

"One day, we can do this by ourselves. That day will come quicker if you take the course."

"Let's not discuss that tonight. You know my feelings on the subject. I need closure first."

"So, what should we discuss?"

I sat in silence, trying to think of another subject, something worthwhile discussing. "Hmm. We should talk properly once in private, back in my room."

"Okay. In the meantime, I can't sit in silence. Let's pretend everything is resolved and you are free to go anywhere in the world with whoever you like. What would you do?"

I picked up a slice of pizza and munched away as I considered the question. Of course, I knew if I could do anything, it would be to find Thorn. But if this was all resolved.

"I would love to travel and see the world without worrying about being hunted down or completing a mission."

"Sounds good. Where and who would you go with?" she said and flashed her eyelashes and sipped her red wine.

"I would like to visit some places I have already been to, but see them properly. I would want to go by myself."

Scarlett coughed as the red wine went down. "By yourself, excuse me!"

"Nothing personal. But I would like time to work out who I am. So much has changed in my life. I have changed so much. I need time to gather my thoughts and explore."

She drank some water. "But surely you've had all the time in the world to gather your thoughts?"

"I have time, but I am locked in a prison and limited access to the outside world. I need a chance to roam and discover what type of person I have become."

She nodded. "Yeah. I think that is a good idea. I would like to do the same. It has been a pretty crazy few years; parents divorced, moved to London, met a boy and fell in love, the boy became a vampire, broken into a military secret research centre, faked my own death, work for a government intelligence agency and kidnapped vampire boy to get him to see sense."

"Yeah. Maybe our paths could cross on our travels. Although I told you before, I am not a vampire. I am a Dragan."

The couple next to us were staring, drinks halfway to their mouths.

I smiled and raised my glass in a toast. "Hi. Just ignore us. We are actors rehearsing for a new TV series. It is a bit of immersive role-play to get into character."

"Oh well, I look forward to watching it," the woman said, and the couple returned to their food. Scarlett grabbed her napkin and stifled a laugh into it.

We finished our pizzas and moved on to some desserts. I wanted to go for the full three-course meal and coffees, anything to spend longer outside the base and increase my chance at finding a friend. I had purposefully asked for a window seat, hoping to spot a friendly face.

We finally finished the meal and I couldn't delay any further.

"Can we have a little walk down the high street before we drive back? It will help my food go down," I asked.

"Yes. I will clear it with the driver," Scarlett replied and left the table to speak to the two guards waiting impatiently.

Scarlett returned and took her coat off the back of the chair. "Yes. It is okay, just once down the high street and back to the car."

We left and strolled down the pedestrianised street. A young couple walked ahead of us, holding hands. I thought about grabbing Scarlett's hand, but it felt too soon.

A group of men walked past on the other side, clearly intoxicated and a couple of them stared at Scarlett and then looked away as I glared back. I paused at the shop windows, feigning interest in the bargains, doing anything to delay the return to the base.

"Keep moving," the trailing guards shouted. I stared back but moved on. I walked past a closed shop doorway with a man sitting inside, covered with a blanket, sitting on a huge bag.

"Hey, mister, can you spare £1 for a cuppa of tea?"

"Sorry, we don't have any cash," Scarlett said, and pushed me on.

"Please, mister, poor old Tommy is feeling the cold tonight."

I stopped and looked back. The homeless man smiled up, his teeth black and gappy, the stink of tobacco and whiskey hitting my senses. I recognised the man. He had saved me after my fight with Giles. The man was rotten Tommy, and he lived at the homeless shelter run by Thorn's friend, Miss Jones. I swallowed and held back my delight. They had found me.

I fished about in my pockets and found some money. Tommy stood up and held out his hand. I put the money in and he grasped my hand in both of his and shook it up and down. "You are a true gent, my friend. This will help Tommy get through the night."

While shaking my hand, he slipped in something and took the money. I dropped the package into my pocket. "No worries, my friend. You take care."

Tommy grinned and gathered up his gear. I guess his job was done. We walked away, but I would have to wait until back at the base to check the package. I sped up the walk, keen to get back, when I heard something I hadn't heard for a long time. I heard the psychic chatter of people. It wasn't

Scarlett's or the guards'. But I could sense Tommy's thoughts.

I pushed my thoughts to his.

'Tommy, can you hear me?' I asked.

'Yes. The package is an anti-spell to the psychic block you are wearing. We won't have much time. Where are they holding you?'

'All the roads signs I have noticed leaving and coming back suggest it is near here, Salisbury. This journey only took fifteen minutes. On the way back, we will head north but stop before a motorway.'

'One day when out, you will spot Giles on a motorbike. Jump on the back and he will take you away. He will have a red helmet and be on a red sports bike.'

'I have tracking devices embedded in my clothes and an ankle tag.'

'I will let them know. They will find you on your next outing. Take care and thanks for the cuppa tea. I can go back to London at last.'

We reached the end of the high street and turned back towards the car park. I picked up the pace and grabbed Scarlett's hand as we walked. She didn't flinch away and walked along. We turned to one another and smiled.

"I have not seen you this happy for a long time," she said.

"It is nice to be out and act almost normal for once."

I enjoyed the night out with Scarlett, regardless of the message from Tommy. When I finally escaped, I knew she would take it personally. I enjoyed being with Scarlett again, even in these strange circumstances, but this wasn't real. For it to be real, I had to be free and I had to know the truth.

Chapter Twenty-Two

Only a few days had passed since meeting Tommy, but time had dragged on. I knew my salvation was close at hand. I was waiting to receive a message on the next stage of the plan. In the meantime, I enjoyed having my psychic abilities back while out of the room. The runes painted on the walls created a significant barrier. The anti spell only negated the talisman I wore. It didn't block out other peoples' talismans. Luckily, not everyone on the base wore one, so I got to enjoy other people's thoughts.

I hoped they had passed a message to one of them. But I heard nothing of any use for my escape. A few of them looked over, wondering why I was kept a prisoner. I learnt more about the base from listening to their conversation and thoughts. As Mary said, the base wasn't supposed to be used as a prison. I was the one and only inmate. For everyone else, this was a multi-purpose building for the military; research, training, and operations control.

One evening, after a heavy training session, I went for dinner. The canteen had windows down one side and I sat next to them. Although already dark, I could see beyond the outside lights into the darkness. I could make out the first set of solid metal fences encircling the buildings. In front of the first ring of fences lay open ground used for training and sporting activities. A rugby pitch ran parallel to the canteen. I had watched a few games and taken an interest in the sport.

I had access to a TV in my cell and watched the weekly games and internationals. I wondered if I would be allowed to get into sports once free. I had never been interested before, as too small and weak, but now I reckoned I would make an excellent rugby player. But I am sure it counted as cheating. I had taken the ultimate performing enhancing drug.

I stared out the window, imagining playing rugby, bulldozing over the competition with my strength and sprinting to the line for the winning try in the rugby world cup.

In the distance, past the pitch, two faint glows appeared. I focused my mind on them.

'V, are you there?'

'Isabella? Marcella?'

'Yes. It is us. We can reach further than the others with our powers.'

'I can see you. I am in the canteen. I am just scratching my head.'

'Yes. We can detect the difference in auras and temperature.'

'Are we going now?'

'No. Next time you go out. We are watching the base. When is it going to be?'

'Should be tomorrow, but I don't know where. They change it all the time.'

'Don't worry. We will be following. Do you remember what Tommy told you?'

'Yes. Giles will be on a red motorbike. I will detect it is him. I will recognise the werewolf's scent. What happens after that?'

'You will find out when it happens. Things may have to be fluid on the day. Get a good night's sleep. We will see you again sometime.'

'Thank you,' I replied.

I picked up the burger and chomped through it, keen to get back to my room and put my affairs in order. Freedom was in sight.

I wanted to write a goodbye letter to Scarlett but couldn't work out how to get it to her after my escape. I could just leave it in my room, as they would search it if I got away. But I didn't want anyone finding it beforehand. My room was checked every time I was out; things were never quite in the same place upon my return and a fresh scent was in the room. I would have to go without leaving her a message. It would be horribly cruel to her, but I had little choice.

I picked my most practical clothes to go on the run in. A pair of jeans, boots, t-shirt, a hooded top and a leather jacket. I played over the likely scenarios I would encounter tomorrow. I would have to act quickly when it happened. And I would probably have to fight to escape. My guards would get hurt, and I would have to take care of the ankle tag as it would track my every movement.

The next day came around and I tried to hide my excitement. I woke early but lay in bed, pretending to be asleep as not to arouse suspicions. I ate a big breakfast in case I didn't get a chance later. I showered, changed and waited for the guards and Scarlett to collect me.

They turned up on time and checked I was wearing the talisman. However, I had the counter to the talisman tucked into the seam of my jacket. They went over the rules again and escorted me to the car.

I psychically listened out for any instruction but heard nothing. During the day, I knew I might not hear from them. I could only communicate psychically with a human if I made contact to hear their thoughts and send mine. I had to hope whoever was watching out for me would pick up the car and follow.

In the back of the car, I looked out for any vehicles following, but I couldn't swivel around enough without alerting the guards. I just sat back and waited to arrive.

We parked by the library and canal in a small town. A cafe sat on the edge of the car park and canal, with metal tables along the grassy verge set back from the canal side. Waitresses carried out plates of food to those enjoying the canal side view while a gaggle of swans picked at the bread scattered on the side.

We walked from the car, across a road into a pedestrianised area of town, and into a small market square hemmed in with cafes, restaurants and shops. As we entered the area, I heard a rev of a motorbike engine. I turned back and saw a black motorbike and a grey helmet. Not my ride.

We looked around the shops for a while and then went for our customary coffee and cake. I spent the whole time listening for messages and looking for someone I knew. Unfortunately, it would have to be from a Dragan and the light of the day made that difficult to get a message. Plus, their faces were known to MI5-S and they would be on the lookout. I would have to be patient. I played along, eager for the time to come while trying to enjoy my last few moments with Scarlett. With our coffee and cake finished and shopping done, we walked back to the car.

I carried Scarlett's two bags of shopping across the pedestrianised square. We were heading back to prison. Another opportunity to escape lost. Then a rev of a motorbike engine rumbled ahead. The red bike parked up on the side of the road. The rider wearing a red helmet, holding another red helmet in his hands. I focused my thoughts and senses.

'Giles?'

'Yes. Hurry up. Time to go.'

I stopped in my tracks. "Here, can you hold these bags for a moment?"

Scarlett took them and I leaned down, held her waist and neck, and kissed her. She relaxed and returned the kiss. I let go. "Don't take this personally. This isn't about you. I need to know the truth."

I spun around and sprinted to Giles.

"Jon," Scarlett screamed.

"Stop. Halt," the guards shouted and chased. They didn't stand a chance. I fired off my magic and blitzed across the pavement. Giles threw the motorbike helmet and placed the bike into gear. I pulled the helmet on and jumped onto the back of the bike. The bike spun away into traffic as the guards sprinted after us. I stuck my middle finger up as we sped away. A guard had a phone to his ear. We wouldn't have long before the area was crawling with police and agents.

The bike weaved through the traffic, left at a roundabout, slipped through a red light to turn left onto a two-lane road, then right again through another red light, cutting through the gaps in the oncoming traffic.

Car horns blared and lights flashed as we dissected the traffic. I held on to the bars on the back of the bike as we tilted around the corner, then turned again and again through a maze of streets. We cut past three car dealers, a van hire shop, and then at a dead end, a high roofed van had its back doors opened up and a ramp laid out.

A figure stood by the ramp, Max. Giles whizzed down the road, up the ramp into the back of the van. The double van doors slammed behind us. Giles slammed on the brakes, tilting us upright and then stopped the engine. We got off and removed our helmets.

I grinned at Giles. "Mate, you rescued me again. I have lost count."

"No worries. We don't have much time. Strip. Your clothes are probably bugged. The van lining will block the signal, but they would have traced us to this point."

I kicked off my boots and pulled off my jacket. I broke off the psychic blocking talisman. Giles grabbed a bag from the corner of the van and laid out new clothes on top of the bike.

I stripped and showed Giles the ankle tag.

"You need to get rid of that," he said.

"My pleasure," I said. I cut through the bond with a claw and put on the new clothes. Giles shoved my old clothes and broken tag into the empty bag and put it on his back.

"Stay in the back of the van. I am going to lead your friends on a merry chase. See you soon." He thumped the side of the van and the back doors opened again. He rolled the bike down the ramp, and then ignited the engine, swung the bike around, and rode down the road.

Max and I pulled the ramp back into the van. "Sit tight in the back of the van, out of sight. We are going for a long drive," he said. I jumped in and he slammed the doors and locked it.

The van pulled away and I held onto the sides. I bumped about on the hard cold floor of the van as it manoeuvred around the roads. The ramp in the back slid about and I had to fend it off with my feet. None of it mattered. A few moments of discomfort were a small price to pay.

I resigned myself to a long, uncomfortable journey and let my body ride along with the van's movement. After a while, we hit a long straight road and the noise underneath rose up. I guessed we had hit the motorway.

After what seemed like hours, the van left the motorway, slowed down, continually twisted, turned, and eventually stopped. I wanted to be sick; my coffee and cake were returning. The back doors flung opened, and I scrambled out the back into the glaring sunshine.

"You're looking a little green," Max said.

"Do you have any water?"

"I don't, but Amber might have some in your pack."

"Amber?"

A car door slammed shut, and I stepped around the side of the van, which was parked down a deserted, small country lane. In front of the van was a grey hatchback car. Amber walked towards us dressed in black tracksuit bottoms and a white crop top. She pushed her sunglasses on top of her blonde hair, holding it out of her face.

"Amber!"

"Yes. Surprise!"

"Amber. I need to tell you something," I said and walked over, my hands held together. "I am sorry about what happened. I should have never used my powers that way."

She tried to force a smile, but it turned into a grimace. "I see Max has been talking to you. I forgive you. Just learn from your mistakes."

"Of course," I replied, and she passed over the car keys.

"The car has a phone on top of the dashboard with directions to an apartment in Leeds. Giles will meet you there in a couple of days. In the boot, there are some clothes for you both, and cash, and a small amount of food and drink."

"Thank you."

"Just look after Giles. Don't let him do anything stupid. This way you can repay me."

"Yes. Of course."

"Take care, Jon. I hope to see you soon," Amber said, and got in the passenger side of the van and flicked down her sunglasses.

"What happens next?" I asked Max.

"Giles has something he wants you both to do in Leeds. Then we will arrange transport to get you back with Thorn. I would love to hear why they kidnapped you, but we need to get this van away from you in case they tracked it. So we should both go. Another time."

"Thanks, Max. Another time."

Max jumped into the van and drove off. I waved goodbye, then grabbed the bag out of the back of the car and found a bottle of coke. I opened it up and slugged it down to wash away the sickness in my stomach.

I got in the car and turned on the phone. It had route directions set to Leeds. I knew what he had planned in Leeds. I clicked cancel and typed in my old address in London. First, I needed supplies.

Chapter Twenty-Three

I waited for Giles in Leeds for two days. He had taken time to throw MI5-S off my trail, and then took precautions he wasn't being followed. I had taken a detour via London to pick something up hidden away in my old house.

I had to stake out my old house and wait for the opportunity to break in through the back door. A woman left the house and I couldn't detect anyone else inside. I went into the back garden looking for the fake rock, which held a spare key. I found it and the key was still inside. It slotted into the backdoor and I twisted it around. The locks hadn't been changed. I wouldn't have to break anything to get inside.

I went up stairs. My old bedroom, which was now painted pink, and had bunk beds against the wall and two high cupboards opposite. I pulled a cupboard across the floor, rolled up the carpet and prised off the floorboard. I reached in, picked up a big glasses case and checked its contents. All good. I stuck it into my coat pocket.

I put the floorboard, carpet, and cupboard back. I exited out the back, locked the door and replaced the key in the fake rock. Then I jumped straight in the car and drove up to the apartment in Leeds.

While waiting for Giles, I wanted to go out into the city centre and enjoy my newfound freedom. But MI5-S would be watching, so I had to lie low until he arrived. I watched TV in the living room of the two-bedroom apartment. I assumed this was one of Thorn's network of safe houses. Considering how much MI5-S knew about her, I was unconvinced this place was still safe.

The door unlocked, and I detected Giles' thoughts and werewolf's scent as he entered. He was alone.

"What took you so long?" I shouted out.

"Ha, ha. I had to take a long route as it took a while to shake off those MI5-S agents."

He walked into the living room and handed over a bag of chips. "I hope you haven't eaten yet."

"No. These are great, cheers," I said and grabbed the hot bag and got stuck in.

Giles dumped his rucksack on the floor and jumped into the armchair next to me. I grabbed us two beers from the fridge.

I ate my chips for a minute and watched the TV.

"You got here all okay then? I assume you know why we have come to

Leeds?" he asked.

"Yes. Got here fine. I guess we are going to wrap up some loose ends."

"I have already been to see the O'Keefe family while you were locked up. We are here to visit Mr May."

"What did you do to them?" I asked, hoping it wasn't too horrific.

"Don't worry. I just scared them a little. Warned them not to mess with our families. I understand they have been steering clear of their old lives anyway, but it didn't hurt to remind them. Made me feel better anyway."

"Mr May?"

"We talked about confronting him about his lack of care. I suggest we head down to the school tomorrow evening and catch him as he leaves."

"Okay. We just talk and find out why he never helped."

"Of course."

I slugged the beer and broke off a piece of battered fish. "Then what?"

"Then you go back to Thorn and work out your next moves. Why did they kidnap you? What did they do to you in there?"

"It is a long story. But basically, they didn't want me to become a full Dragan. They feared I could cure the Dragan infertility issues. They don't want an expanding race of Dragans in case it sparks another civil war and more Turned."

"I can see their point, I suppose. I don't think any of us want to go through that again. Did they treat you well?"

"I was fine. No experiments or tortures. Just a lack of freedom."

"That was Scarlett on the battlefield? So, are you two back together?"

"We aren't back together. However, I did enjoy her company."

"Really!"

"Not like that. Just as friends," I said. I had to limit the truth about MI5-S's theory about Thorn being South. I didn't want to set everyone against each other.

"Okay. So you are looking for revenge on MI5-S?"

I shook my head. "Too difficult. They were wrong to imprison me, but they treated me well. I just want to get back to Thorn. What happened after the battle? I am a little fuzzy on the details," I asked.

"I didn't see all of it. By the time I came back, agents had formed a shield wall. You lay in the middle, with Mary, Scarlett and Ruby by your side. Thorn was shaping up for an attack, but Rip and Cassius held her back. This isn't word for word."

#

'As you lay at Mary's feet, she spoke to them. "Thorn. I will give you a deal. We take Jon and offer him the choice of a human or vampire life. Once he has had a chance to live normally, he can make his own choices to return to you. In the meantime, we let the Dragans go in peace and for you to reign as the Queen. We can work together to control the rising supernatural forces," Mary said.

"He has already made a choice. I don't need your permission to be the Dragan Queen. Now let him go, or I will kill you all."

"No. Don't threaten us. We vastly outnumber you. If you get too close, I will be forced to kill him."

"You wouldn't. He is your friend."

"True. But you can't beat us. We have the numbers. I promise to look after him. As you said, I am his friend."

The other two werewolves went over to Mary's side. MI5-S had the shield wall and a large number of infantry, the tranq unit and the new Hunters, including Ruby, Smash, Bradders and Dunk.

Mary waved her hand in the air and two of the tranq unit removed their helmets and unbuttoned their jackets. Under their jackets, they wore a vest with holders that contained vials of multicoloured liquids. They were both women, a white-haired one and a brunette. The women muttered some words and then removed a vial each and stepped outside the shield wall. They threw the vials at Thorn. Rip stepped out and cut them in half, smashing liquid everywhere, and a strange smoke arose around the Dragans, who coughed on it. "Those spells will cloud the use of magic. You will find your connection to your power source temporarily blocked off."

Thorn coughed. "You had this weapon and held it back?"

"It wouldn't have helped against the Turned, as they don't channel magic. Thorn, just walk away. Save us all from more bloodshed."

Rip pulled Thorn back. "We have plenty of time. They will age. We will not. We will find a way to combat them and rescue him. You have to trust V to return to us."

She shook her arm free of Rip. "I don't care about the numbers and strategic advantages. I don't leave without him."

"Really, after all we have been through together. You want this to all go south," Mary said.'

#

"I don't know what changed Thorn's mind, but she stopped and agreed to walk away," Giles said.

"Mary said, 'you want this to all go south'?" I asked.

"Yes. You know the saying. To go south, as in it to all go wrong."

I kept quiet, as it could have meant 'You want this all to go, South'. Mary may have been talking directly to Thorn's alter ego, threatening to expose the truth to everyone listening. It was the first outside piece of evidence that Thorn might be South. Or it could have just been a saying and Thorn changed her mind.

"They never told me about the witches. I did encounter them when I woke in the lab. They created a psychic barrier around me and the talismans."

"Yes. We know about that. It is probably best to tell you what we did afterwards."

I nodded along and fetched us two more beers for the story.

"The helicopter took you away with Mary and Scarlett and those two witches. Mary arranged for our stuff to be moved out of the base and put into a couple of static caravans in a park. We stopped there for a night and day while Thorn arranged for us to move."

"After that, Thorn and Cassius left. I am not sure why, but there was something else going on. Rip and the Twins stayed to investigate your disappearance. Max and I went back to America."

"Thorn left?"

"Yeah. I know. She freaked out after they kidnapped you. Something wasn't right. Anyway, the Twins investigated and found four likely places where you could be imprisoned. It appears MI5-S had set up decoys. Four bases, each with magical protection around them. Each with an individual detained. Each with a red-haired woman as his jailer. The guys were at a loss for what to do. They had to break the magical barriers, so Rip went off to find out more about magic. The Twins used their powers to learn about the bases.

"They had already ruled out two of the likely places when they received the text message about your whereabouts. Thorn's friend sent in several homeless people to the surrounding towns to spot you. In the meantime, Rip had developed his own spells to reverse the effects of the barriers they had in place."

"He has worked out how to channel his magic to outside his body?" I asked.

"Kind of. He uses blood magic, using his own blood to infuse the symbols and potions from the magic in his blood. He passed these to the homeless agents to give to you. After that, the Twins could pinpoint you, and Max and I returned to spring your release."

"Well, it is good to know I wasn't forgotten about. But Thorn didn't take part in the investigation or planning?"

"I think she was in contact with Rip and the Twins. But she hasn't come out of hiding."

"Weird," I said, but again it seemed to support the idea that Thorn was South. My kidnap and the veiled message by Mary had her spooked.

"Anyway, once we are done with Mr May, we will get you to Thorn. You can ask her yourself what is going on."

We drank through the night and slept it off the next day. In the evening, we drove to the school and parked up like all the other parents along the roadside. A gang of young adults sauntered down the road and hung back from the gates. I recognised them from O'Keefe's old gang. Probably someone else had taken charge.

A man walked out of the school, unlocked the big double metal gates, and clicked them back. A few minutes later, a bell rang inside, and the front double doors of the school burst open and kids poured out.

They streamed out in groups and jumped into waiting cars. Others cycled and walked home. Some students went to the gang and exchanged money and goods.

One kid pointed back to the front gate as two young boys walked out together. I knew what was coming. The two boys walked through the gates and the gang encircled them, blocking their exit. The boys tried to force through but were pushed back. I knew the intent of the gang. Any moment, the boys were going to be punched. It was like watching my own school life on repeat. I had an awful sense of déjà vu.

"I see somethings never change," Giles said, watching the boys.

"Yeah. No one coming to help. No teachers or parents are intervening. Everyone just watching."

"Including us."

"Yeah. But we can't get involved. We have to be careful."

"I am sure that is what the parents and the teachers say to themselves as well."

"It is different."

"You are right. It is different. We can help. Come on. Imagine if that was us."

We stared at the gang jostling the boys and watched the parents and teachers viewing from afar. I didn't have to imagine it was us. I already had that feeling from the moment the gang circled them. Could I really just watch?

I slammed the car door shut and jogged across the road. Giles caught up and we strode over. The noise and our determined march caught their eye.

"Let the boys go, lads," I said.

"Get lost, muppet. This is our patch. Go now before I cut you up," the oldest gang member said. He pulled back the flap of his coat to show a long blade in a sheath.

"It isn't any longer. I am taking over. Now leave."

The gang leader walked up to me and stared up. "Listen to me…."

I whipped my head down and cracked it into his nose. He dropped to the ground, clutching his nose, blood streaming between his fingers.

"You don't know who you are messing with. We will come for you with the rest of the gang. We will get our brothers and dads," he said through his fingers as blood streamed out, coating his hand.

I laughed. "Go ahead. Get as many people as you want. Meet you at the old waste ground at 8 pm tonight. Now run along before I break more bones."

The gang grabbed their leader off the floor and walked away, looking back to throw meaningless insults. The two potential victims had already run away in the chaos. For a moment, everyone looked around. I even heard a few people cheering and clapping.

"Did you enjoy that?" Giles asked.

I grinned. "Sorry, I kept all the fun to myself. You can join in tonight."

"We are supposed to be keeping a low profile. But why the hell not. What is the point of having powers if we can't even save a couple of boys from a gang of bullies? We will be gone tomorrow, anyway."

We returned to the car and waited until the kids had gone and the first of the teachers left. We headed into the car park and met Mr May as he walked out, carrying his briefcase and wearing his patched-up jacket. He saw us, pushed back his swept-over hair, and hurried along to his car. We converged on either side as he opened the car door and got in. Giles got into the front passenger seat and I sat in the back.

"Get out of my car. Who the hell are you?"

This was Giles's show. I let him take the lead.

"Who are we? Come on, Mr May, you were our teacher. Can you not remember us? Due to your lack of care, I was bullied to the point of suicide. My friend had to leave the city and move to London."

He stared at Giles while still clutching his briefcase. "Giles? Jon?"

Giles and I nodded.

"I didn't recognise you. You have grown," he said and looked in the rearview mirror at me and swallowed hard. "Aren't the police looking for you?"

"Yes."

"They said you killed some of the O'Keefes and others in London."

"Yes. I did."

The colour in his face evaporated, and he grabbed at the door handle. I reached over and slammed the door shut again.

"We just want to talk," Giles said.

"I don't have any money."

"We don't want money. We want to know why you never helped us. Why you let the gangs get away with bullying us?"

He let go of his briefcase and cleaned his glasses on a handkerchief. "Do you think I had any choice in the matter? If I could have protected you, I would have. I attended this school. The fathers of these gang members bullied me when at school together. I have my own kid's safety to think of?"

"Your kids go to this school?"

"No. I save every penny to send them to a private school. Couldn't bear to see them here. But these gangs would target my family if I got in the way. Just as they did to the art teacher."

"Just like they did to us?" Giles said.

"I'm sorry, boys. I wish I could do something. I have reported it to the headmaster, who reported it to the police. They came for a while but soon lost interest. Those that do grass get hurt. Everyone in the school knows what happened to Giles. The fact his mum was put into prison instead of the O'Keefe's. It just proved they were untouchable."

"What about my vengeance on them?" I asked.

"Just one family. There are others. People didn't believe it, anyway. They put it down to rival gangs taking over, which they did."

I looked at Giles in disbelief. I couldn't take revenge on Mr May, as he was just another victim. Giles shook his head. "So you can't do anything either."

"All I can do is report it, which I do. The system is broken. No one cares. The headmaster doesn't want the adverse publicity affecting student numbers and budgets. The school would drop in the league tables. Fewer children will want to join, which will mean less budget. In turn, that will limit his chances of getting a better job elsewhere. According to our marketing, this school doesn't have a bullying problem."

"What is the answer?" I asked.

"Get someone to care. The police or the governors or somehow stop the gangs. The gangs use the school as a marketplace, selling drugs and alcohol to the kids. And getting their younger brothers and sisters to steal off the other students."

"We will do our part, Mr May. But you need to stay strong and let us know if help is required," Giles said.

"What can you two do?"

"The same as I did to the O'Keefes. We have a date tonight, 8pm at the old waste ground. Let's see how things work out," I said and got out. That wasn't how I expected the conversation to go. I thought he would deny it all. Not to admit there was an issue. Not actually to care.

Giles and I walked out of the school gates, taking one last look at our old school. The grey concrete building loomed over the courtyard and the red paint had peeled off the gates.

I entered hell each day when I passed through those red gates. Memories of my school life were still an inspiration for vengeance. No matter how many people I had brought to justice. There would always be someone else getting hurt and someone getting away with it. I would redress that balance whenever possible. But for my own justice, who would I do that with, Scarlett or Thorn? Someone was lying.

Chapter Twenty-Four

I woke, stretched out in bed and checked the alarm clock. It was nearly lunchtime. I could hear Giles moving around, so I got up and pulled on my clothes from yesterday. I went into the kitchen and found Giles preparing some breakfast.

"Morning, sleepy. I went out and got some supplies and contacted our travel agents. Do you want to put the local news on the TV and make us some coffee?"

"Cheers. You know how to cook?" I asked as Giles fired up the gas hob.

"Of course, I work in a restaurant. I will do us a Max special."

I flicked on the TV and found a news channel. I put the kettle on and grabbed some cups.

"What did our travel agents say?" I asked.

"I have you on a private charter plane from a local airport. They are delivering some electrical components. They are flying over Thorn's chateau in the South of France. You can leave the plane there."

"They aren't stopping?"

"No. They can't stop as no airstrip, plus technically you aren't on the manifest. We got you a parachute. Is that okay?"

"Well, I guess it has to be. I am sure I will manage."

"Good. I have a flight from Manchester airport back to America."

"Will they not be looking for you?"

"Maybe, but you will have already left the country. I haven't technically broken any laws."

"Helped a prisoner to escape."

"An illegally held prisoner. Were you charged with any crimes?"

"No. I suppose not. I guess it would make it difficult to hold you."

"The last thing they would want is to draw attention to themselves. They may bring me in for questioning but unlikely to hold me for long. If I don't arrive back in America, Max and Amber will start a social media campaign against my unlawful arrest."

"I am sure MI5 have worked it out and will let you go peacefully."

"I hope so. Pour that coffee out and get some cutlery. I am just dishing up."

We carried the food into the TV room and sat at the small table by the sofas. The hot breakfast filled my complaining stomach, and I felt extra hungry after last night's activities. The news switched from national to regional on the TV. A woman behind a desk stared into the camera and smiled as the title music faded out.

"Emergency services were called to the Meanwood estate last night after gang rivalry boiled over into a mass brawl. There were believed to be up to thirty people involved in the fight. The ambulances took away fifteen casualties to the hospital and treated five walking wounded. Others had already fled the scene. The police said the brawl was a power struggle within a notorious gang. No other suspects are being sought. However, a contradictory YouTube video was posted late last night. After the police statement."

The screen changed to show a gang of thirty men surrounding us. The camera was hidden in a pin badge on my jacket.

"I don't understand how you get away with selling drugs and stealing from the school. I am telling you to stop. Where are the police? Why doesn't the Headmaster do anything?" I asked.

"I will tell you before I beat the *beep* out of you," said a tall thug with a shaven head and tear tattoos on his cheeks. "The Headmaster keeps it quiet. He doesn't want the bad press. His school is the model of excellence, with no bullying or drug issues. He wants to move on to another school. No one would employ the headmaster of a failed school. It suits the police as well to have lower crime figures. They all cover it up to protect their careers."

The thug swung a punch and the video showed a fist flying back. The video stopped.

The screen cut back to the TV presenter. "The rest of the video shows it wasn't a gang fight, as stated. It appears to be the work of two vigilantes against the gang of thirty. No one knows the identity of the two who beat the gang. The police and the school have refused to comment on the accusations and the reason for the cover-up."

Giles held up his coffee cup. "A toast to a job well done."

I grabbed my cup and we clinked them together. "To justice."

"You were right. They didn't want to admit to it being just us two against the thirty, but that video will cause chaos. Maybe it will bring about a change."

"Hopefully, Mr May will come forward now."

We finished our breakfast, cleaned away, and packed our bags. Giles drove us to a supermarket car park and pulled up beside a black BMW.

"This is our guy, the pilot. Pick your bag out of the boot and pass over this envelope of money to the driver. He should have an identity card showing you are his co-pilot, and he should have a passport for you. The people at the airport have been taken care of as well. We can easily get you out of the country and into French airspace," Giles said.

"So this is it?"

"Yeah, for now. Come and visit us at the restaurant. Bring Thorn with you."

"Of course, once everything has settled, I will be in touch. Thanks again for the rescue," I said. We shook hands and said goodbye.

I retrieved my bag from the boot and got into the black car next to the driver. I swapped the money for the identity papers and listened to the plan. We went to the airport and were waved through minimal security. I detected an acknowledging nod between the pilot and the passport controller.

I tried to talk with the pilot on the flight over, but he preferred not to talk. He didn't want to get involved, so I thought about what I would say when I finally confronted Thorn.

I couldn't decide what I wanted to hear. If Thorn was South, everything had been a lie. But I could go back to England and try to re-build my life. I could work for MI5-S hunting vampires and other creatures. I could train the new Hunters and make a life with Scarlett.

If Thorn wasn't South, MI5-S had lied to keep me from her, to stop the secrets in my blood from being used. I would always be on the run from MI5-S unless we could come to a deal. It would have meant that Scarlett and Mary both lied. It was a no-win situation. I would lose someone either way.

"Ten minutes until we are over the drop zone," the pilot said.

I left my co-pilot seat and went into the back of the plane. I pulled on the parachute and strapped on my altimeter.

"One minute," the pilot shouted.

I opened the door, and the wind whistled through the plane, buffeting back my body.

"Ten seconds," he shouted.

"Thanks. Take care," I shouted and dived out of the plane.

I held my body flat to slow down and get my bearings, to view the landscape from above and pick out a landmark. I spotted a cluster of lights, which were the local village, and I spun around looking for the lights of the chateau. It looked like every light was on in Thorn's house. Clearly, she was expecting me.

I angled my body around and dived towards the beacon. Once low enough, I opened up the parachute and glided over the thick wood surrounding the chateau, turning around to land on the manicured front lawn next to the long driveway through the woods. I gathered the parachute into a bundle and carried it down the gravel driveway.

The Gothic chateau looked ominous at night. Its sharply arched narrow windows, with intricate grey stonework around the frames. A wide tower overshadowed the main building to the left. In the sloped slate tiled roof, windows jutted out symmetrically to those on the first and ground floor. On top of the roof, black metal spikes stuck out along the ridges of the roof, puncturing the night sky.

I strode up to the main entrance, a big stone porch with pillars and huge double oak doors with studded metal bolts and hinges. I pushed open the big wooden doors. The unlocked doors meant she expected me. I shoved the parachute into the corner of the porch and shut the doors.

I knew where she would be waiting, as I could hear her psychic voice trying to talk to me. I blocked it out. This conversation had to be conducted face to face.

I headed into the storeroom and lifted the trapdoor down into the weapons storage. Then I climbed down the ladder and faced the huge metal safe door. I held my hand against the scanner and the lights shone up and down and went green. The thick metal door swung slowly back on hydraulics to reveal an array of weapons set in racks and shelves.

In front, a column of swords of all different types held in a rack. A red sword was locked in a separate cabinet. It reminded me of the story about fighting the devil and that she had kept the sword. Maybe it was true. Perhaps it was the Devil's sword. It was hard to work out fact from fiction with Thorn.

I grabbed a pistol from a side rack and loaded a magazine of silver bullets. I tapped my inside jacket pocket and felt the glasses box I had fetched from my old house in London. Now I could face her.

I walked back down the corridor, past the main entrance that acted as the central hub for the chateau. I walked past the grand sweeping stairway and tapped the gargoyle on the head at the base of the thick white marble handrail. Just as I had done on the night of my Union.

I paced around the curved corridor of half-height, dark oak panels and white walls flowing around to the back of the chateau. I walked past several doors and classic paintings hanging on the walls until I reached a dead end of two double wooden doors.

The doors would open to the study where we had performed the Union ritual nearly two years ago. Inside that room, I had taken a vow to create a

Union with Thorn, a type of Dragan marriage. In that ceremony, I had promised to always protect and trust her. She had promised to make me, The Dragan King. It was time to put the Union to the test.

Chapter Twenty-Five

At the door, I paused and held the pistol in my hand. I sucked in a deep breath and focused my magic internally, ready for what I would find inside. I pushed the handle and opened the door a crack. Gripping the pistol in two hands, I stepped through, scanning around the room.

Flames crackled in the fireplace. The curtains were pulled tightly shut. In the corner, a black screen had been erected to seal off part of the room. The rest of the room was as I remembered. A big wooden desk and chair to my right. To the other side, a drinks table with red wine decanted and bottles of spirits. On the wall, there were paintings of Thorn's parents. I sensed Thorn in the room, although something felt different.

"Just a moment, V. Pour yourself a glass of wine," Thorn said from behind the screen.

I raised the gun at the screen. She stepped out from behind it and jerked back from the sight of the gun.

"Ah. I saw you go to the weapons store. I didn't realise that was meant for me," she said and spun around a laptop on the study table. The CCTV showed the different rooms and entrances of the chateau. The top left screen showed inside the weapons store.

"Of course it is for you," I shouted. "I want the truth."

"No reunion hugs and kisses," she said and held her arms out and closed her eyes. I didn't move. She opened her eyes again. "I went to a lot of effort and money for our reunion. Organising your escape. I've spent days deciding on what to wear, which room to meet in. This one seemed fitting, as we sealed our Union in here. We have a lot to talk about."

She brushed down her black corset, connected to black silk and thin-netted material skirt going to above her knees. She stood up straight on her black high heels and ushered back a loose strand of raven hair. Her pale skin looked lightly tanned. She looked radiant, her beauty glowing from her body. I even saw mascara and lipstick. She never bothered with makeup, usually. She smiled and her blue eyes sparkled.

"You look as wonderful as ever. Do you have a tan?" I asked. Somehow, I couldn't help but compliment her.

"You are looking handsome as well. Now, do you mind keeping your voice down, and could you put that gun on the table as well, please? I wouldn't want it accidentally going off and bullets going astray."

"Tell me the truth."

"Of course, but just put the gun down."

I paused for a moment and kept it pointed.

"V, I will talk. You deserve the truth. But the gun wouldn't make any difference, anyway. I have had days to gather my powers. I am a full Dragan. Whereas you have been cut off from the magic for months and are no longer a full Dragan. I reckon I could make it past that gun."

I placed the gun on the table and removed the glasses case from my pocket. "Don't worry. I have plenty of rage to fuel my powers. However, I brought something to even the odds," I said, and opened the old case. I grabbed the needle and dropped the case to the floor. I held the syringe in one hand and flipped off the cover. Then I jabbed it into my neck, pushed the plunger down, and the familiar feeling of the Dragan transformation rippled through my flesh.

"Where did you get that? Are MI5-S making the formula again? They have the research details still?"

I gritted my teeth and tensed my muscles through the pain. I stayed stood up, but staggered slightly as the transformation finished.

"No. Remember when I first met you? There were two needles I took from the lab that my Dad tried to hide. I used one in the park on my first change, and I had hidden the other under the floorboards of my old bedroom. It has been waiting there, this whole time."

"Ah. Of course, very sneaky. I forgot about the second needle. So, this would make you a full Dragan again."

"Yes, as long as there was no reversing formula."

"Good. Would you like some wine to celebrate?" she said, and lifted the decanter on the drinks table and poured a glass.

"No. I want answers."

"I am going to have a drink. I think I will need it. So you have some questions. What have those people in MI5-S been telling you?"

I stared at her. She smiled calmly, looking stunning in her black dress.

"I have lots of questions, but it comes back to one question first," I said and took a deep breath.

"Best spit it out, V. The suspense is killing me," she said, and smiled and sipped her red wine.

"Surely, you know the question?"

She sipped her red wine. "There are lots of questions and many answers. But the fact you are aiming a gun means there can be only one question."

"Yes. Are you South?"

She smiled and took a big gulp of red wine and breathed out slowly. "Yes."

"Yes! No denials. You admit to being South. You are even smiling."

"Yes. Of course, I am South. It is a pleasant relief to have it out in the open. I fully planned to tell you after the war. I nearly told you the night before as it was burning me up, but I realised it wasn't the right time. MI5 stole my thunder. Do you know the meaning behind the name?"

"Yes. You are far too obvious; everyone has gotten used to it. South is opposite to North, and North is an anagram of Thorn."

"Oh. I chose that name a long time ago. I know better now."

"Why? Why did you do this to me?" I shouted. I pulled off my golden Dragon Union ring and threw it at her. She caught it and stuffed it into her corset bra.

"Shh, V. Please don't shout. Use your indoor voice. It won't make any difference shouting. I will look after your Union ring until you reclaim it. I promise not to make you beg for it when you return."

"I am never returning to you. The Union is over."

"We shall see. I can wait for a very long time."

"Why did you ruin my life?" I said, lowering my voice.

"Ruined. I have given you what most men fantasise about. You have superpowers, money and a gorgeous woman to enjoy it with. If I hadn't come along, you would still be holed up in your bedroom scared of your own shadow," she said, her voice rising and a slight red tear prickling her eye.

"I could have been with Scarlett."

She glared and took a big gulp of wine. "No. You only met her because you had to move to London. You would have never moved otherwise. Is this about Scarlett?" she said, her voice straining not to shout.

"I would have had a normal life. I would have gone to University and met other people," I said.

"You may have had a boring life. But with me, you have matured and become a strong person. I have not ruined your life; I have saved it. It is called post-traumatic growth."

"My Dad was murdered," I said, tears catching on the edges of my eyes.

"That is regrettable, but it wasn't my idea. I guess they have garnished you with a theory of why and what I did. I will tell you the truth. Now, tell me what they said."

"No. You tell me your story and I will decide how it compares."

"Where to begin? The civil war is all true. I have told you no lies on that part, and I am sure the stories of the other Dragans will back that up."

"Yes. MI5-S agree on this part. So none of the other Dragans knows?"

"Cassius is the only one. I will have to tell the Twins and Rip. Best they hear it from me first," she said, mopping away a red tear line on her face.

"Stop faking it. No amount of tears will drown the pain."

Her face reddened. "This isn't fake. These tears are for us."

I waited a moment, watching her muscles tense and tears build up, enjoying the sight of her in pain. She glared back, boring her eyes into mine. "So, after the civil war?" I said, breaking the deadlock.

"As you know, the Turned did what they do best and turned against us. I couldn't cull their numbers quickly enough. The Original had set up his own kingdom and our own troops were leaving to join him. An uncontrolled Turned army spelt disaster for everyone. They would bring attention to themselves and then to the Dragans. I had to control them, so I sent in my loyal commander. Bramel and I worked together to control the Turned. We set up number limits and used them for hunting down our enemies."

"Why did the Twins and Cyrus survive then?"

"No matter what had happened between the Twins and me, I didn't want them dead. If I killed Cyrus, they would have sought revenge and I would never have convinced them that Cyrus was a monster. So Bramel and I worked together for years, building our empires, gathering wealth and power. Then things changed."

"Genetic engineering."

"Yes. Not just genetic engineering but technology as a whole. The Hunters used technology to hunt us down more efficiently. They created new weapons to kill us and used our digital footprints to find us. They had become a credible threat, and no longer had to stick to controlling the numbers as per the original agreement.

"Genetic engineering had shown promise in unlocking the secrets of the Dragans and Vampires. I knew the stability that Bramel and I had created wouldn't last forever. These two catalysts prompted voices in the Turned to find a new way forward. The end game was upon us. Time to embrace the change. The three-way stalemate between the Dragans, Hunters, and Turned was breaking down.

"So, I let them capture me for their experiments and spent forever in that cell without useful results. Then we heard of a scientist that had amazing results in copying werewolf genetics. I just had to get him to move from Leeds to London and start a new project."

"My Dad wouldn't come."

"Yes. You know the rest of how we convinced him to leave and start a new life in London. We put you in danger, so he had no choice."

"I always thought it was the Hunters that organised the bullying and attacks on Giles and me. But it was you."

"Not true. It was the Hunters. I told Bramel to do whatever he needed to get your father to move cities. I never said to set up the bullying or attacks as a way of encouragement. I didn't micromanage their every move."

"The outcome was the same, even if you didn't organise the actual events personally."

"Let's carry on. I see we won't agree on who ordered it. You came to London and your father's research was brilliant. Same again, you know what happens next. He had encoded the formula to his DNA, and you became the perfect guinea pig. Bramel and Gabriel organised the events around your attacks by Barry's gang and the planting of the vampire formula in the research lab. I just had to encourage you to take it. Again, I didn't order your mugging or bullying."

"You didn't stop it either. You can't blame others for your actions," I said and wiped away the tears.

"Anyway. You took the formula, rescued me from the research centre, and we went on the run. What else do you need to know?"

"What else! My dad's death. My tortures. Giles' being recruited as a werewolf. My possible vivisection at the hands of the Hunters. The final battle."

"Okay. So let me clear this all up. Bramel and I worked together. I told him what to do, but I didn't control every action he took. Sometimes people in the Hunter/Turned alliance did things without his permission. We never had control over the Hunters. Sometimes he had no choice but to let them carry on as expected, else it would have called his leadership into question. I didn't order your dad's murder. You broke into a Hunter's base and stole the files, and they chased you down and killed your father in the fight. It was the Hunters that killed your father. Neither Bramel nor I could have stopped it. They reacted as expected. I tried to get there and save you all, but I was too late."

"It is still your fault. Without you meddling in our lives, he would still be alive," I said.

"I am deeply sorry for the death of your father. But I never asked him to research werewolves and steal files from a secret organisation. Unfortunately, the same is true of the tortures and experiments they performed on you. I never ordered them. But the Hunter organisation expected revenge and furthering of the research and carried on without orders. Bramel couldn't stop them without it being suspicious."

"My Dad still died because of you, and I was still tortured," I said, letting my voice rise again.

"If you stayed with me in America and had not run away and got your dad involved in breaking into a military research centre, your dad would still be alive. You wouldn't have been tortured. It isn't my fault. I tried to protect you. If only you had done as I asked, then nothing would have gone wrong."

"They were your people that killed him and hurt me."

"No. They weren't. The person who killed your father and tortured you was a human and worked for the Hunters. I was never in charge of the Hunters, only the Turned. If you want answers on their sadistic techniques and murderous actions, you would be better off speaking with Mary and MI5-S."

"What do you mean? The Hunters were MI5-S?"

"Yes. They were connected to MI5-S. I thought you knew that, but they lost control of them. This is why they were so keen on stopping them. It was a rogue unit. Where do you think they gained their training, money and techniques from? The Hunter organisations have existed for many years since the peace treaty. They have since been absorbed into every government agency worldwide. Funded, trained and controlled by them, for their own means. The CIA has their own Hunter org as well. Why do you think MI5-S were monitoring them? It is because they are part of their organisation."

I growled and clenched my fists. Mary and MI5-S hadn't been entirely truthful. They hadn't owned up to their mistakes, and I would confront them later. But for now, I still had questions for Thorn. "So you never asked for them to film the fight against the Hunters when they held me prisoner? Bramel never sent this to you?"

"Bramel told me what the Hunters had planned. The Hunters wanted revenge. He promised you would survive. I asked to know what happened. Bramel, being the jealous type, filmed it and sent me a copy to show him defeating you. I wasn't aware of the tortures. Bramel never told me. I only found out afterwards. He let Carmella use you as her plaything. I think he hoped it would take you away from me and give Carmella a distraction."

She took another sip of wine.

"Carry on. Giles and Norris. The final battles," I said.

"They decided a werewolf would be a good way of controlling the Dragan threat. I got Bramel to issue the command that only Giles could fight you. Bramel had become less compliant with my orders towards the end. I am sure he ordered the vivisection. He knew I would have never allowed it. He had become extremely jealous and wanted you dead. After that, Bramel started acting alone, without my approval."

"When did that start?"

"When at the lodge in the Spanish mountains, I contacted Bramel to say we were on our way. I told him to leave and take most of the forces but leave the first-gen Turned lightly guarded. He agreed but sent the army after us instead. He now followed his own path. I tried to contact him afterwards, but I got no response."

"He went rogue and acted alone."

"After that, I had no control. He organised the escape of Cyrus. I suspect he sent us the info to kill the Original to destroy his only possible rival within the Turned organisation. He pushed forward with the plans for the final battle and the takeover of London. All of which he kept a secret."

"But he pleaded for mercy at the end."

"Of course he did. He had betrayed me. He tried to kill us all."

"So that is the entire story. This is your defence. You never ordered these things to happen to me. Others made those decisions and in the end, they stopped following your orders. They actually became the organisation we were fighting against rather than a proxy army. I am supposed to believe it and we can be together again."

"Yes. But you think MI5-S are any better? They kept secrets from you as well. They used you. Mary was put in place to watch your father through you. They faked Scarlett's death. And how long have they known I was South? They let the game play out. They could have prevented your father's death and prevented the tortures. The Hunters worked for them. It was the Hunters that killed your father, tortured you and arranged the attacks. They are not innocent. They have caused you more harm than I ever did."

"You have no proof they just watched it all happen."

"I suspect it is only because of MI5-S needing us we are all still alive. Once magic returned to the world, we became a useful asset. Without magic, I think they would have killed us after the final battle."

I replayed my conversations with Mary after my kidnapping. She had admitted as much. They let the events play out. She was clearly in the area when we stole the files from the Hunter's base, as she was on hand to rescue Scarlett. Maybe they could have saved my father and prevented my tortures.

However, I wasn't giving Thorn the satisfaction of my doubts. "Have you finished?"

"While we are being honest, I should tell you everything."

"There is more?"

"Think about everything I have said. You want to believe I am evil because of a few lies, but this is not true. What if I hadn't sent Bramel to control the Turned? What if I hadn't put these secret plans into action to eliminate the threat of the Turned and kill Cyrus?"

"What if? Explain."

"I stopped Cyrus in the first war. Can you imagine his reign over the Dragans? How long before his gaze turned to the human kingdoms? The Original confirmed Cyrus always intended to rule over humans as well. With Cyrus defeated, I couldn't stop the Turned, but I could control and limit their numbers, stopping them from growing too big and following a similar route. Without me controlling the Turned through Bramel, the vampires would have killed millions. They would have ruled the world."

"Maybe, but it doesn't excuse your betrayal."

She shook her head. "When we met, The Original, you understood. You said we should have thanked Bramel for stopping the Turned from their plans for world domination. But it was me that brokered the peace deal between the humans and the Turned. The humans agreed as I proved to them we could keep the numbers under control by working together. I had introduced myself at that meeting as South and explained that Bramel and I would control the Turned between us. That it wasn't in our interests to draw attention to ourselves.

"I can only assume this is how the rumour of South started. Back then, the humans wouldn't have stood a chance against a vampire army. I have saved millions of people. Without me, you might not have even been born. You should all be thanking me for saving the world, not condemning me. I made hard decisions, but I have no regrets. I did what needed to be done."

I remembered the conversation with The Original about Bramel insisting on peace. I had said without that decision, the world would be a different place. We could have been slaves or just blood bags. But Thorn had saved us. I stared at her in silence. But I couldn't show any change of heart. She had ruined my life.

"You can't be certain. Humans could have won a war. Maybe you just prolonged the Turned instead," I said.

"Really. You have seen the Turned in action and you have met Cyrus.

What do you think would have happened without my intervention? I stopped them the first time around. And this time, I have eliminated the threat once and for all. Cyrus is dead, and the Turned are broken."

I wouldn't be swayed, no matter the strength of the argument. Every pain I had suffered since meeting her flashed before my eyes. I couldn't let her get away with it. I certainly would not thank her. "You are trying to justify your betrayal. Do you have anything else to say before you die?"

"You think hundreds of years ago I set out to betray you? I never knew we would meet and how it would end. I do love you. Remember what I said on our last night together?"

I paused for a moment to think back. "No matter what happens, I should remember that you love me."

"Correct. You said the same."

"True, but I don't think you can hold me to that."

"So, you don't love me?"

I only stared in response and waited a moment. "You knew they were going to tell me?" I said, breaking the silence.

"I suspected they were up to something. But I couldn't prove it. I knew they would turn on us, but even I didn't expect it so quickly. I thought we may have a few hours or a few days for me to explain."

"What does it matter? You lied and hurt me."

"I did what was necessary. My only regret is I may have lost your love. Yes, you may shake your head and laugh. But it is true. When I said I fell in love with you, I meant it and I want you back. However, I realise you may need time to adjust and see it from a new perspective. I promised to tell you my life story if we won against the Turned. Stay with me and I will keep that promise. All will become clear."

I shook my head and focused on my rage to build my sphere of magic. She stepped forward and reached a hand out to my arm. I brushed it away.

She stepped back and continued talking. "Remember what I have told you tonight about MI5-S' actions and how I saved all of humanity, nothing is clear cut. I regret that you have been hurt, but there was a bigger picture. The needs of the many outweigh the needs of the few. You have a big decision to make on who to trust," Thorn said, and lines of red tears stained her cheeks.

I glared at her. "Are you kidding? A big decision to make. I choose to kill you and go back to England and work in MI5-S," I shouted.

"You trust them?"

"At this moment, more than I trust you. I will return and find out the truth from within. At least I know Scarlett wasn't involved in the conspiracy. She is innocent."

Thorn wiped her eyes again and her skin reddened at the mention of Scarlett's name. She held up her hands. "Wait. Listen to everything I have to say first. You don't have all the facts."

"More lies."

"No. I have told you the truth since you arrived and I will continue so you can make your decision. When we first met, I told you I would make you like me one day and I would train you to protect yourself."

"Yes, but these were lies. You can't make Dragans, only vampires. The only protection I needed was from you."

"I've seen your school records, V. You have been bullied your whole life. Plus, I never lied about making you like me. Are you not a Dragan? With that last injection, you will remain a full Dragan unless an intervention is performed."

"It was luck the formula has been slowly changing me. A side effect of the temporary change. You could have never have known that."

"No. There has always been confusion around the formula, which I let continue to hide its true intention and true sponsor. The purpose of the formula was always to change you permanently. The side effects of the formula were the temporary change and not making you a Dragan. Each injection was tweaking your genetics and for that to happen, it granted you the Dragan powers each time. The goal was always to make a new Dragan male. It was no accident."

"Are you saying, you never lied to me then? You have kept your promise to make me the same as you."

"Yes. I had to go along with your statement that I lied. I couldn't reveal the true nature of the formula, else it would have given away my sponsorship. You would have realised I was South."

"But it has done you no good. You may have defeated the Turned, killed Bramel and Cyrus and destroyed the Hunters, but you didn't get the secrets my blood holds," I said.

She pushed her lips together. "Again, not entirely true. The issue with Dragan reproduction has been because of a limited gene pool. I have been pregnant before, but the baby never carried to full term. I believed a new male Dragan would overcome this issue."

"Maybe it would have, but that ship has sailed."

"Yes. Now I want you to stay calm," she said and placed her glass of wine down and walked back behind the black screen.

She walked out carrying a bundle of rags. Thorn looked down at the bundle, then up to me, and smiled. "V, let me introduce you to your daughter, Rose," she said and removed the cover. A baby's face peered out, her blue eyes slowly blinking awake.

I reached out to the table to steady my balance. I blinked several times and stared at the bundle. Thorn offered the baby. I tensed my muscles to get a grip on myself. I opened my arms and Thorn placed her in. "Hold the head," Thorn said.

I put her head in the crook of my arm and looked down. "Now I understand about the stray bullets and shouting."

"I had just got her to sleep."

"Rose, isn't that a bit too obvious even for you," I said and my tears stopped.

"I think it is poetic. A thorn protects its rose. It is perfect. I did think of Hope. But that depends on your point of view."

Thorn stood at my side and rubbed the cheek of her baby. "Rose, this is your daddy," she said and the red tear lines soaked into her skin, leaving it radiant.

The baby smiled, and a little hand pushed out of the swaddling and reached up.

Thorn pulled out a chair. "Take a seat. You are a little unsteady."

I sat down and rested Rose on my lap. Her hand reached out again and I met it with my finger. She gripped it and smiled.

"When did this happen?" I asked.

"The last night we spent together. I guess you were practically a full Dragan then. As I have always said, you were the key, a brand new Dragan male. Everyone was searching for genetic answers, but it just had to be someone outside the limited gene pool."

"Is this why you always wanted so much sex?" I said.

"Yes and no. I like sex and I wanted a baby. It's a win-win. I doubt if it would have made any difference to the amount. I would have wanted as much even without trying for a baby."

"But you always insisted every time I was in a transformed state."

"Yes. But again, it was a win-win. I wanted sex while you were transformed, and I knew it had a better chance of conception. It appears we had to wait for the last change for it to work. I never lied about wanting to continue my race. I said from the very beginning my goal was to reproduce the Dragans."

"True. I suppose I was looking for a scientific answer from my transformation. Something that could be derived from my blood and turned into a drug for other Dragans to use. I didn't realise you meant such an immediate solution."

"It was both. However, this solution was much more fun than test tubes. While you hold her. I can safely tell you the rest of the story without the fear of an overreaction."

"There is more?"

"I realised I was pregnant within a few days, and MI5-S had already imprisoned you. I wasn't risking our baby's life, so Cassius and I left and returned to the Chateau, where we stayed for the duration of the pregnancy. I hope you understand. I had to protect our baby."

I looked into Rose's blue eyes and tears of joy welled up in my own. "I understand."

"Good. There is more you need to hear. As you know, the formula is encoded to your DNA. The Turned and Hunters worked this out and tried to replicate the effect, but it has always failed. The subjects wouldn't take on the Dragan power, but it would just temporarily cripple them instead."

"Bramel said there was another secret. One they hadn't discovered as to why I was special."

"Professor Hickling worked it out. He compared your DNA to mine, Cassius', Rip's and the Twins. All of us share a particular gene that the test subjects didn't possess. It appears you are a descendant of a mage."

"Nothing feels like a surprise anymore after meeting this one," I said, gazing into Rose's searching, sky blue eyes.

"It appears the formula can try to alter a person's genetics, but it can't open the door to magic, which is the power source of a Dragan. However, that mage gene can open the door to magic if triggered, as it was by the formula, which uses the magic to drive the transformation. It appears you are unique."

"I am a mage?"

"Descended from a person with magic abilities, a mage or a witch. Just as the rest of the Dragans are descended from mages."

"So, are we finished? Have you told me everything?"

"No. You commented on my tan."

I looked up in surprise. "Now what? I guess it is a fake tan for some reason."

Thorn shook her head. "Rose has your genetics. She is immune to silver and sunlight."

"That is good to hear, but..."

"Somehow, due to carrying her in my womb, she has affected my blood and body. Somehow it filtered my blood or osmosis occurred between us. Anyway, it appears I have developed immunity to sunlight and silver. Not as good as yours or hers, but I can go outside in the daylight."

"You are joking? It really is a suntan?"

"It doesn't take much sunlight on my skin to tan. I can't go out at the height of a sunny day, but I can easily take in the first few or last few hours of the day. I can bring up Rose like a normal child, help her understand humans."

"Send her to school. Attend parents' evenings. Watch her at school events," I said and laughed.

"Why not?"

"She will stand out. People will ask questions."

"Dragan children don't show their powers until puberty. She will be stronger and faster than all the other kids, but I can teach her to control herself."

I shook my head and gazed back into the big blue eyes of my daughter.

"What is your plan now? Are you still going to kill me?" Thorn asked.

I looked into Rose's eyes. "I should. You are a monster. Regardless of what you say, you ruined my life."

"So you think I would make a bad mother?"

I stood up with the baby in my arms and handed her back to Thorn. "No. I think you would make a fantastic mother. No one would love a baby more. No one could protect her as well as you. I would never want Rose to grow up without her mother, not like I did."

"I knew you would understand. So, why don't you stay with us?"

"I can't. You betrayed me."

"Not for me, but for your daughter. Don't punish her. Stop in one of the spare rooms. Take some time with her and maybe, when you are ready, we can talk some more. I can tell you my entire story. I can help you understand."

I gazed at Rose squirming in her blankets. The idea put a grin across my face. But then I looked at Thorn. How could I stay with her? She had betrayed me. I feared that if I stopped, I would succumb to more of her lies. The alternatives weren't much better. MI5 would lock me away or I would have to go on the run. At least with Thorn, I had a choice. I wasn't being held against my will. Maybe there was truth in her story. I knew the world would be a different place if she hadn't of controlled the Turned. For Rose's sake, I knew the right thing to do.

Thorn's laptop beeped and she checked the screen. "Damn. They have found us."

"Who?"

She spun the laptop around and I saw figures running through the surrounding fields. "Who do you think? MI5-S. We need more time for you to understand the bigger picture. I need you to hear my life story for all this to make sense. I wasn't expecting them to find us so quickly. They have just passed the outer perimeter fence and should be here in about five minutes."

"Hide and I will tell them to leave."

"That will never work. They know I am here and will want to see me. They will want to take you back one way or another."

"I won't go with them."

"They will force you into a decision. Join them or kill them?"

"No. I won't kill them. We can talk it through. In the meantime, you best take Rose and hide."

"No. I will not hide in my own home. They obviously know I live here and will expect to see me. They will search the place from top to bottom."

"Then run."

"I will not run. I will not put my Rose in danger. This is my home. They are unwelcome."

"Okay. Let us just try talking to them. Both of us together may convince them. The odds are in our favour. They won't want bloodshed."

"And when they see Rose, what do you think they will do?"

I looked at Rose and looked back at the door. "Nothing. They will do as I tell them."

"The reason they took you was to stop the possible re-production of the Dragan race. When they see Rose, they will have only one choice. To kill her and to kill me, and possibly you."

"No. That isn't true. Why?"

"It proves I can have children with you. Rose could have children. You can have children with other Dragans. The Dragan race can reproduce and humans fear another war. They will do anything to stop it."

I clutched my head in my hands. I grabbed the gun and pointed it at the door and back to Thorn. "Give me the baby and run. I can protect her."

"No. She is my baby. She doesn't leave me."

"What are we going to do?"

"The outcome isn't set, V. It is your decision what happens next. You must choose. Either protect your daughter and kill the humans. Or side with the humans and kill your daughter. I will leave you with no other choice."

"No. I can negotiate a peace deal. Just as you did hundreds of years ago."

"That was different. The humans would have died without that deal."

"We can talk to them. Explain to them how you saved everyone by acting as South. You stopped the vampires takeover both times. They probably already know. We can agree not to reproduce the Dragan race anymore."

"You are not listening. Let me make this simple. I will not take any risks with Rose's life. I will not lose another child. When they enter this room, I will kill them to protect my daughter. You either stop me or help me. You can't live in two worlds anymore. Time to choose: Dragan or Human, Rose or Scarlett, night or day. Time is ticking."

Footsteps thumped down the hallway, and I kicked the door shut.

"This can't be happening. Thorn, stop, please. I understand what you did, why you acted as South. But I can't forgive what happened to me," I shouted.

"Thank you. But it is time to decide. You know MI5-S are responsible as well. Follow your instincts. Tick, tock, tick, tock," Thorn said, rocking Rose back and forth.

I aimed the gun at Thorn. "Run before they get here. Go out the window."

"No. You are either V or Jon. The King of the Dragans or agent of MI5-S. They are nearly here. Time is running out. Tick, tock, tick, tock. You must decide."

She wouldn't change her mind. I had no choice. Someone had to die.

I lined her up in the gun sights. She smiled, closed her eyes, and forehead frowned. I squeezed the trigger. Bang. Bang. The gun blazed and recoiled twice.

Chapter Twenty-Six

The big wooden double doors burst open. Scarlett stood at the apex of a squad of armed soldiers, pointing in machine guns. All of them kitted out in black combat gear. Scarlett held both hands on a pistol aimed at my head. I held up my hands with the gun still in hand, smoke still wafting out.

"Where is she?"

I nodded behind me and stepped to the side to show a burning pile of ash and embers in front of the empty fireplace. Scarlett walked past and stood over the mound of hot ash. She nudged it with her foot; the embers cascading down to burn the rug underneath.

"You killed her?"

"Yes. She admitted to being South. When you arrived, she was going to kill you all. I had to make a choice. I chose you."

Scarlett suppressed a grin. The soldiers searched around the room, checking behind the black screen, under the desks, and behind the curtains, checking the windows were locked.

"That wasn't part of the plan. You weren't supposed to kill her. Not that it bothers me," Scarlett said.

"Sorry, what do you mean? I wasn't supposed to kill her. That makes it sound like you knew I would come here."

Scarlett blushed. She holstered her gun and walked back to the doors. "Everyone, let's leave," she shouted. "Jon, you coming with us?"

"I have a choice?"

"Of course, and you have already made it, remember? You chose us. Not her," she said, looking back at the ash.

"Wait a minute. What the hell is going on?"

"We knew you would escape at some point. There is no way we could hold you forever. We just hoped to keep you long enough to show you the other life you could have. Show you that MI5-S could be your new family. And we knew, when you escaped, you would come for her. You said it yourself that you needed closure. Well, now you have it."

I holstered the gun into the back of my jeans and took a last look around the room and at the black screen.

"How long has MI5-S known Thorn was South?"

Scarlett shrugged, but I noticed a small flinch beforehand. "I don't know. You would have to ask Mary?" If only I could read her thoughts to confirm her initial reaction, but she wore the blocking talisman as usual. However, she knew the truth, which could only mean one thing. They have known for some time. They let these terrible things happen to me. Thorn was right. I had been used.

"Thorn said she saved humans by acting as South and limiting the Turned," I said.

"Maybe she did. It is hard to deny. But both Dragans and Turned are a threat to our existence. It would have been best for both to die. But with magic returning to the world, we need the Dragan's help. It is a case of better the devil you know."

At the mention of the devil, I thought back to Thorn's story about their fight and the red sword in the weapons rack.

"So, we go back to England and carry on as normal," I said. I would have to play along and act the part of an MI5 agent to discover the true extent of their involvement. No point in directly confronting them. They would just deny it and blame Thorn. She could no longer defend her actions.

"Sort of. Mary will be annoyed that you killed Thorn. She was relying on her to control the supernatural underworld."

I followed her to the doors, and the soldiers gathered in front.

"I can do that. I am the Dragan King, after all. But it means I can't take the reversing formula just yet. I need to stay as a higher percentage Dragan for as long as possible," I said, knowing the last injection would complete my transformation in a few days and would be irreversible. I had no intention of giving up my powers. So I had to keep the last injection a secret, else they would force the reverse formula on me again.

We marched down the corridors to the main entrance.

"We can talk with Mary on our return, but I would prefer you human again. In the meantime, I will arrange for you to move out of the base and into your own house. Now you made your choice. You are free to do what you like, but you can still work for us as well. And I am free to visit whenever I want," Scarlett said and winked.

We walked along the curved corridor and past the sweeping staircase to the main entrance. We stepped out of the front doors and pulled them closed.

"What about the other Dragans?" Scarlett asked.

"I will tell them a gang of vengeful Turned killed her. The Twins will inherit the chateau." I turned my back on the chateau, walked to the fields and the sound of a helicopter.

I had to make a choice. Rose or Scarlett. Dragan or Human. Night or day. Just like when I first encountered Thorn and decided on my path when killing

Barry. On that night, I chose Vampire, Thorn, and night.

However, I had learnt my lessons well. There didn't always have to be a choice, and not all of them were mutually exclusive. I didn't have to follow but one path, excluding all others. I could have options. This time I chose Dragan not Human, but I also chose both Rose and Scarlett, and to live in both night and day.

Epilogue

I listened to the footsteps overhead, thumping across the ceiling and the sounds of muffled voices. My psychic sense could only detect V's thoughts. The others must have been wearing talismans. The doors shut, and the footsteps faded as they left my home. A little hand grabbed my ring finger and pulled it out of their mouth.

"Shh. It will be okay. Sorry, did the loud noise frighten you?" I gently said to Rose.

"So, V has gone," Cassius said as he stepped out of the shadows.

"Yes. He has gone, but he will be back," I said and wiped away a red tear rolling down my cheek.

"How can you be sure?"

"MI5-S will eventually work out I am still alive. When the truth is exposed, his relationship with Scarlett will be destroyed. He has no intentions of becoming human again. Their relationship will never work. As you know, it never does between a Dragan and Human. One gets older and the other doesn't. We have different tastes and desires. We cannot have children between the two races. The differences become insurmountable. He will realise the lies MI5-S told him, now I have sown the seeds of doubt. They must have known who I was for years, but they played the game. They are just as responsible. He has realised it is true, and that I saved millions of lives by controlling the Turned for all these years. For now, it is a bitter pill to swallow."

"He never asked why you controlled the Turned, but also you never told him," Cassius said.

I smiled. "He thinks it was to avoid attention, so we could live in peace, but I barely remember the real reason myself some days. It seems like a dream what happened all those centuries ago and the decision we made. However, the reason doesn't matter; the result is the same. We controlled the Turned and stood guard over the world. They may never know why or even believe us. I sometimes find it hard to believe. But with the release of magic into the world, we will be called upon again to protect it. Regardless of the original reason to limit the Turned, I am glad we followed this path."

"You like the human world?" Cassius said.

"Yes. Of course. All Dragans are part human. The dragons and mages merged to create us, but a mage is just a human with the ability to manipulate magic. I think we forget that we have a human side and so do they. Anyway, there is so much to enjoy in the human world."

"I agree. I wouldn't want it any other way. A Dragan or Vampire led world would have been ordered and disciplined but without the fun. So you think V will return to you?"

"He will see through their lies, eventually."

"Even if he uncovers the truth about MI5, it doesn't mean he will return to you."

"He will. I have his daughter. We have a blood bond. I can be patient. I give it a few years. Less if I wish."

"It might not even last that long. He doesn't realise how much he has changed. He will eventually understand the greater good you serve, whereas MI5 are still covering up. If he ever thinks to ask why we really did it, things may change rapidly," Cassius said.

"I told him half the truth on the plane to Rome, and he saw the red sword in the weapons rack downstairs. There was no point in telling the rest straight away. He is too angry and proud at the moment to have a complete change of heart. He needs time to calm down and think things through. I hoped he would have stayed for Rose. I think he was going to. Then I could have taken the time to explain it, to fill in the second part of the story. But MI5 forced us into an ultimatum."

"In the meantime, is there no other way of breaking his bond with MI5 and Scarlett?"

"Unfortunately, Scarlett appears to be innocent in MI5's games. He may fall out with them, but not her. Scarlett was his first love. He will want to make it work with her. He can also live in daylight, so it will be one less thing to disconnect them. Let him have his human romance and get it out of his system. But even if they split, he will not come back to me straight away. He will need time to discover that only being with other Dragans will make him happy. However, he will return at some point, and I will be ready to welcome him home."

"Always the long game. You played it to the wire with your game of choices. How did you know he would take the offer?" Cassius said.

"He wouldn't kill his own daughter, and he knew I was right about them killing us."

"What if he had killed them?"

"I would have had one less rival in the world," I replied and smiled.

"You left it late to tell him your alternative plan. I thought I was going to be washing blood off the walls and out of the carpet."

“I had to give him no choice but to accept it. I psychically showed it to him in a split second. He fired the gun into the wall as acceptance. We emptied the fireplace onto the floor, and I dropped through the trapdoor behind the screen and under the rug, which he replaced. Always have an escape plan.”

“I know. I taught you that. What’s next?” Cassius said.

“As of today, my daughters have returned and our enemies are defeated. The Turned army is destroyed. Cyrus is dead, and the corrupt Hunter’s organisation is broken. We have a peace deal with MI5-S and the new Hunters, which should secure stability for us. You, the Twins and Rip can work with V to help recruit and control the new underworld created by the release of magic. We will build our forces for the real war to come.

"In the meantime, Rose and I will go to America as planned. We can blend in and pretend to be normal. She will go to school to learn from humans and about humans. The rest of the time, I will educate her to be the Dragan Queen, and you can teach her our history. I will right the mistakes I made with the Twins. I can raise my Rose to be the perfect woman, ready to rule the new expanding underworld and continue our race. No one can stand in our way. The Dragan Empire is reborn.”

THE END

Thank you for reading

Did you enjoy it? Did you love it?
Reviews are the life blood of books. They are quick and easy. It's fangtastic to get them.
I would greatly appreciate a review to spread the word.

You only need to click your number of stars, write a sentence on why you liked it and add a quick couple of words for a title. It will only take you as long as sending a tweet or posting a quick message on facebook.

The link takes you to the product page.

https://www.amazon.com/dp/B09NQLDXDD

Unfortunately, this is the last of the books in the Vampire Formula series. The formula has run its course. However, it isn't the end for Thorn and V. They can have new adventures.

Other books by P.A.Ross on Amazon.

http://www.amazon/P.A.Ross

Printed in Great Britain
by Amazon

60157648R00141